INTO THIS WILD ABYSS

INTO THIS WILD ABYSS

F. J. NEWMAN

Atlantis Publishing
1206 Eruera Street
Rotorua 3010
New Zealand

ISBN 978-0-473-45998-7 (Softcover)
ISBN 978-0-473-45999-4 (New Zealand Edition)
ISBN 978-0-473-46000-6 (Kindle)

Typeset in Garamond

www.atlantispublishing.co.nz

To Jane, John, Olivia and Aedan. You are my everything.

"Then the First Emperor ascended Mount Tabo and sacrificed there to the gods. He entered into a Covenant with them, giving to him and his descendants all lands under Heaven, and in return he and his descendants would rule with justice and benevolence from that day forth."

The Book of Life

"The law of nature is such that plants require earth, lest they wither; fish require water, lest they die; and man requires government, lest he shrivel and return to be among the animals. Thus is the Emperor ordained, by the Covenant, as a Demi-God to rule over mankind, in accordance with the law of nature, and to protect us from barbarity."

The Book of Life

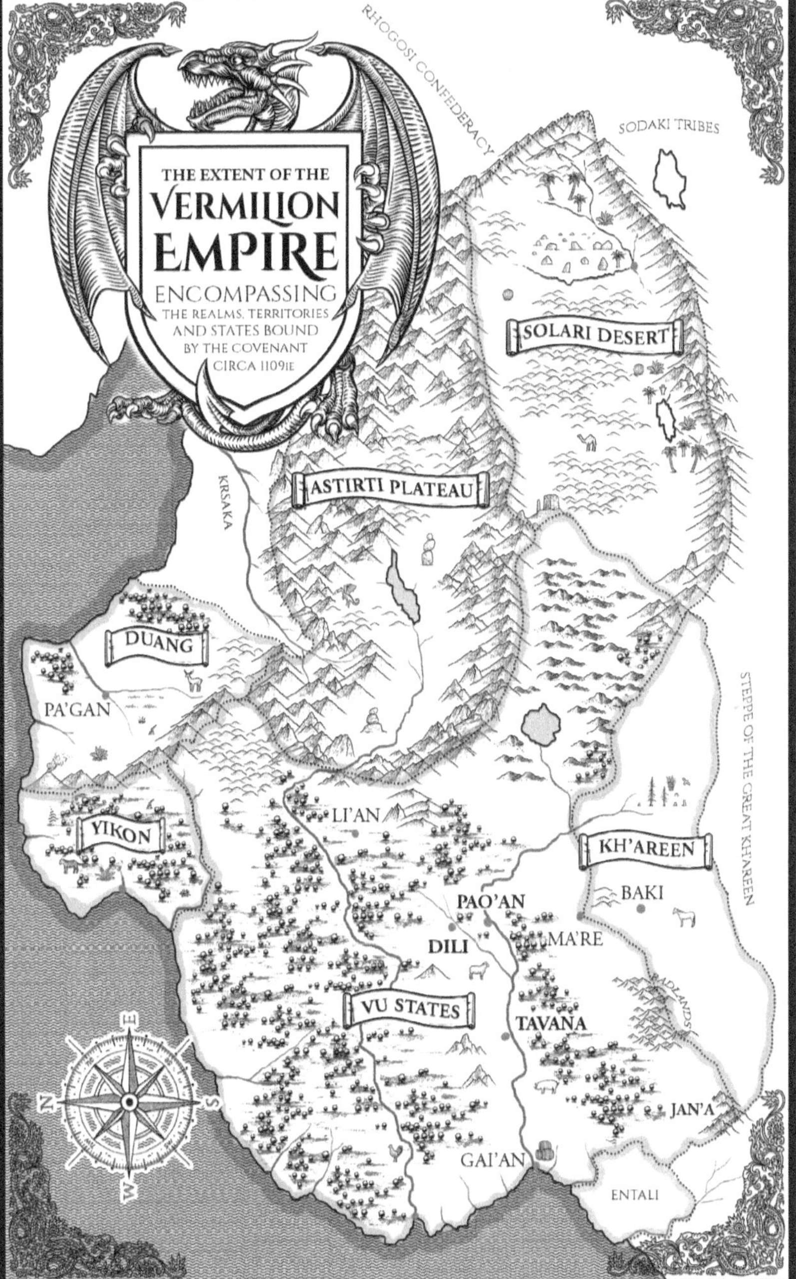

THE EXTENT OF THE
VERMILION EMPIRE
ENCOMPASSING
THE REALMS, TERRITORIES
AND STATES BOUND
BY THE COVENANT
CIRCA 1109 IE
RHOGOSI CONFEDERACY
SODAKI TRIBES
SOLARI DESERT
KRSAKA
ASTIRTI PLATEAU
DUANG
PA'GAN
STEPPE OF THE GREAT KHAREEN
LI'AN
YIKON
KH'AREEN
BAKI
PAO'AN
MA'RE
DILI
BADLANDS
VU STATES
TAVANA
JAN'A
GAI'AN
ENTALI

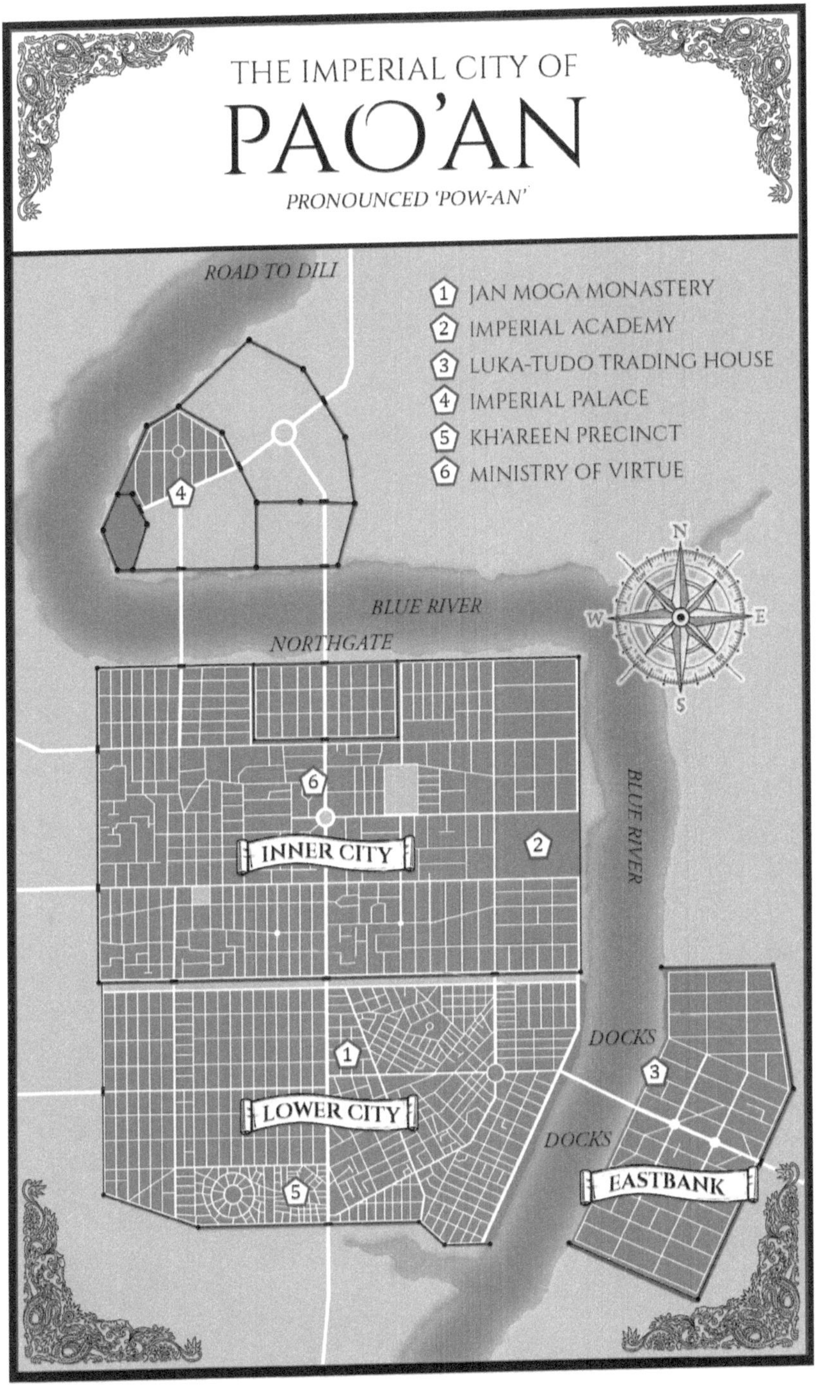

THE IMPERIAL CITY OF
PAO'AN
PRONOUNCED 'POW-AN'

1 JAN MOGA MONASTERY
2 IMPERIAL ACADEMY
3 LUKA-TUDO TRADING HOUSE
4 IMPERIAL PALACE
5 KH'AREEN PRECINCT
6 MINISTRY OF VIRTUE
ROAD TO DILI
BLUE RIVER
NORTHGATE
BLUE RIVER
N
W E
S
INNER CITY
LOWER CITY
DOCKS
DOCKS
EASTBANK

CHAPTER 1

"No city is as remarkable as Pao'an. For over a thousand years it has sat at the heart of a network of commerce, culture and government. From this seat of power rulers claim authority over all under heaven. But there is another side to Pao'an; the side that is made out of bricks and mortar. Fundamentally Pao'an is divided into three parts: the Inner City, the Lower City and Eastbank. The Blue River separates the latter from the former two..."

A Traveler's Guide to Pao'an

Po pressed his nose against the glass. His breath frosted the window pane, covering the books inside in a white, spreading mist.

"Hurry up," Master Dugen barked. "Where have you gone?"

A hand grabbed Po's arm and yanked him away from the shop window. Dugen looked down at Po through his thick brass glasses. His wrinkled skin and shaved head were silhouetted against the sky.

"What did I say? Running errands is a privilege."

"They're books," Po said, pointing.

"Of course they're books. The whole street is bookshops, but we'll never get to *Vaisha's* if we stop and look in each one. Now, can I trust you enough to let go of your arm?"

Po nodded, and Dugen released him.

"Can we look at some on the way back?"

"No," said Dugen flatly.

The door jingled as Dugen and Po entered. Inside was dim, lit only by a lamp over the counter. Po's eyes took a moment to adjust.

"Good afternoon," Vaisha called from out back. The shopkeeper poked his head around the corner and squinted at the pair; the old master in burgundy and the novice in cream — Ba're monks.

"What can I do for you?" Vaisha asked, wiping his hands on an ink-stained cloth.

Dugen handed Vaisha a note, and the two exchanged pleasantries.

"I won't be a moment." Vaisha disappeared out the back and returned with a freshly pressed copy of Asanga's *Foundational Falsehoods of the Vu Religion*. Dugen flipped through the pages and Po admired the woodblock prints.

"So," Vaisha said. "You're with Jan Moga — that's the monastery off Washer's Street in the Lower City isn't it?"

The monk nodded and closed the book.

"This *is* the fifth edition?" Dugen asked, tapping the cover.

"It is. As requested, I'll just need your name here."

Vaisha presented the ledger and Master Dugen put his signature to the paper. While waiting, Po ran his eyes over the floor to ceiling shelves. One day he would have a library like it at home. Of course, that depended on him abandoning monastic life — not an easy thing while his parents paid for his education.

The two monks returned to the street and pushed through the jostling students streaming from the Imperial Academy. At the end of Scholar Street, the masses thinned and the pair rejoined the normal ebb and flow of Pao'an's Inner City. Po would have preferred to walk in silence, but Dugen began a monologue on Asanga's key assertions in dismissing the Vu religion as *'utterly irrelevant and faulty from the very foundations of its thought.'* Po had heard it all before and hurried along in the master's wake, contenting himself with an afternoon off class. Dugen stopped suddenly.

"Looks like some disturbance on South Avenue." Po looked up. A crowd pressed into the intersection, buzzing with chatter. Raised voices carried on the breeze and onlookers leaned from tenement buildings and the windows of the corner taphouse.

"Let's have a look," Po suggested.

"No, best avoid it," said Dugen. "We can take Park Avenue."

"Maybe someone needs help?"

"There's always *someone* who needs help. The question is whether we have the means to give it."

"We don't know unless we look," Po countered. Dugen sighed.

"*Oh* alright. A quick look and we're away. The abbot won't be pleased if we get caught up in anything. I'll have to say it was your idea."

Po bounded ahead of the senior monk, his sandals slapping on the cobblestones. He came to the crowd and edged his way through.

"Excuse me. Pardon me," he said, ignoring the scowls and hot-tempered curses. When he could go no farther, he rose on his tiptoes and caught a glimpse of a man with a bald head and a sharp nose. He appeared to be arguing with someone. Changing positions, Po observed soldiers — and not just any soldiers, but the crimson and bone white armor of the Vermilion Guard. *Imperial business*, Po realized.

"I'm waiting," said the bald man. "Make it easy on yourself."

"I'm a cabinet minister. There are protocols, damn it! We can return to the palace, but I'll *not* go in chains." The crowd murmured in agreement. Po caught a glimpse of the second speaker. He was stocky and shorter than the first but dressed in fine robes of silk and velvet trimmed with fur. His face flushed red and his cheeks quivered.

"Impossible," said the first. "This is a warrant —" a piece of paper rose above the crowd sealed in vermilion wax "— for your arrest, signed by the hand of the Emperor himself. Tell your guards to put down their weapons."

"No," barked the second. "You do this pantomime on the street as if a show for children? Where is your dignity!" A hand fell on Po's shoulder.

"There you are!" Dugen hissed, dragging Po from the spectacle. "Let's go. There's nothing we can do here." Po resisted, planting his feet firmly on the ground.

"Hold on, it's getting interesting." Steel clashed and a man howled in pain. Everyone moved at once. Someone shoved Po, tearing him from Dugen's grasp. Bodies crushed against him, pulling him this way and that.

"Po!" Dugen shrieked. Po fought against the crowd and reached his teacher's side. Dugen stumbled and Po caught him, dragging his teacher as best he could through the writhing mass. He spotted a cobbler's cart and pulled Dugen behind it. There they sat with their backs pressed against the wooden boards. Dugen hugged his book and looked about in terror.

"I can't see. My glasses!" A stone lodged in Po's stomach. He was going to get a good telling off when they returned to Jan Moga.

"I'll go look for them," Po suggested. "Maybe —"

The cart shook, and a weight drove Po into the cobbles. *A person.* Tearing apart, the newcomer pounced into a fighting stance then relaxed. They stared at each other for a moment. Po judged him a clerk or an assistant in an office somewhere; slightly older than Po, perhaps nineteen or twenty to Po's seventeen. Neither was a threat to each other. In the awkwardness that followed Po stuck out his hand in lieu of any better idea.

"Po of Jan Moga," he said. The youth accepted the outstretched hand.

"Dasha Luka-Tudo," he said. "Sorry for landing on you like that."

"Forgiven," Dugen said with the wave of a hand. "Can you tell us what happened?"

"You didn't see?" Dasha asked, joining the pair with his back against the cart.

"We were too far back," Po explained.

"That was the Minister of Revenue," Dasha said, pointing his thumb over his shoulder. "A judge came and presented an arrest warrant."

"Arrest warrant?" Dugen asked.

"You know, one of those paper things," Dasha explained, glimpsing around the edge of the cart. Steel continued to clash in the background. Po peeked over the top. A thick knot of soldiers hacked and stabbed at each other while others lay bloodied and dying. The judge stood apart, signaling down the road. On the other side, the condemned minister seized a poll from his palanquin and joined the fray. Po ducked back down.

4

"You sure it was the Minister of Revenue?" Dugen asked.

"Maga Nodu," Dasha said. "Yeah, I'm sure. My father deals with them. We own a trading house over the Blue Riv—"

"They got him!" someone cried. Po peeped over the cart. A man in crimson armor stood over Maga, the tip of his sword at the minister's throat. The cabinet minister held up his palms in surrender and guardsmen approached with chains ready. Then Po noticed it. Between Maga and the cart was the glint of brass.

"Glasses!" Po exclaimed. He jumped the cart and ran as fast as his sandals allowed. He got halfway before the men at the intersection noticed him. One took a step forward and raised his sword. Po froze.

"*Oi!* Hold it there!" Po glanced back towards the cart, then towards the guardsman. "No closer! This is a security operation." Behind the man, the judge looked Po's way and the two locked eyes. The judge's eyes narrowed in a frown.

"Leave him," said the judge. "Get the minister and go." The guardsman did not respond immediately but scowled at Po before sheathing his sword. Po discerned his chance. He ran for it, skidded, snatched the glasses off the street and scrambled back to safety.

"Hey!" the guard yelled after him, but Po was already back under cover. Dasha regarded him wide-eyed.

"What were you thinking? I've seen some weird stuff, but you priests…"

"Monks," Po said, correcting him.

"Did you not think they'd shoot you?"

"Shoot?" Po asked, raising an eyebrow.

"You didn't see the man with the crossbow trained on you?"

"Oh that," Po said, bluffing. "Yeah, I didn't think they'd shoot a monk." Dasha shook his head and looked back at the intersection.

"They're leaving," he said.

Po took a deep breath and dropped the glasses into Dugen's hand. The monk ran his fingers around the brass frames and held them to his face.

"Crooked and one broken lense," Dugen said. "One scratched. Not much use to me now. I have a spare pair in the dormitory, but you'll have to help me back."

"All clear," Dasha said, standing and dusting himself off. "Well, nice meeting you Po. Stay out of trouble."

"Same to you," Po said. He helped Dugen to his feet. The old monk wheezed and dabbed a handkerchief on a split lip.

"Well," Dugen said after a long silence. "You'll have some explaining to do when we get back."

⁂

On the other side of the city, Natan listened with his ear against the door. Coins slid across the table and dropped into a bag. The tax collector said something, and his father replied, their words muffled. Natan pulled back a lock of his black hair and adjusted his ear against the wood, frustrated that he could not understand what they were saying inside. At eighteen and as the youngest son in the family, information was leverage.

"Natan!" boomed his father's voice. "Natan! Would you come in here?"

"Coming." Natan grabbed the broom he had left propped against the wall and opened the door. "Yes?"

Avi sat behind his desk, his lean frame, hawkish nose and unruly mob of hair framed by the open window behind him. Opposite sat the taxman counting coins into a canvas bag.

"Take this cat away," Avi demanded, motioning open-handed at the ginger cat sitting on his ledgers. Natan scooped the cat up and winced as it clawed his shoulder.

"And shut the window would you?" Natan bit his tongue. The window was just behind his father — he could have done it himself. Natan walked over and slid the window shut. The room immediately darkened.

"Is that all?" Natan asked.

"Yes," Avi said, waving him away. "No, wait. Can you bring me my pipe?"

Natan left with the cat and returned with his father's pipe and a pouch of *dama* leaf. The pouch left a musky, sweaty smell on his hands, so pungent that sometimes Natan thought it was a physical stain, but never there when he looked. Still, the wiry leaf kept his father relatively placid and relieved him of pain. Sometimes he just wished the experts did a better job. The Vu'du holy men tattooed his father's joints, the shaman prayed out the demons, and the apothecary gave him ointment, but Avi kept returning to the pipe — it was the only thing that worked.

"Now," Avi said, grabbing at the pipe. "What was I saying?" He fumbled with the pouch and spilled some of the *dama* on the table. "Yes. It is not an easy time for us merchants. I've never seen it so tough. But somehow you always get your cut *eh*?" The taxman snorted and leaned. The chair creaked under his mass.

"Avi, Avi," he chided. "I've known you long enough and you've never thought business was good. The Empire has its costs. Imagine how the Luka-Tudo Trading House would fair if no one guarded the roads or kept the peace."

"I fear the Worshipful Company of Dockers more than bandits," Avi quiped. The taxman chuckled.

"Plenty of merchants would agree," he said with a wag of the finger. "But the Worshipful Company pays taxes too."

"I'll say it again," Avi said, tapping the table. "Break that monopoly on the river, and I'll halve the cost of grain in the city." Avi lit the pipe and confidently leaned back in his chair, blowing smoke toward the ceiling.

"Easy for you to say," said the taxman. "But the Imperial Government must take all views into consideration. Now think, if we take the monopoly away from the Worshipful Company of Dockers, they'll call for us to strip the rights of the Merchant Guild as well. Before you know it, chaos would reign. Do you want that? Do you *really* want that Avi?" Natan noticed the telltale twitch that indicated his father was angry.

"Well, you do well out of it," Avi snapped.

"There are some advantages to being the cousin of the Minister."

"I'd say. You certainly don't lack any comforts in life." The taxman frowned.

"Don't be like that, Avi. Our little arrangement keeps the auditors at bay. Those things can be a right pain. Everyone does it."

"It doesn't make — what is that blasted commotion?"

Avi swung himself off his chair and opened the window. Natan followed. The yard bustled with shirtless laborers and traders from all corners of the Vermilion Empire. Natan's eldest brother Dan stood amidst them arguing with two men in red and black gambesons.

"Guards," Natan said. Avi leaned out the window.

"*Oi* Dan, what do they want?" The guards spun at the voice and looked to the window.

"We're here for Gupo Nodu. Is he there?"

"Gupo Nodu?" Avi turned to the tax collector. "That's you isn't it?"

"*Er…* yes," he said. "Who are they? What do they want?" Avi turned back to the window.

"What do you want with him?"

"Official business," the guard answered. Avi wrinkled his nose. Natan knew how much his father hated the precinct guards.

"Stay," his father shouted. "He'll come to you."

"We'll come —" Avi slammed the window shut and rounded on Gupo.

"What's all this about?" he demanded. "Did you bring them here?"

"No, no," the taxman said, his hands up in defense. "I didn't —" Something heavy smashed against the front door. His mother screamed from the hall.

"Well they mean business," Avi said. "Downstairs, now."

Avi and Natan pushed past the tax collector to the stairs. Natan's mother Oni stood with the two guards in the hall. She had a stern look on her face, made more severe by her frizzy gray hair tied into a bun.

"Didn't I tell you to stay where you were?" Avi snapped, descending the stairs.

"We've orders," one guard said. "Is that him?" He nodded toward Gupo Nodu behind them.

"It's him. Now, what are you doing in my house? I told you to wait in the yard." The guard drew out a piece of paper covered in blocks of text and fixed with a wax seal and red ribbon.

"'This is a warrant for Gupo Nodu, signed by Chief Justice Loti."

"What does a Chief Justice want with a taxman?" Avi demanded. Natan felt uneasy. *Something* was not right.

"Treason," the guard replied. Natan recoiled. The very word sent shivers down his spine. He jumped the last two steps and hurried to his mother's side. Together they looked up at Gupo frozen halfway down the stairs. The tax collector clutched the handrail with white knuckles. His other hand tightened into a fist.

"Hurry up," the guard barked. Gupo did not move. His narrow eyes became glazed. He collapsed; his body tumbled down the stairs, coming to rest on the hall floor. His limp hand opened, and a glass vial fell from his fingers. From his coat spilled a bag of coins. A dozen silver *li* and a gold *gotti* rolled across the boards.

"Bloody balls of Kive," said the guard.

"Look what you've done," Avi said, barely skipping a beat. "In my house — I ought to have a word with your officer. You had a warrant for his arrest, not to see him killed! Get him out of here." Confidence left the guards. They exchanged looks, dumbfounded. Avi picked up the money bag and returned the coins to it. One of the guards tried to protest, but Avi cut him off. A foul smell wafted through the room. Natan realized Gupo had cleared his bowels. Oni put her hand to her mouth.

"Get him out," she shrieked. "Have you got some way to take him?" The guards stared back at her.

"Well we have a horse, we were —" Oni let out an angry groan. She stormed across the hall and opened the front door.

"Dan!" she shouted for her eldest son. "Dan! Get the donkey harnessed and bring the cart. Quick now." She slammed the door and turned on the guards. "Dan will take you to Eastbank barracks. I trust you can arrange everything from there?" The guards nodded.

"Your capes," she said.

"What about them?" one asked.

"Give them to me. You're not going to take a body out of this house uncovered."

"Well, *er*, yes…" the guard mumbled, removing the clasps and gesturing for the other guard to do the same. Together they wrapped Gupo's body. Dan opened the door and looked in.

"Ready. Wait, is that —?" Avi nodded. Natan avoided eye contact. Oni nudged the guards.

"Dan, I've told them you can go as far as the Eastbank barracks but no further. They can take it from there."

"Is that what I think it is?" Dan asked. Avi put his hand on his son's shoulder.

"Quiet now. Don't need this getting out. Do as your mother says." Dan nodded.

"Natan, you watch the yard," Avi said. "Your mother and I'll clean up inside."

Beads of sweat glistened on the laborers as they strained under their loads. A mule train from the Kh'areen steppe dominated the yard. Everything had to be accounted for, divided up and moved — some to the waiting boats of the Worshipful Company of Dockers, others to the family warehouse opposite the house. Natan found the foreman, shirtless and tan, crouched over a package with one of the Kh'areen traders.

"What are those?" Natan asked, standing over them.

"Terror Bird feathers," said the foreman. "Good quality too." Natan accepted a handful and rubbed them over his palm and between his fingers. *So soft.*

"They're becoming hard to get," said the trader. "Too many people hunting them." Natan eyed the trader. He was stocky and weather-beaten, his face as hard as leather and his clothes tough and utilitarian.

"And you are?" Natan asked.

"Kh'am," said the trader. "Kh'am Daladh'an of Baki. Over there are my two sons; Bayar and Akdu. Next to them is my daughter, Ashara."

At the mention of a daughter, Natan turned. He spotted her straight away, working hard alongside her brothers in much the same garb as her father. She appeared about his age with tan skin and red cheeks from a life in the sun. Her long black hair was tied back in plaits behind her head in the Kh'areen style.

"I'll go help —" Natan began to suggest, but he heard his name called. His middle brother hurried through the yard towards him.

"Where's Dan?" Dasha asked without greeting.

"What are you so excited about?"

"The Minister of Revenue," Dasha said, catching his breath. "He's been arrested. I saw it. They accused him of treason. There was a fight."

"Oh," said Natan, making the connection. Dasha's smile dropped.

"Don't you get it?" Dasha continued. "They *never* arrest cabinet ministers. This is big. They said he plotted against the Emperor. Do you think there'll be others? How deep does this go?"

"Right," Natan said. "You need to go inside."

Ashara had trouble sleeping. It was not the hard ground that caused problems — she was used to that. It was the smell of the city. The locals seemed not to notice it, but in their camp outside Eastbank was a definite smell. Some blamed the cesspits; others said the Blue River reeked of shit and piss. Ashara thought it was both, and more besides.

The first fingers of light touched the tops of the trees and crept up the city wall. Beside her, Kh'am rose and stirred the night's fire back to life. Ashara reached out, grabbed her clothes, and got dressed under the blanket.

"Rise and shine," Kh'am said. "Long day ahead." Bayar and Akdu groaned and rolled themselves tighter in their blankets. Around them, the familiar shapes of the camp stir for their morning rituals, but something was different. They were being watched. Around the camp stood forms, not familiar Kh'areen forms, but strangers. They wore hooded coats and covered their faces beneath the eyes with masks. They stood there, motionless, watching the camp.

"Don't stare," Kh'am grunted. "Don't draw attention to yourself."

"Who are they?" Ashara whispered.

"Virtuemen," her father replied. "The Emperor's eyes and ears."

"Is it about what we saw yesterday at —"

"We don't know what we saw," Kh'am cut her off. "And best not jump to conclusions."

"But why are they watching us?"

"Something is happening," Kh'am said. "I hear the Inner City was locked last night. There's talk of an attempted coup."

"What does that have to do with us?" Ashara asked. "We're not involved."

"Paranoia needs no reason," Kh'am said with a shrug. "Now get the baggage ready and stick close."

A loud discussion erupted on the other side of the camp. Ashara instinctively rose. City guards in their red and blacks had appeared, sauntering between the fires. Virtuemen accompanied them, stopping by selected fires and demanding people's papers. They drew nearer. As they got close, Ashara averted her eyes. The virtueman pointed a gloved finger at Bayar and Akdu.

"Right," a guard said. "Show us your papers. Quickly now." Kh'am produced them from his saddle bag.

"Everything's in order," he said, handing the leather booklet over. Every family in the Vermilion Empire had one. The cover was well worn and pressed with the Imperial Serpent emblem. Inside were multiple loose pages recording pertinent details of each family member and a unique number.

"*Bei-a* and *A-ka-du*," the guard said looking at Ashara's brothers. "Show us your forearms." Kh'am's sons looked to their father and then rolled up their sleeves. Beneath the wrist on each right forearm was a tattooed number. The guard compared the numbers beneath their wrists to the ones in the book.

"Good," he said, passing the papers back to Kh'am.

"So everything's in order?" Kh'am asked.

"Yes — and the girl," the guard said as if an afterthought. Ashara stepped forward and rolled up her sleeve. The guard grabbed her wrist and turned it over. His fingers lingered on her skin longer than Ashara thought necessary. Then, with a grunt, he let go, and Ashara's hand fell to her side.

"All in order," the guard said to the virtueman. The virtueman nodded and moved on to the next fire.

"Well they've never done that before," Ashara said, breathing a sigh of relief.

"They're looking for someone," Kh'am said. "Not sure what they expect to find here though."

An hour later a line of pack animals and carts moved east. Ashara's family had two horses, but these were reserved for Bayar and Akdu who rode among the guard. Ashara walked with her father, leading the family mules. Two miles from Pao'an, the towers of A'an rise above the trees. Approaching the township, Ashara touched Kh'am's elbow and pointed. A squadron of dreadbeasts guarded the road; twelve massive animals, annual tributes from Duang, accompanied by their mahouts and foot soldiers. Ashara had never seen them up close before, and as they passed, she stared, wide-eyed. They were easily fifteen feet tall and their leathery skin ranged from deep gray to murky green. On their backs were fighting platforms for archers and spearmen.

"They're huge," Ashara whispered. "I knew they were big but these are... are massive."

"You certainly don't want them charging your line," Kh'am said. "The horses don't like them. Your great-grandfather's generation learned that." Ashara remembered the stories of the Kh'areen defeat at Ankor-Kh'ondi and the dreadbeast charge that finished them off. She gulped. It had always sounded like a childhood story, something to justify their loss, but seeing the massive beasts left Ashara with a heavy feeling in her stomach.

"I'd be happy not to see them again," she said with a shudder.

"You probably won't," her father replied. "It's been a long time since I've seen them patrolling these parts."

The caravan entered through the gates of A'an and the beasts fell from sight. South of A'an the road continued through the Vu heartland. By the fifth day, the villages had become fewer and far between. Brush on either side of the road became thicker. The traders bunched together and stayed alert. They were a week from the traditional Vu frontier city of Ma're.

Ashara hummed to herself and flicked her sling, feeling the weight of the stone. There was only a small chance of seeing any game this close to the road, but if she saw any she was ready.

"Seen anything?" Bayar asked, riding up beside her. "They say we might get to camp early tonight. Maybe we can arrange a hunting party."

"Alright."

Bayar gave Ashara a look.

"Everything okay?"

"Fine," she said. "Where's Akdu?"

"Where do you think?"

"With the Altan sisters?"

"You've an eye in the back of your head," Bayar said. Ashara glanced over her shoulder.

"He'll have to choose one of them. He can't have both."

"Why not?" Bayar said with a grin. Ashara hit him. "Father won't allow it anyway," he continued. "Not until Akdu can afford his own mules."

Her mule snorted and veered into her, drawing the family train along with it. Ashara snatched the bridle and forced it back, but the mule refused to stay on the middle of the road. It bit at her and shoved her aside.

"Woah," Bayar cried and headed the mule off with his horse.

"They sense something," Ashara shouted. "Check the berm!"

It was too late. The air hissed and cracked in a series of short, sharp pops. Puffs of smoke drifted across the road — right where the mules had tried to avoid. The mules began to panic and veered off to the left. This time Ashara could not stop them.

"Bandits!" Bayar yelled, spurring on his horse.

"Bandits!" Ashara yelled, taking up the cry. There was no time to organize. The gang were already upon them. It was standard bandit tactics: scare the mules, run them off the road and make off with as much as they could before the traders could respond.

Ashara drew her knife and used her sling as a club to hit the closest man. He stumbled and fell with a dull yelp. Then it was her turn. Someone thumped into her, sending Ashara spinning to the dirt. She rolled and corrected herself. The bandit was already pulling at the mules' ropes, leading them in the opposite direction. Ashara kicked out at his shins. The man buckled but before Ashara could knife him someone grabbed her from behind and hurled her aside into the scrub. Twigs scratched her skin and the air blew from her lungs.

"Tanri gosh ba!" the Kh'areen yelled in their war cries. "Tanri is Lord!" Ashara grabbed for her sling and got up in time to see Akdu and others charge the bandits with their horses. Bayar and her father were nowhere to be seen.

"Tanri gosh ba!" Ashara returned the sling to her belt and ran to help her elder brother, jumping on the back of the nearest bandit and slicing upward into the soft skin under his throat. Blood gushed down his front and frothed out the mouth.

"Ashara!" Akdu yelled. "Get away!"

Ashara ignored him. All Kh'areen learned to fight, and she was good at it. She would not abandon her family. Instead she returned her knife, picked up an axe and jumped deeper into the fray. Somewhere she heard Akdu scream. A hooked blade caught her shirt and tore at her upper arm. Ashara fell and rolled, leaping to her feet again to get away. She spotted Akdu in a pool of his own blood. She screamed and became the focus of attention. Blades slashed at her. A stick buzzed by her head. She weaved and dodged like her father taught her, her mind one step ahead. Something hit her. She collapsed, dropping the axe.

"Get her," a bandit shouted. Ashara felt herself thrown over someone's shoulder. He stank. The world was upside down. It was a blur of movement. A man led Akdu's horse by the reins. Brush scratched her face. She wriggled.

"Oi, stop moving." Ashara struggled harder and thrust her weight

to the side. The two hit the ground together. Ashara was all teeth and fists; scratching, punching and biting, her weapons forgotten. The bandit grabbed her by the collar, tearing the stitches. He punched her in the face until the pain turned to numbness. Groggy, her head hit the ground. Somewhere there was a shout.

"Leave her. Move. Before they come after us."

CHAPTER 2

"On Kh'areen and the Vermilion Empire, many an hour could be spent. Here it is only necessary for the briefest of introductions. The Kh'areen are primarily a nomadic people. Their nominal capital is at Baki where they have the Oracle, the spiritual heart of the cult of Tanri. Officially now a client state of the Vermilion Empire, this has not always been so."

Master Suvu's Life of a Scholar

"Remember," Master Dugen said from the front of the class. "Don't write mindlessly. Internalize Asanga's arguments." Po dipped his pen and turned the page of Asanga's *Dialogue on the Nature of Forms*. "I'll be testing you tomorrow," Dugen continued. "You'll need this in the Imperial Exams. Just a hint for those who haven't latched onto the importance of this lesson."

There was an intake of breath across the class. Someone moaned. Po glanced over his shoulder at his friend. Anjan was a skinny student with a face full of freckles. He pursed his lips and frowned at Po.

"Anjan," Dugen said. "That last point was for you. I'm short-sighted, not deaf. This is the second Imperial Exam. The emphasis will no longer be on *knowing* the argument. You must be able to argue it. I —"

The classroom door creaked open and a boy in sleeveless yellow habit tiptoed in. He approached Master Dugen and the two had a hushed exchange.

"Novice Po," Dugen said. "Your presence is requested in the infirmary."

"What, now?" Po asked.

"Yes, now," Dugen barked, waving the messenger away. "Quickly. Pack your things. I don't want anyone else having to clean up after you."

"But the copying," Po said.

"You'll have to come in extra early tomorrow."

Po sighed. Anjan flashed a sympathetic look. Po cleared his desk and headed down the hall past the other classrooms. Master Pani's voice boomed from one. From another Po heard the drone of junior students learning their characters. A monk hit the blackboard and the students started again. Po descended the stairs and exited into the courtyard. He stopped.

The gate was open, and around it gathered a knot of official looking men; at least two virtuemen, three Vermilion Guard and someone from the Ministry of Rites. Po gathered his courage and crossed towards the infirmary next to the gate. The men paid him no attention.

Entering, Po noticed two figures huddled in a corner of the antechamber. *Women*, Po thought. *Unusual.* One looked up, a nun, but the other rested a tear-stained face on the nun's shoulder. Po decided the nun was visiting from Atana Abbey, next to the Imperial Palace.

"You can go in," said the nun. Po muttered his thanks and opened the door to the infirmary proper. The sharp acidic smell hit him. He blinked and squinted into the room.

"Novice," a voice said out of the darkness. Po turned to the sound and approached the figures sitting around a bed. One seemed familiar; old and wise, shrouded in his burgundy and black robes.

"Venerable Biet," Po said. "You requested my presence."

"Yes," said the abbot. "Last week you accompanied Master Dugen to the Inner City."

"Yes," Po said after a pause. Biet nodded.

"You saw the arrest of the Minister of Revenue, Maga Nodu."

"That's what I was told," Po said. "I didn't recognize him." Biet raised a hand and two of the monks crossed to the window behind the bed, drawing back the curtains. Po raised a hand to shade his eyes and took a step back.

"That's him," a voice croaked. Po's eyes adjusted and his spirits fell.

"You're —" his voice trailed off. "The judge?"

"Chief Justice actually," Biet said. "Chief Justice Loti — one of our greatest benefactors."

"What did you call me for?" Po asked, half expecting to be seized at any moment.

"I'm dying," Chief Justice Loti said with a rattle. "I was curious. I thought you were — that day — a Ba're monk. You were brave. Everyone ran away — you ran toward trouble. That's a courage few have."

"My teacher called it stupidity," Po said. Loti shrugged and winced with the effort.

"Sometimes they're one and the same. Are you taking the Imperial Exams?"

"I sit the second exam this month —"

"Top percentile last year," Venerable Biet interrupted. Loti cleared his throat and spat phlegm into a basin held out by one of the monks.

"And will you continue with the monastic life, or take up government service?" Loti asked.

"I must first focus on my studies," Po said, knowing it was the right answer — at least while the abbot listened. Loti nodded in agreement.

"It is good," he said in a hushed tone. "To see my contributions put to good use. The future of the Vermilion Empire relies on young men like you. You're the future. My generation is the past." Loti winced. The sheets were stained dark red. "Tell me," the judge continued. "Let me test you. How many states form the Empire?"

"Come, Loti," Biet said. "That's kindergarten —"

"Six," Po said. "Plus the Entali Protectorate." Loti gestured for Po to continue. "First are the Vu, then the Kh'areen, Solari, Astirti, Duang and Yikon."

"Good," Loti said. "And the provinces in the Vu state?"

"Seventeen. Ja'pa —"

"Enough," Biet said. "You don't need to recite them all. Loti, you'll see our students are well versed."

"Funny thing death," Loti said. "In life I never thought about my contributions. Now I want to know if it all meant something." Biet patted Loti reassuringly and Loti's face settled.

"Chief Justice, Venerable Biet," Po said humbly, his eyes toward the floor. "What can I do? What have I been called here for?"

"To watch and learn," Biet said. "Chief Justice Loti asked for you. He recognized you. I'm sure it was a simple curiosity."

"What happened?" Po asked.

"They stabbed me," Loti said, flushing red. "The feral bastards ambushed me."

"Now, now —" Biet started, but Loti talked over him.

"The Brotherhood of Kive, the armed wing of the Vu'tai Party. Maga Nodu was a prominent member. Traditionalists. Backward thinking dimwits. One had a go at me. Revenge for arresting that bloody Maga. Right here." Loti pointed at the darkest patch of red on the sheets above his abdomen.

"Brothers," Biet said, changing the subject. "Shuffle aside and make room for Po. And those curtains. We don't need the harsh light now." Po took the seat offered to him as the room plunged back into darkness. "Now," Biet continued. "Chief Justice Loti, are you ready? Do you want to see your wife again?"

"I've said what I need to say," the judge said. "I don't want her to remember me like this."

"And do you hold to the teachings of Dasanika, to the Five Tenets and the Way of the Ba're?"

"I do," Loti said.

"Do you understand," Biet continued. "That all things must perish, that life is fleeting, that impermanence is the way of life?"

"I do."

"And do you understand you are near death, on the cusp of oblivion, with a wound that is festering?"

"I do."

"Then," Biet said. "It is our privilege to be here with you, to sit the oblivion watch. When you are ready, tell me."

20

"Venerable Abbot," Loti said. "I am in pain. Help me now." Biet smiled and cupped Loti's trembling hand. He motioned to the monks, and they helped Loti up into a sitting position. Biet turned to the side table and took a small cup.

"This is the Serpent's Gift," Biet said to the monks. "It is a powerful muscle relaxant, allowing us to give the patient further medication without the stomach rejecting it." Biet put one hand behind Loti's head and held the cup to the judge's lips. Loti drank it greedily and then coughed up the last few drops. Biet wiped them from the judge's chin and returned the cup to the side table. He took up a second cup.

"This," Biet said, holding it out to the monks. "Is Oblivion's Kiss. It removes the sensation of pain and helps one on the path." Biet held the second cup to Loti's lips, and Loti drank. When finished Biet returned the cup to the tray and wiped the judge's face with a towel.

"Now let us reflect," Biet said. "You will not be alone." The abbot placed bone reflection beads in the judge's hand. He then took out his own and the other monks followed suit. Biet closed his eyes and began to drone.

"*Kime ki're kima ka. Kime ki're kima ka.*" The others followed. Po fingered his beads, passing his fingers over one bead for each cycle of the sacred mantra. The world fell away around him and Po was alone in his mind, floating on a sea of pure consciousness.

A hand touched Po's shoulder. The room had grown dark — an hour or two had passed. The monks still chanted, but Loti's motionless hands rested on his knees, the beads laying limp across his fingers. There was a slight, almost undetectable, movement of his chest. Po glanced over his shoulder.

"We have visitors," whispered the abbot. "The others can sit vigil."

"And then?" Po asked. He felt foolish as soon as he asked it.

"All things are impermanent," Biet said.

Po stood noiselessly and looked to the door. The sound of voices came from the antechamber and cracks of light leaked around the frame.

"Venerable Abbot, why did you request that I see this?"

"Loti requested you. That is all," Biet said, opening the door. People milled around the antechamber, chatting in hushed tones. When the door opened, they ceased their gossip and stared in the direction of the two monks. One man appeared to command the room, and when he looked toward them, Po felt a vague rush of recognition. He had a firm jaw, a shaved face and short cropped hair. His robes were of the finest silks and the detail work was all done in fine gold thread. The woodblock prints did not do him justice.

Biet offered a deep bow. Po froze, then followed Biet's example.

"Arise, arise," said the man with a dismissive wave. "How is my dear friend?"

"Chief Minister Tomi Mei-Uduga," Biet said. "It is an absolute honor to have you here. Chief Justice Loti is —" Biet looked around the room and chose his words carefully. "Comfortable now but walking the final path with our guidance." Those gathered nodded their heads and Loti's wife buried her face in the arms of the nun. Po guessed those gathered were family and political allies. Chief Minister Tomi clasped Biet's hands in his own.

"I trust you have done all you can to ease his pain. These days have been a terrible, terrible time for the Vermilion Empire. It's good to know there are still people like you around to ease the burden. I have authorized a state funeral for Loti — when the time comes." Tomi turned to Po and extended his hands. Po clumsily extended his own and Tomi took them. "Loti is a dear friend of mine," Tomi continued. "I have nothing but respect for the work you Ba're do. Thank you."

"I am but a novice," Po said weakly. "The Venerable Abbot does the real work." Tomi frowned.

"Your accent — are you from Ja'pa Province?" asked the Chief Minister. Po raised an eyebrow.

"My family is from Li'an," Po answered. "The Alidun family." Tomi smiled, and Po felt himself weaken before the Chief Minister's charm.

"So is my wife," Tomi said. "You natives of Ja'pa must stick together. Not many of you around."

"Yes, Chief Minister," Po said, bobbing his head. Tomi looked to both monks and held out his arms as if to embrace them, but placed his hands on their shoulders instead.

"Now I'm going to do everything I can do find whoever did this," Tomi said, his voice suddenly cold. "They say the Brotherhood of Kive is to blame. I have men right now asking the questions. I trust both of you will let me know if you hear anything?" Biet nodded and Po felt a stone in his throat.

"The Ba're follow the path of nonviolence," Biet said. "It is unlikely we will hear anything but rest assured our interest is in justice and upholding the Vermilion Peace."

"Good," Tomi said. "The Ba're have always been our allies. Maga was a dangerous man. He would have set back our work fifty years."

Po did not know how to respond. Tomi had flicked from charming and personable to cold in a matter of seconds. Someone called Tomi's name, and he was all charm again.

"War Minister Tuno!" Tomi said. "I was just telling the Ba're we were doing everything in our power to —"

"We got them," Tuno said, cutting Tomi off. "Just now."

"Are you sure?"

"Well, we're waiting for the confession, but it won't be long in coming. Cabinet briefing this evening."

"Chief Minister Tomi," Biet said, trying to slip in a few words. "I must excuse myself — I'd like to speak to Loti's wife — Oh Savani, just a moment of your time?" Biet trailed off after a woman with auburn hair and hazel eyes. Po stood before the Chief Minister wondering if he should do the same. Tomi opened his mouth to speak, but a hush fell over the room and heads turned to the door. A monk stood there, his hands behind his back and his head bowed. Loti's wife wailed and Tomi groaned. Loti was dead.

It was the day of Loti's funeral and bells clanged across Pao'an. In his father's office, Natan added columns in a ledger, trying to ignore the sound outside. The door banged open and Avi backed in, shrugged off his coat and removed a wad of banknotes tied in twine. He dumped them unceremoniously on the desk.

"The banks are closed," Avi said, looking down his hawkish nose. "Damn day of mourning for a man we've never met." Avi stomped over to the far wall and removed a painting from its hook. A safe was set in the bricks behind it.

"The banks are closed tomorrow as well," Natan said, not looking up. Avi paused, picture frame still in hand.

"Two days? Did someone else die?"

"No," Natan said. "Festival of Adasa." Avi put the painting down with a huff and fumbled with a key around his neck.

"Those bureaucrats don't know the value of a day's work. Make them rely on what their hands earn and these holidays would all be scrapped." Natan remained silent. It was best to leave his father to his rants. Avi unlocked the safe, stashed the money inside and returned the picture to the wall.

"How is it?" Avi asked with a nod toward the ledger.

"Fine." Avi ran a finger along the columns, sucking air between his teeth.

"Move," Avi said at last and took Natan's place. Natan shuffled aside and retreated to the far side of the desk. Avi took the pen and began correcting Natan's work.

"Were you looking at the numbers?" Avi asked. "Because it doesn't look like it."

"Yes," Natan said.

"Well if you can't add a few columns what are you going to do with your life? Become a dung farmer?" Natan bit his lip and refused to take the bait. "Dan can run this place by himself," Avi continued. "Dasha has his apprenticeship. If you can't do some measly bookwork, what are you going to do?"

"I'm trying—" *Wrong answer.* Avi thumped the table.

"Trying doesn't work. You're lazy, that is what you are. You're eighteen. There are rich people who can afford to send their sons to the academy or college. I can't afford that." Natan disagreed but now was not the time to raise that issue. "You," Avi continued, wagging a finger at his son. "Do you think you can rely on me all your life? Our trade goes steadily down year on year. There isn't a future for you here. You're too young to remember what it was like before the Peasant Rebellion when caravans carried goods from as far away as Krsaka. Taxes were light. Money plenty. Not today."

"Well I could always join the army," Natan blurted.

"You think real wars are like your games in the yard?" Avi snorted. "You wouldn't last."

"No. I didn't say that," Natan insisted.

Avi threw his hands up.

"You're too stubborn. Get me my pipe and let me do this myself."

Down in the yard, all was unusually quiet. The workers had gone home and there were no traders. Dasha and Dan occupied themselves sparring with quarterstaffs. Natan watched them from the door and decided his father could fetch his own pipe.

"I'm next," Natan called, picking a quarterstaff from the wall rack.

"Stand back," Dan shouted as Natan drew near. Natan waited a safe distance and watched his brothers circle each other. They played an aggressive game. Dan dominated with his size, but Dasha was quick and agile. Dan caught Dasha across the knee and Dasha hit the ground. A flash of anger crossed his brother's face. Dasha swept up his staff and jabbed Dan in the groin. Quarterstaffs forgotten, the two brothers ended up on the ground, arms flailing and legs intertwined. Dan finished on top. Natan hauled him off.

"No missing teeth," Natan said. "I don't want to be grounded again." The brothers dusted themselves off, and Dasha wiped the blood from a split lip.

"You next?" Dan asked, nodding toward Natan.

"I'm next," a voice shouted from the gate. The three brothers turned to see their neighbors Niko and Sado No-Meidu lifting the latch. The brothers were Dan and Dasha's age and their parents owned a workshop next door servicing the shipping on the Blue River with ropes, tackle and minor repairs. The five had grown up together. Niko was bare-chested and had the palms of both hands bound in linen.

"You owe me since last time," Niko said, pointing an accusing finger at Dan. Dan grunted and Natan handed his quarterstaff to Niko.

"No head strikes," Sado said. "No broken bones. If you hit the ground, you forfeit."

"Pay attention Niko," Dan sneered. Niko said nothing but swept his staff wide, clearing a space around him. Dan did the same and the two circled each other, taking a measure of each others' strength. Niko attacked first but Dan knocked him aside. Their staves clacked as they pronged for weakness.

"Here," Sado said, holding out a ceramic bottle. Natan took it and downed a mouthful.

"Goddess of Mercy," Natan said. "It's strong." Sado took the bottle back and took a swig.

"To Loti," he said, lifting the drink. "Always grateful for a day of rest."

"The only useful thing he ever did," Natan said, taking the bottle again.

"He deserved it, you know?" Sado said. "Loti was one of the Reformists. They tried to kill Maga but when that didn't work, they framed him instead." Dan gave a yelp and Natan's attention was drawn back to the fight. Niko stood triumphant with Dan on one knee. Sweat ran down his face and dripped from his nose.

"Niko wins!" Sado yelled, sloshing crystal-clear liquor. Natan helped Dan to his feet and what remained of the bottle was passed around. Niko washed his mouth out and spat.

"Niko has some strong opinions," Sado said.

"Eh?" Niko said as he wiped the sweat from his face.

"You and the Reformists," Sado explained. "You don't like them."

"Damn them," Niko said. "Maga was a good man. He was set up."

"How do you know?" Natan asked. "Not hard to believe he played for power."

"I know people," Niko said, shrugging off the question. "Chief Minister Tomi wants control over cabinet—"

"But he's Chief Minister," Dasha interrupted. "He already has control."

"He could always do with more," Niko said. "And the Emperor is childless — who will he adopt as heir? Tomi has a grandson in waiting. Who wouldn't want to be the grandfather to the Emperor? Adan is already the Emperor's godschild."

"It's all speculation," Dan said dismissively, passing his quarterstaff to Natan. "And who cares who's Emperor? I've never seen him, have you? There will always be someone who sits on the throne and it will never be any of us."

"Look at what you have," Niko said, waving around the yard. "Pao'an is the center of the world, and the Vu run it. What will happen to your trading house when the Kh'areen or the Solari are allowed to trade directly over the Blue River? What will happen to our futures when Astirti, Duang and Yikon flood the Imperial Exams and fill all the positions in government? This isn't how things are supposed to go. There is a correct way of doing things, and an incorrect way of doing things. Disrupt this order, and only bad things can happen. This is the way of the Vu. One day you will have to choose sides." Dan huffed as if he found the idea humorous, but Dasha and Natan listened and remained silent. Sado clapped them on the back.

"Come on, who's next?"

"Your turn Natan," Dasha said, shrugging off Sado's hand, and walking back to the house. Natan looked down at the quarterstaff in his hands and up at Niko.

"Protect your face Natan," Dan said. "Niko plays rough."

"It could do with some improvement," Niko sneered, taking practice swipes.

"You can talk," Sado laughed. "Now same as last time. No head strikes. No broken bones. If you hit the ground, you forfeit." Dan and Sado stepped back to make room.

"Don't hold back little brother," Dan said.

"I never do."

Ashara never lost consciousness. At least she did not think she lost consciousness. She lay there gazing at the sky, her vision blurry and her head throbbing. She tried to move her tongue, but it stuck to the roof of her mouth. The dark shape of a hawk, wings outstretched, flew overhead riding the thermals. *This is it*, Ashara thought, *the day I die. The day* — The thought was broken by a cough that tore her tongue from the roof of her mouth and caused her to grip her head in pain.

Survive, she told herself. Ashara rolled over. The grass tickled her cheeks and jabbed her nose. She shuddered. Outwardly the sun glared down on her, but inside she felt cold. Slowly she brought herself up into a sitting position and hugged her knees.

She knew if she was to survive, she had to get up. Something stung her foot. She looked down. Ants crawling over her toes. *At least I can feel them.*

With a deal of pain, Ashara got up and steadied herself. She took a moment to find her orientation. Back at the road, the caravan was gone. Ashara looked up and down the dirt roadway. There was nothing. There was no one. In the ditch she found seven or eight bodies. It was hard to tell between the tangled limbs, clotted blood and matted black hair where one body started and another began. Ashara would have screamed if her mouth was not so dry. The blank eyes of her father stared up at her from amidst the wretched pile. Ashara dry retched and fell to her knees. Someone had taken the time to relieve the dead of their possessions. The presence of flies indicated they had been there a while.

"Dad—" Ashara whispered. She took a moment to compose herself and looked at the other bodies. She nudged one with her foot, then another. Gaining in courage, Ashara climbed into the ditch and rolled one over. Akdu's waxen face glared at her, his face an expression of horror. Ashara jumped back with a yelp and slapped a hand to her mouth. Her courage was gone. She scrambled back up onto the road and hugged her knees to her chin. She was alone.

"Shit," she said into her arms. Though it hurt, she forced herself to think about her situation. Her family was dead. She did not have her identity papers, and without them she was stuck. She had two choices, neither of them appealing. She could proceed to Ma're and hope to catch up with the caravan. It was still a few days away, and the bandits were likely to shadow the column looking for another opportunity. If Ashara failed to catch up before the caravan passed Ma're, she risked being stopped at the border without papers. Alternatively, she could return the way she had come, to Pao'an, and seek shelter until fresh papers were sent from Baki.

A pressure built in her skull and Ashara pressed her eyes with her palms. She forced herself to concentrate. Pao'an was further away but safer. She did not fear distance. As a child, Ashara had been taught to survive alone in the wilderness. All Kh'areen children, boys and girls, did it as a rite of passage and Ashara was no exception. She would return to Pao'an.

"Survive," Ashara said out loud. She looked north in the direction of Pao'an. She looked back down at the ditch. There was nothing she could do for them. From a stranger's undershirt, she made a pair of rough shoes to replace those she had lost. She then checked her sling and knife and started walking, sticking as much as she could to the cover on the side of the road.

That night, Ashara camped by a stream at the bottom of a gully. She washed in the clear crystal water and dried her clothes by the fire. It energised her and restored some hope. As she dried herself off, she picked *dh'azen* berries from the scrubby bushes that filled much of the gully. They were bitter and normally crushed into a drink with sugar, but Ashara ate them whole and picked more for the road.

The next day after a breakfast of rabbit and wild roots, Ashara proceeded on her way, staying close to the road but never traveling on it. She skirted villages and avoided people wherever possible. Towards midday, she took a shortcut across a ridge and through scrub. As she approached the road again, she entered a shaded copse. She froze. There was movement in the shadows. Ashara's hand fell to the sling at her belt.

"No," came a voice. "Don't." He rose from the foliage, his robe falling back over his buttocks as if he had just been relieving himself. Ashara cast an eye over his overgrown hair, and his beard streaked with multi-colored pigments. His robes were made from scraps of linen, cotton and furs. A bone plug went in one side of his nose and out the other, and his earlobes had large rings which made his ears long and droopy.

"No danger," the man said, holding up his empty hands. Ashara's hand hesitated above the sling at her belt. Her eyes flicked across the copse.

"Are you alone?"

"Alone?" the man said with a chuckle. "That is a matter of perspective." Ashara risked a glance over her shoulder.

"What do you mean?"

"Well, how can I be alone," the man reasoned. "When you are in front of me?"

"I mean is anyone else here? Is there anyone watching us?"

"No," said the man. "But spirits live in copses. I can't discount a few of those." Ashara found the man's speech peculiar but his manners reassuring.

"You are a Vu holy man?" she asked.

"A *kebilu*, yes." Ashara relaxed her hand and took a few steps forward.

"Well I mean you no harm," Ashara said. "I mean only to go on my way."

"And what way is that?" the holy man asked. "I ask only because it gets lonely out here."

"Pao'an," Ashara said. The holy man shook his head.

"I am only to Je'ka. But it is a few miles to the turnoff. I will go with you."

"Who said I wanted to go with you?" Ashara said.

"These roads are dangerous," the holy man said. "And people are not safe alone. You will appreciate the protection of a holy man."

"And what if I rob you?"

"Of what? Do you think I'm afraid? I have spent my life in the wilderness. A Kh'areen girl with a bag of stones and a butter knife is not my worry." Ashara rankled at the jibe but decided to trust the holy man. *The company would be nice*, she thought. *Even if it is a Vu.*

The pair left the copse and after some nonsensical small talk Ashara asked him about his earlobe rings.

"Ah," the *kebilu* said. "They are for listening to the gods." He pointed to his upper ear and continued: "We listen to people here. But it is with our earlobes we hear the gods."

"And the nose?" Ashara asked. "Is it to smell the gods?" The *kebilu* gave a deep snort that turned into a laugh.

"No, no. Don't be silly. The gods have no smell." He turned humorless. "Demons," he said. "We smell demons."

"What? And they have a smell?"

"Of course. They stink like the rotten creatures they are. Part of identifying demons is their smell. How else do you distinguish an incubus from a familiar, or indeed a succubus? We have to know them all — or at least the sixty-six chief demons. And that's on top of the five hundred and twenty-seven gods." Now Ashara bit back a snort.

"Five hundred and twenty-seven? How do you remember them all?"

"Remember?" said the holy man. "We don't remember; we *know*. You are Kh'areen, yes?" Ashara nodded.

"You worship one god. You call him Tanli—"

"Tanri," Ashara corrected.

"But," the holy man said, raising a finger, speaking over her. "His real name is Kive Ku'olu, whom the commoners call Kive. His brother is Nulagia the Plague Lord and aurochs-like Sato the Lord of the Battle. They are the sons of the Great Serpent, En, whom the commoners call Heaven —" Ashara shook her head.

"No— We worship Tanri and only Tanri. There are no other gods." The holy man laughed.

"What? No other gods? So, when Tanri is busy, who changes the seasons or causes crops to grow? Who — such as Nulagia — watches over them and keeps them from pestilence?" He said this as if it held an undefeatable logic.

"That's not how life works," she said. "Tanri set the world in motion. He doesn't have to make every blade of grass grow. Do all Vu think like you?" She found it hard to believe the Vu, the very heart of the Vermilion Empire, could survive with such a chaotic worldview.

"No," the *kebilu* said, for the first time almost looking angry, his eyes intense. "There are the Ba're. Godless heathens. They follow the foreigner Dasanika and his nonsense. They think because they can argue from sunup to sundown they must have found some deeper meaning to life." He spat on the ground. "But there are always fools ready to believe them." The conversation promised to go downhill from there, and Ashara was pleased when they arrived at the crossroads.

"Je'ka is that way," the holy man said with the wave of a hand. "Do you know how to reach Pao'an?"

"Yes," Ashara said. "I know the area." The holy man looked stern.

"You're not local. You're not Vu. This is a foreign land to you."

"Foreign?" Ashara said. "Your own gods declare the Emperor rules *All Under Heaven*. I am but a humble servant of the empire."

"You know what I mean," said the holy man. Ashara was glad to see the back of him.

That night Ashara slept in the corner of a field against a stone wall. The next day it became harder to avoid people with plenty of farmers in their fields. Ashara began to travel on the road in case she was caught sneaking by the villages and thought a thief. From their doorways, old women hissed at her and waved their hands as if to ward off any hex she might cast on them.

As the sun went down, Ashara came across a roadside shrine. Heavy clouds promised rain and lights were already showing from nearby villages. Ashara sought shelter under the shrine's thatched roof. Inside she almost changed her mind. On the altar sat a fierce statue of a dog standing on its hind legs, a massive phallus erect. Its bulging eyes seemed to follow her, and its terrible rows of teeth looked ready to snap shut. The bird droppings dripping down its head only made it appear ghastlier.

One night, she promised herself. *Survive.*

CHAPTER 3

"The Imperial Cabinet is a council of senior ministers appointed directly by the Emperor. While the cabinet's role is officially to advise the Emperor, in practice it rules directly in his name. The highest position in the cabinet is that of Chief Minister who, in being Minister of the Imperial Service, is second only to the Emperor."

A History of the Vermilion Empire

Niko stumbled through the dark. He regretted not bringing a lamp. The docks beneath the Inner City were a warren of piers and warehouses, all facing out onto the Blue River. Niko felt his foot squish into something. He hoped it was fruit fallen from one of the barges. From the smell of the surrounding streets, he doubted it. Niko saw the shadow of a building ahead, silhouetted by the starlight behind, and headed toward it.

Suddenly, an arm grabbed Niko from behind and pushed him down into a choke hold. The brute strength hurt Niko's ribs where Natan had given him a beating days before. Niko thrust left and right, trying to break the hold.

"What's a bushel of wheat these days?" the voice hissed in Niko's ear.

"Six copper *jet* but I could do it for five," Niko croaked back. The choke hold relaxed, and Niko pulled away. He straightened his shirt and glared angrily at the attacker. It was Bido. In the starlight, Niko could just make out his features.

"What was that for?" Niko demanded.

"Quiet," Bido said. "Can't be too careful. You still in?"

"Yeah. Well, I showed up, didn't I?"

"Fair enough," Bido replied and took Niko by the elbow. "Come with me." He dragged Niko down an alley and across a side street. They paused to wait for a patrol to pass and then carried on. Ahead rose a row of storage sheds tightly packed and double bolted. Bido took Niko to one and slipped him between the shed and its neighbor. The gap was so narrow Niko shuffled sideways with only a hand's width between nose and wall. Halfway down, Bido dislodged two loose planks and Niko climbed through into the darkness beyond. The man followed and replaced the planks behind him.

"This him? Took your time."

"He was late," Bido replied. Someone lifted the cover on a lamp, and the room filled with a dim light. Half a dozen men seated in a semi-circle. They were dressed in dark clothes and knee-high boots, the same as Niko had been instructed to wear. Opposite them sat a Vu'du holy man crosslegged and puffing on a long-stemmed pipe. Unlike the holy men out on the streets of Pao'an, this holy man was dressed down for the occasion. His matted hair, streaked with dye, was hidden under a woolen hood and the normally vibrant robes were swapped for dirty sackcloth. They would all merge well into the darkness of the night.

"Take a seat," the holy man said without emotion. "Welcome to the Brotherhood. Bido has vouched for you — that will be enough for tonight anyway." Niko took his place among the forms. He felt Bido nudge him as if to say, '*you owe me one*', but Niko resisted a reaction, and out the corner of his eye, he saw Bido turn his sullen face back to the holy man.

"Now, where were we? Yes. Three years ago this so-called '*sage*,' the Master Kalaki, arrived in Pao'an. He carried with him a great deal of books and scrolls that, he argued, showed the '*true reality*' of the world. He argued the world is a sphere and he could place the Vermilion Empire's location accurately on this sphere using astronomical measurement. Chief Minister Tomi, the Great Traitor, used this idea to undermine the Vu'du faith and commissioned a public monument in Covenant Square promoting this *theory*." Niko could hear the scorn in the holy man's last word when he said this.

"The Great Traitor," the holy man continued. "And his ilk are tearing at the roots of Vu civilization. The Vermilion Empire is threatened. The people forget the true source of all power and government in this world and turn to foreign concepts and ideas. This so-called *true reality* of Kalaki's puts the Vermilion Empire not in the center of the sphere, but toward the bottom — a place of no special importance — yet we know at creation the Great Serpent, En, placed Pao'an at the middle of a disk and later, via the Blood Covenant, gave all power over to the Emperors." Niko felt the men stir around him. The air was heavy with their combined heat.

"And this is self-evident," the holy man continued. "For the directions on a compass point east, south, west, and north. Summer comes from the north and winter from the south. If this is a sphere, where does one begin and the other end? Does Kalaki say the scriptures are wrong?" The men murmured.

"And so," the holy man said, getting to the point. "You of the Brotherhood of Kive are gathered here. Tonight we strike…"

Shortly thereafter, dark shapes moved from the warren of storage sheds and along the docks to the piles of rubbish that lined the banks beneath the city walls. Niko brought up the rear, somewhat unsure of himself. Bido had told Niko to come along that night and dress appropriately, but he had not said what they were going to do exactly. Niko, though normally overconfident, did not feel like he was ready. Stuck in these thoughts, he stepped on Bido's heel.

"*Oi*, watch it," Bido whispered.

"Quiet," the holy man hissed. "Or you're both going home."

"Sorry," Niko mumbled. Ahead a fire flickered with figures warming their hands. They were sewer rats; those who made their living picking through the man-sized pipes that crisscrossed under the surface of Pao'an. Shunned as social outcasts, Niko had lived his whole life watching them from afar but never speaking to any in person.

"Brothers," the holy man said, approaching the sewer rats. "Are we on time?"

The sewer rats glanced from the fire and some withdrew quietly, a hand or two placed in their jackets. The rest bowed out of respect to the *kebilu*. A wizened man with a wispy gray beard stepped forward and doffed his Vu-style cap.

"We're all set," the man said. "The guards are turning a blind eye tonight. Jimi will be taking you." The man indicated a young boy, around twelve years old. Niko thought the boy looked more like a pickpocket than a sewer rat.

"But first," the old man said. "You know the drill." The man held out his cap and the holy man dropped a single silver *li* into it.

"It was a pleasure doing business with you," the sewer rat said. "Jimi!" Jimi stepped forward, bowed a second time to the holy man, and took a coil of rope from his belt.

"Here," he said, handing it to the men. "Hold on to this. I lead the way. Don't let go." It was not far from the sewer rat camp to the first culvert leading under the city wall. Normally the iron gates were closed at night and sentries stood on duty. That night the gates hung open and no guards were in sight. Jimi led the men under the city in total darkness.

The sewers were a foreign environment for Niko. Unable to see where he was going, he had to trust the men in front. The water reached to his lower shins and Niko understood then the need for knee-high boots. They sloshed forward, stumbling from time to time. He barely kept up as the men in front moved quickly. They had all done it before. They were used to the tunnels and Jimi had no problem navigating in the inky black.

Niko shuddered as his neck passed under a drip and water ran down his back. Looking up, he discerned a stormwater grate and a lonely star beyond. In that one instant of distraction, he tripped and fell to one knee. Water soaked through his trousers and the rope was yanked from his hands. Niko let out a cry and instinctively put his hands out to steady himself. They plunged down and grasped at the slimy bottom. The column stopped when they heard the splash and Niko soon felt a hand on his shoulder.

"You alright?" Jimi asked.

"Just slipped," Niko said, glad the other men could not see him.

"Better pay attention," Bido sneered. "Won't last long in the Brotherhood if these sewer marches aren't your thing."

"Just getting used to it," Niko said as he took the end of the rope again. "Won't happen again." In the distance, a dog bark echoed up the tunnel.

"Quick," Jimi said. Niko could not see the other men but he felt the mood change. The column set off at a trot.

"I thought you —" the holy man protested.

"No talking," Jimi replied. Niko could hear the dogs getting closer. Suddenly the column stopped and Niko plowed into Bido's back. Bido let out a yelp and fell face first into the sewage, showering the rest of the party in filth. Niko came down on top of him. Both men were soon covered head to toe as they grappled with each other and shouted angry curses. Niko managed to land a good punch to Bido's jaw and Bido landed a blow to Niko's elbow.

"Stop it, stop it at once!" the holy man roared, careless of the sound he made. "Our enemies are out there, not down here." The two men broke apart but not without parting kicks and jabs.

"I don't care who started it, but no more fighting!" the holy man shrieked. Niko flinched at the anger in the *kebilu*'s voice.

"Ummm..." another voice said.

"What?" the holy man barked.

"Jimi's gone."

"Gone? What do you mean *gone*?"

"He's not here."

"Impossible," the holy man spat. "Jimi! Jimi!" No reply. The sound of barking drew closer. The others froze as the reality of what was said, or more rightly what was not said, slowly dawned on them. As if on queue they joined in calling Jimi's name.

"How do we get out?" Bido squeaked, his voice uncharacteristically high pitched.

"Hold on," another said. "I felt something back there. I think it was a ladder. Wait for me." The others waited with bated breath. Niko found the fumes overwhelming, and for an instant he rubbed his nose only to remember where his hands had been. *Shit.*

"Hurry up," someone said, the voice quivering. The group was near breaking point.

"Found it," the man called. The conspirators headed toward the voice and looked up to see a faint silvery light. Someone grabbed the ladder and started to climb. Others joined him.

"Stop!" a voice shouted. "Stop where you are!"

Niko turned just in time to see half a dozen figures holding oil lamps round a corner and break into a run. The water surged around their feet, leashed dogs leading the pack. There was a mad scramble for the ladder. Feet stepped on hands and elbows connected with heads. Niko felt a blow to his temple and dropped with a splash. He grabbed at the rungs and pulled himself up. They were slippery, and Niko almost lost his grip again, but he paid it no heed. He grabbed for the starlight above and his hand felt the rim of the utility hole. The ladder shook as someone jumped on the ladder behind him. Niko hauled himself up and got his elbows and then his face into the fresh, clean air.

"Not so fast," Bido sneered. "Keep them busy." Niko looked up to see the ugly face of the man who recruited him looking down. There was a moment of stunned confusion. A boot connected with his head. The utility hole cover slammed back down, knocking Niko off the top rung of the ladder. Darkness enveloped him and then a bone-jarring jolt caused him to lose consciousness.

Deep within the Imperial Palace, Chief Minister Tomi Mei-Uduga reclined on cushions. His wife, Muni, rested by his side, her hands cupped under her fleshy chin. A minstrel plucked the strings of an instrument, singing an ancient court ballad, and a chained wyvern flicked its tail and paced between two pillars. Guests murmured in conversation.

"What are you thinking about?" Muni whispered, barely audible above the song.

"Nothing," Tomi said, his hands reaching for a fruit platter between them. "Nothing important." Tomi took a half apple and made a show of eating it. His eyes narrowed. Across the room, his son-in-law was similarly reclined, talking with a guest from the Emperor's household. Tomi eyed them suspiciously. He did not trust his daughter's husband.

There was movement out the corner of his eye. Tomi turned his head slightly. A nursemaid approached, shuffling his four-year-old grandson in front of her. She stopped at the required distance, and Tomi waved her forward.

"Your Grace," the nursemaid said. "Your grandson wishes to say goodnight."

Tomi smiled and spread his arms for little Adan, who promptly grinned and fell into Tomi's embrace. The Chief Minister planted a kiss on his grandson's cheek.

"Goodnight, Adan."

"Goodnight, Grandpa. Can you come tell me a story?

"Not tonight," Tomi said. "How about tomorrow?" Adan pulled away and looked at the ground.

"Okay," he said with a huff. "Tomorrow."

"Now, go say goodnight to your grandmother." Muni took Adan by the hand and gave him a wet kiss. Adan curled his lips and tugged to get away.

"Go on, off to bed," she said. Adan nodded and skipped to say goodnight to his parents, nursemaid in tow.

"We must soon think of a tutor," Muni said to Tomi.

"With time," Tomi said. "I have just the fellow in mind."

"You don't mean Master Ajot do you?"

"Of course I mean Master Ajot. He'll be a good tutor."

"I always found him harsh," Muni said, sitting up.

"Court life is harsh. And with what we have planned it doesn't pay to let him be spoilt. He is the Emperor's godschild."

"I guess so. I rather thought we could approach Master Kavati."

"Master Kavati?" Tomi frowned. "He's too busy with his residency."

"Yes," Muni said. "But he'd drop that for this opportunity." Tomi Mei-Uduga waved his hand.

"Leave the poor man alone." Muni looked hurt. "Fine. I'll invite them both to the palace for a chat. How about that?" Muni smiled and nodded.

"That will do nicely," she said, reclining back into the cushions. Tomi rolled his eyes. He would have to find a way for Master Kavati to be otherwise engaged.

Movement. A Vermilion Guard stepped into the dining room doorway and blocked the entrance. Someone was seeking admission. Tomi wondered if it was a messenger from the Ministry of Virtue. They had been busy the last few nights running sting operations against the Brotherhood of Kive and had successfully netted a few coterie.

Tomi placed his unfinished apple down. Around the hall, guests briefly stopped talking and their eyes followed him as he walked toward the door. Seeing, however, nothing of interest they quickly returned to their gossip. Only the wyvern maintained its vigil; its black eyes shadowing Tomi's every step.

"Sergeant," Tomi said. "Who is this man?" The Vermilion Guard did not take his eyes off the visitor.

"He is from the Imperial Courier Service. He carries a message for your eyes only." Tomi eyed the man over. He was turned out in the correct livery. The man avoided eye contact and scuffed the floor.

"Why can't this wait until morning?" Tomi asked. "We have guests. This is not a time for business." The messenger held up the folded paper and raised his eyes to Tomi's chin.

"Your Grace, forgive me," he said. "It carries a yellow seal and can be given to no one but you." Tomi's felt a sudden uneasiness rise in the pit of his stomach. Yellow seals were stamped in only the most serious times of crisis.

"Pass it here," Tomi said and accepted the letter passed over the guard's shoulder. Tomi snapped the seal and unfolded the contents. His eyes scanned the page, and then he read it again a second time.

"Sergeant," he said, his legs weakening. "Escort this man out and raise the household. I want runners sent to each member of the cabinet. I'll meet them in the cabinet room at the tenth bell."

"In the morning, Your Grace?" the sergeant asked.

"No. This evening. As soon as possible. Right away. Tenth bell. No one is to be late." The sergeant snapped his heels and saluted.

"Immediately, Your Grace."

Two hours later, Chief Minister Tomi waited alone in the meeting room of the Imperial Cabinet. The lamps cast a flickering glow over the dark, archaic fixtures. A stone table dominated the middle of the room and at one end stood Tomi's hardwood chair, that reserved for the Chief Minister of the Imperial Cabinet. Around the table were smaller chairs, each inscribed with the name of their office. One was removed, leaving a gap yet to be filled. *How many more will be empty before this is over?*

Members of the cabinet began to arrive in various states of official dress. On entering they nodded respectfully to Tomi and then bowed to the statue of the Great Serpent in its alcove by the door. Some took out balls of amber resin and dropped them in the bowl of hot coals before the statue. The scent offerings soon filled the cabinet room with a sweet odour. The last minister to arrive was the Minister of War, Tuno Bago-Nula.

"Your Grace," he said. The ministers waited silently as Tuno Bago-Nula shuffled over to his chair and took his seat.

Tomi looked around the table. The cabinet ministers returned his gaze. Each would want to know why they had been summoned so late that night.

"Gentlemen," Tomi began. "One thousand, one hundred and nine years ago the First Emperor ascended Mount Tabo and there made a covenant between gods and men, sealed with the Vermilion blood, to rule with benevolence, to uphold justice, to remember the poor, the sick and the widowed. In exchange, the gods promised him an empire — an empire that would rule all under Heaven." The ministers nodded, well familiar with the formal Vu style.

"There have been challenges," Tomi continued with a shrug. "Sometimes the gods have tested us with adversity. Sometimes we failed. And when we failed the gods saw fit to punish us. Emperors have come and gone, dynasties have risen and dynasties have fallen, but still the covenant remains."

"But rebellion, treason, and civil war," Tomi said with a nod toward Maga's empty chair. "Are not part of the covenant sealed those many years ago. These go against the divine mandate. Whoever does these things goes to war, not just with humanity, but with the gods." Tomi cleared his throat as if to emphasise what he was about to say.

"Tonight I received word of just such a thing. General Jano Maretaki, commander of the 7th Army, is questioning the arrest of the traitor Maga. In doing so he questions the legitimacy of this cabinet. And — to the matter I brought you here for — he is, as we speak, marching on Pao'an."

⚜

Ashara smelt Pao'an before she saw it. The odor of half a million people and animals wafted for miles, and though it assaulted her senses, she found comfort in the familiar smell. She quickened her pace and joined the main road just east of the first watchtower where Pao'an became visible through the trees. She paused a moment, noticing the changes. Workers bent their backs digging out the ditches beneath the ramparts, while others raised additional watchtowers and walkways.

Odd, she thought to herself.

At the city gate she joined a queue, but had no trouble getting in. The guards appeared more interested in collecting tolls than checking beggar girls for the right paperwork. She worked her way through the jam of carts and stopped at an intersection.

"Which way's the Blue River?" she asked a fruit seller.

"Bugger off," said the vendor, reaching for his cleaver. "Paying customers only." Ashara bunched her fists and took a step forward, but the vendor stood his ground. "You deaf?" he continued. "The guards are only a shout away."

"Just asking," Ashara sneered and slunk away to check a street sign and see if she could understand the Vu script. Before long she noticed eyes on her, and an old fellow leaning on a crutch approached.

"This's my corner," he said. "Find yer own."

"Just looking for the Blue River," Ashara said. "Which way is it?"

"Sure," said the man, rolling his eyes. "You're sightseeing. You need a better cover than that. Now shoo." Ashara retreated. She'd walked these streets many times before, but only ever when following her father. She made the best guess and followed her instinct, soon proving herself right. Tenements transitioned into workshops and warehouses, and along the banks of the river the tops of masts became visible over the berm. Not far from there she found the row of trading houses, factories, and riverside storage firms that her family always visited when they had come to Pao'an. Ashara walked down the street checking the signs. Above one particular open gate hung an old wooden sign, faded and worn with age but still readable: *Luka-Tudo Trading House*, and underneath, *Established 1063 Imperial Era*.

Ashara paused at the gate. Inside traders and workers went about their tasks loading and unloading two dozen pack animals and ox carts. *This is it.* She stepped inside and skirted the activity. Avi was talking to a trader — an animated conversation by all appearances. She waited and listened.

"I'll accept nine copper *jet* per unit," the trader was saying.

"Nine coppers?" Avi answered. "I'll pay five."

"Come on, Avi. With war on the horizon prices are going up."

"Five is still the government benchmark," Avi said. "More than fair."

"You and I both know the benchmark is slow and without a Revenue Minister this crisis will be over before the price is adjusted."

"I could go up to six," Avi countered.

"What? And sell it at ten over the river before the next hour bell rings? Eight."

"Six," Avi said with a little more force this time. The trader shrugged and turned to leave.

"Seven," Avi said.

"Look," said the trader. "I don't want to waste your time. I can get nine coppers by going down the street. I'm happy to do eight just so I don't have to go any further."

Avi's face turned sour and his shoulders sagged.

"Eight copper *jet* it is then," Avi said, holding out his hand. The trader shook on it and yelled for his men to unload the goods. Avi's eyes fell on Ashara.

"What are you doing here? Out. No begging. We're a business, not a charity house." Ashara threw a forearm across her face, expecting a blow.

"Kh'am Daladh'an," she yelped. Avi stopped. *He recognizes the name.*

"What do you know of him?" Avi snapped.

"He's my father," Ashara said. "Was my father."

"Was? Talk sense and make it fast."

"We were here two weeks ago. When we left, our column was ambushed by bandits. My father and brothers died." His eyes drilled her's. The features of his face softened. He massaged his hands as if they caused him pain.

"You had two brothers," he said.

"Bayar and Akdu," Ashara said. "I'm Ashara Daladh'an."

"What do you want from us?"

"Please, if I may," Ashara said. "I don't want charity. I need somewhere to stay while I can get my papers sorted — no, no, not charity — I can work for my keep. It is just, well, your's is the only house I know..."

Avi folded his arms and stood silently. Ashara gnawed her lower lip. Without a word, Avi crossed to the house and returned with Oni close behind. Ashara had only met her once, and though she had been nice enough, her appearance was severe with intense eyes and gray hair tied into a tight bun at the back of her head. Avi talked to her as if Ashara was not there.

"The caravan was attacked, and somehow she escaped. Wants a place to stay while she gets herself sorted."

"And this is Kh'am's daughter?" Oni asked.

"So she says. Looks familiar and the timing is right."

"Well, I could do with help."

"Can't you get Natan to do it?" Avi asked. "He seems to have plenty of time on his hands."

"You'll need him in the yard no doubt. War has a way of making labor hard to find."

Avi sucked on his teeth and ran a hand through his mop of black hair. Ashara picked at her elbow and shuffled her feet. Time seemed to stand still.

"Right," Avi said, finally turning to Ashara. "You can stay here. But — before you get too excited: you'll do as you're told, sleep in the kitchen, and take your meals after the family has eaten. And I don't envisage any wages being necessary. This isn't charity. You'll have your shelter and your food."

Ashara toyed with asking for even one copper *jet* a week, but Avi struck her as the sort to throw her out on the street rather than part with real coin.

"That's fine," Ashara said. "I don't want charity. Just a fair opportunity to work."

"That's the spirit," Avi said.

"Let's get you cleaned up, shall we?" Oni suggested. She extended a calloused hand.

A cat sat watching her. Judging her. Ashara turned away and slipped into the fresh clothes Oni provided her. The cat meowed.

"*Oh,* stop watching me," Ashara said, half imagining the cat would reply. She looked back. It swished its tail and sniffed the air.

"Do they fit?" Oni asked from the doorway. "I have some others you could try."

"They'll do. Your fabric is so fine. Are you sure I can wear them?"

"They were my sister's, they don't fit me," Oni said. "Now come help me. We've things to prepare."

Down in the kitchen, a fire flickered in the hearth. Ashara gaped at the food. Sausages, onions and sprigs of thyme hung from the rafters, and a leg of lamb roasted on the spit. Against the back wall lay piled cases of vinegars and oils, hogsheads of pork, salted sardines, and rolls of cheese. *How could the Kh'areen ever compete with this?* Ashara wondered.

Oni touched her arm and indicated the counter.

"We're making pastries," she said. "For tomorrow."

"What's special about tomorrow?" Ashara asked.

"Nothing." She indicated the flour and showed Ashara how to knead the dough.

"What's happening at the wall?" Ashara asked after a time.

"The wall?" Oni said. "They're getting it ready. There's a war — or so the men say. A general marches on Pao'an."

"Are we safe?"

"I wouldn't worry about it," said Oni. "These things happen — can you pass the butter? — Thanks. Avi said three whole armies are being moved here to reinforce the city. It'll be sorted out before the traitor even gets here. I —"

The main door banged open and a worker yelled for Oni to come.

"Quickly! They have him! You've got to come. They have your son!"

Oni exchanged glances with Ashara, and both women ran for the door.

CHAPTER 4

"In the early days of the Vermilion Empire, the land was dominated by powerful lords and ladies. Their relationship with the Emperor was a constant source of tension and unrest. To combat this a series of reforms were introduced stripping the nobility of their power. All land was turned over to the Emperor and divided up into 'Gifts' by the Ministry of Land. A peasant coming of age would then gain a Gift for the length of their natural life in exchange for a set annual rent or goods in kind. This of course required a large state bureaucracy and the setting of rents a matter of political tension."

A History of the Vermilion Empire

The exam was finished, and the students were allowed one night off to venture into the city. Though they were under a strict curfew and not allowed to take money with them, this did not stop the novices' excitement at being allowed out.

"Hurry up," Po said. "I want to go see that play."

"Hold on," Anjan replied. "Just a little longer." Anjan's eyes fixed on a puppet show. To the amusement of the crowd, a caricature of General Jano Maretaki sneezed and the general's helmet fell off. Po rolled his eyes.

"The play will be more intelligent."

"This is funny," Anjan protested, palms out. "Enjoy yourself."

A puppet dressed in flamboyant soldier's gear bent to retrieve the helmet and accidentally backed into Jano's second-in-command. The second-in-command squealed excitedly. That was enough for Po.

"Right, we're going." Anjan groaned and followed Po through the crowd.

"Okay," he said. "But I choose what we do after the play." Po did not respond. Ahead he could see the stage the actors were using. Above it in vibrant colors hung banners proclaiming that the entertainment was paid for by the Emperor for the "*Edification of the Populous.*" The play was *The Deification of the First Emperor* and had lofty undertones. There were not so subtle references to General Jano and other current political figures. Without the slapstick, it did not take long for Anjan to lose interest.

"Eh?" Anjan said, nudging Po. "If General Jano is so bad, why did they make him a general?"

"He was a rebel leader in the Peasant Rebellion. At the Peace of Tabo he brought the rebels over to the Emperor's side. Listen, and they'll tell you."

"Yeah," Anjan said. "But that was like twenty years ago. That's plenty of time to get rid of him if this is all true." Po shrugged.

"I guess so. But people change."

"I think they're afraid."

"Who?" Po asked.

"The government," Anjan explained quietly. "They're afraid people really like Jano." Po looked around to see if anyone was listening.

"We can't talk like this," he hissed. "You'll get us in trouble."

"I'm just stating the obvious. Besides, this play is boring. I think they wrote it in an awful hurry." Po had to concede Anjan had a point.

"Fine," Po said, giving up. "What should we do now then?"

"Let's go exploring," he said.

The pair were shortly lost in the side streets leading off the great avenue. They found rows of tightly packed eateries and alehouses with lanterns hanging outside and tables scattered over the cobbles. The influx of soldiers and laborers into the city kept business brisk. Po carefully picked his way through the crowd.

"House Ale! House Ale!" one man yelled from a doorway. "One *ku'net* a pint!"

"Dancing beauties," hollered another. "Beauties from far Pa'gan! One *jet* entry and first drink on the house!" Po and Anjan gave the second place a wide berth.

"Not sure we'll find much down here," Po said, looking back over his shoulder.

"Roast pork and potatoes," a young lady called, a chalkboard with prices propped up in her arms. "Five *ku'net* a plate. Seasoned with our special blend."

"*Argh*," Anjan groaned, rubbing his belly. "What I would give right now for a meal." As if on cue, a woman rose from a stool at the open front of a restaurant and moved to intercept Po and Anjan.

"Holy ones," she said breathlessly in an Astirti accent. "Please, come with me."

"We're fine, thank you," Po said.

"No, no. Come, sit," she persisted. "Free — a gift. You are Disciples of Dasanika, no?"

"We are Ba're novices," Po corrected. He realized her confusion. The Astirti recognized Dasanika as a god-like figure, while the Ba're considered him human.

"The difference is not so great," the woman insisted. "You bring good luck to my business, yes? Maybe Dasanika will protect my sons."

"That isn't how it works," Po said, but Anjan cut him off.

"We would love to sit and talk," Anjan said. "But you don't have to give us food."

"No, no," the Astirti said, shaking her head. "You sit, you eat." Po was about to protest when Anjan winked at him and guided his friend inside. The mother led the way to the back of the restaurant where there was a raised stage.

"For a worried mother, yes?" she kept saying. When they were seated, and the woman had disappeared to the kitchen, Po leaned over and whispered in Anjan's ear.

"What are you doing? You know Ba're don't believe in the concept luck. It's superstition. You give false hope."

"You tell her that," Anjan said. "I believe in making mothers happy."
Po sighed.

The woman returned and pushed two large mutton platters in front
of the novices. The mutton swam in a heavy butter sauce laced with
pepper, in the style of the Astirti's homeland. The woman plonked
herself down opposite the pair.

"You eat," she commanded. Po and Anjan exchanged glances and
began to eat.

"Now," she said, fetching a small wooden box. "These are my two
dear sons, Taljat and Serik." The woman flicked a latch, and the box
sprung open to reveal two panels with bronze frames. On each panel
was a portrait of a young man. "They are with the Sixth Army, Fourth
Banner," the woman explained, a twinkle of pride in her eyes. "They
serve under General Nulu. Brave boys. And strong. You would not
believe how strong."

"You must be proud," Anjan said between mouthfuls, butter running
down his chin.

"Oh yes," the woman said. "They make their mother proud. But I
also worry. I understand there is a war. I hear General Jano wants to
attack Pao'an."

"We have heard," Po said before Anjan could say anything.

"So I worry for my sons," the mother explained. "War is a terrible,
terrible thing. My boys will come shortly to reinforce Pao'an, I'm sure
of it."

"I know there is nothing you can do," the woman continued. "You
are not military leaders or politicians. But promise me you will keep my
sons in your prayers. May Dasanika keep them safe from harm."

"We..." Po began, but Anjan kicked him under the table.

"It would be an honor," Anjan said. The mother dabbed an eye with
the corner of her apron.

"You are good boys. May Dasanika bless you for the kindness you
show me."

Po and Anjan left the restaurant with an invitation to come next time they were *"in the city."* Realizing that curfew was quickly approaching, the two novices hurried in the direction of the monastery.

"Well, that was awkward," Po said.

"You need to enjoy yourself," Anjan said. "Relax. The woman wanted hope."

"Yeah and you encouraged her in her superstition. What would Dugen say?"

"Dugen can keep his opinions. Po, you're smart but when it comes to people, you're as thick as a dreadbeast's arse. You —"

A man collided with them and dropped a pile of papers.

"Sorry," Po blurted. "Here, we'll help —"

"Never mind," said the man in a fluster. "You two look educated, here — take two of them." He offered up two folded fliers and stuffed the rest into his coat. Po and Anjan accepted and the man disappeared among the crowds.

"That was weird," Anjan said. They looked down at the leaflets in their hands.

> *General Jano comes to save you.*
> *Tomi is the Great Traitor.*

Small block print filled the rest of the paper in essay format. Anjan exchanged glances with Po and without a word they tucked the leaflets into their robes. Some things were best read in the safety of their cots.

Eastbank lay under a lazy afternoon sun. Natan and Sado played a game of *sa'na* in an upstairs room of the No-Meidu residence, taking turns rolling four-sided dice and moving their counters around an elegantly carved board.

"Two," Natan said, glancing at the white dots on the pyramid-like dice. "Damn." He chewed his thumbnail and added a new counter to the board. Sado laughed and took the cup with the dice in it. He rolled.

"Wrath of Heaven," he said, returning Natan's token to the side. "Not your day is it? Your turn." Natan retrieved the dice and paused in thought.

"So you really don't know where Niko's gone?" He rolled and moved a counter the required distance.

"Nope," Sado said. "No one knows." Sado took his turn.

"Three," Natan said. "Goddess of Mercy. I'm safe." Sado slapped his thighs in mock outrage, picked up a porcelain cup and sculled the contents. His face flushed red and he shuddered. Natan took the bottle and went to pour another cup.

"We're out," he said.

"There's another one in the cupboard."

Natan crossed Sado's room to the cabinet.

"Which one do you want to open?"

"You choose," Sado said. Natan returned to the table with a suitable bottle. Sado nodded in approval.

"You don't think he's run off to join the army, do you?" Natan asked, seated once again.

"I doubt it," Sado said. "He would've said something. And you know what he thinks of this lot — the Reformists in the Imperial Palace. No, if my brother joined anyone it would be General Jano and the Vu'tai — but Jano is far away, and Niko disappeared before we all heard."

"A mystery alright," Natan said. "How're your parents?"

"You saw," Sado said. "Trying to be strong. They've got their business to run."

A door banged downstairs, and Sado's mother called up.

"Sado! Can you come down please?"

"Soon!" Sado called back, rolling his eyes.

"Quickly!" his mother shouted and slammed the door.

"I can't get a break anymore," Sado said, lowering his voice. "Now I have twice the work." Natan put the dice aside and swept crumbs from the table.

"You go, I can wait," he said. Then he cocked his head. "Lot of noise outside."

"Some customer will be disputing the bill," Sado said. "They agree to everything and then think the total is up for discussion."

"Yeah, we get that. They only do it once."

A scream carried from the yard, followed by a string of shouts. Natan looked to the window and Sado jumped from his seat.

"Soldiers!" Sado said. "Outside."

"They're what?" Natan scrambled from his seat stood at the sill. "Not soldiers. Those are guards. And look - virtuemen."

"What's that?" Sado asked, pointing to a wooden frame being erected beyond the gate. "Is that a gallows?"

"We need to get out. Quick."

"Wait, that's my mother!" Sado screamed, grabbing for the window latch. He threw it open and pulled himself through onto the roof. Natan tried to follow but boots stamped on the stairs and guards burst into the room. He wheeled on them and raised clenched fists."

"Stop!" yelled a captain in a crested helmet. "Hands on your head where we can see them."

"No," Natan said, hoping to buy his friend time. "First, what's this about?"

"This house harbored a traitor," said the captain as his men spread through the room. One lunged at Natan, but Natan sidestepped and drove his knuckles into the man's jaw. In a spray of blood and teeth, the guard went down on all fours. The others raised their batons and charged. Natan fell into a fighting stance and shouldered the first one into the wall, kneeing him as he went down, and snatched the baton.

Just like our games, he told himself. *Think of it like that. You can beat the neighborhood, you can beat these men.* Two more came at him. Natan slipped to the side, giving himself room. In a blur of batons, wood crashed on wood and one man swore. Another threw a chair which broke over Natan's back. He fell to one knee and struck his attacker's kneecap. The man howled and fell onto Natan. The two grappled on the floorboards and more piled on. The air drove from Natan's lungs and someone pinned his hands.

"Bastard. You'll hang for this." They dragged him to his feet and led him downstairs. In the doorway, Natan lurched, smashing a guard into the post. For an instant he was free, then a baton drove into his stomach. Natan wretched.

"Listen, you mutt!" Blood dribbled between the man's bronze teeth. "You're dead." Yanked to his feet, they led him to the scaffold. Violent hands tugged a noose over his head and pulled the knot tight against the nape of his neck. Natan cleared his mind just long enough to see Sado standing next to him, vainly trying to ward off the hands dragging the rope around his throat.

"Stop!" Natan heard. He did not know from which direction it came. Blood surged to his head and a growing pressure felt like his head would explode. "Stop!" The pressure relaxed and his legs went out from under him. Hands forced Natan to his feet. An officer stood before him in full dress uniform.

"These two young men, they can be sold to the penal battalions," the officer ordered.

"But sir."

"Don't you *but sir* 'me," the officer spat. "You heard me. Penal battalions. They need the hands; we can do with the commission." Slower fingers this time loosened the knot around Natan's neck and hauled it over his head. They prodded him in the direction of a cart. Sado stumbled along behind him. The cart already had the majority of the household workers in it and there was little room for Natan and Sado, but they managed to slip awkwardly into the back, where they collapsed.

Natan gasped for breath. It felt like the rope was still around him. He scratched at his throat and for the first time tasted blood in his mouth. With his tongue, he noticed a tooth was missing.

"Fuck," he croaked. He looked at Sado. His friend nursed a swollen eye.

"Quiet," the officer roared above the din. To Natan's horror, five people still stood beneath the scaffold, Sado's mother and father among them. "Listen," the officer continued. "This family — the No-Meidu family — has been found guilty of treason in collaboration with the Brotherhood of Kive. Their son — Niko No-Meidu — was arrested on an active mission with the terrorist Brotherhood. By the law and the instructions of the High Court, Niko's parents are to hang by their necks until they are dead. Others found at this address are to be sold into the penal battalions so they can work off their associated guilt in the service of the Empire." The officer gestured toward the soldiers holding the ropes. "You may begin."

The victims left the ground. Their faces flashed red. Their bodies convulsed. Their feet clicked together. Natan turned away.

"What is going on here?" *Father.*

The officer wheeled on the newcomer. They exchanged curt words, with Avi gesturing toward the cart. Natan could not hear what was said, but the meaning was clear enough. Avi wanted Natan back. The officer stubbornly refused. Shortly, someone came and grabbed Natan's wrist, revealing the tattooed identification number. There was more discussion and Avi went back to the house to fetch the family papers.

"Natan," Oni screamed, entering the yard. Natan's mother tried to approach the cart but virtuemen cut her off. A young woman Natan did not recognize pulled Oni back.

"Let my son go," Oni shreaked. "Let him go."

Avi returned to the yard with papers. The officer took his time looking over them, then passed them to a clerk. The clerk scratched his chin and returned them to Avi.

"Pay him," Oni screamed, louder than was wise. "Damn it, Avi. Pay him."

"Get that woman out of here," the officer ordered. Oni resisted, but the young woman at her side held her tight and took her away. Avi resumed his discussion with the officer, wildly gesticulating and habitually running a hand through his unruly black hair.

"Ten coppers," Natan heard. The officer laughed and pushed Avi away.

"Is that a joke?" the officer barked. "Twenty silver *li.*" Avi threw his hands up.

"He's not worth that much to you," Avi shouted, spit flying from his mouth.

"He is now," the officer said, a smirk on his face.

"One silver *li,*" Avi said.

"No deal." The officer motioned for his men to get the cart moving. "I see no agreement can be reached."

"Two," Avi said. He grabbed the officer's arm but the officer yanked it away.

"Don't touch me," he hissed. "Or you're in the cart too."

The cart moved. Natan dug his nails into the side and screamed inside wild curses at his father.

"Pay him," Natan said, though no one heard. The cart rattled down the street. The guards fell in behind it. "Pay him."

The young woman from earlier returned. She crossed over to the clerk and whispered something in his ear. From her clothes, she took a bag and placed it in the clerk's hand. He opened it and peered inside. He fished about with a finger.

"Captain Davodi," the clerk called from the back of the column. "Captain Davodi!" The officer halted the cart and picked through the bag. Avi stood dumbfounded.

"Release him," the officer shouted. "Release this man's son."

Natan climbed down from the cart. Some of the guards, still showing their injuries, leered at him. Natan avoided eye contact.

"Natan!" Oni threw her arms around her son. "Never do that again."

"Sado," Natan croaked.

"Get back home," Oni said. "There is nothing we can do for Sado."

"Please!" Tears fell shamelessly down his face.

"Home," Oni said. The Luka-Tudo family returned to their house. Avi walked sullenly behind the rest, muttering to himself.

"How much did you pay them?" he demanded as they entered the home.

"None of your business," Oni said, her face red. "It was from my own savings."

"We could have negotiated him down," Avi sneered. "Silly woman."

"I got our son back," Oni snapped. "I think that is what matters."

The monastery dining room vibrated with the dull hum of subdued chatter. Anjan pinched a pea between thumb and forefinger

"A bit undercooked, don't you think?"

"Dovo will hear you," Po said. "You'll add to his worry lines."

Anjan flicked the offending pea to the floor and returned to his meal. Po finished his mouthful and prepared to speak, but a hand clamped on his shoulder.

"Po and Anjan," Biet said. "Could you come with me please?"

"Our meals —" Anjan began.

"Brother Dovo can look after them. At the rate you were eating, they were going to be cold anyway."

The pair returned their trays to the kitchen and followed Venerable Biet through the Great Hall, past children memorizing the *Sudo Ba're Datai*, and into one of the reflection rooms hidden behind a waxed paper screen. Biet sat on a plump cushion and waited for the two novices to do the same.

"Do you know why you're here?" Biet asked.

"No," the two said together. Biet waited but neither changed their response.

"Perhaps you should think about it," the abbot suggested.

Po considered the room, thinking perhaps the abbot had left a clue. The walls were familiar enough; painted with scenes of high Jan'a, the greatest monastery in all the Ba're faith, perched like a mountain fortress on the far frontiers of the empire. He contemplated the wyvern, weaving through the rolling gray clouds, and the sabertooth perched on a rock watching a flock of goats. *Sabertooth*. Something clicked.

"I honestly don't know," Po said, hoping Biet did not see through the facade. The abbot shook his head and spoke in a low whisper.

"The world outside is full of danger. General Jano has sacrificed to his gods at Mount Tabo, making a covenant with them in the image of the First Emperor. Gai'an and Tavana have fallen. Generals Lot and Gako haven't been heard from — perhaps they've joined the conspiracy. And as we speak the Sixth and Eighth Armies are entering Pao'an to reinforce the defences." Biet paused and considered each novice in turn. "Do you know why I'm telling you this?" They shook their heads. "To stress," Biet continued. "How unbelievably *stupid* it is for you both to have these in your possession. Not just contraband by rule of this monastery

— criminal contraband under the Vermilion Law." Biet removed two pamphlets from his robe and placed them in front of the novices.

"Tomi is a traitor? Jano is coming to save? Do you know how much trouble these could get you in if the Ministry of Virtue found you carrying them? It is good that Master Dugen found them during a routine inspection. I will shortly have these burned. That removes one problem. But the question remains: What are we to do with you both?" Po dared not respond. Anjan cleared his throat but said nothing. His face had paled, causing his freckles to stand out the color of *kaja* beans.

"I was young once," Biet said after a silence. "I've seen wars, scandal and intrigue. There's nothing new in this. There's always something to excite the mind. But you have both come here as students — to learn the way of the Ba're. Are these studies not hard enough for you?" Anjan mumbled something.

"Speak up," Biet snapped.

"No, Venerable Abbot."

"Then how did you find the time for this?" Biet asked.

"I can explain —" Po said, but Biet raised a finger.

"I will hear from Anjan," Biet said. "Where do you find the time?"

"When we were in the city," Anjan stammered. "Someone gave them to us. I forgot all about them."

"Anjan, I've talked with Master Dugen. He says you're smart but not applying yourself. Starting tomorrow at the fifth bell you are to report to Brother Nikodima in the infirmary. Outside classes, you are to report directly to him. This will keep you busy and set your mind to something practical."

"Understood," Anjan said. "How long for?"

"Until I've decided you're ready. I'd suggest an improvement in your grades would be a good start."

"Thank you," Anjan said.

"Now Po," Biet began. "You've done well in the exams and Master Dugen and I both agree you should become my student. You need a challenge — and obviously, from this incident, you're not getting enough of one. At fifth bell tomorrow, and that *is* in the morning, you'll report to me. Is this understood?"

"I understand," Po said, dreading his loss of freedom. He returned his attention to the wyvern flying across the painted wall. *One day I'll be like them,* he thought.

Biet indicated the door. Po and Anjan bowed to the abbot and headed for the exit.

"Oh, and novices," Biet called after them. "After class today, report to the kitchen. Bidovi thinks Brother Dovo could do with the evening off."

Po was quick to discover it was not easy being Venerable Biet's student. The routine never changed. At the fifth bell, Po got up and prepared the abbot's robes and placed a warm basin of water beside the bed with a razor. Venerable Biet then shaved, washed and got dressed before the two climbed the steps to Biet's study.

In the study Biet always chose the book. He ran his finger, along the spines on the bookshelf before picking out an appropriate volume or treatise. Without a word he would give it to Po, before settling down to his own study.

Before morning meditation Biet looked up and closed the book he was reading.

"Now Novice Po — what have you been reading?"

It was the same question every day. Biet expected a point by point breakdown of argument and logical progressions. Invariably the abbot would stop and say, "and what do you think?"

CHAPTER 5

"In the year 853 of the Imperial Era the cult of Tanri began in the far-off land of the Kh'areen. One night, or so the story goes, the woman Sala Gobayar received a revelation saying their pantheon of traditional gods were, in fact, one god called Tanri. Armed with this message, Sala Gobayar united the tribes and established her capital at Baki where she built the Oracle. She is now known simply as the Chobi and book she received - if we can believe that - is called the Chobi Ghada."

Master Suvu's Life of a Scholar

Avi booted open the door and held out the cat.

"Will someone take this?" Ashara dropped the clothes she was mending and took the cat in her arms. It pawed at her and latched onto her shoulder. Ashara winced and put the cat down on the sewing table. "Anyone seen Natan?" Avi continued. "Our foreman hasn't come in today. I need Natan to run some errands."

"He's gone out," Oni said.

"Where the hell to?"

"Never mind. He'll be back late afternoon." Avi looked as if he was about to leave, but then turned back.

"What about Ashara. I need —"

"She's got the afternoon off," said Oni. Ashara blushed. Avi narrowed his eyes and squinted down his hawkish nose.

"Off? Who said she could have an afternoon off?"

"It's been four weeks," Oni said. "Time she was allowed an afternoon to herself."

"And what's she going to do with it?"

"You ask her," Oni said, threading a needle.

"I'm going to get my papers sorted," Ashara said. "If that's okay with you." Avi flexed his fingers and without a word left the room. Ashara looked to Oni for guidance.

"He'll calm down," she said. "Give him time."

"I need my papers," Ashara said, feeling like she was wrong for wanting time off. "Maybe I can see what he wants? I could go help him now."

"No," Oni advised. "It won't change his mood. He'll manage with what he's got." They returned to their sewing.

After lunch, Ashara set off for the Kh'areen precinct, walking with a spring in her step and basking in the details of a city she had visited many times but never lived in. The smell of the river faded, replaced with spices and musks, and the scent of the various alehouses and workshops. Dressed in her Vu clothes, hawkers shouted to her their wares and ran after her, trying to get her to spend a single copper on one thing or another. She waved them off and feared if she opened her mouth it'd break the spell.

On reaching the precinct, Ashara gazed about the houses in the old style and sniffed the smells of home. She wandered a while, not certain of where she was going, but following the erratic back streets of the precinct. She came to the outer wall where the workers were still working at preparing the defenses. Back into the warren of streets, Ashara browsed shop windows and listened to the sounds of her language chattered in alleys and doorways. Memories cut through the fog of her loss —

"You looking for something?" a woman demand from a doorway. Ashara broke from her nostalgia and considered the woman in stunned silence. The woman narrowed her black eyes and creased her brows.

"The Temple," Ashara stammered.

"Keep going," the woman said with a jerk of her head. "Follow the street and you'll come to a square. The Temple is opposite." Ashara thanked her. "And a word of advice, young lady," the woman continued. "We know a newcomer when we see one. Best not loiter."

"Thank you," Ashara repeated and hurried in the direction the woman indicated. Passing a window, she glimpsed her reflection and halted on the spot. *I look Vu*, she realized. She touched her face and ran her fingers over the hair Oni plaited that morning. Her eyes fell to her clothes and back again. *This isn't me.* She pulled out the hair ties and unwound the intricate plaits, then redid them in the way she was familiar with. *Better.*

Further down the street Ashara found the square hemmed in on three sides by shops. On the fourth side was the temple; large, majestic and commanding. She crossed the square and climbed the stairs, taking a moment to admire the red-brick dome and the cupola-capped towers that surrounded it. Entering the foyer, eight women stopped gossiping and gave Ashara the once over. *Look normal,* she reminded herself. *You belong here.* Ashara smiled and passed them into the hall.

Light pooled on the floor and voices echoed off the high ceiling. Ashara followed the noise, her feet squeaking on the marble. Between the columns, a priest in clerical robes sat on a chair teaching catechism. He was forty-something with a fatherly face, black wiry beard and eyes of obsidian. Children knelt at his feet in absolute obedience, engrossed in his every word. Ashara pulled up short and stood in the shadows, listening.

"Catechism fifty-one," the *sabka* said. "What does it ask, Narali?" A little girl of about eight rose on her knees.

"It asks: what is the *Chobi Ghada*?" The *sabka* congratulated the girl. He put a mark next to her name on a chalkboard in his arms.

"Good girl," he said. "And Altan, what is the answer to the question?" A chubby boy raised himself on his knees, a look of excitement on his face.

"The *Chobi Ghada* is the written word of Tanri given to the first Oracle."

"Good boy," the priest said, adding a mark to Altan's name. "And who can tell me the answer to twenty-four: who is the Oracle?" The children stirred, and a few hands went up.

"Otgani?" The girl looked excited to be chosen. She appeared to be the youngest of the lot.

"The Oracle is the messenger of Tanri."

"Good, but if you can tell me the name of the first Oracle, before she became the chosen one, I will give you an extra point."

"Her name was Sala Gobayar." The *sabka* grinned and made the required mark.

"Now, that is all we have time for today." The *sabka* reached under his stool, drew out a wooden box and lifted the lid. The children crowded around him, clutching sweet treats between their tiny fingers. The children shouted their goodbyes and ran to meet their mothers at the door. The *sabka* closed the box and tucked it under his arm.

Ashara approached, and without looking her way the priest spoke.

"Young woman, I don't believe you are a regular with our congregation."

"No," Ashara said. The priest removed his spectacles, blew on the lenses, and wiped them on his woolen vestments. "I, well, I've come for your help," Ashara continued. "If you are willing."

The priest turned and considered her.

"And what can I do for you?" He offered her a space on the mat and Ashara knelt before him as the children had done.

"My name is Ashara Daladh'an, daughter of Kh'am of Baki. My father was a merchant running caravans between Baki and Pao'an. We were ambushed. My father and two brothers were killed. I was lost in the wilderness, but found it safe to Pao'an. Now I have no family, no papers and no way to return home." She tasted salt on her lips as a lone tear trickled down her cheek. "Now I stay with a Vu family. They give me lodgings in exchange for work."

The priest ran fingers through his beard and leaned forward.

"And what would you have me do?" he asked. "You have not said how I can help you."

"Write, please, to Baki, and have new papers sent so I can travel."

"And what will you do with these papers?"

"What will I do with them?" she echoed. "I'll be able to travel." The priest nodded, but his fingers massaged his knuckles in a nervous gesture.

"How can I put this?" said the priest slowly. "You'd not be the first... asking for papers. Sometimes young women — and men — want to run from their families, to become independent." Ashara began to protest. "Now," the priest continued, his hands up. "I'm not saying this is you. But it does happen. I don't know you. You come here wanting paperwork. We have to be careful. That and with the war coming, you'd be in good company if you want to leave the capital."

"Are you saying you can't help me?"

"No, no," the *sabka* insisted. "I think I haven't chosen my words well."

"So you'll help me get papers?"

"We'll see," the *sabka* said. "It takes time. I'll make enquiries." He crossed to a cupboard and returned with a writing board, pen, ink and paper. He dipped the pen in ink. "Now, let's begin."

His script flowed like lace upon the page, working from top to bottom and right to left. He paused after a few lines and asked Ashara to show him her tattoo. She complied and the priest copied her identification number. He then probed her for details about her name, age, parents and the other families that traded alongside them. He finished off the document with an elaborate signature.

"Do not worry," he said, holding the letter to the light. "The enquiries I make are just a precaution. If you speak the truth, there is nothing to worry about."

"Thank you," Ashara said. "I guess."

"This will go with other dispatches," he explained. "But it may be a few months before we receive a reply."

"That long?" Ashara asked. The priest shrugged.

"Questions take time," he said. "Roads take even longer. Do you pray?"

"Do I — yes," Ashara said, catching herself.

"And do you recite the *Chobi Ghada*?"

"I try to," Ashara said. The priest nodded in approval.

"From now on," the priest said. "You recite and pray every day. You will come here regularly. This is how we will stay in touch. When I am comfortable you are who you say you are, and I have received them from

Baki, you will get your papers. I would invite you to evening prayers, but Pao'an is not safe for a young woman after dark. I suggest you get going now. We will meet again another day."

Ashara kicked a lump of fallen masonry and sauntered into the yard. Natan and Dasha played with their quarterstaves, while Dan watched from the side, buffing his boots.

"The wanderer returns," Dan said. "We were getting worried. Well, Dasha was anyway."

"Shut up," Ashara snapped. "I had the afternoon off."

"Someone's cranky," Natan said. Dasha glanced Ashara's way and Natan's staff drove into his knee. "I win. Who's next?"

"Fuck," Dasha groaned. "I'm going inside. The goal's to win, not to cripple."

"Dan?" Natan said.

"No. I'm keeping this face beautiful for the army. Ladies like a man in uniform."

"The army?" Ashara said. "You're joining?"

"Soon," Dan replied. "Hey, it's one *jet* a day and we'll likely march around and be disbanded by autumn. Can't complain about that."

"Come on," Natan said. "That face is never going to win you any hearts."

"I'll do it," Ashara said, taking a staff off the wall.

"You?" Natan scoffed. "I don't fight girls."

"You'll regret that in the morning," Ashara said and jabbed Natan in the chest with the staff. Natan stepped back and knocked her second jab aside.

"Knock it off," he said. "It's not funny." Ashara persisted.

"Careful Ashara," Dan warned. "Natan plays rough."

"I know. I've watched him. Pity he's a coward." Natan fell to a crouch and thrust the staff end up at her. The staff grazed Ashara's collarbone as she jumped aside and brought her stick down on Natan's knuckles. His hand leapt from the shaft and he unleashed a torrent of abuse. Soon the yard echoed with the furiousness of their fight. Each blow threatened to splinter the wood and sent jolts down their respective hands.

"Not the face!" Dan yelled, but it was too late. It felt like a mule kick. Blood splattered the back of Ashara's throat and she went down. Hard. Her ears rang. Stars twinkled in her vision. Numbing pressure threatened to burst from her face. Dan's voice echoed in her ears. "What did I say? Not the face! You can't treat the *servants* like that." *Servants*.

Ashara rolled to her feet and put distance between herself and Natan while she returned to her sense. She shook the fog from her mind and readied the staff for another go.

"You don't need to go again," Dan said. "Don't be silly." Ashara ignored him. She probed the back of her teeth with her tongue and spat bloody phlegm. *They're all there.* "What are you trying to prove?" Dan continued. "We know you can take a beating."

She charged. Natan pirouetted and struck her off balance. Ashara stumbled and regained her footing before attacking again. Her staff connected with Natan's jaw. He spun and dropped to his hands and knees.

"Stop!" Dan shouted. "Okay, enough. You've both bested each other."

Natan shook his head and massaged his jaw.

"Okay," he said. "I didn't see that coming. The girl has teeth."

"Name?" the clerk asked, not looking up.

"Dan Luka-Tudo."

"Papers?" Dan placed a stamped letter in front of the clerk. Beside his brother, Natan sighed and scuffed the dirt of the city square. They had been waiting in line since breakfast. His stomach rumbled and Natan craned his neck, looking for signs of a food cart somewhere. Nothing.

"Have you served in the army before?" the clerk asked.

"No," Dan said. The clerk marked the book in front of him.

"And you bring your own armor?"

"Yes," Dan replied, indicating the bag Natan carried.

"Good," the clerk said. "Sergeant?" A man stepped forward and gave Dan the once over.

"Lift your arms and turn around." Dan compiled and the sergeant grunted.

"Right," said the clerk. "I'm assigning you to Sixth Army, Third Group. The sergeant will show you where to go."

Shortly Dan and Natan stood in a second line.

"You remember to help when I'm gone," Dan said. "They'll need it."

"Mother will miss you," Natan said, changing the subject.

"She'll get used to it. This is my big break. I'm going to be a soldier. A real one."

"I wish I could join you." Dan gave Natan a serious look.

"No, you don't. Dad was right. Eldest first. You help with the trade."

"I'm eighteen," Natan said. "More than old enough to enlist. Father never lets me —"

"Next!" There was no clerk this time, just a ragtag bunch of soldiers shaving the heads of every recruit. "Right, quick now," the man in charge continued. "That your brother? Time to kiss goodbye. Leave your bag over there." Natan shrugged the bag off his shoulder and left it where indicated.

"Look after yourself," he said to Dan.

"You too, little brother. Don't let father get to you."

"He won't," Natan said.

"He's as much a victim of himself as you are," Dan continued. "I wouldn't want to be him." Natan wiped his nose. Rather than continue the conversation, he thrust his hand out. Dan accepted it.

"Get a move on," the soldier barked. Natan's fingers tightened around his brother's hand, but Dan slipped free and took his seat on the stool. Natan lingered, watching the first cuts of Dan's hair. His fists clenched. *I should be there.*

Natan meandered through the back streets and alleys, frequently finding his path blocked, for soldiers flooded the city's alehouses and taverns, streaming out the doors and clogging the streets with their revelry. The banging of hammers echoed off the tenements as shopkeeps shuttered their stores, and by the time he reached Eastbank the ways out of the city were choked with wagons and handcarts.

"No weapons may leave the city," a virtueman shouted, hands cupped on either side of his mouth. "Empty houses may be used to billet troops. Five *jet* reward if you hand your keys into Eastbank barracks."

At the end of his street Natan paused, feeling about in his pocket for a little paper bag. There was something he was putting off. Not wanting to see his father any time soon, Natan turned back into the press and headed to Fletcher Street two blocks away. He walked the rows of shuttered shops, wondering if he was too late. He was not. In the midst of desertion stood a lone apothecary still open. He tried the latch and the door opened with a groan and a tinkle of a bell. He squinted into the shadows. The apothecary rose from his seat behind the counter.

"Mr Luka-Tudo," he said. "What do you have for me today?"

Natan approached the counter and found room between porcelain jars with peeling labels to put the paper bag down. He unfolded it and pushed it towards the graying man.

"Teeth?" the apothecary asked, turning each with his index finger. "Wolf?" Natan nodded. "Not up to your usual quality," the apothecary said, shaking his head. He reached into a drawer and removed three bronze coins.

"I'll want more than that," Natan said. "The siege will put prices up."

"For wolf teeth?" the apothecary snorted. "They're used in aphrodisiacs. Not much demand for *those* during a siege. You don't have anything else?" Natan shook his head.

"We haven't had a caravan through in a week," Natan said. "Not since they executed the traitor Maga. Trade is dead."

"Well, I can't pay you for things you don't deliver," the apothecary said. "You'll have to think of something. Now do you want these coins or not?" Natan slid the coins off the counter and into his hand. *Father won't miss the teeth, but I'll miss the coins.*

"Better than nothing," he said. The apothecary took a jar, removed the stopper and tipped the teeth into it. "So," Natan continued. "What do you want?"

"Oh the usual. But I'll tell you what —" He placed a wrinkled piece of paper in front of Natan. "If you see anything from there, you know, on the black market, they'll be worth a coin or two."

"What's that?" Natan asked, scanning the piece.

"News sheet," said the apothecary. "The Imperial Academy's been conducting a dig in the Valley of Kings — in hiatus now but not before they found lost artifacts. See, there's a print of the copper horse dug from one of the tombs. Meant to be a whole lot there not yet discovered. It won't be long before some of these start popping up for the right buyers."

"You think some might come our way?" Natan asked. The apothecary shrugged.

"Doesn't hurt to keep an eye out, does it?"

"I'll pay extra attention," Natan said. "I take it then you're not planning to close?"

"Me? No. People will still need their ointments and elixirs." The apothecary sighed and wiped down the counter. "That, and the road north is a restricted area now. My son's in Dili but I've no way to get there."

"When did that happen?"

"Announced three days ago," the apothecary said. "Soldiers patrol the Blue River and the roads have shut down to traffic. I have a friend, runs a high-end apothecary on the corner of Northgate and High Street, says there have been strange goings on. *Official* convoys going all hours of the night. People leaving."

"I thought soldiers were moving into the city."

"The soldiers are," the apothecary said. "But, well, other branches are moving out, aren't they? Why else do they send things north?" He tapped his bulbous nose. "They're preparing to lose the capital."

Natan slowly absorbed the information. He searched the apothecary's face for signs he was joking with him.

"No way," Natan said at last. "Have you seen how well the city's defended?"

"I have," said the old man. "Walls can become death traps, as surely as a coffin."

Natan stepped back and turned to the door. He wrung his hands.

"I doubt it," he said.

CHAPTER 6

"The Temple of Tanri in Pao'an is a great example of Vu and Kh'areen architecture working side by side. Originally set up as a guild hall for Kh'areen workers in the old settlement, the building slowly expanded and was bought out by a committee of locals in 921 Imperial Era to be consecrated as a temple for communal worship. The main prayer hall was constructed in 937 and administrative wings at an unknown date after that. In 1042 the Vermilion Emperor paid for a complete overhaul of the temple and established the grandeur we see today."

A Traveler's Guide to Pao'an

Ashara picked her way down South Avenue. A dog ran across the deserted cobbles. Somewhere a door slammed. She scanned the surrounding buildings and pulled her clothes tighter about her.

Dark shapes in the direction of Southgate shimmered in the distant haze. Soldiers camped out on the broad avenue around their fires. Washing hung from trees, and weapons lay stacked close at hand.

"Stop," a sentry said, holding up a hand but not drawing his weapon. "Where're you off to?"

"The Temple of Tanri," Ashara said. "Kh'areen Precinct."

"You can't go past this point," said the soldier. "Take that street and turn left at Brick Lane. Don't be out too long." Ashara thanked the sentry and hastened the way he directed, casting a brief glance over her shoulder.

The temple rose above the other buildings, pigeons roosting around the towers. Sounds of chatter drew her to the square, but they were soldiers. *Kh'areen soldiers*, she realized, for she recognized the language. They milled about while some of their number drilled with batons and staves, and others played at target practice with their slings.

"You return," said the priest from the top of the stairs. Ashara climbed to meet him.

"What are they doing?" she asked.

"Them?" said the priest. "The Emperor — may Tanri shine upon him — has allowed us to raise a self-defense force. They're training."

"Do you think it will come to that?" Ashara asked.

"Unless Jano is stopped, there will be a siege. But maybe Jano will have a stroke? Maybe Tomi will sue for peace? Who knows? It is up to the will of Tanri."

"Some of them look very young," Ashara persisted. The priest nodded but stood his ground.

"Too young to die?" he asked. "Or too young to defend themselves? I don't think we have a choice. Look —" He pointed beyond the square. "That's the city wall right there. When the enemy comes, that's where they'll be, and we'll be in their path."

Ashara unconsciously put a hand to her stomach. It was all so *close*.

"Lots of people have left," she said, following the priest inside. "Maybe the Kh'areen should do the same. Take yourselves out of danger."

"Some have already gone," he replied. "But do you really think they'll all abandon their homes and lives? What will they come back to? No, we have our plans. Don't worry. Tanri's in control. When — *if* — General Jano stands outside the city, the women and children can come inside the temple. It will offer them protection."

"And yourself?"

"I'll minister to the people. That'll be where they need me the most."

"I'd like to wait out the siege here," Ashara said. "Among my people. I know a thing or two about medicine and I can fight —"

"Ashara, you are a fortunate one. Maybe you don't feel it, but you have somewhere to go. Here is the last place you should be. Eastbank is safer. Many would go there if they could."

"But —"

"No." The priest was sterner this time. "Enough with this. Have you remembered your prayers?"

"Yes, every day. Like you told me."

"Good, you'll be pleased — your letter is sent. Now we wait. Though, compared to other things, perhaps the wait is not too bad."

"Hopefully not too long," Ashara replied. "It's tough living here. The Vu have very strange ways. I'd be happy to be back in Baki." The *sabka* narrowed his eyes.

"Tanri does not judge where someone was born," he said. "But the choices they make afterwards." He motioned to a group of figures kneeling at the front of the hall. An acolyte walked among them. "They are converts," he went on. "Some are Vu, some are lapsed Kh'areen, yet others are Solari, Astirti, Duang and Yikon. All are welcomed into the temple." Ashara hung her head.

"I am sorry," she said. "I mean this family is … tiring. The father, Avi, rants and raves. When he isn't blaming someone for a problem of his own making, he's smoking storm clouds. His youngest son, Natan, bears the brunt of his bullying, though I guess Mistress Oni gets a lot too, and Natan just passes it on to me..." Ashara stopped, realizing what her problems sounded like in the precinct.

"He suffers," said the *sabka*. "Poor man."

"Both of them apologize," Ashara said. "But they forget."

"They are their own victims," said the priest. "Understand that."

"But Mistress Oni is good," Ashara said. Her face brightened. "At first I thought she was afraid of Avi, but I've seen she's stronger than I imagined." The priest nodded.

"Tanri has put you there for a reason," he said. "It's best you remember that. I —"

A bell chimed a single note. Stillness. The priest glanced heavenward, to the great dome. His lips whispered in prayer.

"It's not first —" Ashara began, but then the bell chimed a second time.

"Jano and the Seventh Army are here," said the priest. "They call the defenders in from outside the walls, and prepare for the siege."

"Here? Now?"

"You should go," said the priest, marching her to the steps. "Get home. Run."

"Po, wake up. Po."

Po rolled over and pulled the blanket over his head. The pestering continued. A finger poked him.

"What is it?" he moaned under the covers.

"It's Anjan," a voice whispered. "Come quick." Po sat up, rubbing his eyes and suppressing a yawn. One of the other novices snored in the corner.

"What time's it?" Po asked, chewing his tongue to remove the dryness from his mouth.

"Just after the fourth bell. You've got to be quiet." The voice worried him. Po accepted the offered robe and slipped out of the cot and into his sandals. "This way," Anjan added without explanation. Po followed him. They slipped from the dormitories and moved noiselessly down corridors and up stairs. Anjan took a hooked stick from the wall and pulled down the hatch to the bell tower. Putting a finger to his lips, he pointed at a door.

"Master Dugen's room," he whispered. Po nodded and climbed through the hatch. Anjan followed. They came out onto a platform with all the ropes and pulleys for the bell system. Another series of ladders led up to the bells themselves.

"Keep going," Anjan said, indicating a second lot of ladders. Po climbed and Anjan came immediately behind. The ledge above was thin and just enough for one person to stand on. Po held tight to the tiled railing and gazed out over the sleeping city. Sunrise was still two hours off. Even the street lights had flickered out — but there, off to the west, lights flickered. Po tried to make out what he was seeing. It was too far to discern individual shapes, but he thought the lights came from the city wall.

"So the army is up?" Po said at last, rubbing his eyes. "I'm going back to bed." Anjan grabbed Po's sleeve.

"No, listen." Po held his breath and strained his ears.

"Trumpets? Maybe."

"And…"

"Drums?" The darkness beyond flashed in a series of bright, flickering, pulsing lights. Thousands of bright specks rose into the night air, no higher than a thumb width considering the distance, and gently fell back down. Similar flashes happened, closer this time and more specks rose up and fell back down.

"What are those?" Po asked.

"Fire wagons," Anjan said. "That first lot I think was from the outside firing in. The second lot was the inside firing out."

"Do… should I tell the abbot?"

"Why?" said Anjan. "He can't do anything. Just watch. You're up in an hour anyway."

Po slipped into Biet's study, lit the lamp and got a fire going in the grill. From the other room footsteps padded on the wooden floor. Biet entered with a shawl over his shoulders.

"Good morning," he said. "All ready for the day's study?" The kindling caught and crackled. Po stood and dusted off his hands. "You didn't get much sleep I take it."

"Pardon?" Po asked. He touched his face.

"Bags under your eyes," Biet said. "Be seated. We'll begin."

"Jano attacked overnight," Po said. "I could see the fire from the monastery."

"And do you think Dasanika gained enlightenment by watching the outside world? Or was it inner reflection?"

"They had fire wagons," Po said. "A lot of fire wagons." Biet sat at his desk and knitted his fingers.

"And did you watching them help in any way? Did it change a thing?"

"No," Po admitted.

"Right, so pull up your book and let's start." Po hesitated, his mind giddy, and focused his attention on the present. After a few breaths he took Master Sudodlma's *Treatise on Spiritual Materialism* off the shelf and pulled up a chair.

Brother Nikodima tapped gently on the door and poked his head into the abbot's study. Biet glanced up from his work. Po tried to ignore the interruption.

"You might want to see this," the monk said. Biet set aside his pen, closed the ink bottle and motioned for Po to follow.

"What time is it?" Po asked, stifling a yawn.

"Just after seventh bell," Nikodima said. "They started coming half an hour ago. Brother Dovo's gone to get the monks and fetch water."

They crossed the courtyard and left the gate.

"Are we going far?" Biet asked.

"Just to the avenue," Nikodima said. "Not far."

The monks reached the intersection and paused, watching the trickle of soldiers traipsing toward the Inner City. Early morning sun glinted off their eyes, but behind they were gray and dead. Many leaned on their spears. Blood soaked wounds. Arms hung in makeshift slings. A wagon creaked along with an ox straining at the yoke. Limbs hang out the sides, limp and waxen.

"Po, help me with this," came a voice from behind. Po broke his eyes from the horror and turned to help Dovo lug up a barrel. The older monk was red-faced and sweating with the effort. They broke the barrel open and began ladling out lukewarm water. The walking wounded sucked at it, grabbing at the ladles and monks' hands. Water splashed down Po's front and the cobbles became a sticky mess of water, grime and blood.

"Hey, not too much," Brother Dovo barked. "If you want a drink you've got to be nice about it." A soldier promptly tried to drink directly from the barrel and Dovo rapped him over the back of the head with his ladle. "You hear me? Line up. One scoop each."

The soldier sneered and Po stepped in front of Dovo. The anger passed from the soldier's face and slunk back into line.

"Thanks," Dovo said.

Brother Bidovi arrived with a steaming cauldron of soup and more monks to help. Civilians also appeared. Brother Nikodima walked among them, checking their injuries and sending them with novices to the infirmary.

"No soldiers," Nikodima told the novices. "Civilians only. The army has their own aid stations. Quicky now. Divide the wounded from the non-wounded. Keep families together. No — no soldiers."

For some, it was too much. Po ran to help a man who collapsed beneath one of the avenue trees. Sticky red blood coated his lips and pooled between his teeth. Black eyes stared uncomprehendingly at Po as he checked for the source of the injury.

"Leave me," the man groaned, pushing him away. Po refused to go but sat next to the dying man holding his hand.

"I'll be here if you need me," he said. The man leaned his head against the trunk of the tree and closed his eyes. His breathing rattled and slowed. Blood bubbles formed around his nostrils, popping with each exhale.

"Po," Anjan said, coming up. "There are more coming. We need you."

"I said I'd wait with him," Po said.

"He's gone, Po. There's the living that need you." Reluctantly Po peeled back the man's fingers and got to his feet. What was previously a trickle had become a stream and then a river. Towards midday, columns in Eighth Army colors marched through the wounded and milling crowds. A company of heavy cavalry galloped past, sending people scattering.

"The fighting's the other way," Po grumbled. "Why are *they* pulling back?" Anjan wiped the blood from his hands onto his cream robe and shook his head. The next column that passed he made eye contact with the captain.

"Where are you going?" he said. "The fighting is in that direction."

The captain huffed.

"Do your own job, monk. We'll do ours."

Moonlight cast silvery light on Natan's bedroom floor. A rat scuttled somewhere in the ceiling cavity. Natan rolled over and stared at the wall, his hands cupped under his head. Outside nothing stirred. Not even the hour bells rang. After what seemed like an eternity he got up, pulled a chair over to the window and rested his head against the sill, still warm from the heat of the day before. He wondered where Dan was with his unit; doubtless somewhere in the city ready to defend the walls at the blast of a trumpet.

Down on the street, a single horse and rider trotted in the direction of Eastgate. The horseshoes clattering on the cobbles sounded demonically loud in the stillness. A cat yowled and a series of dogs started barking, setting each other off one after the other. Black shapes moved in the wake of the horse, their feet muffled. Rank upon rank of them marched twenty abreast. The odd piece of equipment chinked and tinkled, but their passing was eerie in its quietness. And they kept coming; Natan lost count.

He poked around on the floor for his clothes, found his trousers and stumbled around getting his legs into the right holes. In the corridor he tiptoed to Dasha's door. Dasha snored lightly.

"Dasha," he whispered. Natan tried the door handle and slipped inside. "Dasha," he whispered again. "You awake?" *Movement.* Metal scraped against wood. "It's me," Natan hissed. "Something's happening outside."

"What? Quiet down, you'll wake…"

"Soldiers are on the street," Natan cut him off. "There must be thousands."

"So? The city's under siege. What time's it?"

"They stopped the hour bells at midnight."

"Fuck, Natan. Get some sleep. What happens will happen."

"You're the one with the knife next to the bed," Natan said. "Besides, something's up," he insisted. "I *know* it."

Floorboards squeaked and Dasha pulled back the curtains. Moonlight streamed into the room, revealing his naked body.

"No one on the street now," Dasha said.

"The dogs still bark," Natan countered. "Do you want to go for a walk? I want to see the Lower City. I can't sleep cooped up in here."

"You serious?" Dasha said. "There's a curfew. You know what sort of trouble we'd be in if spotted." Despite his words, Dasha was already picking his clothes off the floor.

"When have you been the one to worry about consequences? We've been getting in trouble for years."

"Fuck it. Go wait in the corridor."

The stairs creaked with each footstep; Natan winced and held ever tighter to the balustrade. A faint smell of jasmine tickled his nostrils, causing his stomach to flutter.

"What are you doing?" Natan almost fell off the last stair.

"Ashara," he yelped. "*Shhh,* what are you doing up?"

"You *shhh* me? You both sound like dreadbeasts in a chicken house."

"You didn't answer his question," said Dasha. "What *are* you doing up?"

"What do you think? Neither of you thought to sleep by the door tonight."

"Go back to the kitchen," Natan hissed. "The sun'll be up soon."

"No," said Ashara. "You're going somewhere. Where?"

"*Oh,* fuck off," Natan retorted. "This doesn't involve you." He crossed to the hall door, feeling her clothes brush against him in the dark, and fumbled with the lock.

"I'm going with you," Ashara said. "If you make me stay, I'll tell your parents."

"You're a real bitch sometimes," Natan sneered. "You wouldn't dare."

"How bad can it be?" Dasha said. "She can come with us."

"She'll get us caught," Natan said. "This is stupid."

"I thought we didn't care about consequences? I'm older and I say she comes with us."

"Fine," said Natan, and he pulled the latch.

The three slipped into the night; sticking to the darkest shadows, ever mindful of what was around them. Not far from the house, loud thuds shook the street. The earth trembled and every animal on Eastbank started awake.

"What was that?" Natan asked, perched uneasily on his toes. A hand touched his shoulder and squeezed gently. It was Ashara.

"Quiet," she said in his ear, prodding him to keep going. They came to Bridge Street and crossed from corner to corner till they came to the massive arch that spanned the Blue River. Natan expected guards to be posted somewhere on the bridge, but saw none.

"Okay, I'll go first," Dasha said. "Wait for my signal." Natan and Ashara nodded and crouched beside the road. In the faintest light from the graying sky they watched Dasha weave from post to post. At the middle of the bridge, just where he would disappear over the arch, Dasha put up his hand and waved the all-clear. Natan and Ashara ran to catch up. Dasha stood against the rail, looking north at the Inner City.

"Bleeding Goddess of Mercy," Natan swore. There was a gap in the Inner City wall — a large gap. Bits lay strewn down the bank and into the Blue River, cloaked in a rising cloud of dust.

"The city is breached," Dasha said. "It's fallen."

"*Ummm*," said Ashara. "If they made a hole, why aren't they storming it?"

"But where is the enemy?" Ashara asked. "If they made a hole, why aren't they storming it?" Dasha tugged at their sleeves.

"Never mind," he said. "Off the bridge. We're way too visible here."

The Lower City beckoned them, embracing them in the back alleys and side streets. Not far from South Avenue, boots clattered on the cobbles and the three ducked into the cover of a night soil cart. A column of troops moved north in the dim morning haze. They waited for the column's tail to disappear from sight, and the three then continued.

"At least some soldiers are still about," Natan said.

"Onto that wagon," Ashara suggested. "We can get onto the roof from there."

"Why the roof?" Natan asked.

"Ashara's right," Dasha said, already climbing. "Good views up there." Ashara beamed at the support and flashed Natan a wink. He scowled. She scrambled past him and in a series of quick movements pulled herself onto the roof above. Dasha, slower, came second.

"You need a hand?" he hissed.

"I can do it myself," Natan said. With effort he joined them. "See?" They crawled across the terracotta tiles and peeked over the edge. Columns of soldiers marched in rhythm up the broad avenue. Their light green and black banners were limp in the breeze-less air.

"These are Jano's men," Dasha said, the disbelief evident in his voice.

"Seventh Army colors," Natan confirmed. Behind the infantry rode heavy cavalry, resplendent in their gear. At their head rode an armored man on a white horse.

"Look," Natan said. "That man down there — in front of the cavalry. Who does he look like?" Ashara and Dasha looked for only a moment.

"General Jano," Dasha said.

CHAPTER 7

"In the early days of Pao'an only Vu lived in the walled city. Migrant workers set up their own townships south of the capital. These migrants worked in Pao'an during the day and returned to their homes at night. As Pao'an expanded these townships were swallowed into the bubbling metropolis. Today you will find the Kh'areen, Astirti and Solari precincts, in particular, reflect the old style."

A Traveler's Guide to Pao'an

Po felt like an ancient sage, an ascetic, struggling with carnal nature to reach true understanding. Or that was what he told himself. Stiff, miserable and with the distinct taste of dirt on his tongue, Po rested his head against the brick wall and waited for dawn. Minutes ticked by like hours. Occasionally someone knocked on the monastery gate and Po stumbled groggily over and let them in.

Hammering on the gate interrupted his thoughts. For a moment, Po stared blankly at the dark oak panels until his mind clicked.

"Coming," he grumbled and removed the lock bar. Hands pushed on the gates from the other side and Po only just got out of the way as they slammed against the wall. Soldiers jogged into the courtyard, followed by an officer on horseback, then more soldiers. The officer paid no attention to Po, but trotted to the center of the yard, removed his crested helmet, and ran a hand through his oily hair.

Though early, some monks were already about their chores. Faces appeared at windows and stood behind the colonnade railing. Having spent the day before with soldiers of the Eighth Army, Po knew these were not the same.

"Pao'an is liberated," shouted the officer. "The traitor Tomi Mei-Uduga has fled the capital. Civil control is now in the hands of the Seventh Army. Curfew is between ninth and seventh bell. Those found sheltering deserters and subversives will be dealt with harshly." He looked around the yard and thumped his clenched fist to his chest. "All under Heaven."

"None of those here," Venerable Biet said, descending the steps to the Great Hall on the arm of Master Pani. "Would you like me to show you around?"

"That shouldn't be necessary," said the officer. He raised his hand and his men broke into squads and began the search. Po worked his way around the yard and came to Biet's side.

"Can I do anything?" he whispered.

"No," Biet replied.

Almost immediately, people started shouting and the infirmary door slammed open.

"Captain!" came an excited voice. "We have wounded men in here."

"Wounded men?" the officer asked, raising an eyebrow in Biet's direction.

"Only civilians, I assure you," Biet said. "No soldiers."

"Bring them outside," ordered the officer. "Let's see for ourselves."

"Sir," Po burst in. "They're wounded. It's best not to move them." The officer took one look at Po and his lips curled to one side in a sneer.

"Keep that mouth shut if you know what's good for you."

Assisted by monks, the soldiers brought the wounded out on stretchers and laid them in the dust. The officer dismounted and walked among them.

"The blood is still fresh," he said, kneeling to inspect a wound. "And under these bandages? Burns? These are all recent." The officer took a patient's jaw in his firm grim and twisted the head. "What's your name?"

The patient's eyes bulged and he stuttered inaudibly. The officer ignored him.

"These men," he raged. "Were in fighting yesterday."

"Collateral — I assure you," Biet said. "No one came in uniform. No one brought weapons."

"A likely story," the captain snarled. "Execute them." His soldiers jumped to the task, raising their spears and thrusting them down into their victims.

"Stop!" Po yelled. All attention turned to him.

"Stop?" said the captain, advancing on Po. "Stop? You don't know what's best for you, do you?"

"They've done nothing wrong," Po protested. "We refused all soldiers. These are innocents you're killing." The officer seized Po's elbow and yanked him forward.

"Get down on the ground with them," the captain said. "Since you care for them so much." Po knelt between two wounded men and set his eyes on the ground four feet ahead. *Breath*, he told himself. *Focus on your breathing.*

"Captain," came Biet's voice. "This is a novice monk. You can tell he's no soldier and not someone you're looking for."

"Silence!" yelled the captain. "Examples must be made. This city will be pacified or so Kive help you. Now, boy, what's your name?"

"Po, sir."

"Do you feel brave now, Po?"

"No," said Po. Steel ran against leather and the sun cast the silhouette of the sword on the ground before him. *All things are impermanent,* he told himself. *Suffering comes from attachment to impermanent things. People live in an illusion of permanence. There is a way to reach a state of quiet contentment. This is the way of the Ba're. Kime ki're kima ka, Kime ki're kima ka.* The sword swung.

"No!" screamed Anjan. Po's concentration broke. Anjan ran towards them. "Take me! I'll take his place." The captain laughed.

"A holy order of heroes today," he said. "We could do with you lot on the front line." He turned to his men. "Fuck this novice up a bit. Teach him a good lesson. Let's see how they break." Hands gripped Po under his armpits. A brute of a sergeant removed his gloves and landed a punch to Po's gut. The pain spasmed through his body, but Po focused on the *Ba're. Pain is an illusion. It's an experience. It's not me.* A second blow landed and a third.

Someone twisted his arm behind his back and drove his chin into the ground. The muscles and tendons screamed. *Think of Jan'a,* Po commanded himself. *You're on the mountain. The wind against your cheeks. The wyvern soaring above. A warm meal in your belly.*

"Stop," the officer barked. "I told you to fuck him up. Why isn't he screaming for his gods?"

"We could cut him?" suggested the sergeant. "Peel off some skin?"

"We're soldiers," said the officer. "Not savages. Leave it. They've got the message." The sergeant grumbled and slipped back on his gloves. Someone offered Po a hand and Anjan drew him aside.

"You okay?" Anjan asked.

"I'll live," Po said. His stomach muscles spasmed and he clutched his abdomen as if holding his body together. Anjan rubbed his back. Back among the soldiers, the officer turned to a second sergeant. "Sergeant Davadi, what did you find?"

"The usual. Millet, oils, lentils, some *kaja* beans."

"Take it. These monks can consider themselves lucky. Abbot, what money do you keep?"

"None," said Biet. "Our lay community manages the accounts. We don't keep coin."

"Then in lieu of a fine for harboring criminals, you should provide me with aid. These men — they were in your care, yes? I'll take twenty-five monks with knowledge of medicine."

"I cannot command them to go with you," Biet said.

"I'll go," said Brother Nikodima. "We don't need more violence." Nikodima sought out the faces of his infirmary assistants. Quietly they stepped forward. Anjan slipped has hand off Po's back.

"Anjan, no," Po whispered, but his friend already had his hand up.

"It's what we do," Anjan said under his breath. "We make sacrifices."

"You don't have to."

"Neither did you."

"Twenty-three," the officer said. "Close enough. Get your things. Sergeant, keep an eye on them. We're leaving as soon as this stuff is packed." Then to Po: "Consider yourself fortunate the gods smiled upon you today. It won't happen twice."

Rubble lay strewn across the street, and cracked timbers jutted from piles of tumbled bricks. Some buildings were just frames, gutted from the inside. Others stood unharmed amidst a sea of carnage. Ashara picked her path between the debris, making her way toward the now familiar temple. Around her, residents sifted through the wreckage, retrieving what they could. Here and there a patrol marched through, clearing the way with shouts and spear butts.

"A coin, young lady," said a beggar, holding out her cap. "Just a ku'net to wet my parched lips?"

"I have nothing," Ashara responded, pulling out her pockets in sympathy. "I wish I did."

The square lay ahead, and as Ashara approached, a knot tightened in her stomach. Over the week since the fall, word had spread of the devastation among the outer communities. She was now seeing it for herself, and it did not bode well. Someone had sectioned off the square, driving stakes into the earth and lashing them together with leather and twine. Green and black banners hung limp from the buildings, and watchtowers stood at each corner. *They've garrisoned the square*, Ashara thought to herself as she skirted the perimeter. She arrived at a barricade.

"No one past this point, sorry," said a sentry. "You'll have to turn back."

"But the temple —" Ashara began.

"No one past this point," repeated the sentry. "Go back the way you came." Ashara huffed and craned her neck. Beyond the checkpoint rose the temple steps. Soldiers loitered about, leaning on their spears, casually chatting to each other. *It's a barracks?*

"Step back please, miss," said the sentry. Ashara shot him a glare and stepped back.

"Fine," she said, turning back the way she came. She continued on around the corner and clutched her stomach, nausea sweeping over her. Her head spun and Ashara staggered to a wall and squatted, her back against it. Acid stung her throat and in a wave of dizziness, she pressed her hands to her face. *What have they done?*

Uncertain, Ashara slid to the ground and sat hugging her knees to her chin. Any sense of certainty, of protection, of a clear path home had vanished. She would have to do it without papers. She was on her own. Her fingers wiped a tear from the corner of her eye and she glanced up at the nearest watchtower. They were pointing at her. Ashara grounded her teeth and rested her cheek on her knees. Was she ready to walk back to her homeland alone and paperless?

"You don't look so good." Ashara froze. "You're not sick, are you?"

"No," Ashara said, slowly turning to the sentry. "I just need rest." The sentry frowned and wandered off, returning a minute later with two others.

"Sick?" a newcomer asked. The sentry shook his head.

"No. Just conveniently loitering," said the first.

"Time you should move along young lady." Ashara rose unsteadily and held a hand against the wall for support. "What's your purpose in being here?" the newcomer continued. "What're you doing?"

"I came for a walk," Ashara said, rubbing the snot from under her nose. "I wanted to see the temple."

"So you're one of *them*," he said. "Papers?"

"I left them at home," Ashara lied. The newcomer examined her and scratched his chin with his thumb.

"Then you won't mind coming with us," he said. "Just for a chat in the shade." Ashara gagged and put her fingers to her lips. Her eyes probed the brown eyes of the sentries. They were not joking.

"I just came for a walk," she said. "It's hot." The first sentry took Ashara by the arm and the other two fell in behind them.

"You're not in trouble," he said. "Just a few questions we'd like to ask."

So much for shade, Ashara thought, looking about the tent. The flaps were down and blue-gray smoke hung heavy and rank in the air. Opposite her, a captain tapped more *dama* leaf into his pipe and lit it. He sat watching her, the pipe loose between his lips.

"A walk?" he said at last. "You're a bit far from Eastbank."

"The temple's here," Ashara said with a shrug.

"You had much involvement with the temple?" he asked.

"Been once or twice." She gripped the sides of her chair and leaned forward, trying but failing to contain her nervousness.

"And what was the purpose of those visits?"

"I'm Kh'areen. It's what we do."

The captain cleared his throat and leaned forward, removing the pipe from between his lips.

"What do you know of the Kh'areen Self-Defense Force?"

"Nothing. Who are they?"

"They've given us grief," the captain said. "It was created before the siege to protect the precinct. Some hotheads have continued their efforts."

"Oh," Ashara said. This time he paused and the muscle beneath his right eye twitched.

"You do know something," the captain said. "You're not in trouble. Say it."

"I heard of guard companies," Ashara said. "Before the siege."

"Who told you?"

"I overheard it," she said. "In the market." This appeared, on the surface at least, to satisfy him. He leaned back in his chair.

"Your Vu is good. You were born here?"

"No. Baki. But my family ran mules my whole life." The captain nodded and picked out a blank piece of paper. Ashara crossed her legs and swallowed down bile. Behind her the tent flap stirred and a beam of yellow light briefly fell on the camp desk. A figure breezed past her and whispered in the captain's ear. The captain sat blankly and folded his hands in front of him.

"Well," he said. "We have a problem."

"What…"

"Tell her what you told me," the captain said to the messenger.

"We sent someone to the Luka-Tudo Trading House to fetch your papers," said the newcomer. "They said you don't have any."

"So," said the captain. "Don't lie to me. Tell me the truth. Where are your papers?"

"I've told you the truth," Ashara insisted. "Why —"

"Where are your papers?"

"But," she stammered. Ashara looked sheepishly towards the dirt floor. "I live there. And I told you before — I recently moved."

"Irrelevant," said the captain. "You either have papers or you don't, and it turns out you don't. You lied to us. What else have you been less than truthful about?"

"I live there…" Ashara groaned.

"Stop." He raised a hand. "We can't sort this out here. As I'm unable to continue, I'm letting the Ministry of Virtue sort this out. We can't take too many chances in this environment."

The captain watched her as if expecting a reaction. The messenger grinned with his rotten teeth showing. The tent flap moved behind her, a stab of light once again cutting down the middle of the tent. Ashara dared not turn, but she sensed the person behind her.

CHAPTER 8

"It is been estimated that Pao'an requires a thousand ton of food a day. Pack animals cannot carry this burden alone, so the majority is via the Blue River. And this is no small trade. With an average capacity for one hundred ton, the Worshipful Company of Dockers commissions, controls or exercises levy rights over one hundred and forty-seven river boats — officially. Some suspect the number is much higher."

A Traveler's Guide to Pao'an

Crows perched on the crossbeam. Beneath them swayed six men and a woman, hemp ropes tight about their necks. Biet turned his face, but Po stared in fascination at the empty sockets that once were eyes. Signs about their necks declared them traitors, reactionaries, and saboteurs.

"Why don't they cut them down?" Po asked.

"A warning," Biet replied, leaning heavily on Po's arm. "Their final duty."

They continued in silence. Biet's weight drew down on him. Po realized for the first time how much his mentor had aged. The stresses and strains of managing the monastery through the crisis were getting to him.

"We can stop here if you want," Po suggested. He indicated a bench on the side of the street.

"No," Biet said. "Let's just keep going." Po did not want to insult Biet's sense of independence, but neither could he let the abbot wear himself out.

"Or…" he suggested. "I could go by myself?"

"No," Biet said again. "Judge Bodai is an important benefactor. I must go. He would not take kindly to a novice turning up and asking for money."

They came to a square packed with people. Signs announced: *"One Copper Jet & Three-Square Meals," "General Jano Stands Against Chaos, Do You?" and "Enlist Today."* A crowd gathered in front of a series of camp desks, some with their families, others alone. By the drop off station were tearful farewells, and behind that were rows of chairs where raw recruits were shaved and washed down with buckets of water. The two monks skirted the whole affair.

Not far from the square Venerable Biet and Novice Po came to a row of mansions. They approached a red door with a large number 15 on it. Biet rapped the door knocker against its iron backing and stepped aside.

"Now let me do the talking," he said. "I —"

Bolts clicked, and the door opened. An elegant woman with auburn hair poked her head out, looked the pair over, and checked the street with a glance in each direction. Po sucked in his breathe. *She's beautiful.*

"Savani," Biet said. "Your husband was expecting us."

"He was," she said, stepping aside. "Come in. Would you like anything to drink? He'll see you shortly."

Biet waved a hand in dismissal, but Po had had enough of the abbot's modesty.

"The Venerable Abbot would like water," he said, trying to sound polite. Savani flashed him a smile. Her hazel eyes met his. In a land where black hair and brown eyes dominated, Savani was unique. *Where… the face… yes.* He had seen her the day Judge Loti died; Biet had talked to her. She led them through into an atrium and disappeared through a kitchen door. A fountain bubbled and the sweet scent of flowers spilled over the side of hanging baskets. Exotic birds chirped in their cages, and two cats lay on the sun-baked tiles. Savani returned and placed a tray on a low stone table.

"How is the monastery?" she asked, passing first the abbot, then Po, a drink.

"We can't complain," Biet replied. "The whole city suffers."

"It won't be long now," Savani said. "The Emperor has set himself up at Dili and the Third Army is coming to reinforce them. You'll see. They'll recapture Pao'an and we'll root out the Vu'tai as the real traitors."

"We can only hope," said the abbot. "You're not tempted to join them?"

"Bodai's job is here," Savani said. "We're safe as long as we don't make our opinions widely known. If I can say one good thing about Jano, he has tried to pull the bureaucracy together again." She cocked her head as if to a sound and excused herself, only to return a moment later. "He's ready for you."

They followed Savani down a corridor and through a double door into an office with views out over a courtyard garden. In the center behind a desk sat Bodai e Unuga. His eyes brightened when he saw Biet.

"Venerable Abbot," he said, rising to his feet. "What a pleasure."

"A pleasure indeed," Biet said. "May I introduce Novice Po, one of our best students. Novice Po, this is Judge Bodai e Unuga, Chief Judge of the First Circuit Court." They exchanged pleasantries, and Bodai motioned for them to be seated. Po sank down into the upholstered armchair, then sat up straight, self-conscious of his company. Venerable Biet appeared relaxed, exchanging small talk with the judge, and then moving on to a conversation on legal ethics. The judge leaned forward, asked questions, and listened to Biet's answers while massaging his beard with thumb and forefinger. After a while he regarded Po.

"And what do you think?"

"Your Honor," Po said. "I — I..."

"I confess," Biet said, cutting in. "We have not spent much time on legal ethics. Po, however, has been reading up on Asanga, Kadopi and Suvu of Ja'na. He is a remarkable student."

"Indeed," the judge said. "The Venerable Abbot must see something in you, Novice Po. He's not easily satisfied."

"Top of his class," Biet said smiling. "We'll make an abbot of him yet."

"That is quite an endorsement," Bodai said. "We could do with scholars like you entering government."

"That is not yet decided," Biet said, politely cutting off the judge with a dismissive gesture. "It is unwise to jump too quickly."

"That is true," Bodai said. "A strong house is built with strong foundations. Count yourself fortunate, Novice Po, you are not a student of the Imperial Academy. I worry about them. The Academy is closed and half the buildings damaged in the breaching of the city wall. I can't imagine when things will return to normal."

"Your wife said the Emperor has gone to Dili. Is it true?"

"I believe it is," said the judge. "It would make sense — Tomi buys time. I'm sure once the Third Army arrives they'll have the strength to retake Pao'an. In the meantime, Dili is easily defended. Meanwhile, Jano is here with a massive hole in his wall. But this is politics. How's the monastery?" Venerable Biet moved to the edge of his chair.

"In dire straits," he said coldly. "We've opened our gates to the sick and wounded and handed out food to the poor. But three times now soldiers have seized our stores. We're low on almost everything, without enough food to last the fortnight." The judge reached for a pen and paper.

"Tell me everything," he said. Biet held up both hands.

"I don't think we need to make an issue out of it," he said. "You and I both know it will cause more issues than it is worth." Bodai shrugged and uncorked an ink bottle.

"Just my private notes," Bodai said. "The Vu'tai reign of terror won't last forever. One day there will be a day of judgement. All their acts will be exposed to the harsh sunlight of public opinion and the law. I simply prepare for that day." Biet sighed and began to speak, telling the judge about the three times soldiers had come to the monastery. Bodai listened and wrote as the abbot spoke. When Biet finished, Bodai blew on the paper and considered it. He made corrections, then put it on the corner of his desk.

"I'll file it away later," he said. "I have quite a collection. You wouldn't believe what I hear. One day we could make a bound book out of everything. The Vu'tai are dangerous."

"You don't need to convince me," Biet said, then regarded Po. "Us," he added. Po nodded. "You have our support and thanks."

"That's what I wanted to hear. The Ba're have always been valued allies to the Reformists. Now, what is it you want?"

"We could do with material assistance," Biet said. "Po has counted one hundred and seventeen mouths to feed."

"You ask a lot," Bodai said. "How much is grain now? Fifteen? Twenty *jet* a bushel? Half the city is starving. And grain only gets you so far. As Master Kalaki says…" Bodai paused as if he forgot the exact quote. He clicked his fingers.

"Millet is not a sufficient diet," Po said. "But meats and vegetables are needed in equal portion." Bodai looked at Po, surprised.

"You're familiar with Master Kalaki's treatise on public health?"

"My father," Po said, then remembered some topics were out of bounds for monks but proceeded anyway. "Is Sanitation Officer of Li'an. Master Kalaki was a favourite of his."

"Well then," Bodai said. "As Novice Po said, millet will not solve all your problems. It'll be tough to find fresh vegetables and meats — though I guess we can find legumes and beans."

"We are aware we ask a lot," Biet stressed. "We wouldn't ask it lightly."

"And how do I know," Bodai went on. "That you don't fill your pantry, only for everything to be seized again?"

"I've convinced the abbot to divide the food up and hide it in the ceiling cavities," Po said. "Leaving just enough in storage to satisfy any visitors." Bodai considered Po then turned to Biet.

"He's a tricky one. Since when did the Ba're engage in deception?"

"Since lives depended on it," Biet said. "General Jano does not deserve this food."

"Very well," the judge said. He slipped a piece of paper across the table and wrote a number on it. He showed it to Biet. "Will that help?"

The cell door opened. Ashara sat up and picked straw from her face. The virtueman in the doorway held up a single candle, casting his features in heavy shadow. Ashara scrambled away from him into the corner and stood with her back against the wall. The man grunted, and placing the candle in a wall niche, took shackles from his belt and waved Ashara forward. Ashara knew already the penalty for refusing. She held out her hands, palm upwards, and stepped forward. Cold iron bit into her skin and the locks clicked.

"This way," the virtueman said. They marched through the grim interior of the Ministry for the Promotion of Virtue and Elimination of Vice, and up flights of stairs to an interview room. Natural light fell in shafts from high windows. Ashara shielded her face with her forearm. The virtueman yanked on the chain and made her sit in a chair with cuffs on the armrests. He switched the manacles for the cuffs.

"Your interviewer will be along shortly," he said, and left the room, locking the door behind him. Ashara looked about her. There was a table in front of her with a chair opposite. Ashara tried moving her wrists, but the cuffs were bolted through the armrest.

The door opposite opened and a man entered, different from the others in a solid black coat, velvet gloves and high leather boots. Around his neck he wore a gold chain which ended in the head of a serpent. The newcomer placed a folder on the table and took his seat.

"Ashara Daladh'an," he said. "Daughter of Kh'am Daladh'an. Is this correct?" Ashara nodded.

"I'm Inquisitor Lukan. My colleague is, well, otherwise engaged. Now, I don't believe I have your mother's name."

"She died when I was a child. I just knew her as Mother."

"And how long have you been in Pao'an?"

"Spring sometime," Ashara said. "Time's lost meaning. It is all such a blur. Could I have something to drink?"

"First you answer my questions," Lukan said. "Then, when I'm happy, you can eat and drink. Tell me, you were not entirely honest with us. Why was that?"

"I was scared. I thought the problem would go away. I hadn't done anything wrong."

"And you were on the way to the temple. Who do you meet there?"

"No one," Ashara said. "I haven't been here long." Lukan adjusted himself and read the notes in front of him. He looked up from the page.

"Does the name Takich Kh'undit mean anything to you?" Ashara shook her head.

"Is it a person?" she asked. The inquisitor's lips curled into a smile and he came around the table, Ashara's eyes following him, until he leaned over and whispered in her ear.

"You are in trouble, young lady," he said. "You have no documentation. You don't exist. You have lied to an imperial officer, and now may be lying to an imperial inquisitor. It's not hard to link you to the Kh'areen Self-Defense Force. It's safer for us if you disappear, no? Convince me otherwise." His breath assaulted her nostrils. *Sardines and millet beer.* If she had food in her, she would have purged it.

"I've never heard of them," Ashara said, straining at her cuffs. "I don't know who they are."

"That's not what you told my colleague."

"What I mean," Ashara said. "I know nothing other than they exist." Lukan returned to his seat and tut-tutted to himself.

"When," he asked. "Did you first meet Takich Kh'undit?"

"I told you — I've never met him!"

"So," Lukan said, knitting his gloved fingers. "Let me get this straight. What you're telling me is; you go to the temple, meet no one, and have never met Takich?" When said like that, Ashara realized she sounded silly.

"There was the priest," she said. Ashara described the priest and the interviewer nodded along.

"Have you seen him since the liberation?"

"No. I was looking for him that day." Lukan pushed the folder aside and crossed his arms.

"I'm struggling," he said. "I believe you're just a naïve provincial in over your head. Others say you're in cahoots with Takich. I want to help you. But you're not giving me much to go on. Let me save you."

With that, Ashara broke. She opened up about the ambush, the loss of her family and her arrival in Pao'an. She gave details about the Luka-Tudo house and the visits to the temple to get fresh papers sent from Baki. She talked about the priest and their conversations, and finally she talked about that day she went to find him again. "Is that what you wanted?" she demanded at the end. "Are you happy?"

"I think that's about it," said Lukan. He stood and knocked on the door. "Enough for this afternoon anyway." The door opened. "She's behaved today. Take her to the dining room and get a meal into her. After that return her to her cell."

⁂

Muni Mei-Uduga reclined on her couch and checked her teeth in the mirror, picking at the remains of lunch with a metal toothpick. A servant waited with a velvet cushion for her to finish, her clothes ruffling in the wind. Around them from the citadel balcony spread the magnificent vista of the Dili Valley, from the walled city beneath, to the sprawling tents of the gathered armies, to the Gray River, and the forested hills beyond. Muni laid the mirror and toothpick on the cushion and waved the servant away.

"Call Captain Vatoni," she said to another. "Immediately." She lay back and closed her eyes, the sun glowing through her eyelids.

"Your Grace?" Muni did not move. She knew the voice.

"Captain, what were those noises downstairs?"

"The Emperor's concubines," Vatoni said. "They lost something."

"Lost something?"

"Just a comb, Your Grace."

"And the citadel doesn't have enough of those?"

"The concubine in question wanted her own. It was left behind in Pao'an."

"Of course it was, what did they expect? This is war."

"Yes, Your Grace."

"We should send them further on to safety," Muni said. "Then tip off the rebels to their location." Vatoni remained silent. *Wise.* "You see, you're on my detail, and while you were servicing the imperial strumpets, I was here alone."

"We're ever vigilant, Your Grace."

"Well, that's a relief," Muni said with a laugh. She got up and walked to the balcony rail. "You see —" She pointed across the valley, a ringed finger indicating a patch of wood. "What do you see?"

"Trees?"

"Not impressed, Captain. Use the same eyes you ogle the concubines with."

"Flashing. It's a signal."

"And none of your men spotted it?"

"Could be one of our's?"

"Well, go check. I shouldn't be doing your job for you."

Shortly, a portly signals officer stood on the balcony.

"Not one of our's," he said.

"What's it saying?"

"Not our codes," the officer said. "It appears to be a string of questions with long pauses. Someone is replying."

"From *inside* the city?"

"It would appear that way." Muni threw up her hands and turned her back on the two officers.

"And why is it left to me to figure this out?" she demanded, rounding on them again.

"That would be a question for the Ministry of Virt—" Muni cuffed the signalman. He shrunk back and covered his face.

"Captain," she growled. "Take this man out into the valley. You'll see where the signal is coming from inside the city. Don't come back until you've sorted it."

"Your Grace," babbled the signal officer. "It's very likely they'll be finished..."

"*Awww,* do you want to pack a picnic? Bottle of wine? Captain Vatoni, take a pair of pliers. If he complains too much, cut out that tongue."

Later that day Muni burst into a war cabinet meeting and dumped the contents of a bag onto the table. Ministers and generals alike recoiled in horror as severed heads rolled this way and that, and came to rest amidst their glasses of wine.

"What the flaming—" General Nulu began and cut himself off.

"Good grief, woman!" Minister Tuno spluttered into his handkerchief.

"Perhaps," Tomi said coldly. "My wife can explain why she comes into a meeting — a meeting she isn't invited to — and dumps these... these... abominations on the council table. Assuming you haven't found my lovers, these must be somehow connected with the war." Order somewhat restored, the attendees smiled at the humor. Captain Vatoni cleared away the heads and servants removed the wine cups.

"They were spies," Muni said. "In the city."

"And how did you get them?" Tuno demanded. Muni rolled her eyes at the old war minister.

"My Vermilion Guards collected them for me. Or would you prefer a more exotic story? More importantly, Minister Tuno, I would like to know why I had to get them. Where are your soldiers? How many men do you have in the valley? One hundred thousand? No one noticed the signals coming from the hills opposite?" Minister Tuno glowered.

"This is not your business," he said. "This could have been a counter-intelligence operation..."

"Calm it," Tomi said. "I think we can all congratulate Muni for her dedication. Now, darling, we have a meeting here. May we continue?"

"You haven't told me what you're going to do about it," Muni said.

"Well it seems you've taken care of the problem," Tomi said. "Or did you have something else in mind?"

"These were Vu'tai spies," Muni said. "The traitor Jano knows we're here and already prepares to march against us."

"He'll fail," Tuno interrupted. "The Third Army will be here soon. With General Mamot's men we'll outnumber him two to one. This really isn't a concern for you."

"I don't think Mamot's coming," General Nulu said. "He's taking his time."

"Has anyone had reports of his progress?" General Duju asked. "He could be months away."

"I have," Tomi said. "He's being slow, but he'll get here."

"Chief Minister," General Nulu said. "I don't have your confidence. The Vu'tai reach is far."

"Vu'tai?" Tonu scoffed. "General Mamot's... nothing traditional about him."

"Yes," Nulu said. "A general who doesn't fight, or heel when he's called."

"Enough!" Tomi yelled, hammering the table. "Point made. We'll need two plans. One for *when* Mamot comes, and one for *if* he doesn't. Now, darling, can we continue?"

"With pleasure," Muni said. "Good evening gentlemen." She turned to the door and Captain Vatoni fell in behind her.

"You didn't mention the traitor, Your Grace," he whispered in the hall.

"I'm not certain which one it is yet," she said.

CHAPTER 9

A Traveler's Guide to Pao'an

"And this is how you both feel?" Avi demanded. Dasha nodded. Natan did not move. "No. I forbid it."

"You let Dan enlist," Dasha said. Avi swept the papers off his desk.

"And have you heard from him since? Am I to lose all my sons?"

"You don't care," Natan snapped. "You..." Avi bounded towards him and drove him into the wall, Avi's forearm against Natan's throat.

"You ungrateful bastard. Everything I do is for this family. How dare you!"

Natan pushed back and Avi lost his footing. Natan's clenched fist connected with Avi's cheekbone. His father grunted and sat stunned on his desk; his tattooed fingers probed his cheek.

"You fucking punched me," Avi said coldly. "You hit your father." Natan watched his feet.

"I'm sorry," he said. Dasha drew in his breath. Natan glimpsed his father's eyes, twinkling again with fire. *Well that was a mistake.* Avi rushed at him and Natan hit the floor clutching his stomach. Natan struggled to get up, but Avi's booted foot thumped into his rib cage.

"Stop!" Dasha cried. "Father, he made a mistake."

"He's a little shit," Avi said. Natan protected his head. He hit the door frame.

"Hit him again and we're both joining," Dasha yelled. "Try us." Avi rounded on his middle son and lifted a fist, but Dasha was ready with a paperweight. Avi dropped his hands and put the office desk between him and his sons.

"Out," he said. "You have a day. Both of you. Go fucking join the army — you've made your feelings known. After everything I've done for you, you've clearly decided this is not your home. One day you will realize what a good father I have been. But don't expect to come back here when you're crippled and begging on the corner for two *ku'net* a day. You'll be dead to me."

Dasha took Natan's arm.

"Come on," he said. "We'll get the papers ready."

Natan followed his brother. Oni stood in the hall, her eyes red and puffy.

"You heard?" Natan asked. She nodded. The two sons hugged their mother and fetched the family papers.

They waited in a queue at the Eastbank barracks for the best part of an hour before approaching a desk.

"Endorsement letter?" asked a clerk. Dasha said it was and prompted Natan to hand over the papers. Natan laid the palm-sized book in front of the clerk.

"My brother, Natan Luka-Tudo, and myself, Dasha Luka-Tudo."

"Very good," the clerk said and flipped through the papers before going out the back to check the file system. He returned with a folder, thumbed through the pages, found the appropriate information and selected two forms from a pile on his desk. The forms would confirm Dasha and Natan's identity and that they were of '*reliable character*'.

"Could you do a third one?" Natan asked, watching the clerk stamp the forms with a red seal. Dasha raised an eyebrow.

"Another endorsement letter?" asked the clerk. Dasha tugged on Natan's sleeve as if asking for an explanation. Natan ignored him.

"I want to sort something out," Natan said. "Just an introduction to the family." The clerk absently scratched his brow.

"You're after a Letter of Introduction," he said. "Different form. Endorsement letters are free, but the introduction will be three *jet*."

"Hold on," Dasha said, pulling his brother aside. "What are you doing?"

"Trust me," Natan said. "Mother'll need the help." He turned back to the clerk and put the required coins on the counter. The clerk put the money in the drawer and selected a larger piece of paper.

"Anything in particular you want noted?"

"Say my father is a member of the Merchant's Guild, that we own the Luka-Tudo Trading House, he has three sons, no daughters and we're all of reliable character." The clerk checked the file to confirm these details.

"Anything else?"

"That is all," Natan said.

"You're mad," Dasha said as the pair approached the red-brick edifice that dominated the corner of South Avenue and Imperial Way. "Father's going to freak."

"We're dead to him, remember?"

"He'll forget that," Dasha said. "I'm half convinced I should wait outside."

"If you want," Natan said. "Here, give me the letter. I'll go in alone." Dasha fidgeted and looked up and down the street.

"Nah, I'll come with you. Shit, they'd kill me if I let you go in there alone."

"Fair enough," Natan said and opened the door to the public entrance. The marble in the foyer squeaked under foot, and above the front desk a sign swung on a chain until the door closed. It read: *Ministry for the Promotion of Virtue and Elimination of Vice.*

"Good afternoon," a woman said, standing up. "Can I help you?"

"I'd like to make a report," Natan said, placing the Letter of Introduction on the counter. "My name is Natan Luka-Tudo. My family owns a trading house on the Blue River. I believe one of our employees is in your custody." The woman looked over the letter in front of her.

"And what do you think you can add to the case?" she asked.

"The Luka-Tudo Trading House can vouch for her activities and whereabouts. You see, my brother and I are about to enlist in the army, and that will leave our parents alone to look after the house. I would go off to fight for the empire a lot easier if I knew that our employee was there to look after them."

"I see," the woman said, reading the letter a second time. "Who did you say your employee was?" Natan told her. "I see," the woman said a second time. "I will go speak to someone."

"No going back now," Natan said as the woman ducked out the back, noticing his brother's white fingers on the counter edge.

"You've got the balls of Kive," Dasha said under his breath. "She's taking a while."

The woman came back with a man in black with a gold chain around his neck. *An inquisitor*, Natan realized, his own knuckles turning white.

"Come this way," he said curtly. "We have a few questions." Dasha motioned for Natan to lead the way. They followed the inquisitor down corridors and up stairs to an interview room.

"Take a seat," the inquisitor said.

A rat scurried down the corridor and disappeared into a crack between the tiles. Ashara wondered why a creature would choose the bowels of the Ministry of Virtue for a home — even vermin should have more sense. They climbed a flight of steps and turned into a vaulted hall with diagrams of the human body splayed out like the flayed flesh of a defeated enemy. Ashara shuddered. She hoped she would never get used to it. At the end of the hall they came to two doors. The virtueman took out a brass ring with a half dozen keys. He picked one and unlocked the door on the right.

"Wait," Ashara said. "Where are we going? That's a different door." The virtueman ignored her and pushed Ashara through into the checkered corridor beyond. They arrived at a green set of double doors and once again the virtueman selected a key. Harsh sunlight flooded the hall and fresh air brushed against Ashara's skin. Ashara blinked and stumbled out onto the courtyard. For one brief moment she sensed freedom, then the putrefied stink of death leached into her nostrils, overpowering her hope and crushing her spirit.

Cadavers hung by their necks, gently swaying from the rows of gallows. Crows hopped across the stone slabs, fighting over strips of festering flesh. Ashara put a manacled hand to her nose.

"You're going to kill me?" she asked. The virtueman locked the double green doors and turned to her.

"It's what happens to traitors," he said. "But not today."

"Oh," Ashara said. The virtueman led her along and coughed into his sleeve. A door at the other side of the yard opened and two more virtuemen entered. Behind them trudged Natan and Dasha. Ashara bit her thumb and forced herself to contain her excitement.

"You know those two?" her virtueman asked. She said she did. One virtueman opposite shrugged.

"Orders are orders," he said. "Ashara Daladh'an, you're to be bailed to the Luka-Tudo residence with temporary papers." He held out a sealed document. "Do not come to our attention again." Her virtueman unlocked her manacles, and the other turned to Natan. "And you have sworn under oath. You are now responsible for her conduct. Better take that seriously." The third virtueman opened an exterior gate to an alleyway beyond. "Off you go then."

At the house Oni threw open her arms and Ashara ran into her embrace, breathing in the familiar jasmine and rose fragrance of her mistress. Natan and Dasha raced to explain how they got her back. Avi was less emotional.

"You're back," he said. "Hope you didn't drag this house into your drama." Oni rolled her eyes.

The next day the two brothers waved goodbye at the gate and Ashara accompanied Oni inside. As she swept the hall, conversation drifted in through the open front door.

"A Ba're monk," Oni said, watching over Ashara's shoulder. "At least he's a customer."

"Ba're?" Ashara asked. *Them*, Ashara remembered. The *kebilu* had talked of the Ba're. "He doesn't look scary."

"Scary," Oni said with a laugh. "They're about as boring as you get."

Outside Avi was getting animated and the monk nodded along. Eventually they shook hands and Avi left with the letter of credit. The monk turned and for a brief moment they locked eyes. Ashara smiled. His face flushed red.

"Ashara!" Avi called. "Where is she? There you are. Here's an order. Load the donkey. You'll need to make a few trips to avoid the Worshipful Bastards."

"The who?"

"The river workers," Oni said. "Keep it to a bag and you can cross the bridge."

"Absolute rort," Avi fumed. "I'll say it again: Break that monopoly on the river, and I'll halve the cost of grain in the city."

An hour later Ashara arrived at Jan Moga. Finding the gate open she guided the donkey into the colonnaded courtyard and tethered it to a railing.

"That was quick," a monk said. Ashara recognized him as the monk from earlier. "Let me take that."

"It's heavy," Ashara warned. The monk ignored her and hefted the sack onto his shoulder. The muscles in his neck ran taught and his face reddened. "We can carry it together?" she suggested. "It's why I brought the donkey." The monk relented and they carried the millet through to the monastery storeroom. Done, the monk dusted off his hands.

"Thanks for the help," he said. "When you bring the next one ask for me. I'm Po."

"Ashara," she said, offering her hand, but he held back.

"Sorry," Po said. "It's forbidden."

"I didn't know," she said.

"You're Kh'areen?"

"Why do you ask?"

"I want to show you something," Po said and without further discussion breezed past her to the door. Ashara paused, finding the monk odd, then hastened after him.

"When Pao'an fell," Po explained on the way. "We took in the wounded. It all became quite a mess. Most have gone home now, but others have needed more intensive treatment." He opened a door and Ashara caught the acidic tang of sickness. "One of them's an elderly Kh'areen man. We've had trouble understanding him."

"What's wrong with him?" Ashara asked.

"Flesh wound," said Po. "It never healed, and while we've done what we can, he recently developed a fever." They shuffled between the rows of patients and came to the back corner. Po drew back the curtains, revealing the eddying pools of dust. The patient gazed up at them, his face a waxy yellow and the skin hanging from the bone. The whites of his eyes, where not bloodshot, had turned a mustard color and beads of sweat collected on his brow. It was the *sabka*.

Ashara stared blankly into the twilight. Candles glowed from the Great Hall and the droning of monks echoed off the monastery walls. Sandals scuffed the tiles behind her.

"I brought you food," Po said, joining her on the step. Ashara accepted the bowl and rested it in her lap, the heat radiating through her thighs.

"Thanks," Ashara said. "He's not going to make it you know."

"I know," Po said. "I'm sorry."

"He was like family," she said. "When I needed help, he was there. I don't even know his real name. Do you think he'll wake soon? I can't be here too late..."

"The Brothers will do their rounds and they'll wake him. When you talk with him, does he make sense? When you speak to him I mean. I saw you just sit there and both move your lips."

"We're reciting the *Chobi Ghada*," Ashara said. "It is our holy text."

"And it helps?"

"It is comforting. And it is said — I don't know how to translate it? If the *Chobi Ghada* is on your tongue and you die, you will be with Tanri in the life beyond."

"Tanri is your god?" Po asked. "You've mentioned him before."

"The only god," Ashara said. "Is it true the Ba're are godless?" Po flinched back at the question, but he steadied himself and measured his words.

"Yes," he said. "We don't believe in gods, or you could say they're irrelevant." Ashara opened her mouth in surprise. Regaining composure, she indicated the images of people carved into the pillars of the colonnade.

"Then who are they?" she asked. Po laughed.

"They're not gods," he said. "They're carvings; masters and sages, and people from stories.

"But," Ashara protested. "How can you say there are no gods?"

"How can we? Dasanika said if there are gods, what do they do? Rain falls on the believer and the non-believer. A flood hits a village and washes away those of all faiths. Everyone dies — what faith has saved someone from that? And when the body weakens, praying to one god or another doesn't extend life. This is what Dasanika meant when he said gods, if they exist, are irrelevant. You believe in Tanri — what does he do for you?"

"Easy," Ashara said. "He makes the sun rise and the sun set. He made all that is around us. He provides comfort to the poor and punishes the bad. He is..." Ashara paused, searching for the Vu word. "Civilization." *Close enough.*

"The Vu'du make the same argument," Po said. "Yet the people of Krsaka have some of the greatest legal minds in the world. But they don't know Tanri, nor the Vu gods. You say this is Tanri. The Vu'du say the Great Serpent. Krsakans say the Ancient Wisdom."

"Well they're wrong," Ashara said. "We know. Tanri revealed himself to the Chobi, and she testified to the tribes." Po fell silent and contemplated the bottom step. Ashara watched him and then turned to her meal.

The next day Ashara leaned over the priest's bed and adjusted the blanket under his chin. Purple blotches marked his cheeks and his breath rattled in his throat. It unnerved her. *No papers now*, she thought, but as soon as it came to mind she chastised herself for thinking something so selfish.

"How's he doing?" Po asked.

"Same as before," Ashara said. "But the breathing slows." The blanket moved and the priest's eyes crept open. His lips cracked into a smile and he whispered something.

"What's he saying?"

"I don't know," Ashara said. The priest drew his hand from under the blanket and pointed his index finger at the mattress.

"*Kh'or*," he said.

"He's choking," Po said. "I'll get a cloth."

"No," Ashara said. "I think he means *under*."

"Under what?" Po asked. Ashara ignored him and got down on her knees and drew a bloody canvas bag out from under the bed.

"Oh that," Po said. "He brought that with him." Ashara held it up to the *sabka*. He nodded so gently it was almost undetectable.

"*Ba'ee*," he grunted. *Open*. Ashara loosened the ties and drew out a rectangular object wrapped in lambskin. She put the lambskin on the bed, unwrapped it and withdrew a book of blue leather and gold embossing. Ashara gasped.

"It is a *Chobi Ghada*." She turned the pages, each one handwritten and beautifully illustrated. "Done by a calligrapher."

"It's beautiful," Po said, leaning in to her. "Can you read it?"

"Not well," Ashara said, running a finger over the flowing script. "We memorize it as children. But I have never owned a book. Ever." She turned to the beginning and stopped. Someone had pasted a piece of paper onto the page before the dedication. With time the paper had yellowed and fallen from the page. It was now loose against the spin.

"To Takich," she said out loud. Her eyes widened. "Takich Kh'undit." She slammed the book shut.

"What does that mean?" Po asked.

"Nothing," Ashara said. "Nothing important." She stuffed the book back into the bag, but the priest stopped her.

"I think he wants you to take it," Po said.

"Why me?" Ashara said. *No*, she screamed inside.

"Well you're Kh'areen. You said he was like family."

"Yes, but…" She looked at the book and back at the priest. "Takich Kh'undit?" she said. "Is it you?" He nodded and grunted as if trying to clear his throat.

"I will get him something for the pain," Po said. "You sit with him. It'll not be long now. Sometimes they wake to say goodbye before the end."

CHAPTER 10

"I now must give some account of Vu infantry. They are primarily divided up into squads, companies and banners. Twenty men to a squad, 240 to a company, and 2,880 to a banner. Beyond this, their banner groups and armies become somewhat arbitrary."

The Travels of Odam Yusufkas the Solari

"Shields!" Captain Mako yelled. Soldiers swung shields forward and braced them between those of their neighbors. "Spears!" The front ranks dropped their spears level, and the back ranks bristled like a porcupine. Natan blinked sweat from his eyes and struggled to focus on the patch of field in front of him. Drums rolled the advance and Natan shuffled forward, keeping his timing.

"Keep those shields together," Sergeant Bi'reke yelled. "Keep the beat!"

"Stop!" Mako roared. "Bloody hell." He drew his sword and pointed at individuals. "Dead, dead, dead. You bastards broke ranks. Someone speared you and now you're pissing yourselves, crying for mommy. Let's do it again." They repeated the drill, then repeated it again and again until Natan's muscles burned and his arms felt as heavy as wagon wheels.

The sun shimmered over the western horizon when Mako stopped them. Barrel-chested and as grim as death he surveyed the troops in formation; twenty men across and ten ranks deep.

"Sergeant Bi'reke!" he barked. "Your squad looks like it's enjoying itself. Can't have worked hard enough. Two miles to camp — run it and light the fires. I think we deserve a good meal tonight — who's up for ration cakes?" Muffled moans reached Natan's ears. Mako narrowed his eyes. "Some of you might think I'm a right bastard. And yes, it's true. But I've been here before. I know what you're going into. You're the 37th Auxiliary. Act like a unit or when pitched into the hellstorm of battle you'll be chewed up and become the shit of the gods. Look to your squad mates. Look to your sergeants. Promise each other you'll do your bloody best. Got me?" The company cheered.

"All under Heaven!" Bi'reke shouted, and the men took up the cry. Captain Mako raised his hands for silence.

"That's the spirit. Now, Sergeant Davati, was that your squad earlier? Your men can join Bi'reke. Go!"

Fires flickered as far as the eye could see. Natan massaged his legs and longed for a bucket of hot water to wash them in. At least the day was over.

"So where do you think we're going?" one of his squad asked, chewing his ration cake.

"Who cares," said another. "As long as it's one copper *jet* a day and three square meals, I'll go anywhere."

"Three square meals?" Natan said. "I've tasted better rat shit."

"You're a connoisseur of rat shit are you?" the first man said. "Even rat shit's better than no shit. And imagine the plunder when we win. We'll live like priests."

Natan bit his tongue. He had to remember his family was probably one of the richest in the company.

"Is a Natan Luka-Tudo here?" came a voice. The soldiers glanced up at one of the company's drummer boys. When no one responded he continued: "You Bi'reke's squad?"

"Who wants to know?" the earlier speaker asked, spitting into the fire.

"Captain Mako," said the kid. "So is he here or not?"

"Here," Natan said, cursing under his breath. "Show me where the tent is." The drummer boy scampered off barefoot between the fires. Natan followed, grumbling as he went. They found Mako in his tent working by lamplight.

"Natan," he said, cutting off a formal greeting. "I understand your family owns a trading house." Natan said they did. "And you're good with a pen?"

"Well enough," Natan said with a shrug. Mako passed him a piece of paper.

"If you can read it, I'm going to need your help with a report." Natan's eyes scanned the page. "Outloud," Mako added.

"Of course," Natan said, clearing his throat. "*Captains of the 14th Banner, tomorrow we push north for the final battle. Prepare your companies. Assemble at sixth bell on the Imperial Way. Logistics group will work through the night. Get your requests to them now.*"

"Good enough," Mako said and handed Natan a second piece of paper. "Run around the squads and compile a list of equipment we require. Bring the list back here, I'll stamp it, and then you can take it to logistics group for them to fill."

Natan stared down at the paper with dead eyes. *So much for rest*, he thought. Mako evidently noticed. He rummaged about in a satchel for his purse and drew out three copper *jet*.

"It'll be worth your while," he said and dropped the coins into Natan's hand.

"And these are for?"

"37th Auxiliary, 14th Banner," Natan said to the gray-haired clerk at logistics headquarters. The clerk on the other side of the desk scanned the order and marked it with a pen.

"I'm sure we can do that," he said. "Just a few changes." He crossed out some items. "And how are you off for bandages and dressings?"

"Fine, I believe."

"You didn't ask, did you?"

"No," Natan said. The clerk chewed the end of his pen and considered Natan for a minute.

"You're new to this, aren't you?" Natan nodded. "Better pay attention next time. You'll be the scapegoat for everything. Now your company will get the supplies sometime during the night." Natan thanked the clerk. "One more thing," the gray-haired man said. "How are you up for a little side business?"

"Side business?" Natan asked.

"Yes, well. How about I sell you a pound of *dama* leaf for two copper *jet*. You can then sell them to your squad after payday."

"Two coppers? That's twice the going rate in Pao'an."

"So, you know your stuff," the clerk said. "But think about it. You're out in the field. Where else will bored soldiers spend their money?"

"With someone cheaper," Natan said. "How about two pounds for three coppers?" The clerk took out a canvas one pound bag, the sort Natan often saw pass through his father's yard.

"Give that a smell," the clerk said. "Fresh *dama* leaf. Worth every copper." Natan gave it a cursory whiff and hated it. It reminded him of his father.

"Not the best quality," Natan said. "I'll leave it." He turned to leave.

"Wait, wait," the clerk said, rubbing his brow with three meaty fingers. "Three coppers for two pounds." He offered Natan his hand. Natan hesitated then accepted it. The exchange done, Natan returned to his squad, and finding everyone asleep, buried the two packs of *dama* leaf at the bottom of his bag where others were less likely to find it.

Ashara cleared the bowls from the table.

"You're not going to finish?" she asked. Oni rested her head in her hands. Her frizzy gray hair hung down about her shoulders as unruly as her husband's. Avi coughed into a clenched fist and settled back with his pipe.

"Put them in the kitchen," he said. "Maybe we'll feel like dinner later." Ashara considered the porridge and thought that unlikely.

"There's some sausage," she said. "You'll need something good in you."

Avi waved her off and stared blankly at the ceiling blowing smoke rings in his brooding.

"Mistress Oni? I'll go put the bedpan on the fire and boil ginger water for you."

"No," Oni said. "I'll be fine. Just a sniffle."

Ashara retired to the kitchen and hung the kettle over the hearth. Oni surprised her by coming to help with the washing up.

"I can do them," Ashara said.

"No," Oni replied. "Let me feel useful. No sons to fuss over." Ashara relented. She peeked at Ashara's bowl. "You're not having any vegetables with your porridge?"

"I leave those for you," Ashara said. "I see how few there are." Oni grunted and leaned heavily against the countertop. Ashara lay a concerned hand on her shoulder. Oni jerked away as if the touch stung her.

"Sorry," Oni said and left the kitchen. Ashara watched her go, considering how far Oni and Avi had deteriorated over the week. To an extent she recognized the numbness; she too had lost her family, but there was something else. She heard a thud from the hall.

Ashara dropped what she was doing and ran. Oni lay at the foot of the stairs, like a doll cast away by a bored child.

"Mistress Oni," she cried, falling to Oni's side. "Are you hurt?" Oni groaned and rolled on her back, her arms flopping to her side.

"Avi!" Ashara called, but she heard no response. She slapped Oni on both cheeks and failing to get any response, dragged her to her feet and wrapped Oni's arm around her shoulder. Somehow they managed it up the stairs and into the master bedroom. Ashara got Oni into bed and tucked the quilt tight about her chin.

"What happened?" Avi demanded from the doorway, his hair wild and more unruly than usual.

"She collapsed," Ashara said. "She's got a temperature." Avi came to the bed, his foot dragging on the floor, his movement languid.

"Fetch the doctor," he said. "I don't remember his name. Down on the corner of Eastbridge and..." his voice trailed off and he dropped into the chair next to the bed. "I think I've got it also."

"I'll find him," Ashara said. She snatched coins from the side table, ran downstairs and bounded out the door. Eastbridge Street was not far from the trading house, just a few blocks, and Ashara cut through alleys and through the yard of a wagon station to get there. In the darkness by the light of a lamp, hung a sign of the Vu goddess A'lu. *This is it.* Ashara knocked and waited. Floorboards creaked and a slot opened.

"Who is it?" demanded a woman.

"We need a doctor," Ashara said. "The Luka-Tudo Trading House." A bolt clicked and a gray head popped out.

"He's out," said the woman.

"Will he be long? My mistress collapsed. She has a fever." The woman tut tutted and motioned Ashara inside. Inside was the strong tang of vinegar. Ashara curled up her nose.

"Everyone does these days," said the old woman. "People are dropping like dice on a gambler's table. It's typhoon fever I'm afraid. Too many soldiers and broken sanitation." They came to a cluttered kitchen and the woman started opening and closing clay pots.

"How're her bowel movements?" she asked.

"Excuse me?" Ashara asked. "I don't know."

"Any rash or spotting around the eyes?"

"Not that I saw."

The woman muttered to herself and began collecting an assortment of dried herbs from different jars and wrapped them in a tight wad of paper.

"Give your mistress this," the woman said. "It'll purge the sickness from her and settle the fever. It's best you keep her warm and stop any bad air coming in. I'll send my husband when he is home." Ashara took the paper and clenched it in her fist.

"What do I owe you?" she asked.

"Three *jet*," said the woman. Ashara counted out the coins and ran back to the house.

The cat perched on the edge of the kitchen counter and watched Ashara stir the pot.

"It's only millet," Ashara said. "You don't like it." The cat meowed, jumped to the floor and stroked its chin against Ashara's legs. "No," she repeated. "Go away." She pushed it with her foot and the cat retreated to a safe distance and continued to watch her. All of a sudden its ears pricked and it twisted towards the laundry door. The door knocker hammered against the backstop.

"Coming," Ashara called and hurriedly moved the pot from the fire. She drew the bolt and opened the door a crack, keeping her foot jammed behind it. "Po?"

"Good morning," said Po. "The front gate's locked."

"No business these days," Ashara said. "Can I help you?"

"Maybe," Po said. "I was thinking about the book, can I come in?" Ashara opened the door and let Po through to the kitchen. The cat took one look at him and scampered off to the hall. "You told me one day at the monastery you wanted to return to Baki?"

"I do," Ashara said. "But I don't have time —"

"I did some research," Po cut in. "That book's worth at least three silver *li*."

"Mistress Oni is sick," Ashara said. "I don't have time to think about home."

"How sick?" Po asked. "Typhoon fever?"

"Come see," Ashara said. He followed her through the house and into the master bedroom. Po put a hand to his nose. Even Ashara, familiar now with it, drew in a sharp breath at the smell of the stale room.

"How long's she been like this," Po asked.

"A week," Ashara said. "She gets weaker by the day." Po shook his head, crossed the room and opened the windows.

"Wait," Ashara protested. "The doctor said we need to keep the bad air out."

"She needs fresh air," Po said. "Keep these open. Is she getting enough to eat and drink?"

"Trying to," Ashara said. "She's not hungry."

"And her bowel movements?" Ashara frowned.

"Why does everyone ask that?" Po appeared not to hear. Instead he indicated his shoulders.

"What's her skin like around here?" Ashara pulled back the edge of the quilt. Oni's skin had a red rash about the shoulder blades. Po nodded and Ashara patted the quilt back down.

116

"We've been told to give her this," Ashara said, showing Po small wads of paper. He took one and sniffed the contents. He then poked around with his finger.

"Hawthorn, dandelion and *geli* root," Po said. "Was she constipated before this?"

"No," she said.

"You've called on a Vu'du doctor?" Ashara nodded. "Well there's your problem." He snatched up the remaining wads and threw them from the open window.

"What are you doing?" Ashara demanded.

"This is wrong," Po said. "Those were diuretics. The Vu'du think it helps flush the disease from the body. But it is weakening her. She needs energy to fight the fever."

"What do you know?" Ashara said. "You're not a doctor."

"No," Po said, raising his hands. "But forty of our monks are down with typhoon fever and I've seen just as many lay cases. She needs fresh air, cinnamon, *topu* root, and the fungus called *votimi*. Do you have these?"

"I've no idea what you're talking about," Ashara said. "But Avi will be furious once he sees what you've done."

"I'll talk to him," Po said. "He needs to listen if he wants his wife alive. Have you got coin?" Ashara indicated the side table. "Take it. We'll go see what we can find. Come."

They were back within the hour and Po busied himself in the kitchen. Upstairs they propped Oni up on her pillow and gave her the black steaming drink. She took tiny sips and they patiently waited for her to finish.

"It smells sweet," Ashara said, sniffing the cup.

"I added honey," Po said. "She hasn't been eating enough."

"This better work. You know you'll be blamed if anything happens."

"Trust me," Po said. "Where's Avi?"

"He'll be back this evening. Some meeting of the Merchant Guild or another."

"Has he got any symptoms?" Po asked. "Fever? Temperature? Blotchy skin?"

"He did," Ashara said. "But he has no soul. He brushed it off." Po removed the empty cup and checked Oni's temperature.

"I have to go now," he said. "But you tell Avi he has to listen — and wash everything down with vinegar. Keep surfaces clean and cook your vegetables. I'll be back when I can."

Ashara walked the monk down to the door and waved good-bye. She then returned to the bedroom and did as Po said — after all, the doctor's house *did* smell of vinegar.

The front door slammed. Ashara jolted awake and glanced around the room. The curtains ruffled in the breeze and a light haze fell over the bed. Oni's snores reached her ears. *Avi.* Ashara ran to the top of the stairs. Pots banged in the kitchen. She took the stairs two at a time and reached the kitchen door. Avi sat slumped on her bedroll by the fire, an empty pot rolling at his feet. His face was flushed red.

"You're drunk," Ashara said. Avi garbled a response. "I thought you didn't drink."

"Why not?" Avi managed, his voice slurred.

"Come, we'll clean you up and get you to bed." Avi rolled his head against the counter and muttered to himself.

"What?" Ashara demanded. "You stink."

"Leave me alone. I…" his voice faded to nothing. Ashara glared at him, then removed her things from his proximity and returned to the master bedroom.

The next morning Ashara rose early, stepped over Avi's snoring form, and prepared Oni's medicine. Oni was already awake when she brought it to her.

"How do you feel?" she asked.

"Better," Oni said. "What's this you're giving me?"

"Something new," Ashara said. "It seems to be working."

"It does," Oni said. "Who was that man last night?"

"A friend," Ashara said. "A doctor." *Liar.*

"I didn't recognize him," Oni said. She drank the brew and rested back into her pillow. "Where's Avi?"

"Downstairs. He'll be up before too long." She decided not to mention the drinking. "Would you like some breakfast? We've still got that sausage." Oni agreed and Ashara returned with a tray on which was a steaming bowl of porridge, a cup of hot *kaja*, and a saucer of sliced sausage.

"Any word from my sons?" Oni asked as she ate.

"None," Ashara said. "But no news is good news, right?" She did not mention the Seventh Army had marched north a week before.

Feet fell on the stairs and Ashara spotted Avi's head from the door. He came and stood in the doorway, his eyes bloodshot and his clothes disheveled. He looked about the room from the clean sheets to the open window as if struggling to understand what had changed. His hawkish nose twitched as he sniffed the air.

"Who did this?" he asked, his voice like ice.

Natan knelt by the stream and dipped a bucket in the crystalline water. He cast his eyes about looking for movement. Wooded hills ran ragged up from the far bank. In the distance a wolf howled. From behind him drifted the chatter of sentries at the picket. Natan laid the bucket down and reached into the pouch on his belt. He drew out a wad of banknotes and counted them. Seventeen *jet*. His dealings with the logistics people had been lucrative. He just wished they were paid in coin; it was a lot easier to spend. He folded the banknotes and put them back.

"Counting your earnings?" Natan spun around and snatched at his camp knife. Captain Mako picked his way down the hill to the stream. "You need to pay better attention. I could have bloody slit your throat and you'd be none the wiser."

"Just fetching water," Natan said. "Nothing too dangerous."

"You should tell that to the 42nd," Mako said, scanning the far hills. "They had a sentry snatched. The bastard was found this morning strung up from a tree."

"Do you think we're being watched now?" Natan asked. Mako shrugged.

"Buggered if I know, but if you're smart you always keep your wits about you."

"Yes, sir." Mako removed his helmet and ran water over his shaved head. Natan glimpsed the scars and shuddered, imagining the injuries that caused them.

"What were you counting?" Mako asked.

"My pay," Natan said.

"Bit much for a common soldier," Mako said. "The boys say you're selling *dama* on the side."

"It's not illegal," Natan said defensively.

"No," Mako said. "But I *can* make your life bloody difficult. Let's see. You sold two pounds. Probably cost you, like, what? Four *jet*? You sold it probably for ten. So that's six coppers profit for a week's work. Blimey, you've almost doubled your pay."

Natan remained silent. *Actually better than that*, he thought. But no point correcting his captain. Captain Mako rubbed the stubble on his chin.

"Now, I'm not a bloody moron," the captain said. "I knew this'd be your gig and I sowed the seeds. A soldier never gets rich on his *official* salary. So let me cut you a deal. I don't get in your way, your sergeant stays off your back, and you get access to logistics. But, and this is the important part mind you, I get half the profits, so in this case you give me three *jet*, two which I keep and one to Sergeant Bi'reke to turn a blind eye. Understood?"

Never accept the first offer, Natan remembered his father saying. He scratched the back of his neck, feigning uncertainty.

"Business has costs," Natan said with a shrug. "But fifty-fifty's a bit much isn't it? That better be for an exclusive. I don't want anyone undercutting me. And it sounds like you should have some flesh in the trade."

"What're you suggesting?" Mako asked, lowering his voice.

"If you want a half cut," Natan explained. "You have to guarantee I have no competition. That, and you need to put some money up front. Just to help buy more product."

"You don't understand how this works," Mako said. "I make the demands, you do as I say."

"Fine," Natan said, picking up the bucket. "But I thought this was business and you wanted a healthy return. Put the money in and I'll give you your cut. Ten coppers should do as a start." Captain Mako glanced about and then stabbed a finger at Natan's chest.

"If you play games with me, I'll fuck you up. You got that? I give you this money trusting a good return. And if you take it, I expect sixty percent." Natan nodded and offered his hand. Captain Mako shook it.

"You'll see," Natan said. "I'll turn it into thirty by the end of the week." Mako peeled off the notes and handed them over.

"Remember what I said," he growled. "I —" A trumpet blasted from the camp, then another and another. Mako and Natan looked at each other and together they ran back towards the picket, water sloshing everywhere.

"Put the bucket down," Mako shouted.

"No," Natan wheezed between breaths. "I'm not going back for another one."

Running past the sentries, Natan noticed they were all on edge, standing firm with shields and spears, scanning the perimeter for danger. At the squad's campfire, Natan put down the now half-empty bucket and fell in line with the 37th Auxiliary.

Three other companies joined them on parade. Captain Mako huffed and paused before surveying the ranks. He nodded to his sergeants and took up position with the standard-bearer carrying the gold gilt saber-tooth head. Natan exchanged looks with his squad.

"What's happening?" he whispered under his breath.

"Some officer arrived," the man next to him said.

"Silence in the ranks!" growled Bi'reke. "Eyes forward. Straighten those backs."

Horse hooves pounded the dirt and a rider on a black mare reined in before the troops. The plume on his helmet ruffled in the breeze. The sun glinted off the Y-shaped links of his armor, and the emerald cape draped over the back of his saddle. The officer whirled about and trotted up and down the parade lines a few times, then stopped once more before them.

"Soldiers of the 14th Banner," he roared in a parade ground voice. "I'm your commander. You've done well sweeping these hills, but now is the time for the final push. The traitor Tomi Mei-Uduga holds the Dili valley. Elements of the Seventh Army already look down upon the enemy positions. We must push up to join them. Our objective is the near bank. To this end you break camp in one hour — yes, a night march. But the end is in sight. Do your general proud." He ended his speech by holding a clenched fist to his chest. "All under Heaven."

"All under Heaven," repeated the soldiers. The commander spurred his horse and galloped off. From the fringes, staff officers and a bodyguard raced after him.

"You heard him," Mako bellowed. "Get some food in you and prepare to break camp. Dismissed!"

The squad returned to their fire and set the kettle to boil.

"Any of you ever been to Dili?" one asked. Most shook their heads.

"Nope," said one. Another opposite Natan piped up.

"Once," he said. The soldiers turned to their companion.

"What's it like?"

"Dunno. Alright, I guess."

"Nah," said another. "Like, what's the ground like. What can we expect?"

"It's a valley isn't it?" said the soldier. "Hills on either side. A river down the middle. The city's on the northern hills rising up the slopes. The citadel is well positioned."

"So we're crossing a river and assaulting a city?" someone asked.

"Resisted the whole way," Natan added. "What's the river like? Deep and wide like the Blue River?"

"Nah," said the soldier. "I don't remember it well but I'd be surprised if you couldn't wade across in most places. A lot of stones. Bad for footing. When I was there the banks were mostly overgrown."

"A battle for a river," said one of the older men. "Is still a battle for a river. Doesn't matter how deep or wide."

"I can't swim," someone said. "W— will we have to swim across?"

"Swim?" the older man said with a hoot of laughter. "Boy, if you fall in the water you'll drown under all the weight of your armor. No, we'll be fighting for ground every inch of the way — river included."

An hour later, the trumpets blew and weary men rose to their feet, shouldered their bags, and fell into formation ready for the march. Mako and the sergeants laid about them, stressing the need to stick together and not get lost in the dark. All fires, lamps and torches were banned. There was to be absolutely no singing or anything that would give their position away. Drums began to roll and columns staggered forward, then fell into step. After a while the drums stopped and they proceeded in silence.

It was another six hours before they arrived at the Dili Valley. Natan was yawning when he first caught a glimpse of the fires below.

"Goddess of Mercy," he said. The pinpricks of ten thousand campfires glistened, with a wide, black, no-man's-land between them. Unseen, Natan knew, around those fires were two of the largest armies to ever assemble in a generation. And he was part of it all.

CHAPTER 11

"The Vu Fire Wagon is a multiple rocket launcher developed by the College of Alchemists and deployed during the war with Duang between 1010 and 1016 of the Imperial Era. Being able to fire two hundred steel tipped javelins, the fire wagon proved particularly effective in killing the eight-ton dreadbeasts favored by the Duang court."

General Janovi Kalavanti, Encyclopedia of Military Thought

On the other side of the valley, Tomi Mei-Uduga watched the same fires. Dili echoed with final preparations; horses clattering down streets, hammers hammering, soldiers running riot through the taverns, and the final residents clogging the only side gate open to civilian traffic.

"You're up early," War Minister Tonu said. Tomi turned his head ever so slightly.

"I haven't slept yet."

"It looks like they haven't either," Tonu said, nodding to the city streets. "Still, if it's their last night alive, it is better spent awake. Isn't it?"

"I don't think I'd have a say in the matter," Tomi said. "We never know when death will strike." He regarded the Minister of War, his aged face deep in shadow. "Did you want something?" Tonu sighed and took three steps forward, leaning heavily on his walking stick.

"I'd like to join you on the battlefield," he said. "As minister it is my role to be down there, close to Generals Nulu and Doju."

"I'll be down there," Tomi said. "They are both capable generals. They know what they're doing. Why put yourself in harm's way? We hold the river, and our's is the righteous cause. Stay here with the Emperor. If not finished tomorrow, we'll be done the next."

"Come on," Tonu said. "Give me a command. How about I command the aid station? The soldiers will be pleased we're taking their care so seriously when they see a cabinet minister take charge."

"They would," Tomi said, shaking his head. "But then you are no doctor, and they already have a qualified commander. Best let him be."

"Signals?" Tomi laughed and War Minister Tonu chuckled along.

"Come on," Tomi said. "We both know *that* wouldn't work."

"Yes," Tonu said, gazing up at the night sky. "They'd need to use my one good ear. I do say though, back in the day I'd be relishing time on the front line. That desire for danger, the excitement of not knowing what will happen, it never really leaves. True, it gets dim with age, but so does everything."

"We'll find something for you," Tomi said, placing his hand on Tonu's arm. "You've got life in you yet."

"I guess I'll wait in the citadel," Tonu said. "With everyone else. Awaiting victory or death, whichever comes first."

"No," Tomi said. "How about we put you in charge of the citadel. You'll have the Vermilion Guard under you, and be responsible for the Emperor, the imperial household. Think about that, who could say they held such responsibility during an important battle?"

"And you'd trust my old bones to the task?" Tonu asked.

"Of course. You'll have General Vasha anyway. He'll do all the legwork."

"I think we have a deal then," Tonu said, extending a wrinkled hand. Chief Minister Tomi took it.

"You'll do us proud," he said. "If the tide turns, you'll be the last valiant defender of Emperor Gotti VII. An honor to be sure." Tonu smiled at this.

"I could die for that," he said.

Behind the two gentlemen, guards snapped to attention and General Nulu strode onto the balcony, his armor polished, his helmet under his arm, and his hair slicked back in a horsetail. He dipped his knee in respect.

"Greetings," Tomi said. "The enemy will break when you take the field." General Nulu grunted. His one good eye did not blink. It unnerved Tomi, and he looked away.

"Your Grace," Nulu said, his voice hoarse. "Jano's moved up more men. A reconnaissance party spotted siege equipment. Look's like they're going to force the river crossing."

"We knew they would," Tomi said. "How many men does he have now?"

"We'll have an estimate at first light, Your Grace."

"Reasonable," Tomi said. "So you still think today's the day?"

"Positive. Jano's never been one to sit about."

"The gods smile upon us," Tomi said. "If only we had General Mamot. Those extra troops would make a big difference."

"He's not coming," said Nulu. "If Jano's a man of action, Mamot's a man of inaction." There was a moment of awkward silence, then Nulu continued. "But with your permission, I'll return to my men." Tomi reached out and put a hand on Nulu's pauldron.

"Be strong," he said. "Fight for the Emperor and the gods, for this is indeed to be a righteous battle." Nulu fell to one knee and bowed his head.

"Your Grace, you honor me."

"Stand," Tomi said. "The day awaits and the earth thirsts for Jano's blood."

🪶

Bells tolled the hour over Pao'an. Flocks of sparrows, disturbed, took to the sky. Ashara clutched the priest's book close to her breast and hurried, head down and shoulders hunched. Avi had ranted and raved, closed the windows and called on the Vu'du doctors. If he was not going to listen, then she was going to sell the book and prepare to go home.

The afternoon was stifling hot. Pao'an smelt of smoke. The streets were dirty and on the most part void of people. Piles of litter collected in drifts on every corner, while shuttered shops, taverns and homes proved targets for burglars and vagrants.

"Money for m' starving children?" a beggar asked holding up a cup.

Ashara avoided eye contact, feeling bad for the wraith-like woman kneeling in the dust.

"Not today," she muttered. Ahead lay one of the avenues leading to the Inner City and over the tops of the buildings rose a column of black smoke. As she drew near the smell became acrid with a tangy sting in the air. There was a slight earthiness to it, a mustiness of rot.

She came out onto a square and pinched her nose. There was a smouldering pyre in the middle, surrounded by people throwing more wood and rubbish on to it. Blackened limbs and bloated stomachs protruded from the charcoaled timbers and wisps of smoke. More bodies lay in the backs of wagons waiting to be added to the fire. The workers seemed to be preparing a new pile, their faces masked behind handkerchiefs, their eyes red from the smoke.

Ashara stopped and stared. No one really noticed her. They were too intent on their work. A Vu'du *kebilu* chanted, anointing the wagons with oil and smoke from a censer. An Astirti ascetic sat in the dust beside the embers, rubbing ash onto his skin. A woman with a baby tied to her back used a forked stick to roll bodies off the wagons and into wheelbarrows to be taken to the pyre. Besides the Vu'du holy man, everyone worked in grim silence.

The horror of it struck Ashara dumb. Her stomach rumbled and she felt like she needed to puke. She turned from the scene and continued along the avenue. She passed two more wagons collecting the bodies of the dead and asked the driver of the second what was happening.

"The dreaded fever," the driver said from behind his mask.

"Is there a cure?" Ashara asked.

"Only in the lap of the gods," the man said.

At the drawbridge into the Inner City, no guards watched the gate to wave her through. In the guardhouse a man, shivered beneath a quilted blanket, a hot mug of steaming *kaja* beside him. He looked too old for the job, but Ashara had heard all the young guards had joined the army on promise of better pay. She hurried past. Further down the road three men loitered outside an open door. Their eyes followed her and as she drew near they approached her.

"What've you got there?" one of them asked. Ashara considered him and drew back a step. The man, much like the two behind him, had missing teeth and bloodshot eyes. His cheeks flushed red and the heady mix of body odor and liquor reached her nostrils.

"Nothing," Ashara said.

"Come on," said the man. "Give us a look." He reached for the book and Ashara sidestepped. His fingers grazed the bag and he stumbled clumsily. The other two men looked at each other, then laughed at their friend as he planted himself face first on the cobbles. He looked up at Ashara with blood running from his nose.

"You'll regret that," he said, spitting out a mucus laden glob of blood. Ashara ran and the men stumbled after her, huffing and puffing and calling for her to come back. She put on a burst of speed and one by one her pursuers fell behind and gave up. At a red brick arch, she risked a glance over her shoulder. *All clear.* She stopped. Over the arch was a sign in Vu which she couldn't read, but from her conversations she understood it was Scholar Street where she would find all the bookshops. A uniformed guard sat on the steps of a squat building just beyond the archway. Ashara checked, and he confirmed it was the street she was looking for.

"Not going to find much open I'm afraid," he said.

The first open shop she came to was a printer's. It did not look like a place that dealt in old books but Ashara tried anyway. The old man behind the counter was nice enough, but when he looked at the book, he shook his head and offered her four *jet*, only a fraction of what she expected. Ashara put it back in the bag and tried the next shop. The offer was slightly higher, but both shopkeepers seemed to think her a fool. She *knew* it was worth more than they said.

The third shop was narrow and musty, with cobwebs in the windows and thick coatings of dust on the shelves. The books were positively antiquarian and the floorboards creaked as she crossed to the counter.

A bird hanging in the corner flapped its wings so feathers and birdseed scattered about the cage and the floor around it.

"*Customer!*" it cawed.

"Alright, alright," said a woman, shuffling onto the shop floor with a tray of *kaja* mugs.

"Hello," she said, seeing Ashara for the first time. Ashara explained why she was there and placed the book on the counter. The woman brought a lamp over and examined the book. She *ummed* and *erred* and then offered Ashara two silver *li* for it. It was a lot more than the previous two offers, but still not enough.

"You better be careful," said the woman as Ashara put the book back in the bag. "A lot of people are going to be asking why a Kh'areen girl has such an expensive book under her arm."

The next shop mostly stocked textbooks of uniform shape and size, but half the shelves had sheets thrown over them, reflecting, perhaps, the fact none of the schools were open. The owner sat in a chair by an empty fire, his head in his hands and a bottle of liquor beside him. As Ashara approached, he stirred and looked up at her, blinking back whatever grogginess he felt.

"Sorry," Ashara said. "Wrong store." She turned to leave, but he called after her.

"What're you after?" Ashara relented and explained she had a book to sell. She took it out of the bag and showed it to him. Just when he was about to take it, she pulled it away, noting the ink stains on his hands.

"They're old ones," the bookseller grunted. "Come on, give me a look or I can't buy what I don't see." Ashara handed it over and the bookseller inspected it.

"It could be worth a bit," he said at last. "Where did you get it? I don't handle stolen goods."

"It was my family's," Ashara said. "We've fallen on hard times."

"Well that has a ring of truth to it," he said. "I'll need a closer look." He slipped on a pair of glasses and ran his fingers over the pages. He then shut the book and returned it to the bag. Ashara waited expectantly.

Instead of returning it to her, the man put it under the counter and looked at her blankly.

"What are you doing?"

"Doing what?"

"My book," Ashara protested. "Give it back."

"It's not your book," he said with a shrug. "Now run along." Ashara stomped around the counter, but before she could take the book the man wrapped an arm about her throat and shoved her towards the door.

"Le' go," she gasped, squirming in his grip.

"Listen, kid. It's stolen. Now, go quietly or I call the guards. They don't like thieves." Ashara gave two vicious twists and the bookseller's forearm came in range of her teeth. She bit down and thrashed her head. The man yelled and dropped her to the floor. Ashara hesitated and looked toward the counter, deciding whether she had time to grab the book or not. The man's boot decided the matter. Ashara went sprawling.

"Little bitch," he yelled and kicked her again. She rolled out of the way of the next kick and jumped to her feet, avoiding his arms as he lunged at her. Ducking, Ashara drew back a fist and drove her knuckles into the man's groin. He landed on his backside with a bone-jarring thump.

Ashara ran from the shop and collided with three men standing outside. They gave a cry and she caught the whiff of alcohol and stale sweat. Falling into the arms of the nearest one she grappled with him and kicked his legs out from under him. The second launched at her, pinned her arms behind her and swung her around.

"Where's your bag?" demanded the man with a bloody nose.

"I lost it. Le' me go."

"You need to learn some manners," the man sneered, drawing a rusty knife and tickling Ashara's chin with it. "Hand over all your money or I'll stick this in yer belly." Just then they were interrupted by a whistle, shrill, loud and clear.

"*Oi!*" a guard yelled. "What's going on? Stop right there!" He blew the whistle again and came running. Ashara seized the opportunity to wiggle out of the drunk man's grip and, having fallen to all fours, used her weight to drive up into him, toppling him backwards. She rolled with him and sprang aside, putting distance between herself and her attackers.

"Everybody stay where they are," the guard said. He waved his baton and advanced on the man with a knife. "Put that away."

Ashara caught her breath and glanced around for a way to escape. Suddenly the bookshop owner was in the doorway pointing at her.

"Stop thief!" he shouted. "Get her! Thief!" Ashara did not wait for a response. She chose her path and took it, sprinting down Scholar Street in the direction of the city wall. She grabbed at a lamp post and used her momentum to swing herself onto a side street going in the direction of the Imperial Academy. Behind her the whistle blew again.

In front she came to the academy's iron gates. They were locked with all classes suspended. Ashara grabbed the bars and, hauling herself over, landed nimbly on the other side. She ran. Behind her she heard the *oomf* and swearing as her followers tackled the gate. Not daring to look back, Ashara took off down the side of a building, jumped a waist-high fence and crossed a grassy field. A caretaker stood in the shadows raking leaves. When he noticed her he shouted at her to get off the grass, and then when he saw her followed by the city guard, he took up the hue and cry.

Ashara's chest heaved. She gulped down breaths. She started to see stars in the corners of her vision. *I must go on*, she told herself. *I must go on*. Ashara rounded a corner and found it a sight of desolation. The buildings there, all the way up to the breach in the wall, were ruins, cleaned of everything useable. Ashara avoided the cracked beams and piles of bricks and sprinted to the gap in the city wall. Earth had been piled up and stakes hammered in on top, forming a palisade some eight feet high. Ashara jumped up, clutched a wooden support near the top, and scrambled with her feet to pull herself over. She was almost over the top when a hand latched onto her foot. She was stuck.

The valley echoed with shouts, trumpets and stamping of feet. Pennants rippled amidst fields of spears. Only the Gray River separated the two armies arrayed for battle.

Natan shuddered, wishing he had pissed before forming up. He squinted over his shield's rim at the opposing army. Dan was out there — somewhere — going through exactly what he was going through, just for the other side.

"Hold those shields," Bi'reke barked. "This isn't the practice ground. Close up there — *oi* Natan — you dozing off? Keep focussed." The sergeant uncorked a flask and gave a mouthful to each man in the squad. Natan licked his lips. His mouth was dry with fear. When it was his turn he gulped a mouthful down. He gagged, but the acrid aftertaste lingered in his mouth.

"What's that?" he spluttered. Bi'reke had moved on but he turned his head.

"Courage," he said. "A good strong brew of *kaja* beans and *dama*." Trumpets peeled and Bi'reke flinched. "Stand ready boys!" Drums rolled and Bi'reke ran for his spot at the end of the line. "Advance at the march!" The same orders echoed off the hills and the army took its first steps forward. Ahead of them rolled the massive siege equipment for crossing the river; veritable bridges on wheels pushed by veteran Seventh Army soldiers ready to establish and hold the first bridge heads.

All morning Vu fire wagons had exchanged fire, but now that the siege equipment lumbered forwards, the volume from both sides increased. Volleys of iron tipped javelins rained down on hosts of packed men, punching through anything they hit, whether shield, armor or flesh. Screams rent the air; gurgling sounds cut off with the last breath; sobbing wails of those too terrified to move.

Natan watched the enemy pack in close to the banks, ready to oppose any landing. Behind him someone yelled '*fire*' and a volley of crossbow bolts arched over, and down into the advance ranks opposite.

The lead wagon sloshed down into the water and the ramp at the far end fell onto the opposite bank. Defenders rushed forward, and attackers streamed onto the bridge and braced for a fight. Other bridges rolled down into position and this scene carried itself out, a dozen, ten dozen, then a hundred times over.

To his left Natan heard a roar. Then to his right the ground shook. Through gaps in the line came charging squadrons of dreadbeasts. These huge creatures, decked out in spiked armor with archers and spearmen on top, easily waded the Gray River and rose up on the bank opposite, to aid those who held the crossings. Their Duang mahouts gave up a great ululation as they plunged into battle, tossing men left and right. From Natan's position he saw a body thrown in the air, only to come down on a dreadbeast's spikes.

The charge of the raging beasts worked for it gave those crossing the river time to form bridgeheads. With waving banners, trumpets and a steady drumbeat the 37th and the rest of the 14th Banner were ordered to the river bank. Natan marched forward, fully aware that his life depended on holding the line.

As they drew closer, showers of bolts came amidst them, thudding into shields, helmets, flesh and ground. A shaft whispered past Natan's ear and buried itself in the man behind him. The man grunted and collapsed. Natan closed his eyes and took a breath. He could die any moment, he thought. *Just push on.*

"Join the bridgehead!" Captain Mako yelled, leading the first ranks of the 37th across. Natan, encouraged by his captain's valor, took up the shout of those around him. Wooden boards bent under their weight. Water bubble up through the cracks and soon the crossing was awash, but it held. Next thing he knew he was on firm ground, glancing to the left and right to check his squad were all still with him.

The ranks of the company drove into the spearmen opposite. Shields clashed. Spears poked and weaved. Men screamed. Natan had to break ranks to haul casualties back, lest they created an opening. The line edged forward as the enemy gave ground. Natan stomped on something and slipped. He looked down and saw a human leg. He repositioned his feet and banished the memory from his mind.

133

Soon he was at the front, holding the shield wall. He pushed and jabbed with his spear, searching for openings. His whole world narrowed to the few feet in front of him. He had no thought for the rest of the battlefield. His spear caught and when he yanked back it came with a spray of blood. Natan had no time to think of the damage he inflicted. He was shortly fending off another attack.

Sticky wetness ran down into his eyes. He blinked but it only got worse. Panic. A hand on Natan's collar yanked him back. He landed on a shield and was shoved forward. Raw fear paralyzed him and a primordial scream left his lungs. Only his desire for self-preservation kept his spear firmly in his grip. More hands clutched at him and pulled him backwards again. A rough texture smothered his face and Natan could see again. He blinked. Someone wrapped a bandage around his head twice, thrice, then tied it off in a knot.

"You'll be okay," a sergeant yelled over the din of battle. "Back in line." Natan babbled. Even he could not understand the words he wanted to form. He crooked his spear in his arm and felt his head. *Where's my helmet?*

"Back in line!" the sergeant bellowed and tossed Natan forward. He was then three ranks back from the killing zone.

"They're breaking!" someone screamed excitedly. Indeed, Natan saw the enemy in front falter then the wall of shields backed away, causing bloodied ground to appear between the two armies.

"Hold!" Captain Mako bellowed over the battlefield. "Hold your positions!"

"My squad to me!" Bi'reke called. Other sergeants did the same. Natan pressed forward and rejoined the front rank. Warm liquid ran down his leg and his trousers clung to his skin. He looked down, fearing it was blood, but saw nothing. *I don't need to piss anymore.* Natan steadied himself. Soon the battle would start again and he was at the front this time.

Signals passed down the line and drummers began rolling out a beat. Captains and sergeants took up the call to advance. Natan lowered his spear and edged forward, taking small, careful steps in line with everyone else. The gap closed between the two armies.

The air buzzed with iron slugs. Slingers from amidst the enemy ranks launched volley after volley into the advancing formations. Shields shattered with the impact. Flesh and bone did not stand a chance. Out the corner of his eye something flickered, then he heard a crack like the slapping of a wet towel on stone. He glanced to the side and saw the man next to him was gone. Before he could grasp the significance, his leg splintered in agony. He fell to one knee, catching his chin on his shield rim on the way down. Every attempt to move caused pain. He screamed and the world went black.

Po bolted the wagon's tailgate and rested his hand on the sideboard in quiet reflection.

"Ready?" the wagon driver asked.

"Ready," Po said. The wagon rolled over the courtyard cobbles and rattled towards the gate. Po watched it go, the bodies of seven fellow novices and Master Pani inside. He swatted at a fly buzzing about his face. The stink of disease hung heavy on the air.

"We did what we could," Venerable Biet said. "I've written to whom I can."

"I know," Po said. A hand squeezed his shoulder. He sniffed. The Venerable Biet had written a number of letters to the leaders of the city, pleading for immediate intervention. The sewers, damaged when the loyalists left, needed to be fixed. The regular collection of night soil had to be restarted, and money from the treasury had to be used to bring in fresh fruit and vegetables for the sick. So far, his words had fallen on deaf ears. There was no money, no workers and no fresh fruit or vegetables for miles around. Instead it was said fever had spread to over half the population, and of those that got it, a full three in ten died in agony, their vital organs failing, their flesh melting away, and their skin turning a placid yellow.

"We'll make a special dinner," Brother Dovo promised. "In name rather than substance."

"How's Brother Bidovi?" Po asked.

"On the mend," Dovo said. "If only it wasn't so hot."

"Is it your first time managing the kitchens alone?" Dovo nodded.

"Bidovi will do fine," Biet said. "He's over the worst of it."

Monks drifted from the yard. Po sat on the steps where he'd once talked with Ashara.

"Can I join you?" Master Dugen asked. "How are you doing?" Po shuffled aside, giving the monk room.

"I've never seen so much death," Po said. "It's draining."

"You're doing well," Dugen said. "Novices are giving up and returning to their families. Monks are shivering in their cots. It isn't easy to stay and face your own mortality."

"It's a noble duty," Po said. "Tending to the dying."

"It is," Dugen said. "How is that young lady who helped you here?"

"Ashara?" Po said. "She — she, well I suppose she's fine. Her mistress has typhoon fever."

"You visited them?" Dugen asked. Po massaged his hands.

"Well, the priest left something for her," Po said. "You know. They have a trading house over the river. The Luka-Tudo Trading House. So I visited. Just for a while. The mistress was sick and I helped get her comfortable."

"I see. Will she live?"

"I don't know," Po said. Dugen nodded as if leaving something unsaid. Just then the bells rang for midday reflection. Those inhabitants of the monastery able to walk appeared at the doors and headed towards the hall. Po joined them.

Venerable Biet led the reflection from the dais under the bronze hand of Dasanika. It started with reflection and chanting of the *kime ki're kima ka*, and ended in a sermon on mortality.

"I want to tell you a story," Biet said humbly after a brief preamble.

"Long ago when Dasanika still walked this earth, he came to a city called Sraka. In this city lived a young scholar called Pretivati. He lived a life of surety and surplus. His every want was met by his father. One day Pretivati's father became gravely ill. The young scholar heard Dasanika was at the city gate. Pretivati put on sackcloth and went to see him. *'Teacher,'* he said. *'My father is gravely ill and will surely die. Help me.'* Dasanika said, *'Take here my begging bowl and return with it filled with oil.' 'Is that all?'* Pretivati asked. *'No. You must take it from a house where no one has died. When you find such a house, say 'My master Dasanika wishes for a bowl of oil. Will you grant his request?' And when you have done this, return to me.'* So the young man took the bowl and hurried to do his allotted task."

The Venerable Biet cleared his throat and adjusted himself on the dias. A young novice approached with a cup of water, which Biet took and sipped.

"That afternoon," Biet continued. "Pretivati returned the bowl to Dasanika. *'What, no oil?'* Dasanika said. Pretivati looked at his feet with shame. *'Teacher,'* he said. *'I should have known. Death in this world is more common than millet in a field. No house was free of death, no matter lord or lady, worker or slave, all life ends in death. I now know nothing is permanent.' 'Congratulations,'* Dasanika said. *'Everyday people go about in the illusion of permanence. They think things will remain the same, and thus they do not value what they have, and they desire what they do not have. They spend their days wishing to be somewhere else. And when on their deathbed, they wish to relive it all again. For in truth all we have is the here and now, and even this passes from moment to moment.'* Pretivati was impressed and said *'Teacher, show me your ways.'* And from that day forth he became a disciple of Dasanika."

Po's mind wandered and he had to consciously bring it back to Biet's words. He wondered how Oni was doing, and how Ashara would cope with the inevitable.

"You see," Biet said, standing and stepping off the dais. "We like to tell ourselves our lives are permanent. We like to tell ourselves the things around us are permanent. We take meaning from our families, our homes, our jobs. But all these will pass away." He flicked his fingers and let the following silence preach its own sermon.

"Even mountains," Biet said after a pause. "Slowly fall back into the ground. A stone, the foundation of a mighty fortress, can whither to a grain of sand. How much more our own lives? For surely the wheel turns in one direction, and never the other. One moment passes to another, and the next that too is gone. All we have, if we truly have anything, is the now."

"And this becomes the source of our discontent — this failed belief in certainty. It is only when you break through this illusion, to realize you have lived a life of deception, that you can get on the path of the Ba're and break the chains of discontent."

Biet wrapped up the sermon with a few parting words, extolling listeners to stick to the good path and take refuge in the teachings of Dasanika. He then rang a bell and the reflection was finished.

Po rose and in deep contemplation shuffled towards the door.

"Po," Biet said. "Can I see you in my study, please?"

"Shouldn't we do the rounds?" Po asked.

"In a while," he said. "Master Dugen, can you join us?"

Soon the three were climbing the staircase to Biet's study. It had been weeks since Po had spent time with Biet going over the books in the early hours of the morning. To be back in the study brought a certain comfort to Po, along with fond memories for a more peaceful time.

"Take a seat, please," Biet said. Po sat cautiously and held himself straight and rigid. "Po," Biet continued. "Dugen and I have been impressed by your diligence in looking after the sick. Under normal circumstances you would be well on your way to studying for the next exam, but I do have a concern. A fairly major concern actually. This woman, Ashara, you've had a few dealings with her, haven't you?"

"I guess you could say that," Po said, shifting his attention from Biet to Dugen and back again.

"And you've continued to help because her mistress is sick?"

"Yes," Po said. "She helped us. I thought I'd return the favor."

"A noble gesture," Biet said. "It is in accordance with the Ba're. But I'm afraid your interest is beyond helping the family."

"Beyond?"

"You have grown attached to this woman."

"It's not like that," Po protested, realizing immediately how foolish he sounded.

"What does Dasanika say on women and relationships?" Po closed his eyes and gathered his thoughts. Then he opened his eyes and spoke carefully.

"Dasanika made it a rule that monks could not have relationships. It is the life of a monk to avoid attachment and anything that may take him from the good path."

"And you understand how this relationship with Ashara may distract you?" Dugen asked.

"It isn't a relationship," Po said. "I want to help her. Her family were killed and now she has no one. She just wants to return to her homeland, but she can't do that while her mistress is sick. That is all."

"So," Biet said. "Your desire is to help, but is it out of compassion or passion?"

"Compassion," Po said.

"And if you helped her, but never saw her again — no chance of gratitude — would you still aid her?"

"I would." But Po realized too late where this was going.

"And would you help her with the same vigor?"

"No," Po said reluctantly.

"Then you must admit that at least part of your desire to help is in your attraction to her." Po slumped in the chair and held his head in his hands. "And this attraction has become an attachment. And this attachment is now causing problems for your wellbeing."

"Yes," Po said. But the abbot wasn't about to give up.

"Do you believe this attachment is healthy, Po? Is it in keeping with the Five Tenets? Does it draw you away from those things that are important and cause you to waste time on things that are unimportant?"

"It has become an attachment."

"Now what do you propose we do about this?"

"Break the attachment," Po said.

"I was a young man once," Biet said. "I know attachment is not so easy to break. This is not the last time you will face it."

"So what should I do?" Po asked.

"You'll not see her again," Biet said.

"But," Po stuttered. "Her mistress —"

"— will live or die, regardless of your help. You told them what to do. Trust them to do it. There are people here who need your help."

Po bit his lip and swallowed hard. Between his fingers a teardrop ran down his face.

"Can we do the rounds now?" he asked.

The sounds of battle continued to echo over the Dili Valley. Steel clashed and trumpets blasted. Men screamed as they were pulled from the ranks, blood gushing from their wounds. General Jano's men fought with their backs to the river, their flanks at risk of collapse as the overwhelming might of the loyalist armies pressed in about them.

From her balcony, Muni Mei-Uduga could see the whole bloody engagement. She grasped the rail with both hands, her knuckles whitened, straining her eyes to pick her husband out from the seething mass of faceless men. Vatoni approached and coughed to get her attention.

"Eyeglass, Your Grace."

Muni shoved it to her eye and scanned for sign of her husband. Following a few minutes of frantic motion, Muni found him high on his horse, surrounded by officers and Vermilion Guard. She sighed and patted her chest in relief.

"Your Grace, there's something else." Muni turned.

"What's she doing here?" Muni demanded, drawing back from the snotty nosed, knotty haired girl before her. A second guardsman had a gloved hand on the girl's shoulder.

"She's the daughter of the stable master at the Blue Swan Inn," the guardsman said.

"And this means something to me?"

Captain Vatoni put his hands up.

"Your Grace, the Blue Swan Inn is on Guard Street," Vatoni said in a hushed tone. "Opposite where we found the enemy spies..."

"*Oh*," Muni said, her brown eyes widening for an instant. "You saw something didn't you?" The girl averted her eyes and they all waited.

"Come on, tell Her Grace what you told me," the guard said at last.

"A man," the girl said. "We played on the street. A man used to come by every day."

"And?" Muni asked. "Who was this man?"

"Dunno," the girl said.

"Yes, you do," the guard said, yanking on her sleeve.

"He worked in the citadel," the girl said. "One day we were very loud and when he came out he kicked little Jadi and told us we're all nuisances. So I followed him and pickpocketed his purse. That's when I saw him come here."

"Did you keep the purse?" Muni asked. "You did nothing wrong, sweetie."

"No," the girl said. "I took the coins and chucked the purse."

"Was there anything else in it?" Muni asked. The girl shook her head.

"Captain Vatoni," Muni said. "It can't be a coincidence. That man was feeding the spies information. Take her down to the servant's hall and see if she recognizes anyone."

"Yes, Your Grace."

"And Vatoni, be discreet."

Muni entered her apartment and sat with her grandson at the table. Adan ignored her, preferring the pen and paper in front of him. A maidservant was showing him how to write basic Vu characters. After a few minutes he glanced up with a twinkle in his brown eyes.

"Grandma!" He held up the paper. On it were the characters for '*grandma*' and '*grandpa*'.

"Good boy," Muni said. "How about you go put that on the dressing room table so Grandpa can see it when he comes home? Then we can do something for your Mummy and Daddy."

"Okay," Adan said and ran off with the paper clutched in his eager hands.

A fist hammered on the exterior door. The handle rattled.

"Who is it?" Muni called.

"Captain Gobi of the Vermilion Guard," the voice said. The name was unfamiliar to her. "You're under orders to stay in the banqueting hall."

She opened a slit in the door and spied the red armor and cape outside. An eye appeared at the slot.

"Who's orders?" she asked.

"War Minister Tuno's."

"We're safe here," Muni said. "At least no more in danger than down there."

"They are his orders, Your Grace. Can you open up, please. We're to escort you down."

"I am aware of the orders," Muni said. "But I am quite comfortable in here. If Tuno would like me to take Adan down to that hall with the sickly stale air, he can come discuss it with me himself."

"It is for your own good," Gobi said. "The War Minister and General Vasha want to know where everyone is. There is a battle going on, Your Grace. It requires certain precautions."

Muni considered her position. She knew the banqueting hall would be packed with senior officials, cabinet ministers, and all their families. There would even be members of the imperial family, though the Emperor himself would be kept elsewhere. In the banqueting hall they would indeed be protected by the Vermilion Guard, but she would be confined there, with little room to move, no way to check the progress of the battle, and if anything went wrong, it was a death trap. But she had little choice.

"Grandma, what's going on?" Adan asked, returning to the room.

"We're going down to the banqueting hall," Muni said. "We're going to wait for Grandpa down there."

"Is Mommy and Daddy down there?"

"I presume so," Muni said. "Hold on while I get the key." She fetched the key from the fruit bowl and opened the door. Captain Gobi and two other red-cloaked Vermilion Guards stepped into the room.

"Anni," Muni said to her handmaid. "Bring Adan's bag, will you? We won't be long." Her handmaid curtseyed and shuffled Adan towards his grandmother. When all was ready, Gobi ushered them from the room and into the corridor. He walked in front, the two other guards went behind. The citadel was an ancient building with many alterations over the years. Some corridors led to nowhere. Others wound about and turned back on themselves. Gobi seemed familiar with the way and led them down a flight of steps, along a collonaded gallery and down another flight of steps.

Muni held Adan's hand and asked him what he would like to write next. He said dreadbeast, as he had been promised by his father he would be allowed to ride one after the battle. Muni suggested a simpler word, like cat or dog.

Music drifted along the corridor. It came from stone-latticed windows that looked down into the banqueting hall. Muni peaked over the edge and spotted familiar faces milling about the hall. They sat in groups drinking, playing games, and snacking on fruit platters. Up on the stage sat the Emperor's family behind paper screens, but from Muni's vantage point she could make out the different concubines and servants attending them.

Gobi led them around another corner into a corridor lit only by wall sconces. Muni felt something brush against her hair. Thinking it was a spider she reached up to slap it. Suddenly a cord pulled tight around her neck, catching her hand within it. It bit into her flesh and left her gasping for breath. Panicking, Muni thrashed about. Adan screamed.

"Grandma!" In the corner of her vision, Muni saw Gobi tug Adan away from her and draw a knife from his belt. Muni kicked, trying to connect her feet with someone. Anyone. Her head throbbed. It felt like it was expanding, like a pastry in an oven. She grunted and pushed the guard behind her into the wall. He pushed down on her, refusing to let go of his grip.

Muni's eyes fell on Anni, struggling with a garrotte around her neck. Her face was crimson red and her eyes bulged in their sockets. Gobi, his hand clutching Adan's shirt, advanced on Anni and plunged the knife into her neck, opening up her skin in a torrent of blood. He yanked the knife sideways, cutting her down to the bone. Her body went limp and fell to the floor.

Stars flashed in the corners of Muni's vision. Intense pain pulsed through her head. She felt her body slow and relax, as if entering the final stages before the gates of oblivion opened. *This is it,* she told herself. *Dasanika take…*

The grip relaxed and with a sudden rasping air flowed back into her lungs. Muni fell forward onto her knees then rolled onto the floor, her body limp, her head spinning as if drunk. Her ears rang like gongs in the temple, but through the swirling experience of her consciousness she heard steel on steel. It became louder. Someone was shouting, coming to her as if through water. It was Vatoni. She recognized that voice. Hair brushed across her face and Adan nestled up to her. Slowly life returned to her body.

"Your Grace," Vatoni shouted through the haze. His hands were on her. They lifted her and carried her like Tomi did on their wedding night. "We need to get you out of here. Your Grace, the traitor is Tonu. It was his chief manservant taking information to the enemy. It's a coup."

"Adan?" she gasped, her voice sounding gravelly even to her.

"We've got him," Captain Vatoni said. "Don't worry."

Captain Vatoni carried her back the way they had come, but instead of returning to her chambers they went down another passage towards the west wing. From there they took the steps down into the servant's courtyard two at a time. The yard was deserted. The horses were all gone from the stables. Captain Vatoni put Muni down. She put a hand against the wall to support herself.

"This is a postern gate," Vatoni said as he tried to break the bolt. "It will take us outside the city. We can then hide in the woods."

"Grandma, I'm scared!" Adan said. Muni patted him on the head. There were only the four of them: herself, Vatoni, another bodyguard, and Adan.

"What happened to the girl?" Muni asked. Vatoni went over to a woodcutting block and came back with an axe.

"She pleaded to be let go," he said. "I let her slip into the kitchen. She was no use to us anymore." The captain swung the axe and broke the bolt away from the aged timber frame of the door. He pushed. It did not move. Vatoni threw his weight against it with his shoulder. The postern gate was as immovable as the wall around it.

High in the citadel, a bell began to toll. Muni's eyes darted around for another way out. She did not know what the bell meant but knew it could not be good.

The other red-cloaked guard pointed to a well by the stables.

"The rope," he said. "We'll go over the wall."

Muni rolled up her sleeves and joined the two men in dragging up the rope. Vatoni used the axe to sever the rope from the well.

"To the wall," he said. "Do you need me to carry you?" Muni shoved him away and grabbed Adan's hand. The postern gate was fitted into a section of wall that lay at one end of the courtyard between two towering wings that dominated their view. An ancient timber set of steps led up to the battlement. At the base of the wall, Vatoni scooped Adan up and the three adults took the stairs two at a time. At the top Muni put a hand to her head, feeling woozy.

"We've got to go on," Vatoni said, offering her a hand as the other guard set up the rope.

A whistle blew. Muni looked back into the courtyard. Red-armored Vermilion Guard raced towards them, swords drawn. Captain Vatoni drew his own and adopted a fighting stance at the top of the stairs.

Muni glanced over the parapet. It was a long way down.

"Your Grace, we don't have time," said the guardsman.

"Can you take Adan on your back?" she asked.

"No — I want to stay with you."

"Adan," Muni growled. "Be brave." *If only I could be the same.* Suppressing her fear, Muni swung her legs over the edge and gripped the rope in her hands. The fibers scratched her soft skin. She grimaced. Steel struck steel and Captain Vatoni screamed to hurry. Muni pushed off and dropped, hand under hand, with gritted teeth. The rope jerked about as the guardsman and Adan joined her. Eight feet from the ground she let go, fell and rolled.

"To the ridgeline," the guardsman said. He sounded out of breath. "We need to keep going."

"Grandma!" Adan cried. "We did it." *He thinks it's a game. Oh to be a child.*

"Yes, Adan. Hold my hand. You need to run. Can you do that for me?"

They dashed for the ridgeline. Just beyond was the thick primordial forest that hemmed in the Dili Valley. Muni glanced behind her. Vatoni had freed himself from the fight and reached the ground. His former companions in the Vermilion Guard were at the top of the battlement and looked baffled as to what to do next. One of them tested the rope. Then after an animated exchange they left the wall.

"Into the forest," Vatoni yelled, waving his hands wildly. He caught up with them and they stumbled and scratched their way to the ridge and down the other side, into thick brush that soon turned to trees. Twigs cracked and leaves rustled as they waded through a waist deep carpet of ferns, brushing aside vines and hanging sheets of moss. Gnarled trunks towered over them and birds called out in warning at the sudden disturbance beneath them. Vatoni led the way, the other guard took up the rear and Muni carried Adan in the middle. Muni looked about, wide-eyed, in complete disbelief. She could not process what had just happened. Her breathing was heavy. She felt Adan cling to her. His little fingers held tight around her neck. The excitement had exhausted him and his breathing was shallow. She sensed him slowly drifting off to sleep.

"I'm sorry Adan," she whispered. "I'm sorry."

After a time, Vatoni stopped and put a hand up for silence. Muni hesitated, then crouched down into the ferns. She was mindful of the noise they made. In the enclosed space around them it seemed incredibly loud. If anyone was out there, there was no way they could miss them. Vatoni edged forward. Muni followed then stopped. Ahead of them was a wide gully and on the other side wound a leaf-covered path cut into the hillside. Through the ferns Muni sensed movement. Then six horsemen appeared, trotting along in single file.

She squinted and strained her eyes. The horsemen wore armor and one of them was helmetless; his black hair tied behind his head, and an eye patch over one eye.

"General Nulu!" Muni cried. "General Nulu!"

"Your Grace," Vatoni squealed in shock, pulling her down. But Muni put Adan down next to her guard captain and ran towards the road, stumbling here and there on hidden branches. Five of the riders stopped and drew their weapons, but the eye-patched one up front saw Muni, dismounted and ran towards her. Muni jumped into his arms. Nulu looked confused and patted her lightly on the back. They broke apart.

"I never thought to see you again," Nulu said.

"And I you. What's happened?"

"We've lost," Nulu said. "I'm sorry Muni."

"And my husband?" Muni asked, wiping tears back from her eyes.

"The gates of oblivion are wide today," Nulu said. "He died a hero, Your Grace."

CHAPTER 12

"In the year 839IE Gotti I ascended the throne and issued an edict that all religious institutions be exempt from taxation. This came to be known as the Orange Edict, as the vermilion ink used for all such documents was sabotaged and turned orange once dried. For some, this was reason enough to dispute the legality of the text."

The Memoir of Master Todo A'lidun

Ashara shivered in front of the fire, steam rising off her undergarments. She stretched out her bare feet and felt the flames tickle her toes. Beside her, water dripped into a puddle on the stone slabs from her clothes hung to dry above.

"I thought I heard you return," Avi said from the doorway. Ashara covered her breasts and twisted on the spot. "You look a mess," he added. "Got yourself in trouble again?"

"I fell in the river," Ashara lied. "There was a scramble for fresh vegetables down at the docks." Avi nodded.

"Did you get any?"

Ashara raised an eyebrow.

"I ended up in the water — no. No, I didn't."

Avi grunted. He crossed the kitchen and took a bottle from the cupboard.

"Have you eaten?" Ashara asked. "I can put some porridge on."

"Not hungry," Avi said and removed the cork with his teeth.

"Mistress Oni? How's she?"

"She'd be a lot better if you hadn't thrown out her medicine and opened the windows like that. You leave her to me. You can take her some weak porridge when you're dried off. I don't want you bringing that dirt through the rest of the house."

The room lay stagnant in the darkness. Ashara set the bowl on the side table and swallowed the bile that rose involuntarily at the smell about her. Oni moaned.

"Some porridge," Ashara whispered. "Would you like it?" No response. Ashara knelt beside her mistress and put a hand to her forehead. It came away sticky with sweat. *Po was right. They're killing her.*

"Natan?" Oni moaned. "Is it you?"

"It's Ashara," she said soothingly, placing Oni's hand atop the quilt. "I'm here." She patted the hand. "What do you want?"

"Water," Oni gasped. Ashara took the bowl of porridge and dribbled some onto Oni's tongue. "Dasha?"

"He's not here, either. Avi's downstairs."

"Avi? My husband?"

"Yes," Ashara said, stroking Oni's hand. Her mistress let out a long breath, rattling through her throat, and kicked her feet. The head rolled to the side and continued ragged, irregular breathing. Ashara waited. Avi came and went, eventually returning to sit at the foot of the bed with his pipe. They said nothing. They had nothing to say. Ashara had tried what she could. If Po was there, he could have said something, she reasoned. But it was too late. The breathing weakened and the restlessness waned. Oni's bony fingers tightened around Ashara's palm and relaxed. As the city bells chimed sixth bell, Ashara leaned over and put her ear to Oni's lips.

"She's dead," she said.

✦

Crows circled in the azure sky. Natan coughed and tried to swallow, but his tongue was swollen and his mouth too dry. He groaned. His body refused to move, every inch of his skin prickled in discomfort, and his insides felt numb. Slowly memory of the battle returned; the sounds and smells, the screaming of men and the taste of blood.

Shadows passed about in his peripheral vision. A weight fell on his chest and a wrinkled face regarded him. Something rough and metallic entered his mouth. It forced his jaw open.

"*Agh*," Natan gargled.

"I think he's alive," someone said.

"Not for long," the face above him growled, positioning a set of pliers on Natan's front tooth. "Nice teeth he has too."

"G'us a look," the other voice said. The first man screwed up his nose and made room. Another face appeared, this one youthful, and considered Natan before grunting and shoving the older man away. "He's one of ours," the younger man said. "G'me that bottle."

The cold steel touched his lips and fiery liquor burnt his throat. He coughed and gagged, setting off a sequence of stabbing shots through his body.

"Don't move," the man said. "We've got you." Soon others were about Natan and they lifted him onto a stretcher. From the stretcher, Natan saw for the first time the field of bodies all about him, with people scavenging amidst the carnage.

"Can you hear me?" a stretcher-bearer asked. Natan nodded then grimaced. "You're messed up, but you'll live."

"Stay awake," another said. "Don't want the surgeon to think you're past it." Natan managed the slightest nod of his head and gritted his teeth as the stretcher began to move in jerky motions. Due to his position on the stretcher, he did not see the medical pavilions until he was almost under them. Crowds of people stood about, some the walking wounded, others burdened with stretchers and a few with bodies carried in their arms. Surgeons moved among them and directed them to different tents depending on their need.

A surgeon approached Natan in an orange cap and white mask, designating him as one from the College of Surgeons. He prodded and poked at Natan, noticing with apparent enthusiasm Natan's groans and contortions.

"He's got good life in him," the surgeon said. "Over there, pavilion twelve."

They carried him over and were greeted by a young woman in the brown tunic of the army's medical group. She had them set him down at the end of a row. Natan was glad for the sudden stillness. He raised a hand, but the soldiers had their backs to him. The young woman saw the motion and came over, kneeling beside his stretcher with a flask, a bucket and a towel.

"Keep yourself still," she said. "My name's Nimi."

"Natan," he croaked. Nimi put a finger to her lips.

"*Shhhh.*"

She dipped the towel in the bucket, removed the bandage around his head and began washing him. The water soothed his burning skin and was a distraction from the pain.

"That's a nasty cut," Nimi said, probing with the towel around his forehead. Natan maintained eye contact with her and Nimi smiled back before putting the towel away. She opened the flask and set it to Natan's lips. He gagged and coughed half of it up. The tart taste left him chewing his tongue and pulling faces. Nimi laughed, rolled him onto his side and left him to sleep aided by the vile tonic.

Someone was screaming. It took a while for Natan to consciously realize he was awake. The light had faded and flies buzzed about the tent. One landed on his cheek and Natan slapped at it. The jarring pain in his skull that followed jolted any other thoughts of sleep from him. He rolled onto his back and glanced in the direction of the screams. Surgeons worked on a man by lamplight. Two women held the patient down and a surgeon ran a jagged saw back and forth. The patient howled and shrieked, kicking about with his legs and thrashing from side to side.

The arm came off and a red-hot brand was placed on the open flesh. The screaming stopped. The body went limp.

Natan's mouth dropped open in horror. In a moment of doubt he reached for his legs. One was heavy and did not move. His hands found bandages and a splint. He patted the rest of his body down, finding it intact. Someone, at some point, had removed his armor and left him only with his shirt.

"Are you okay?" A figure approached.

"Is Nimi here?" Natan asked.

"Who?"

"Never mind."

By day the aid station busied itself and Natan watched the comings and goings from his stretcher, unable to get up. At some point breakfast was passed around, and then it seemed to take forever for lunch. The temperature rose and bloated blow flies buzzed aimlessly about.

He heard Nimi before he saw her, doing the rounds and chatting to the patients. In the light of day she appeared younger than he first thought, perhaps fifteen or so. When she came to Natan she took one look and said he looked fine.

"Wait," Natan said, inwardly berating himself for sounding desperate.

"What? Others are waiting."

"Do you have some of that —" he searched for the word. "Tonic? My head hurts." *Okay, that's true enough.* Nimi looked to her supervisor, reached into her apron and removed the flask.

"Here," she said. "Not too much." As he drank, Nimi stepped behind him and massaged his neck. Natan flinched. "You were hit on the head," Nimi explained. "Sometimes that means your neck is out of alignment." Whether the magic of her touch, or the alignment of his neck, the pain in his temples waned and he relaxed back down, falling into a deep sleep.

Days passed in the muggy heat and it turned out Natan was the only soldier in the tent who could read and write. With many a person desperate to write home, Natan occupied himself writing letters for a copper *jet* per page. On the afternoon of the eighth day, Nimi approached and asked if he could help her write a letter.

"I prepared a copper," she said, drawing the coin from her apron.

"Keep it," Natan said. "You helped me buy the paper."

"Everyone else pays," she said.

"You're not like everyone else," Natan said. Nimi blushed.

"How so?"

"You're different. I mean the others are soldiers."

"Would the priest pay?" Nimi asked.

"Yes, but—"

"And the Master Surgeon?"

"Yes, but they've got money, haven't they?"

"And here's my money." She pressed the coin into Natan's palm and closed his fingers.

"Who am I writing to?" Natan asked.

"My mother."

"They'll need more than that to deliver it," Natan said. Nimi blushed and said of course they would. She gave her family name and her hometown of Katani in Talu Province. Her mother lived there with her stepfather, and she had not seen her in three years. Nimi wanted her mother to know she was well, had travelled many miles and seen many things, was still a good girl and said her prayers before bed every night.

"Do you?" Natan asked, looking up from the paper.

"No," Nimi said with a laugh. "But my mother will worry if I didn't. And tell her I was at the battle and saw the Emperor rescued by General Jano and how it's good to think there's finally to be peace."

"Three years," Natan said, finishing it off. "Do you not miss them?"

"Sometimes," Nimi said. "Our relationship, you could say, improves with distance."

"Same with my parents," Natan said. "I guess they'll never understand what we've been through here."

"This is our family now," Nimi said. "The Seventh Army. Jano says he's our grandfather, the officers the parents, and all around us our brothers and sisters. It's how I think of it anyway."

"That is a welcoming thought."

Natan blew on the paper for the ink to dry, folded it, and wrote the address on the front. Nimi tucked it into her apron and thanked him. She was getting up when a sergeant wandered over.

"You got a Natan Luka-Tudo here?" the sergeant asked.

"That's me," Natan said.

"*Oh*," said the sergeant, suddenly drawn up short. "I'm from the 13th Auxiliary. Your brother, Dasha Luka-Tudo, was in my squad. He died yesterday of his wounds. He wanted me to find you."

"My brother's dead?" Natan was unsure if it was the medicines in his system, or the trauma, but he felt nothing.

"Yesterday," the sergeant reiterated. "Pavilion three. They'd amputated his leg but the fever spread. A lot of fine men have died on this field. And women. Your brother was a good soldier. Ready for anything."

"He was a clerk before the war," Natan said, staring into the distance. "We used to play soldier. We never thought we'd be them."

"Life doesn't make sense, does it? Anyway, I thought I'd let you know before we march out. We've got our orders — no, don't get too excited. The wounded stay here. You'll be on a long path to recovery. Some of the officers have already been driven back to Pao'an for the officers' hospital, but, well, we're the common grunts aren't we?"

"I guess we are," Natan said, lying back down.

"But it's peace," said the sergeant. "At least they say it is. Tomi's dead and the Vu'tai once again control the cabinet. It was not in vain."

"Thanks for bringing this news," Natan said. "I know it was not easy for you."

"Like I said," the sergeant said, rubbing the back of his neck. "Sorry about your brother."

A breeze ruffled the pages of Po's book and the fire in the grill flickered violently, casting dancing shadows over the study walls.

"The summer rains are coming," Po said. Biet mumbled. "Is something wrong?"

"Not good," Biet said. "Not good at all." Po waited for the abbot to fill the silence with an explanation. But he only added: "I never thought I'd see the day."

"What is it?" Po asked, his curiosity getting the better of him.

"What?" Biet said, looking up. "It looks like I'll be eating breakfast up here. Can you go arrange it? Don't dawdle, I'll need you after that."

Po left for the kitchen and spotted Dovo approaching under the colonnade.

"A bit early to be out of the kitchen," he said.

"I was looking for you," Dovo said. "Come quick before the others arrive for breakfast. Someone's here to see you."

"Ashara?" Po asked. "A woman?"

"Don't know. Didn't catch her name." *Her.* Po scampered after the monk, their sandals slapping the tiles. In the kitchen Brother Bidovi stood by the oven fanning himself and looking busy. When the pair entered he spun about, then relaxed.

"All clear?" Bidovi asked. Dovo stood in the dining room door and checked the outside hall.

"All clear," he said.

"You can come out now," Bidovi called. The pantry door opened and out stepped a tall, slender woman beneath a travelling cloak.

"You're not Ash—" he began, but his words died in his throat. He caught a glimpse of auburn hair. "Savani?" The judge's wife drew back the hood and revealed her grim face. "Wait — what are you doing here? Why the secrecy? You called for *me*, right?"

"So you *do* remember me," Savani said. "I was worried."

"Yes —" Po said, still trying to orientate himself to developments. "You're Savani e Unuga. Your husband's a judge."

"*Was* judge," Savani said. "I don't have much time. He's been executed and I have to leave the city. We need your help. We need someone unknown who won't stand out. He mentioned you."

"Executed?" Po said. "You should be speaking to the abbot."

"No," Savani said. "I need someone with your energy who won't draw attention to himself. Please take this." She drew a canvas bag out from under her cloak and handed it to Po. He turned it over. There was nothing on the outside. He opened it and drew out a clump of loose papers covered in small, precise handwriting. At the top of the first page was written the title of the manuscript: *The Secret History of Jano Maretaki,* by Judge e Unuga.

"If anyone doubts the content," Madam e Unuga said. "There's a reference at the back for where to look for evidence. Unfortunately almost every witness is dead." Po flicked through the papers. From the headings he knew how serious the allegations were contained within. Chapters included *Corrupt Practices, Political Assassinations, Inappropriate Liaisons, Debt,* and *Betrayal of the Empire.*

"But…" Po said. "To even to be found with such a document would mean certain death."

"One day," Savani said. "This document will be his legacy. I don't want it wasted. But that's why it can't come with me. I'm fleeing Jano's spies, but how long will it be before they catch up?"

Po showed Bidovi and Dovo the document. Bidovi began to read but Dovo shoved it away.

"Don't show it to anyone," Dovo said. "If you want to keep your head, learn some discretion."

"Your friend is right," Savani said. "Hold on to it. Keep it safe. Don't let the enemy take it. You'll know when and how to use it. Even if not in Jano's lifetime, may it one day be used to curse his memory." Po hesitated and returned the manuscript to the bag. Savani's hazel eyes drilled into him. Gone was the elegant woman who sent him giddy. She was a tigress protecting her husband's work and eternal reputation.

"Take it," Dovo said. Po tucked the bag under his robe and Savani nodded in satisfaction. Bidovi opened the kitchen door to the alley behind the monastery and poked his head out.

"All clear," he reported. Savani slipped on her hood and said her hurried farewells. Po stood frozen and unable to respond. She squeezed his shoulder, leaving a lingering scent of jasmine, and slid out into the alley.

Po knocked on the study door and entered. A breakfast tray lay on the desk between piles of papers and books. *Dovo's already been.*

"You took your time," Biet said, waving to the chair opposite.

"Just something to see to," Po said. The manuscript was under a floorboard in the dormitory. Master Dugen would not find it there. "Anyway, I'm here now. What are we doing?" Biet shuffled through the papers before him and selected an official looking document.

"The new Chief Minister Jano has wasted no time," Biet said, passing Po the letter. "Effective immediately, the Orange Edict is abolished, meaning — for our purposes — the monastery will be liable for tax. We're to prepare a report for the Ministry of Revenue to assess."

"Can they do that?" Po asked. Biet shrugged.

"They make the laws. Of course, it doesn't apply to the Vu'du establishments."

"That's not fair."

"Fair has nothing to do with it," Biet said. "It's politics." Po's eyes skimmed down the page and landed on the second part.

"That's… that's not possible," he said. "How will they… no… there's too many. Is this — no."

"So you've seen it then," Biet said. "Only Vu'du schools and the Imperial Academy may submit students for the Imperial Exams."

"But what about all the monasteries? All the students here? What about the Solari and Astirti schools, or the Kh'areen sponsoring their own students?"

"They're not saying Kh'areen and Ba're can't study," Biet said. "Just that they must go to an ideologically approved school."

"What've we done to deserve this?" Po asked, staring at the page. "The Ba're are the bedrock of the civil service."

"Maybe that's the problem. Mediocrity hates success."

Po returned the letter.

"But — what are we going to do?"

"What can we do?" Biet asked. "We'll complete this report. Then think about our options. But it seems like students will have to go home or find other schools. Maybe some can continue as monks, but without parent donations we won't be able to maintain a large community."

"And me?" Po asked. Biet massaged his temples.

"You," he said. "I guess you'd be a prime candidate to remain here. But we both know your ambition and talent. You won't be happy doing that."

Lightning flashed across the night sky and rain pelted the tiled roofs. Ashara hurried from cover to cover, bunching Oni's robe about her. Water dripped off the hood and her feet were sodden and *squished* with every step. Still, this was the weather she wanted. No one would be out on a night like this, and the noise of the rain would cover a multitude of mistakes.

She had slipped into the Inner City before sundown and found cover on the stoop of a temple. When the bells struck midnight, she headed for Scholar Street, splashing from shadow to shadow and shelter to shelter. The streets were deserted. Only the occasional light showed in a window. Even the guards stayed inside that night.

She hesitated under the great arch at the entrance to Scholar Street. Lightning blinded her, momentarily revealing the dark forms of shops with their shutters closed and hanging signs yanked this way and that in the wind. Ashara paused to regain her night vision. It had taken her two weeks to gather the nerve, and find the right time to do this.

It was hard in the dark to find the right shop. Only the infrequent flashes revealed the facades. Once found, Ashara crouched down opposite and watched, trying to catch any hint of light in the shop, or in the apartment above. She crept closer, her hood over her head, water dripping off her, and put an eye to the crack in the shutters. Nothing.

She raked her memory, trying to remember what the window behind was made of. Most residences and the poorer shops used shutters and loose canvas, sometimes with a grill. But the more well-to-do shops had panes of glass supported in frames of lead.

Ashara drew out her knife and slid it between the wooden shutters, testing for contact. At first the shutters resisted her probing, then the knife dug deeper between the two panels. It hit something solid. *Probably glass*, Ashara thought. A leadlight window would be difficult to break without causing a commotion even the storm would fail to hide.

She tried the front door but it was locked. Her fingers probed the keyhole, feeling for some weakness. There was no way she could pick the lock. That was not one of her skills. *Bother*, she said to herself.

Ashara splashed around the back and found the rear entrance. A little gate led into a yard and she fumbled, found the bolt and left the gate open. The back door was much the same as the front. It was made of solid wood planks and had an iron lock with a round orb-like handle above it. Try as she might, the lock did not give.

Then in the briefest of moments when lightning clashed, Ashara saw a side window, not too big, just above head height. It took some muscles, but she maneuvered some of the junk from the backyard under the window and climbed up to have a good look. This window was covered in canvas and did not have any bars. Out came her knife and the canvas peeled back one thread at a time. Before climbing through, Ashara removed her robe and shoes, tucked them off to the side as best she could without leaving them in a puddle, and then pulled herself up head first into the gap.

Inside, the bookshop smelt of solvents. Ashara guessed the back room was used as a workshop, but she had trouble seeing anything beyond the vague forms of equipment. She tiptoed onto the shop floor and quickly realized she was not going to be able to find her book. Everything looked the same in the inky blackness around her. She felt around for a lamp she remembered on the counter. Her hand touched something and she ran her fingers over it. *The lamp, now for flint,* she told herself. *It must be kept nearby.* But she could not find it.

Quickly, she said to herself, feeling vulnerable in the darkness. She imagined any moment a door opening and light falling across her. Her hands dropped behind the counter and ran along the tops of books, sheets of paper and an ink bottle. She bumped into something. It was a chest of drawers beneath the counter. She opened the top drawer and rummaged inside. Pain bit into her finger and she stuck it in her mouth, tasting the iron tang of blood.

Ashara tried the next draw. It did not move. She felt for a lock and her fingers brushed against a clasp. With her knife she pried it open. Coins *chinked.* Without being able to see them, Ashara was limited to identifying them by touch. There were copper *ku'net* and *jet,* silver *li,* and at least one gold *gotti,* as well as paper notes of nondescript form.

This will pay for the book and more, she told herself. Suddenly, breaking into the shop seemed worth it. The owner deserved to pay dearly for what he did to her. She would take it all. *Well,* she thought. *Maybe not all. But enough. How much is enough? I wish I had a light.* Then she paused as another thought struck her, and she sat down heavily, her legs splayed out on either side of her.

What have I become? She asked herself. *Is this me that I should steal?* She tried reasoning with herself. The man had stolen from her. He had taken one of her few possessions, and now she could not afford to return home. He *deserved* it. She needed the money and he had taken it from her. She was just, she reasoned, returning the favor. *Or was she? What would Tanri and the Chobi say?* She clenched her fists. *What have they done for me? I fend for myself. But is this me?* Paralysed by doubt, Ashara felt a tear slip down her cheek. *This is not me.*

Ashara stood and returned her knife to her belt. She hesitated. If she left now, she told herself, she could still have self-respect. Thunder rolled outside and the building shuddered. Ashara made up her mind and snuck back outside via the small workshop window. All the way home she questioned whether she did the right thing.

Dawn arose gray and sombre over the imperial capital. The storm had not slackened in its fury, and the Blue River, brown with mud and clogged with branches, had swelled up to cover most the docks. Ashara donned her still half-sodden clothes, warm from the fire, and headed back out into the rain.

By the time she reached the monastery, it was not possible for her clothes to collect any more water. She dripped from her nose to her undergarments. Ashara was just glad, it being summer rain, she was still warm and not in danger of a cold.

She rang the bell at the monastery gate. There was no response. She looked about for signs of life, but the street was deserted. Ashara rang the bell again. This time a slot opened and a voice shouted through. She said her name and explained she was there to see Po, a novice, as she had something to tell him. The slot closed and the speaker went away, only to return shortly after with the message that Po was *"otherwise indisposed."*

"Can I leave a message?" Ashara asked, her mouth up to the gap in the door.

"I don't think that would be appropriate," the voice said. *Inappropriate,* Ashara said to herself. *What is he on about?*

"When will he be available?" Ashara asked.

"I don't rightly know," the monk replied. Ashara stamped her foot and leaned against the door.

"Listen," she said. "I have come this far. I am wet. I need help. This is Jan Moga right? Maybe someone else will speak with me?" There was a long paused.

"What's your name again?" the man asked.

"Ashara." Nothing. Ashara peeked through the hole. The speaker had gone. *Damn Ba're.* They could be so infuriating. Eventually, the door opened a crack.

"Come in," the monk said, waving Ashara into the dry patch beneath the gate. Another monk, older and in burgundy, stood in the shadows. He pushed a pair of glasses up the bridge of his nose and regarded her for a moment. Ashara shivered in the midst of a growing puddle.

"Ashara," the older monk said. "I'm Master Dugen. Po's teacher. How are you? It's a wet day for a visit."

"Fine," Ashara said. "I thought I could see Po."

"That's not really possible," Dugen said. Ashara's eyes widened and hand went to her mouth.

"He wasn't — he didn't get the fever did he?"

"No, he's well. We just have rules about fraternization between men and women. Things were a bit different after the fall."

"Fraternization?" Ashara said. "I don't understand." Dugen let his silence communicate the meaning. Ashara went stiff and she bit back a laugh.

"You think I... we... were interested in each other? Is that all you can think about? We're *friends*. Po's nice. He's helpful. But I'm Kh'areen. So, therefore I can't see him?"

Dugen shrugged.

"They're the rules," he said. "They're for your own good as well as his. I hope you can respect that. Now, how can I help you?"

"Forget it," Ashara said. "I thought you Ba're were different." She reached for the gate but Dugen put his hand on it.

"Stop," he said. "Control those emotions. They'll only get you into trouble. I'm here because you helped us. We're returning the favor. Now explain what you need." Ashara twisted her fingers into claws but forced down her anger. At least Dugen *seemed* honest, she thought, even if annoying. She told him about her need for money, the priest, and the book and how it was stolen.

"That's better," Dugen said. "Now, let's think about this. Which shop took the book?" Ashara explained where the shop was and what it looked like. Dugen nodded, then asked for a description of the bookseller and the book itself. Ashara obliged him with everything she knew.

"Right," Dugen said, standing up with some difficulty. "Leave it with me."

Rain lashed the Dili valley and a heavy mist rolled in between the hills. Water dripped from the boughs of trees and the ground around the aid station turned to mud. Parts of the Gray River broke its banks, flooding the surrounding farmland that was weeks before a battlefield. During one gap in the rain Nimi sloshed through the mud towards the pavilion, a basket under one arm and a crutch under the other.

"Natan," she said. "We've got to pick some herbs for the clinic before the rain returns."

"Me?" Natan said. "My leg..."

"You've still got a leg, haven't you? Get off your lazy arse and give me a hand." Natan looked about the pavilion. He was doing better than most. In truth, if it was not for the rain clogging the roads he would probably be back in Pao'an already.

"Okay," he said, accepting the offered crutch.

"How's it feel?" Natan tested his weight.

"Alright I guess. Something to get used to." Nimi nodded and set off in the direction of the forest. Soon they were under the cover of spreading trees with water dripping from burdened leaves. The path led ever upwards, winding into the side of the valley.

"Do you know what *votimi* looks like?" Nimi asked, helping Natan over a fallen log.

"No," Natan said. "I've heard the name. It's a bark isn't it?"

"Fungus," Nimi said. "Here... see under the bank. It's growing on that exposed root." Nimi left the path and scrambled up through ferns to the root. She took a knife from her belt and cut the fungus away into her basket. On the way back she stumbled and Natan caught her, briefly holding her in one arm as she regained her balance.

"Here, you dropped one," Natan said, bending over as best he could to retrieve the fungus. "What else are we looking for?" Nimi indicated with her fingers a tiny plant no taller than her little finger.

"Green, we'll see it under some of these ferns if we look hard enough."

"And what do you call it?"

"*Vate're*," Nimi said. She pulled aside a sheet of hanging moss and knelt at the base of a tree amidst the ferns. "It's not this, but it's similar. This is *takiva*. You'll get sick if you eat that. See how the underside is rusty? That's the difference." Natan poked about in the ferns with his crutch.

"Like this?" he asked. Nimi picked her way over.

"Don't be silly — that's nothing like it. That's a *talolo* sapling." She pointed at the canopy. "They're like that when fully grown." Natan's cheeks burned and he began to turn back to the path. "Don't be like that," Nimi said. "Keep looking." Her fingers wrapped around his arm and her lips gave his cheek a quick peck. "I need the help."

Natan locked eyes with her and her gaze drifted down to his lips. The crutch fell from his side and his arms embraced her, pulling her to him. Her fingers ran along his back and her breasts pressed into his chest. They kissed. Their lips moved slowly at first, but then their tongues met and Natan kissed her deeper and more passionately than he knew possible. They stumbled backwards. Nimi came to rest against the trunk of a tree. Her hands fumbled with Natan's trousers. Keeping his weight on his good leg, Natan picked her up, his hands under her thighs, and entered her.

It was over way too soon. They held each other in the same position. Natan listened to Nimi's breathing. She giggled and buried her lips in his neck. Slowly he let her feet back down to the ground.

"You'll have to teach me what to look for so I can come with you more often."

For a week Natan went out with Nimi daily to forage for herbs and other things the aid station could use. The activity helped his body to recover, and the passion lifted his spirit. One afternoon the pavilion was in the charge of a certain Ba're monk called Nikodima. The men thought him humourless and accused him of dosing them up to make them sleep.

That day Natan lay on his stretcher, his hands cupped behind his head, thinking of home. It'd been two days without heavy rain and it wouldn't be long before he could take one of the wagon trains back to Pao'an.

"*Psst*, Natan," a soldier whispered. "Do you think they'll let us go into Dili?" Natan glanced towards the surgeon's station, behind which steam rose off the fields in the shafts of sunlight breaking through the clouds.

"Not with this monk in charge," Natan said.

"I'm going to eat my hand off if I stay here another day."

"It'd be an improvement on the soggy ration cakes. Any other body parts going?"

"Eat your own damn hand. I'd kill for a warm beer."

"Silence!" Nikodima's voice rang across the tent. "This excitement isn't good for your nerves. Another word from either of you and I'll give you enough medicine to put a dreadbeast to sleep for a year."

"How's he hear us?" the soldier hissed.

"Kuvu! I know it's you!"

"He's a monk," Natan said. "I think they have powers." Nikodima stalked between the stretchers and stood at Natan's feet, eyes locked with his.

"Natan Luka-Tudo, do you have problems following instructions?"

"No, sir."

"Then maybe you have too much energy. For the sake of everyone who needs rest, I find it necessary to give you something to do. We need fresh *vate're*. I believe you know what it looks like? You've volunteered yourself."

"I do," Natan conceded. "But I —"

"Excuses," Nikodima said. "Do you have any idea how many patients we're caring for? You are one of the healthier ones. You can start earning your one *jet* a day. Or do you think this is a charity?" Natan did not reply but put on his studded boots, tightened his belt and checked his money pouch and knife were secure. He was not leaving any valuables behind for the others to riffle through.

"You can take this bag," Nikodima said. "The last owner doesn't need it anymore." Natan thanked the monk and fetched his crutch. Without a word he set off for the forest. Walking in the forest was not the same without Nimi. It was an unfamiliar environment, one where every smell and sound was something new. Pushing on along the path the trees grew thicker. His leg began to ache. It was easier to ignore when he was with Nimi. Now it drained him.

Pushing about in the undergrowth Natan began filling his bag, determined to return with a good quantity. Each patch he found took him deeper into the forest until he was farther than he had been before. Ahead the trees opened to overgrown fields, where once peasants had dug terraces for their crops. The remains of two houses, their roofs caved in, lay buried beneath a tangle of shrubbery.

Out in the open, something caught Natan's attention. A sound carried on the wind; a human sound not found in the forest. *Bells.* Natan turned and saw the city of Dili opposite, cast in a brilliant pool of sunshine cutting through the gray clouds. At first it was hard to tell, but then Natan noticed smoke rising from the buildings. The citadel itself was on fire. Flames licked up the side of the towers, curling from the windows and creeping along the spires.

Natan stood, transfixed, trying to comprehend. *Danger.* He dashed back down the forest path as fast as his crutch allowed, slipping and sliding in the mud. By the time he got near the valley floor he was caked in mud, his bandaged leg soaked through, and his exposed skin cut on branches and twigs. He panted, out of breath, and ignored the pain. *Smoke.* The sense of dread grew. He approached a fallen log and peeked over the top, careful to keep himself out of sight. The aid station burned. Bodies lay strewn about, some still with arrows and spears sticking out of them.

Nimi, he yelled silently within himself, fighting back the urge to cry out. Men moved amidst the devastation. They wore drab uniforms caked in mud and grime, but their shields were quartered yellow and black with the emblem of a terror bird emblazoned in silver.

Natan stared in disbelief, too exhausted to think clearly on what he should do. He had not seen the shields before but remembered something about the emblem. Before the battle soldiers had talked about *maybe* facing the Third Army. General Mamot had arrived — too late to save the Emperor, but ready to reap his revenge.

Some bodies wore brown tunics. Others were clearly wounded soldiers. *No survivors.* Natan's fingers gripped the handle of his knife. He wondered how many he could kill before they overwhelmed him. *But that's chucking my life away as a gesture to the dead.* Reality dawned. He'd arrived too late. He was no use to anyone. Anger turned to grief. For the second time in his life he had failed to protect those he loved.

Never again.

Natan pulled himself up on his crutch. As he did so someone shouted.

"Over there!"

CHAPTER 13

"On the distant fringes of the empire in the mist-wreathed mountains called the Graytalons lies the Ba're monastery of Jan'a. It was built in 634IE as part of a campaign to stabilize the border regions, and while other projects of that era have faded, Jan'a has become the center of Ba're learning."

A History of the Vermilion Empire

Jan Moga Monastery lay damp and dreary under the gray sky. For once the rain had stopped, but buckets still collected under drips and the courtyard was a lake for the sparrows. Bells tolled a mournful note, calling the Ba're to reflection. In twos and threes, novices and monks approached the Great Hall, their sandals leaving wet tracks on the tiles.

Po joined his companions and sat cross legged on the floor. Beneath the Hand of Dasanika, Biet leaned on the lectern, his fingers clawed about the sides.

"Today," Biet said. "Is our last reflection as a school." He blew into a handkerchief. "Master Dugen has arranged for transfers to the Imperial Academy. Those who wish to return home will be given a reference letter. I wish this was not the end. I wish we could all remain in fellowship, but this is not the way of the Ba're. Today as we enter reflection, remember this."

Biet moved to his cushion and rang the bell. The gathered monks bowed their heads and repeated the sacred mantra. *Kime ki're kima ka. Kime ki're kima ka.*

After reflection Master Dugen sat at a desk and took the names of those who wished to be transferred. Po hung around towards the back, his mind in agitation. The novices thinned. Soon he stood before his teacher.

"You should get a good position," Dugen said without looking up. "Your results will see to that. I just need your signature." Po checked the form and his hand paused on the pen. "And novice, I'll need you to come with me this afternoon. I'll fill you in later."

"No," Po said.

"No?" Dugen said.

"No, I mean I can't sign this," Po said. "I haven't decided."

"Of course you have," Dugen said. "You'll be a master before you put down the pen."

"I can't," Po said. He turned and ran from the hall.

In his dorm room he lifted the floorboard and removed the manuscript. As long as it existed it was a weight around his neck. He considered burning it, but Judge Bodai had given his life to get the message out. No, he could not do that. He could not take it to the Imperial Academy either. That would be like dressing up as a lamb and walking into the sabertooth enclosure in the Emperor's garden.

"There you are," Dugen said, entering the dormitory. "What's going on?" Po stuffed the manuscript back into the hole but he was too slow. "I saw that. Give it here."

"No," Po said. Dugen put out a hand and stepped forward.

"Is that your favorite word today? You sound like a child. Give it to me." Po handed his teacher the manuscript, feeling like he was pulling the noose around Dugen's neck. Dugen read, his face impassive.

"Where did you get this?" he asked after finishing a half dozen pages. Po explained and asked for Dugen's silence. "No," Dugen said. "We're taking this to the abbot."

"We can't. It's too dangerous." But Po had no choice. Dugen was already out the door.

"When were you going to tell me?" Venerable Biet demanded from behind his desk. Dugen sat beside him in brooding silence.

"I wasn't," Po said. "I wanted to keep you safe."

"We've had this discussion before. You *know* the rules." Biet pinched the bridge of his nose. Po had never seen him so stressed before. "So, what are *you* going to do about it?"

"Me?"

"You want to be independent. What are you going to do?"

"I was going to hide it."

"Not here," Biet said. "Neither will you take it to the Imperial Academy, but I guess you've realized that."

"I did," Po said, flicking his attention towards Dugen's stone-chiseled face.

"It needs to be somewhere Jano will never find it."

"Like Li'an?" Po asked, referring to his hometown.

"Too political," Biet said. "It's a provincial capital."

"Jan'a?" It was a suggestion born of frustration, but Dugen and Biet exchanged glances.

"That's not a bad idea," Biet said. "Abbot Vaina is a friend of mine. Or was when we were your age. The Graytalons are about as far as you can get."

"Essentially impenetrable," Dugen added. "And the monastery grounds are sovereign territory if I know my history."

"Which I'm sure you do," Biet said. "We'll write a recommendation letter and Po could continue his studies there. He just couldn't sit the exams."

"Less likely to get in trouble," Dugen said. "No temptations of the big city — or young ladies."

"Hold on," Po interrupted. "Do I get a say in this?"

"Do you have a better idea?" Biet asked.

"No."

"Well, that settles it," Biet said.

"So I'm leaving? By myself?"

"You'll have a few days to get ready. I'm sure we can see in the meantime if anyone else is going that way. Now, can you go with Dugen

to the Imperial Academy and deliver these enrollment forms. He asked
if you'd accompany him."

Po blinked, still processing all that had happened.

"Sure," he said.

The streets were gray and sullen. People stayed indoors and smoke from
wood fires drifted along the cobbles like mist. Po kept a wary eye to the
sky and trailed along behind Master Dugen.

"Your friend visited the other day," Dugen said once they were inside
the Inner City.

"Ashara? She was at the monastery?"

"Yes, needed help with something." Po ran to keep up, suddenly interested.

"What did she want? Can we help her? Is she well?"

"Something about a book," Dugen said. "Someone stole it from her.
She wanted our help getting it back."

"Did you offer it?" Po asked. "Can we do anything?"

"Well, yes. We're going there now. It's not far from the academy." He
then explained the circumstances as relayed to him by Ashara. "But stop
with the questions," he said at last. "You used to be the quiet student. I
liked it better that way."

Scholar Street was much as Po remembered it. Dugen wanted to check
on *Vaisha's Books and Stationers* but the pair found it shut with timber
nailed across the front and the glass windows broken behind. Dugen
held his glasses to get a closer look and peered inside, muttering about it
being a waste of good books. Po tugged at Dugen's sleeve.

"Which shop was it that took Ashara's book?"

"Around here somewhere," Dugen said, pulling himself away from
Vaisha's storefront.

They found the shop and the shopkeeper welcomed them with a
big grin until he realized what the monks were after. The book had
sold, he explained. He honestly believed the girl had stolen it. Dugen
launched into a diatribe on honest belief and theft, essentially accusing

the shopkeeper of the later and was going to call a magistrate in to settle the case. The shopkeeper could not risk the courts getting involved, so Dugen and Po left the shop with eight silver *li* in a purse.

"Do you think we pressured him too hard?" Po asked once out on the street.

"Nonsense. He was clearly crooked."

A big 'CLOSED' sign hung over the open gate of the Luka-Tudo Trading House. The ginger cat sat nearby, watching with practiced disinterest as soldiers and revenue clerks searched the warehouse and stables. Inside the house, Ashara shook Avi at the kitchen table.

"Avi, wake up. There are men here to see you."

"We're closed," Avi moaned. "Tell them to come back tomorrow."

"They're from the government."

"I don't give a pig's arse. Make that noise stop!"

"That's them. They're pulling everything apart."

Avi rose his head from the table and knocked over a half-empty bottle. It rolled off the table and smashed on the floor. His unruly black hair clung to his face and his eyes were bloodshot.

"What in the name of Asata're are they doing?"

"They're in the warehouse."

"Who opened the door?"

"I did. They made me."

"Bollocks," Avi said and tried to get up, but the rush of blood caused him to grip his head and swear. "What do they want?"

"I didn't understand," Ashara said. "They had papers. Some list. Here, let me help you." Ashara got Avi to his feet and he clung to her arm as she led him outside. As soon as the sunlight hit his face, Ashara felt his muscles tighten.

"Look here boys!" a sergeant roared. "We've got ourselves a drunkard." Soldiers stopped what they were doing and laughed. One of them pointed.

"Look, the old bugger's wet himself." Ashara wanted to drop Avi and run away, but some sense of loyalty remained.

172

"This is my master," she said. "Treat him with some respect."

Avi pointed a finger, his voice slurred.

"What's the meaning of… this… here?"

The sergeant waved a bookish man over. The man looked down through spectacles perched on the end of his nose, and carried an open book with him. A copper brooch on his lapel identified him as being from the Ministry of Revenue.

"This is my good friend De'reke," the sergeant said. "We're just keeping him safe from rogues like you."

"Yes, well," De'reke said, looking decidedly awkward. "Sorry to be the bearer of bad news. Are you in a position to read this document, sir?"

"Get on with it," Avi growled.

"Righty-o, sir. So basically, in short if you will…"

"Oh, give it here," the sergeant said and snatched the paper from the book. "This here is entitled the *Decimation of the Reformists*. Being the desire, blah blah blah, justice, loyalty etcetera, the Chief Minister Jano Maretaki hereby declares, blah blah blah, the families of those who provided soldiers, for the failed attempt at kidnapping the god-like Emperor Gotti VII, blessings and honor to him, shall forfeit a one-off tax ten percent of their assets to the Imperial treasury." The sergeant grinned at Avi at over the top of the letter.

"You think I have money to pay," Avi said. "I'm broke. I have nothing. So go tell your bosses…"

"In the absence, sir," De'reke said. "Of any inventory here, your only real asset is your business, otherwise called and herein known as the Luka-Tudo Trading House. This, in accordance with a ruling in council, is assessed following the *katikati* method as twenty-nine golden *gotti*, seven silver *li*, and ten copper *jet*."

"What! Where?" Avi barked. "I have nothing. That might have been the business' worth, but it isn't now."

"Therefore," De'reke continued. "I compute a tax of one thousand and ninety-five copper *jet* in the common currency."

The sergeant whistled.

"Goddess of Mercy, that's a lot."

"Stop tormenting him," Ashara said. "It's obvious my master doesn't have it. Which family didn't supply a son to the army?"

"We're just following orders," De'reke said.

"So what happens now?" Ashara asked.

"We take him with us," said the sergeant. "He can't pay and he's drunk. He'll have money somewhere — they always do. Once he's sober and cooled his heels he'll cough up."

Soldiers stepped forward and manhandled Avi towards their wagon. The sergeant ordered the rest of his squad to take what they could from the house.

"That will reduce what he owes off the total bill," he said with a wink to Ashara. She said nothing. The sergeant put his hand on her cheek. His fingers were rough on her skin. He forced her to look at him.

"You called him master. Does that mean you come with the house?"

"No," Ashara said.

"Can't accept servants unless caught in the commission of a crime," said De'reke casually.

"Only joking," the sergeant said. "But you'll be alone in a big house tonight."

"That's enough," De'reke said. The sergeant sneered.

"You ink trotters ruin all the fun." He patted Ashara on the cheek. "You appreciate a good laugh don't you?" Ashara bit down on the wrist in front of her. The sergeant yelped like a wounded puppy. "You bit me," he cried. "Balls of Kive, you bit me!"

"You deserved it," De'reke said. "Go help your men." The sergeant sucked on the wound.

"You'll pay for that you will." Ashara refused to move. She did not want to show weakness. She had to look after herself. De'reke put his hand on the soldier's shoulder, but there was a fire in the sergeant's eyes. He swung a fist at her and she ducked too slow. The gloved knuckles grazed her ear and drove into the back of her skull. Ashara stumbled and blinked back the fog of stunned confusion that threatened to overwhelm her. She corrected herself and closed with him. *You can't run. Fight.*

Like you were taught. Her knee connected with the sergeant's groin and her fingers knotted themselves behind his head as he buckled forward, bringing his face down onto her other knee. Flesh met bone. Twice, three times she struck. The sergeant's face came up a bloody pulp.

Ashara did not wait. She ran for the kitchen where she found her things. She fumbled with them, eventually fastening her belt and checking her knife, sling and stone pouch. The rest could go in her bag.

From the yard came shouts. Ashara looked to the laundry door, then back to the hall. The sergeant stood there silhouetted by the sunlight of the open front door. Two soldiers entered behind him, entreating their squad leader to drop the matter.

"You took it too far," one of them said. "Captain Gidi doesn't want trouble on his watch."

"De'reke said he'd report you if you don't come out now," another said, his voice shaking. The sergeant shook them off and drew a knife from his belt.

"Blood for blood," he said. "Just a little slash across that face and we'll be off."

Ashara backed towards the counter and held out her hands, indicating she held no weapon. She flexed her fingers, hoping her attacker was distracted by them and did not see the knife at her side. He came at her and she stepped into his slash, ducked under it and skipped aside. He slashed madly at her again. This time Ashara got under him, drew her knife and thrust it under his chin till her hand hit flesh and blood gushed out over her fingers and ran down her arm.

"Kive!" a soldier yelped. The other was already running from the kitchen. Ashara drew the blade from her victim and allowed his body to fall to the floor. The last soldier backed away.

"That was between you and him," he said and scampered for the yard. Ashara wasted no time; she wiped her blade on a kitchen towel, grabbed a spare blue travelling cloak from the laundry and ran out the back door.

Natan landed shoulder-first in the wet loam of the forest floor. His fingers sank deep and as he got up he peeled a leaf from the tip of his nose. Behind him he heard the sound of pursuit. There was no time to lie around. He took his crutch, gritted his teeth, and continued his flight, doing his best to ignore the spasms of pain through his injured leg.

He risked a glance over his shoulder. Two men appeared over a rise between the vegetation. They carried round shields and hand axes typical of Astirti warriors. Natan only had his crutch and a blade no longer than his hand. There was no way he could beat them in a fight, but neither could he outrun them forever.

At the next rise, he looked again. They had halved the distance. Natan wheezed and pleaded with his muscles to go on. He plunged into the valley, twigs scratching at his face and ferns grasping at his feet. Something moved ahead. He stopped. If an ambush, he was done for. Forcing his breathing to a minimum, Natan peered into the forest dimness, noting at once the unnatural movement of a cluster of fern fronds. An animal rose out of the cover like an oversized chicken, the entrails of a beast dripping from its iron-like beak. Its eyes narrowed and its head bobbed. Blue and green plumage rippled as it stalked forward on oversized talons. Natan had never seen a terror bird before, but he recognized the feathers. It froze him as if the bird's eyes had cast a spell. A scream caught in Natan's throat and would not come out. The creature did not come directly at him, but stepped carefully around the forest floor, approaching in an arc.

As the terror bird passed behind a tree, it broke eye contact. Life returned to Natan's limbs and he broke for the ridgeline behind him. His heart pounded in his chest and his lungs cried with stabs of pain. Knowing he could not make it, he rolled over the top of a fallen log and landed on his back on the other side. In a panic he wriggled into the gap between log and ground, fumbling for his knife and waiting for the predator's head to look down at him.

"There he is," came a shout. General Mamot's men crested the rise and pointed at him. They broke into a run. Suddenly, there was a screech and the log shuddered as two massive talons kicked off from it. The terror bird jumped overhead and the two men shrieked.

The bird hit the first man and threw him to the ground, its talons wrapped around his chest and its beak drilled into his face, cracking his skull. The second man chopped with his axe and the axe head bounced from the bird's neck in a spray of red mist. Angered, the bird jumped at him and pinned the man between his shield and the ground. The Astirti soldier cried out in his own tongue and screamed in wild terror. The bird toyed with him, nipping at the warrior's exposed flesh until it was a bloody mess. From under his shield the Astirti retrieved his knife and slashed about wildly, scoring a blow to the underside of the bird's breast. The beak flashed down and tore out the man's throat, ending the cries and returning silence to the forest.

Natan dared not move. The terror bird was wounded, but still deadly. He watched it feed on its prey, tearing off strips of flesh and digging between bones to pull out the innards. Everything about this was wrong. Natan knew terror birds existed, but it did not seem right they would come so close to civilization. None of the soldiers had worried about them and their threat was not mentioned by the officers. The war must have dislodged the predator from its normal roaming grounds. He'd have to be careful in the future — if he survived.

The terror bird stopped eating and wavered about, cooing softly in an odd manner for such a fearsome killer. It ambled past Natan's position and out of sight. Natan rose to follow the bird's route. It was gone. Natan walked slowly over to his pursuers. A trail of blood smeared over leaves and branches led from the carnage. He took an axe and shield and followed the trail. Not far away, he found the bird curled on the ground, weak but still alive. Its eyes followed him as he approached but gone was the fierceness of before. Natan almost felt sympathy for it.

He reached out a hand and the terror bird snapped at him. He looked down at the axe he carried. It would be easy to end the creature's life.

Part of him even felt it was the right thing to do, but he could not bring himself to do it. Natan turned his back on the bird and returned to the bodies. Both wore heavy quilted gambesons, one of which was still fit to wear. Natan took it. The other was torn and splattered with blood and pieces of human flesh.

Though tired and in pain, Natan knew he had to put as much distance between himself and the scene as possible. He picked a direction and walked until he could go no farther, stopping then and clearing a space between the sprawling roots of a giant tree. Time was meaningless in the perpetual twilight of the forest floor, but ever so slowly it darkened until Natan could not see his hands and unseen animals grunted in the undergrowth. An owl hooted and at one stage during the night something screamed, followed by a thrashing of branches. Natan tried to sleep, but lay half the night clutching his knife. His stomach growled. He reached into his bag and ran his fingers over the *vate're* leaves he had collected. In his mind he wondered what they tasted like and how they were prepared. He was hungry, but didn't want to poison himself.

The dawn chorus woke Natan as first light filtered through the leaves. He startled awake, surprised he had fallen asleep. He glanced about, fearing danger, but whatever had made noises during the night had long since returned to their burrows and bolt holes. His stomach growled and there was a pounding in his head from thirst. Hauling himself to his feet, Natan continued his trek, stopping here and there to suck rainwater from the occasional leaf. It was never enough. He was soon on all fours, dragging himself through the ferns, and thought he imagined it when he heard the trickle of water ahead. He dipped his hands in the stream, then put them to his mouth, feeling the water run over his dry lips.

Further down he found duck eggs among the reeds and set up a fire on the bank to cook his new-found meal. At heart he was a city boy, but he knew some people lived their whole lives in the wilderness. Natan was determined to survive, and one day he would make it out and have his revenge.

A fiery sun sank over the Imperial City, the sky a rich crimson with streaks of pink-silver. From the trees of South Avenue came the raucous cacophony of birdsong, and street vendors cried their final specials of the day at grossly inflated post-fall prices. Po returned along Washer's Street and through the monastery gates. He carried a basket of peanuts and dried fruit which he dropped off to the kitchen before climbing to the dormitory to pack and re-pack his bag.

"Almost ready?" Dugen asked, making his rounds.

"I don't think I'll ever be," Po said. "Still, I'm leaving in the morning whether ready or not. There's a long way to go before winter."

"I've got something for you," said Dugen, sitting on the corner of the cot. "This is my copy of the *Sudo Ba're Datai*." He handed Po the leather book with peeling edges and dogeared pages. "My teacher gave it to me, and his teacher to him, and so on. I guess it's time for you to have it. If we're not going to be a school any longer, then I suppose you're my last student."

"Thanks," Po said, accepting the book, then looking at his bag. "I'll have to make room. Who *really* needs three pairs of undergarments?"

"I don't suppose," said Dugen. "You can burn this manuscript and stay in Pao'an? It's a heavy burden for such young shoulders."

"No," Po said without hesitation. "Someone died for it. It's not mine to destroy."

"And you're right," Dugen said with a sigh. "You're right. I shouldn't have asked. And besides, Jan'a is a jewel in the Ba're crown. You'll do well there."

"So what will you do?" Po asked.

"Me?" said Dugen, staring at a blank spot on the wall. "I don't rightly know. It's been forty years since I've lived anywhere else." They were quiet for a few minutes as Po rearranged his bag to fit the book. A thought occurred and he looked up.

"You'll remember to give Ashara her money?" Dugen nodded and patted his belt. "Good."

The bells rang for dinner and the two monks made their way to the dining hall. A dozen or so novices huddled in a tight knot, chattering furiously.

"What's going on here?" Dugen demanded. "Silence at the dinner tables. You're not at the Imperial Academy yet." The novices glanced at their teacher and parted ways, revealing the cause of their discussion.

"Anjan!" Po cried. Anjan jumped from his meal and ran across, throwing himself into Po's arms. They spun about and laughed, each talking at once as if they had their entire life stories to complete.

"Alright, alright," Dugen said. "The wanderer returns. Quiet now. Slow down."

"But, but," Po said. "Anjan, you were with the army? Where's Brother Nikodima, Brother Lito and the others?"

"Just me," Anjan said, his brown eyes suddenly downcast. "I ran away. Army life wasn't for me."

"We heard the aid station at Dili was lost. You weren't there were you?"

"No," Anjan said. "I left in the chaos after the battle. I only heard about the aid station yesterday."

"Hold on," Dugen said. "You *ran away*? You *deserted* the army, and now you have your dinner here?" Anjan sniffed and kept his eyes at Dugen's feet. "You have some explaining to do," Dugen continued. "Well I never, I thought I was going to miss this teaching game, and now I remember what drove me to want retirement all these years, Novice Anjan Tadi'a."

Monks *never* used surnames and the two novices flinched as a result.

"I — I couldn't stay there anymore," Anjan said.

"So you thought the monastery would be a safe place. Did you think what'd happen here if you were discovered?"

"Well actually..." Anjan began, but Dugen took him by the arm and led him to the door.

"We're going to see the Venerable Abbot right now. Po, come along please."

Po looked to his friend, then at the serving counter and felt his stomach rumble. It was going to be the last hot meal he would have in a long time. He looked at the disappearing forms heading out the door, shrugged, and hurried after them.

"Ah, Po," Biet said, looking up from his desk. "I've just completed this map, copied from Katavi's *Atlas of Empire*. According to the tables at the back you've got a trip of about seven hundred miles to get to the Graytalons. You'll —" Anjan entered the room. "Anjan?"

"He's back," Dugen said, stepping in behind the novices. "We need a word."

"Yes, certainly," Biet said, clearing his desk and waving at the chairs. "What's it about?"

"Anjan ran away from the army," Dugen said. "*Deserted* in legal parlance." Biet looked at Anjan sternly and folded his arms.

"Is this true?"

"Yes, Venerable Abbot," Anjan said, avoiding eye contact.

"And what does this have to do with Po?" Biet asked.

"Well," said Dugen. "I thought it obvious. Anjan can't stay here and he'd be caught if he went to the Imperial Academy — that is *if* they accepted him. We can make this problem go away by sending him to Jan'a with Po."

"Jan'a?" Anjan stuttered. "That's like... like..."

"South of here, seven hundred miles," Biet said. "Cold, mountains, wyvern. You'll get used to it."

"But," Anjan began. "With Po?" Po looked to the abbot, wondering if he should say anything, but Biet shook his head.

"Yes, with Po. He's transferring there. I can write you a letter of recommendation if you like? Po's leaving in the morning."

"I don't think that's appropriate," Dugen said. "The monastery's already under a heightened sense of scrutiny. It would be best if they left tonight before Anjan can sleep under this roof."

"Tonight," Po and Anjan both said, but Biet raised a hand.

"That would be more appropriate. There's just one other thing. Brother Dovo has asked to go with you. We won't need two cooks now the school's closed, and he'd like to get out of the city."

"Is it wise?" Dugen asked. "You know who he's travelling with." Biet sucked in his breath and knitted his fingers as if looking for the right words.

"He expressed he understood Po's situation. I think it's why he wants to go with them." Dugen's eyes widened then settled down.

"Three monks would make the trip safer."

"You can be responsible for telling him they leave tonight," Biet said. He blew on the map, folded it and handed it to Po. "It's a shame the departure is so rushed. Po, can you see Anjan has a bag and all the things he'll need for the journey?"

The monks gathered in the kitchen. The three companions stood ready, bags on their backs. Each wore a roughspun traveling cloak over their monks' robes. Dovo carried the extra weight of frying pan, implements and camp kettle. They made a noise every time he moved.

"Bedrolls," Bidovi checked off on his fingers. "Sewing kit. Underclothes. Map..."

"We've gone over it already," Brother Dovo said. "We'll be fine."

"Of course," Bidovi said. "I've made you breakfast. Here." He fetched three parcels from the windowsill. "Just heat."

"The gates open at sixth bell," Biet said. "You'll get a few hours sleep before the day begins."

"Remember your daily reflections," Dugen added, fussing over each of their traveling cloaks in turn. "If you get wet, dry your clothes. Eat well. You'll be surprised how hungry you get."

"We know," Po said, desperate to get out the door. He thanked those gathered for their friendship and support over the years and said a few words to each in turn. Brother Bidovi wiped a tear from the corner of his eye with his apron, but the others remained stoic.

Dovo unbolted the kitchen door to the alley. Outside a mangy street dog looked up, startled at the sudden intrusion into its world, and pattered off into the darkness. Po paused on the threshold and looked back into the kitchen. Anjan touched his arm, directing him forward. He resisted at first, then raised a hand, waved goodbye, and with that, he set his mind on the journey ahead.

CHAPTER 14

"The profession of the wristcarver is much misunderstood. In the popular imagination, they perform their diabolical art by cutting into the flesh of their client and removing or rearranging their identifying tattoo. In reality, they prefer much subtler arts and employ many different tricks to change someone's identity."

The Account of Inquisitor Sudotaka

Savani e Unuga walked down the gangplank onto the dock, a single piece of luggage in her hand. Around her sailors secured ropes and laborers struggled under their burdens. The captain looked up from a discussion with a government official.

"I told you we'd make good time," he said. "Just in time for your sister's wedding."

"Thank you," said Savani. She did not wait for the captain to say anything else. She turned her face from the ship and crossed the dock to the stairs leading up the riverbank to the town above.

"Welcome to Tavana," a boy said, tugging at her coat. "Do you need help carrying your luggage? Where you going?"

"I'm fine," she said.

"Come on, miss."

Savani swatted away his hand as it reached for her pocket.

"Touch me and I'll call the guards."

The boy disappeared amidst the dockworkers. Savani reached the top of the stairs, to the broad street that ran along the top of the flood bank. It was faced with shops and warehouses, with streets leading off it as if spokes of a wheel. Tavana rose up the hill behind, its houses and temples culminating in the ramparts of the governor's mansion above. She looked about. The streets looked much the same, and she had not been to Tavana before. She chose the safest option, the middle street. It was not straight like the streets in Pao'an, but twisted this way and that, and at times so steep that steps had been cut into the rock.

Almost every ground floor was a shop. Savani felt eyes on her from under awnings and behind counters. She knew she was just being paranoid. No one in Tavana knew her.

The street opened into a plaza with a statue of a general on a horse and market stalls around the base. Savani picked among the fruit and vegetables, picking out a half dozen apples and a bag of roasted peanuts. Casually, she enquired about a shawl and after a brief period of haggling bought it to replace her scarf, hoping it would throw anyone off her tail.

Near the plaza was a budget tavern. She entered the downstairs common area and regarded the figures in the smoke-filled room. Some looked up at her. A couple of working girls snorted and returned to their gossip.

"How can I help you?" a bearded man asked.

"I'd like a room for the night," Savani said. "Nothing too fancy."

"For the one —"

"Just I," Savani said. "I'm catching up with my husband tomorrow."

"One night then? That can be arranged. What do we call you? You got papers?"

"Tasani," Savani said. "Tasani Mei-Bandoni. Here are my papers." She drew out the leather pouch with her forged documents, procured from a wristcarver upriver. The barman fingered through them with grubby fingers, adding to their history and authenticity.

"I'll show you the room," he said.

The room was dark and bare. The only window was a handbreadth wide and covered in grimey canvas. Savani tested the bed and reconciled herself to a sleepless night. The mattress was stuffed with prickly straw and she felt fleas already jumping on her skin.

"You said two *jet* a night?"

"Yes, payable now," he said, his arms crossed. Savani studied his face and felt her coins in her pocket.

"Do you charge everyone so much?" she asked.

"Just you."

"Me? Why me?" The man unfolded his arms, put his thumbs in his belt and leaned forward until Savani smelt the garlic on his breath.

"You come here, all fancy-like, with a posh accent and square shoulders, but wearing common gear. What am I to make of it? You just walk in, a single woman, not a working girl, with some story about meeting her husband, and I'm supposed to believe it?"

"It's true," Savani said. "And how do you know I'm not a working girl?" The man snorted.

"Two *jet* for the room, and five for my silence." He stuck out his hand. Savani reluctantly paid.

"There you go. I told you there was something to hide."

"You misunderstand," Savani said. The weeks of hiding were getting to her. She was making mistakes. Stupid mistakes.

"Sure I do, sweetie," he said with a wink. "You want me to bring anything up to you?"

"I'm fine," Savani said. "Thank you."

As soon as the door closed, Savani's head fell into her hands and she choked back a sob. She lay down on the bed, too tired and emotional to remove her clothes. In the corner, a rat squeaked and scuttled under the bed.

Some time passed with Savani falling in and out of sleep. The walls were thin and her room was adjacent to the stairwell. People came and went, thumping up and down the stairs, calling hello and goodnight and fumbling for their keys. As the sun outside slowly set, music from downstairs drifted up, and a headboard down the corridor pounded rhythmically against the wall. Savani promised herself she would leave Tavana in the morning.

A key jiggled in the lock. Savani tensed and sat up, but whoever was outside stopped, burped, and moved on to another door. She lay back down again. The evening wore on and the music began to slow and then stopped with the last bell. Patrons were rounded up and kicked out to the street, with drinking and singing continuing outside Savani's window. Sometime later guards moved them along.

When she woke again, it was dark and silent. Not even night workers made their customary cries. The stairs creaked. A rat squealed. Savani was too tired to worry anymore. She cupped her head in her hands on the pillow and rolled over. A fist pounded on her door.

"Open up."

Savani stumbled from the bed, her blanket tangled about her legs. She checked the window but it was too small. A voice outside called for the owner to bring his keys. Savani glanced up at the ceiling. She wondered how secure the boards were. Climbing on the bed she gave them a shove. Dust spilled down, stinging her eyes, but the wood moved. She pushed again and a hole opened up. Desperate now, she began to work furiously at the other beams. The door slammed open, banging against the wall. Savani stood frozen in the lamplight. Hands grabbed her and a hooded figure yanked her wrist into the light. He spat on it and rubbed his thumb over her skin. The tattoo, subtly changed with makeup and ink, became clear.

"It's her," the voice said. A bag was pulled over her head.

A door slammed and a servant crossed the alley with a bucket of slops. Ashara sat in the shadows, counting the footsteps. He saw her and paused.

"What time is it?" Ashara asked. The servant glanced over his shoulder as if he suspected an ambush, then relaxed.

"Just after fifth bell," he said. "You slept here all night?" Ashara nodded. The servant dumped the slops and returned to the house. Ashara got up and dusted herself off. It had been months since she had slept rough and her body was no longer used to it. Her back ached and her arm had gone numb. She noticed the dried blood still on her skin and clothes. Ashara poked her fingers into the cracks between paving stones and the wall of the building she slept against and scooped up tiny amounts of sand and dirt. She rubbed it on her skin until her hands were raw and red, but the blood was gone. The worst of it was on her sleeve, but without water she could do little about it.

The door to the inn opened and the same servant returned. He put a bowl of water on the ground with a few mint leaves sprinkled on top. Ashara pointed to herself in confusion, and then drank the offering.

"Now you best be going before my master wakes," the servant warned, retrieving the bowel.

Ashara thanked him for the kind gesture and wandered down to a street of shuttered shops. It took time to get her orientation, but as the city bells struck six, Ashara came into view of Jan Moga. She suspected the front gate would be locked, so she traipsed around the back and found a monk by the kitchen door with a bucket of water and a brush, scrubbing paint off the bricks.

"What does it say?" she asked, not wanting to startle the monk. He flinched and looked about cautiously, but said nothing. "You're scrubbing words off the wall," Ashara continued. "What do they say?"

"Ba're go home," said the monk.

"Not very imaginative."

"I guess not. We're all born in the Empire." The monk returned to his work as if the conversation was over. Ashara waited awkwardly until he glanced her way again.

"Can I see Master Dugen? Is he about?"

"You know Master Dugen?" He looked her up and down. "It's a bit early, but he might be up." Ashara offered to scrub the wall while the monk went to fetch the master. He gave her the bucket and brush and shut the kitchen door behind him. The bolt clicked from the other side. It took a while but the monk returned with Master Dugen in tow. Dugen removed his glasses and rubbed bloodshot eyes. His jaw was dark with stubble and nothing in his manner indicated pleasure in seeing Ashara.

"Ashara," he said.

"Master Dugen," she replied. He took out a small leather pouch and tossed it to her. It landed in her hands with a *chink*.

"That should be enough," he said. Ashara did not need to count it. Her eyes widened.

"Thanks," she said. "I'm leaving today. Can't stay around here for long." She dared not tell him why. "Can you say farewell to Po for me?"

"No," Dugen said. "He's no longer here."

"Gone?" Ashara said, surprised. "But — where is he?"

"I don't believe I'm at liberty to say," Dugen said. "Now, excuse me as I have the day to prepare for." Dugen scratched his stomach and yawned. "I wish you safety on your journey. Brother Bidovi, I'm done. See you at breakfast." He ambled off to the hall. Ashara was left holding the bucket and brush. Brother Bidovi appeared again and took them off her.

"You're looking for Po?" he asked. Ashara nodded. "They left by the south gate about half an hour ago. If you hurry you might catch up."

There was a commotion at the south gate. Ashara approached with caution. Guards scrambled over a bullock cart and were busy tossing boxes and bags off the back. A Solari ecclesiastic stood nearby in his sky blue robes and yellow cylindrical box-hat, ranting angrily at them.

"You have no right!" he raged. "Get off my cart."

A guard stood on the back of the cart and wiped his nose with the back of his hand.

"This is temple property," he said. "You know full well you can't take this out of Pao'an while the tax is being counted."

"It is *my* property," the man said. A guard opened a sack and removed a gold ceremonial instrument.

"Hey, look what we have here," he called. "Goddess of Mercy this is a lot."

"Nice try priest. I think you should come talk to us." Ashara slipped past them as the Solari ecclesiastic was pulled off to the side. No one seemed interested in bothering with her.

"Hey, wasn't it a Solari who murdered the priest of Nulagia two days ago?"

"So it was," another said. Ashara quickened her pace. She shuddered to think what treatment awaited the Solari priest when he got to the guard house.

Outside the city, the road continued on due south over rolling desolation. What once was farmland was now spoiled and turned to weeds. A village half a mile up the road was a shell. The bricks still stood, mostly, but all the timber frames and thatch had been burnt away. Further on, desolation turned to scrub and scrub turned to woodland with a scattering of villages. Farmers worked in the fields and smoke drifted from the chimneys of the cottages. It was a familiar setting for Ashara.

After two hours with the fields steaming in the sun, Ashara turned a bend in the road. Three figures walked ahead side by side, their heads shaved and their sandals slapping. They looked just like children going off to catechism. She could not help but laugh.

"Po!" she called.

The middle figure spun about, bewilderment on his face.

"Ashara?" His two companions looked to him, but Po ignored them and ran for her. They stopped ten paces apart.

"What are you doing here?" Po asked.

"Going home," she said. "A monk said you'd gone this way."

"Did Master Dugen give you the money?" Ashara tossed the leather pouch in the air and caught it again, the money making the appropriate noise. "So you're going alone? You should wait for a convoy or sign up with an escort. It's not safe."

"No," Ashara said. "I killed a man." Po's mouth dropped. "He attacked me," Ashara added. "It was self-defense. A soldier."

"Are they looking for you?" Po stammered. "Are you okay? Is... is that your blood?" He stepped forward to check her. She put up a hand to stop him.

"I'm fine. But I have to assume they're looking for me." Po did not seem convinced, so she rolled up her sleeve to show him her arm was unhurt. "We're taught to fight as soon as we can walk. The Vu didn't stand a chance."

"I'm sorry," Po said. "I was forbidden to see you again. Maybe if I helped you earlier this wouldn't have happened."

"It's okay. Dugen explained it to me. You didn't make the rules." *You just follow the silly religion.* "And you, why are you leaving? I thought you had a permanent home at the monastery."

"Nothing's permanent," Po said with a shrug. "You're not angry?"

"Not at you," Ashara said.

"Friends?" he asked, offering a hand. Ashara paused, noting the significance of the gesture.

"Friends," Ashara said, accepting the hand.

Po's two companions approached. The taller monk in burgundy put a hand on Po's shoulder. Po jumped.

"What's going on?" asked the monk. "You're full of surprises." Po introduced her, then in turn she was introduced to Anjan in the cream robes, and Dovo in the burgundy. Anjan was about the same age as Po, thin and boney but with a cute, almost childish, face full of freckles. Dovo was considerably older, perhaps in his forties with worry lines and ruddy cheeks.

"We're going to Jan'a," Po said after introductions were made.

"Jan'a?" Ashara asked. She had never heard the name before. Brother Dovo unfolded a hand-drawn map. It was very simple, but it had major landmarks and roads. She studied it.

"Those mountains are the *Tashik Sha*," she said. "Right on the border with Kh'areen."

"We call them the Graytalons," Po said. "Right on the frontier."

"Do you know them?" Dovo asked.

"No," Ashara said. "Only stories. They're about as far from Baki as we are now." As she spoke she noticed Po moving his weight from one leg to the other.

"Can you come with us?" Po blurted once she stopped talking. Anjan and Dovo looked shocked and Dovo apologised for the outburst. He took Po by the shoulder and led him off the road for a talk. Ashara and Anjan exchanged glances. He shrugged.

"No one tells me anything," he said. "So, don't ask me. Anyone would think we're on a secret mission." Anjan had such a boyish charm that Ashara could not help but giggle. "Sounds fun," she said. "Us against the world."

"Rescuing a damsel in distress," Anjan said. "But I guess you'd insist on being the damsel and you're here."

"I could be here to save you," she suggested. Anjan gave a self-deprecating bow and pretended to doff an imaginary hat.

"That, my lady, is more than possible. Indeed, I'd say it's probable." Then he whispered behind his hand as if revealing a great secret. "Po can't even light a fire by himself." Dovo and Po returned to the road.

"Did you want to join us?" Dovo asked. "Po explained to me — nevermind. That's behind us. This isn't the monastery. It would be nice to have someone familiar with the ways of the road."

"It'll mean a longer journey for you," Po warned. "But we're safer in numbers."

"You can leave any time," Dovo added. "But I'd suggest we go to Danma. You can then cut south of the Badlands to Baki. In your situation, they're less likely to watch for you there."

Ashara felt three pairs of eyes looking to her for her answer.

"I'd love to," she said.

CHAPTER 15

"Passing from village to village we came across many shrines to an eagle-headed god. Locals said this was Basatu, the god of strangers and travelers. We found them well stocked with firewood and a reasonable shelter against the elements."

The Travels of Odam Yusufkas the Solari

Natan gripped the edge of a well and looked down into the murky blackness. A chunk of mortar crumbled under his fingers and fell with a splash.

"Water," he gasped through cracked lips. The very act of speaking hurt his throat. There was no bucket to draw the water. Natan sank down with his back against the stone. His vision swam and his head throbbed. For days he had wandered the wilderness heading, he hoped, in the vague direction of home. He had lived off nothing but his wits and had made it this far. *Don't give up,* he told himself.

Through the haze Nimi approached. Natan was unsure if it was a dream or reality. On some level he did not care. She knelt down beside him and kissed his forehead, running her hands over his body and settling her fingers on his crotch. *Nimi,* he whispered in his heart.

A sharp pain jolted him awake. An old man stood at his feet, jabbing him with a walking stick. Natan pulled his one good leg in and covered his vulnerability with his hands. The old man pulled back the walking stick and rested both hands on it, content now it seemed he had Natan's attention. He watched Natan, and Natan watched back. The man was bald, with liver spots. He wore a blue apron and mustard tunic in the peasant style, with leather sandals on his feet.

"Vu'tai or Mamot?" he asked through thin purple lips. Natan took a moment to grasp his meaning, and the man repeated his question.

"Vu'tai," Natan whispered. "Please help me, I can pay."

"Seventh Army?" he asked, ignoring Natan's request for help.

"37th Auxiliary, 14th Banner," Natan answered. "Seventh Army." If the man was an enemy, Natan had no way to escape. The man nodded and walked away, leaning heavily on his stick.

"Come back," Natan gasped. "I can pay… I can pay…" A woman appeared. She was easily as old as the man, though she carried a certain energy about with her. Her clothes were simple but bright, and her gray hair was combed and braided. Yellowing eyes regarded Natan, and then the woman was at his side. The ceramic edge of a jar pressed against Natan's teeth and a sickly, sweet mixture poured into his mouth and down his chin. He gagged and the woman pulled it away.

"More," Natan said instinctively, chasing after the jar with his hands.

"No, no," the woman said. "Not now." Instead she put a chunk of peppery sausage on his tongue and told him to chew.

"Where am I?" Natan asked, finally gathering the strength to sit up and look around. The man stood over his shoulder, watching him.

"Ido village," the old man said.

"Mamot's men are coming," Natan said. "An army."

"We know," said the woman. "His outriders have been here a few times. Most recently last night. They say we're liberated. Foolish men."

"I thought the war was over," Natan said.

"There's no end to war," the woman said, clicking her tongue. "Now, let's get you inside." The woman lent Natan a hand and Natan rose with the help of his crutch. For the first time he was able to fully appreciate his surroundings. He was at the base of a shallow valley. Woodland extended up on either side, but this was broken by terraced farms and fenced-off orchards. Ahead, past a grove of katsura trees, appeared a gathering of a dozen cottages in the country style, each cottage being attached to a walled courtyard. The woman led Natan towards the closest of these, and through the open gate. The man hovered behind, keeping an eye on their guest.

Inside the cottage, Natan was offered a seat by the brick stove, and while vegetable stew was heated up for him, the couple plied him with questions, wanting to know everything about the battle and how Natan had come to be by their well, and what he had seen and knew about the new threat of the Third Army. Natan told them what he knew, and was glad to stop answering their questions when a steaming bowl was placed before him.

"We've had a few stragglers through here," the old man said, watching Natan eat. "But few offered money."

"I'm serious," Natan said, looking up with a spoon before his lips. He did not want to be a burden on anyone. "I can pay."

"No," the man said, a wave of his hand dismissing the idea. "That isn't the Vu way. But it is nice to think you didn't *demand* it. Mamot's soldiers last night wanted a goat slaughtered, and a keg of beer breached."

"And did you give it to them?"

"Of course," the man said with a satisfied grin. "But we put *tavu'na* berries in the beer so they'll get the shits later today. That won't be pleasant on horseback."

Natan stopped chewing and looked down at the mixture in his bowl.

"Don't worry," the woman said, pouring three cups of *kaja* from a boiled kettle. "We don't do that to those who ask nicely."

"I'm glad," Natan said, returning to his meal a little shaken.

"Anyway, what do they call you?" the man asked.

"Natan. Natan Luka-Tudo. I'm from Pao'an."

"Ah," the man said. "A city boy. It explains a lot."

"And can I know the names of my hosts?" The woman clicked her tongue and made some form of a sign with her fingers.

"I'm Pa'tavi, and my husband is Jen'gu. You may call us by those names." Natan sensed some disquiet about sharing this information. He finished his meal in silence, and then Pa'tavi insisted on checking his bandaged leg. She clicked and hissed, making an odd gurgling sound at the back of her throat as she unwound the bandage to reveal a bruised, smelling, discolored leg. She made another sign with her fingers.

"Goddess of Mercy," she said, stretching her hands over the flesh and intoning a prayer. "You'll be lucky to walk straight again. You're going to need plenty of rest."

"But I have to get back to Pao'an —"

"No, I forbid it," the wife said. "Absolutely not. If you walk on that leg again anytime soon you'll be a cripple. We'll put a mat near the stove and I'll rebandage that leg. Did you even notice the splint was cracked? You've given it some rough treatment."

Natan protested some more but it was no use. Jen'gu fetched water and a fresh splint, while Pa'tavi prepared her ointments and bandages. Before long, Natan's leg was bound up once again.

"Now let me have a look at that head," Pa'tavi said with her odd clicking sound. She placed her wrinkled fingers on Natan's scalp and sniffed him, almost like a dog hunting for a scent. Her nostrils flared with each breath.

"There's a darkness over you," she said. "Make yourself comfy on the mat and we'll see what can be done." Natan obliged and Jen'gu gave him a cushion on which to rest his head. Pa'tavi took time to prepare; boiling more water, crushing bark and herbs, straining liquid and cleaning bowls.

Eventually she sat beside Natan. He watched her take coals from the stove and put them in a bowl with herbs and amber. Smoke wafted up and she began to chant an incantation. It was old-Vu, but Natan recognized the invocation of "ram-headed Kive and aurochs-like Sato" and a myriad of other greater and lesser gods.

She lifted up a bowl and offered it to Natan. He sat up and took it in two hands and sipped it hesitantly. The acrid contents were gritty and bitter, with bits of bark floating on the surface, but he drank it all and lay back down. Pa'tavi's incantations droned on and her words drifted from old-Vu to incoherent syllables.

Jen'gu came to the foot of the mat and began to play on a reed flute. The tune was mournful, but it merged in harmony with Pa'tavi's prayers and the smoke pooling about the rafters, like all three became one. Natan felt his body sink as if the floor had turned to feathers and he was weightless. His vision swirled and images from his childhood began to appear as vivid and crisp as fire cutting through the night.

Unbidden, he found himself sitting on his mother's knee, watching Avi scold Dasha for unfinished chores. Dasha answered back and Avi slapped him across the cheek, leaving an angry red mark. Oni covered his eyes with her calloused hands. Another image appeared. He was going off to the temple for classes when Avi snatched up his slate and demanded Natan show him his writing. When not good enough, Avi broke the slate in two and said the classes were not worth the half-*jet* a week. From that day forth, Natan worked in the trading house, counting receipts and doing labor.

Natan's mind began to speed up. Other incidents flashed before him, coming and going like notes from the reed flute, rising and falling and disappearing amidst the smoke. He remembered the day a customer had tipped him for carrying a bag for her, only for Avi to take it from him for *'safe keeping'*. Natan remembered when he started consistently winning fights in the yard, Avi told him there was more to life than brute strength, but then when Natan wanted to resume classes, he was told he was not smart enough and it was a waste of money.

Screams cut into Natan's memory, but they were blunt and felt bruising rather than sharp. He was watching Sado's parents hung, jerking about at the end of ropes. Avi stood there, haggling over the price of his son. Natan felt a burning rage. *I hate him,* he heard himself scream. *I hate him.* An arm was around Natan's throat. He could not breathe. Suddenly he was awake, in the one-room cottage throwing up into a bucket while Pa'tavi held his hair back. He realized he was crying, but the noise, the sensation, did not seem to come from him; he was disembodied, floating about inside his body, but not of it.

"It's okay," Pa'tavi clucked. "It's okay." Natan struggled to understand her words, hearing them as pure sound devoid of meaning. Then he realized he was babbling himself, spilling out his thoughts on his father and unable to stop. He sank back down, his vision fading with the sounds of battle raging in his head. At once he was in the Dili Valley staring over the rim of his shield. Steel clashed and people screamed. A spear tip came for his head and just as it grazed him the attacker stumbled back and was crushed by a spearhead the size of a man. Natan spun about. This was not part of his memory. Beside him stood a god-like creature, a giant cow on two legs, no — a minotaur, its eyes burning a fiery red, and its body covered in rippling muscle. In its enormous hands it wielded a spear with a shaft as thick as Natan's thigh, thrusting it again and again into the Reformist lines.

The battle took on familiar forms once again and Natan saw the lines break apart as the air buzzed with iron slugs. Slingers from amidst the enemy ranks launched volley after volley into the advancing formations. Natan knew what was coming. He braced for the pain. Then the minotaur was out front, taking the brunt of the iron slugs itself and striking them back into the enemy with a cart-sized shield. One of the ricochets struck Natan's leg, another his head, but he did not fall. Instead the minotaur had him in his hands and carried him out of the battle before laying him tenderly on the ground, out of harm's way. The vision faded.

"Aurochs-like Sato," Pa'tavi chanted. "Lord of the Battle, protect your young warrior. Shroud him in the armor of your protection. Bless him with victory in battle, and a place with you in the hereafter. Aurochs-like Sato, Lord of the Battle, heal this young warrior. Let him be as tribute to you..."

"I see him," Natan moaned. "I see him." Looking up at the ceiling, the smoke from the censer formed shapes that came to life. Two eyes looked down on him, red and fiery. Natan's moans caused Pa'tavi to pray more furiously.

"Aurochs-like Sato, Lord of the Battle, he who is present, accept this young man. Let him be as tribute to you. Aurochs-like Sato, Lord of the Battle, make him your vessel. Repair his body and soul."

Once again Natan found himself sitting over the bucket, vomiting, and crying, and moaning, somehow numb to his senses, yet aware of the noise and the turmoil within his head. This time Pa'tavi did not sit behind him holding his hair, but knelt over him straddling his legs. Her wild eyes and hair shivered amidst the smoke. She took the bucket away and cupped his hands in her's, massaging life into them with her fingers as she chanted.

"Aurochs-like Sato, Lord of the Battle, he who is present…" Natan felt full sensation return to his fingers and palms and sank back, but Pa'tavi prevented him by tugging him up. His head lulled and his eyes drooped, but he felt something press in around his fingers — no, his fingers pressed in around it. His hands held a wooden carving of aurochs-like Sato, Lord of the Battle, uncannily familiar to the one he saw in his vision. As Pa'tavi chanted, she took a strip of red silk and wrapped it around Natan's hands, with the carving within. She had Jen'gu stop playing his flute and help her hold it, dripping wax from a simple peasant's candle onto the red silk to seal it. From a small bag she scattered bone disks on the mat beside Natan, picking out each that was face up, and again and again until only one was left. There was a carving engraved on it, but it made no sense to Natan. Pa'tavi pressed the carving down into the wax seal, leaving an impression.

"Aurochs-like Sato, Lord of the Battle, he who is present…"

Light streamed into the cottage, sending Natan falling back onto the mat, his world continuing to spin, but now he could see nothing but light as white as the sun and a thousand stars. The feeling, or lack of it, in his body began to dissolve, replaced with feelings of joy and fullness. It was not that Avi was forgotten, but that he did not matter.

"… accept now this offering, Lord of the Battle, and may this young man be reborn." Warm liquid splashed onto his skin and dribbled down his cheeks. Some fell onto his tongue, sending off waves of sensory information: *blood*.

"As a child comes with blood, now accept this young man; Natan Luka-Tudo, adopted of Sato."

※

Tuno Bago-Nula stood amidst a sea of tents and raised his arms. Soldiers looked back at him and snickered.

"Well, aren't you going to search me?" Tuno demanded. The officer in charge gave a polite bow and motioned towards a large tent.

"General Mamot doesn't require it. He said the day he worries about a gout-ridden old man is the day he stops being general." Tuno lowered his arms and bit back a snarky reply. He accepted the return of his walking stick and hobbled towards the tent.

Mamot sat alone behind a raised table, eating his dinner with pudgy fingers. Tuno effected a courtly bow.

"Ah," Mamot said in his booming baritone. "My old commander. Tell me, how much did Jano pay you to betray our Emperor?" Tuno's cheeks flush. *Control your tongue.*

"He paid with peace," Tuno said. "That's all I asked for." A lie, he knew, but it felt better.

"I heard fifty thousand *gotti*," Mamot said, ripping off a leg of roasted fowl and stuffing it in his mouth. He chewed it noisily with his mouth open. "No wonder Jano is taxing this and taxing that. He'll bankrupt the Imperial treasury."

"General," Tuno said. "I didn't come here under a flag of truce to be insulted like this. I bring a message from Chief Minister Jano and the Emperor."

"Fifty thousand gold and now a glorified errand boy," Mamot quipped. "Go on, I'm all ears." Tuno straightened his shoulders and drew a deep breath. Mamot put down his food and leaned forward in mock interest.

"Chief Minister Jano wishes to extend the hand of peace," Tuno began. "He understands you marched on Tomi's orders. Tomi is now dead, and the war is over. This leaves you in an awkward position. Take your armies and go home. All will be forgiven." Mamot belched and put a hand to his mouth.

"Pardon," he said, dabbing his lips with a clenched fist. "But how long will he let us live once we go home? Jano is only generous while our army is in the field. And who says my men want to go home? They've tasted blood." Tuno eyed up his former subordinate. *He wants to be paid*, Tuno thought. But he could not appear too eager.

"This is a one-off offer," Tuno said. "If your army remains in the field, it shows a clear intention to stay in rebellion."

"See, we have a problem," Mamot said. "Did you see my levies? They've been promised glory and plunder. Do you think they will go home so easily? They couldn't face their families empty-handed. And what about my Astirti? They've heard of the persecution."

"His Grace Jano respects all subject peoples," Tuno said. "He does however limit their activities in the Imperial capital. But this does not pose a threat to their interests. I'm sure the Astirti can understand. Don't they limit what Vu can do in their capital? It is the way of things." Mamot laughed and pounded the table with a fist.

"Wait, you're not joking?" he said, stopping. "That's first-grade dreadbeast dung! How are the other peoples of the Empire supposed to take these changes? How can they trust a traitor turned tyrant?" Tuno nodded and stood stoically before Mamot's passion.

"What would you suggest?" Tuno asked.

"I have eighty-thousand men," Mamot said. "Two hundred and fifty-thousand gold *gotti* should convince them to go home."

"That is more than a year's pay per man," Tuno protested. "Be reasonable and we might end this bloodshed."

"I am being reasonable," Mamot said, emphasising each word by stabbing his index finger on the table. "There's a lot they'll have to forgive."

"And your army is innocent?" Tuno said. "How many people did you put to the sword? Thirty thousand? You're lucky you aren't put on trial."

"Dili betrayed the Emperor," Mamot said with a shrug. "Of course, I didn't know it was you at the time." Tuno narrowed his eyes. *Of course Mamot knew. He just wanted the plunder.*

"Still, that's a lot of families to be paid off. They'll all seek the Emperor's justice."

An officer took the opportunity to indicate he had a message. Mamot put out a broad, hairy hand and accepted the note. He read it, put it in a candle and let it burn until the flames licked his skin and he dropped it on the table.

"Interesting," Mamot said. "Did you tell Jano that Tomi's wife and grandson survived?"

Tuno stiffened.

"What business is that to you?" he snapped. "They have no legal title."

"And General Nulu," Mamot said. Tuno glanced involuntarily to the tent flap.

"It isn't common knowledge," Tuno admitted.

"I think," Mamot said. "You have not told Jano of this failure of yours. He'll be very surprised to learn the grandson of the martyred Tomi yet lives, a miraculous survivor of your betrayal. And while the boy has no legal title he was godschild to the Emperor. The people like heroes."

"He's four years old," Tuno said icily.

"So were you once," Mamot said. "Now you're an old man who gets up six times a night to piss. I bet it's like milking a calabash through a pinhole."

"There's truth to that."

"I think our price just went up," Mamot said. "Though you should now consider your own position. Jano doesn't forgive betrayal. You betrayed your last master and now you hide critical information from your current. You play a dangerous game." *It's true.*

"I must report to Jano," Tuno said. "I bid you farewell."

"When the time comes," Mamot said. "I suggest the poison *kavili* washed down with hard liquor. Quick and mostly painless."

"The advice is appreciated," Tuno said, a hand on his acidic stomach as he departed the tent.

Ashara looked up at the inky black clouds rolling in from the west, bringing with them the gray haze of rain on distant fields. It would not be long before they were all drenched through to the skin.

"We need to find a place to camp," she said. The monks seemed less concerned.

"They said there is a village over this hill," Po said.

"I don't think we'll make it." Thunder rumbled above and a sudden gust blew leaves and twigs across the road. Ashara pulled her clothes tighter around her and braced for the inevitable dollops of cold rain.

They rounded the top of the hill and looked down into a steep valley. At the bottom lay a village beside a river with a mill and water wheel. Ashara was right, they did not make it. Halfway down the zig-zag path the heavens opened and the rain came in torrents, thrashing the trees and causing rivulets to run down muddy slopes. By the time they got to the village,

Ashara's clothes clung to her and her shoes *squelched* with every step.

"Over there," Brother Dovo said, pointing out to them a shrine to the travel god Basatu. The companions headed for it and were relieved to find the shrine well stocked with dry firewood. Soon they had a fire going and water on the boil.

Ashara watched Po carefully unpack his bag and check the contents.

"You do this every time it rains," she said.

"I don't want anything ruined," Po said with an edge of defensiveness. "There are books in there."

"It's three weeks since we left Pao'an," Ashara said. "It has rained more than ten times. Those are oil skins. Your things are safe."

"I hope so," Po said.

"Can't be too careful," Dovo said. "Now who wants *kaja*?" They all agreed and settled down. Ashara was happy for the distraction. Three weeks on the road and some of her companions' habits were getting to her. When travelling, Kh'areen aimed for speed. These Ba're took their time. Kh'areen avoided contact with locals. Po and his fellows stopped at every village to offer assistance and take alms. To Ashara, their progress felt painfully slow.

"Well, this is it for the day," Ashara noted as they drank their *kaja*. The others nodded their agreement. Time did not matter so much to them.

The eagle-headed statue of Basatu looked down at her from his alcove. Some ancient artisan had carefully crafted the eyes out of obsidian. It had a terrifying aspect, at least to her Kh'areen sensibilities.

"Don't you find it odd sleeping in a Vu'du shrine?" she asked. The monks looked to each other then Po shrugged.

"Where else will we sleep?"

"But you don't believe in their gods."

"This wasn't built by their gods," Dovo said. "It was built by mere humans for mere humans."

The monks finished their *kaja* and settled down to reflection. Ashara retreated to the back wall and rested with her back against the bricks. The monks' lips moved silently in the *Kime ki're kima ka*. Their fingers slipped soundlessly over their reflection beads. She wondered what it was like to pray to no god. Brother Dovo and Po had tried to explain the concept, telling her it was not *praying* as she knew it. Instead they were focussing on the mantra and thus gaining deeper insight into the five tenets.

After a while, villagers appeared. Ashara was now familiar with the process. She watched them place their gifts of food before the monks and then sit opposite them. Some carried out their own rituals, while others just watched the strangers with vacant eyes.

Dovo's hand stirred and his fingers rang a small bell he kept around his wrist. This signalled the end of their devotions. Almost immediately, villagers began talking and motioning for attention, pushing their offerings forward for the monks. One had a letter, sent from a son in the army. Po took it and read it out to her. Another had a rash and a third wanted a recording of his final will and testament.

Others came and it was late afternoon before all the requests were met. As Dovo prepared the evening meal, a farmer stood under a nearby tree watching them. Water dripped on him, but he appeared unconcerned. He just watched.

"What do you think he's doing?" Ashara whispered. Dovo and Po managed not to look, but Anjan glanced over at the man.

"I don't know," Po said. "Don't worry about it."

"Probably first time he's seen Ba're monks," Anjan said.

"Travelling with a Kh'areen woman," Dovo added. "This isn't the main road to anywhere and these people don't see outsiders that often. They are probably equally suspicious and fascinated by us."

"I don't like it," Ashara muttered. "It's not right. What if he's a thief or a bandit? He's watching us for something."

"No one robs Ba're monks," Po said. "It isn't done. That's why we are forbidden to travel with money."

"I have money," Ashara hissed, then glanced about self-consciously.

"He doesn't know that."

"How do you know?"

"Well," he said. "Did he look inside your bag?"

"No. But he could guess."

"Guessing and knowing are —" Po began before Dovo cut him off.

"Dinner's ready," the cook said. "Now eat up before it gets cold."

The next day Ashara was extra cautious, but nothing came of it. They wound their way up the valley, down into another and out onto an open plain. As night fell, they saw lights in the distance and Ashara looked forward to a warm fire and food in her belly.

"Won't be long now," Dovo said. "I can almost taste the *kaja*. Who wants me to use tonight that cheese we've been saving?"

"And the peppered sausage," Anjan said. "What about the *saka* beans?"

"They need soaking. We can do them tomorrow if we find water."

"Sausage, cheese and warm bread," Po said. "I hope they have bread to spare." The mention of food made Ashara's stomach rumble.

"I can buy some flour next time we have the chance," she suggested. "Then we don't have to rely on charity at every stop."

"A noble gesture," Dovo said. "But it's heavy. It'll just weigh us down. So far the locals have been generous, and we've repaid their kindness ten fold."

The smell of log fires drifted towards them on the breeze and Ashara knew they were getting close. Soon she could see the dark forms of cottages and a lone tree by what looked like the village well.

"Do you see a shrine?" she asked. Her companions each replied in the negative, though it was too dark for them to be certain.

"Stars are out," Dovo said. "Doesn't look like it'll rain. Let's sleep by the well." No one could come up with a better idea so they found a dry patch and dropped their stuff.

A dog barked from one of the houses and then another and another. Voices carried in the night across a vegetable garden. Anjan was just getting a little fire going when doors opened and three torches appeared.

"Please be warm bread," Anjan said. "Please be warm bread."

"They don't sound friendly," Ashara said. She checked her knife and sling and kept them ready beneath her cloak. She stood and placed herself slightly to the back of Dovo, giving her room to maneuver if they were in danger.

204

"They'll be fine," Anjan said. "Come sit down."

"Let's see what they have to say first," Po said, clearly following Ashara's lead. Anjan relented and stood up as the three figures became clear in their firelight. Four big dogs strained on their leads and a barrel-chested man held them back with a clenched fist. He wore a blacksmith's apron and had a thick black beard with flecks of gray. His companions were rough village types with matted hair and lean bodies.

One of the dogs growled and that set the others barking until the blacksmith yanked on their leads and shouted a command.

"Good evening," Dovo said as soon as the dogs were quiet. "We're Ba're monks on the road from Pao'an. Is anyone in your village in need of assistance?" The big man narrowed his eyes and glanced back at his two fellows.

"We don't know you," he said. "No one trusts strangers around here. We'd be a lot happier if you moved on."

"Moved on?" Po said. "Now?"

"Now," the blacksmith said. "No offense to you personally. Strange word about. We're just not taking chances." Anjan took a step forward to say something and a dog growled and snapped at him. The leash pulled tight feet from his face. Anjan yelped and hurried to the back of their group.

"We have come a long way," Dovo said. "I'm sure you won't deny travelling monks a place to sleep."

"I said what I have to say. Move on. Pick your stuff up and we'll escort you out."

They were left no choice but to agree and packed their things again. Ashara made a concerted effort to stay out of their torchlight and never let her hand stray far from her blade. She was convinced, though she did not know how, that these men were connected with the watcher the night before.

"How peculiar," Dovo said once they were escorted beyond the fields on the other side of the village and the men returned to their homes. "I've never been treated like that before. They looked angry."

"Maybe they don't like Ba're," Po suggested.

"Rubbish," Dovo replied. "It hardly matters to the common folk outside the cities."

"You should try being Kh'areen," Ashara said. "No one wants us in their villages."

"So they were angry at you?" Anjan asked.

"No," said Ashara. "They couldn't tell. And I don't think they were angry. I think they were trying to be confident. But you could tell they were scared."

"You mean frightened?"

"Yes."

"Of us?" asked Po. "Why scared of us?"

"Maybe not of us," she said. "But scared of something."

They set up camp on a barren stretch of road. Ashara cast about for signs of water but found none in the dark. She sat and watched Dovo get a fire going, but it was pitiful and made a lot of smoke with little flame.

"Looks like it is sausage and cheese tonight," Dovo said. "This won't heat anything."

"No *kaja*?" Anjan asked.

"Nope," Dovo said.

"Better save the water," Ashara said. "I don't think we'll get more until tomorrow."

After their simple meal the monks went to sleep, wrapped in their robes, using their bags as pillows. Ashara stayed awake worrying about the day. Before drifting off, she laid her sling beside her with a stone in it.

"Alright, wake up," a voice barked.

Ashara sat bolt upright. The three men from the night before stood ten feet away, their dogs sniffing the remains of dinner. Ashara was up in an instant, slinge ready. Po, Anjan, and Dovo yawned and looked about in groggy surprise.

"On your feet," the blacksmith ordered. "And put the weapon down."

One of the men now carried a hunting bow. He drew back an arrow and aimed it at Ashara. She looked down at her sling and up at the man.

"Stop," Po said, stumbling between Ashara and the archer. "What are you doing?"

"Out of the way," Ashara hissed.

"Put the bow down," Po insisted, ignoring her. Ashara returned the sling stone to its pouch. Her hand brushed the handle of her knife, but it was pointless at ten feet against an archer.

"What's the meaning of this," Dovo demanded, rubbing sleep from his eyes.

"You're coming with us," the blacksmith said. "You three and the witch."

"Witch?" Ashara spat. "You think I'm a —"

"Keep those lips shut," the archer said in a voice born of terror. Ashara spotted the other man make a sign with his hands. She had seen that motion before when villagers warded off evil. She rolled her eyes.

"Right, grab your things," the blacksmith ordered. "You're going to walk in front of us nice and slowly like. No fast moves. Nothing stupid, okay? If I think you're going to play games, I let go of the dogs. Got it?"

"Where — where are we going?" Po asked.

"To meet someone. That's all you need to know. Now move it."

CHAPTER 16

"Of the Ba're there are two major schools. The Sudo Ba're are by far the most common, but the Tika Ba're capture the popular imagination. The name means Narrow Path and these ascetics reject civilized life, taking up lives in the wild."

Master Suvu's Life of a Scholar

Ido echoed with singing and the crashing of cymbals. Natan watched as excited children threw branches of the *daka* bush onto a large fire. The dried seed pods exploded with *cracks* and *bangs*. Ju'gen played his reed flute accompanied by a neighbour on the lute, and villagers danced merrily in the open space between the fire and the musicians. The whole valley had turned out for the marriage of two of their young ones.

"Don't they dance in Pao'an?" a woman asked, offering Natan her hand. She was about ten years older than Natan and large for a local. Not fleshy as some in Pao'an became, but big boned from a good diet and hard work.

"Sorry," Natan said, indicating his crutch. It was three weeks since his arrival in Ido and while his recovery was miraculous, he wanted to be careful.

"That's no good is it," the woman said, and asked if he wanted a drink instead. Not wanting to say no twice, Natan accepted the offer. She returned shortly with two tankards of locally made fermented potato liquor mixed with crushed fruit.

"There you are," Pa'tavi said, appearing around the corner of a cottage. Natan was caught with the tankard to his lips. She took it off him and chugged it back, finishing the tankard in one go.

"Don't look at me like that," she said, clicking her tongue here and there at random points. "You need to look after yourself. No drinking today. And you Nasali, you know better than to get our guest drunk."

"One drink won't hurt," said the woman. "All a bit if fun, eh? He looks like he could do with some." Nasali winked at Natan as she sauntered off to rejoin the party.

"Keep an eye on that one," Pa'tavi said. "Her husband died in an accident last year. She's trouble."

"Don't worry about me," Natan said raising his hands in mock surrender. Pa'tavi pointed towards the groom's home.

"They'll announce lunch soon. Come on, we'll go together."

Natan took Pa'tavi's arm and they walked over to the house. It was early for lunch, but already some guests gathered in the yard smoking, spinning yarn and catching up on the local gossip.

Large trestle tables were laid out around the yard, weighed down with fresh vegetables cooked with butter, garlic and plenty of cracked pepper. Natan cast his eyes over steaming piles of butternut squash, pumpkin, carrot, cabbage, leek, potato and parsnip and his stomach growled. The groom's father roasted a sheep over an open fire. The mother fussed with dinner plates.

"Just be polite and stay off the drink," Pa'tavi repeated for the dozenth time.

Dinner was called and guests packed around the tables. Natan looked about at the generations present and was quite suddenly irked at their cheerfulness. *Don't they know there's a war on?* Pa'tavi passed Natan a platter of potatoes and nudged him.

"I know what dark thoughts haunt you," she said, tapping her nose. "But be cheerful for their sake." Pa'tavi nodded towards the bride and groom at the head of another table. The groom wore fresh blue linens, and the bride was adorned in white with a crown of flowers upon her head. They laughed with their friends. *Nimi*, Natan thought. She would have been the same age as the bride.

One of the guests called a toast, then another and another. Pa'tavi made sure Natan's tankard was always filled with plain blackberry juice without the added alcohol.

"So you're a soldier eh?" a man from up the valley asked. "I heard about you."

"Good things I hope," Natan said awkwardly.

"Oh good enough. You were with that — what was his name dear?" the man asked leaning over to his wife.

"Jona," the wife said.

"Jano," Natan corrected. "General Jano. I was just an auxiliary."

"Still, a soldier's a soldier," the man said. "I fought once. Years ago now." He held up a hand and showed off the stumps of two missing fingers.

"Battle of Totna Field," he said. "Lucky they didn't cut my arm off."

"Come on dear," the wife said, pulling her husband's hand under the table. "This is a wedding — no time to talk about missing fingers."

"Righty-o," he said. "So what did you do before the war?" Natan explained how his family owned a trading house and they talked for a while about the day to day activities of doing business in the city. It was a difficult subject, and the more Natan talked, the more he realized he did not miss it. He missed the idea of home, but not home itself. It made him sick to think he would have to go back there.

"Your parents must be worried," the man said, suffering the reproving glare of his wife for hinting at the war again.

"Oh, I don't think so," Natan said. "My mother will. Maybe. Avi, my father, well, he probably hasn't noticed I'm gone." Pa'tavi put her hand on his shoulder and suggested Natan try the lamb.

"Absolutely delicious," she said. "Such a treat." The man took the hint and turned to another guest.

"They don't see many newcomers," Pa'tavi whispered. "You don't have to answer every question, Son of Sato."

"I know," Natan said, his face downcast.

A shout went up from the head table. An uncle of the bride announced it was time for the bedding ceremony. Natan twisted in his seat to watch. Male guests went for the groom. Female guests went for the bride. As was customary, the pair of newlyweds resisted and tried to get away, but they were grabbed and hoisted on guests' shoulders. The parents led the way to the couple's new home next door while Jen'gu and the musicians followed behind.

Natan got up and with Pa'tavi followed the shrieks of merriment. The house was too small for everyone to fit inside and guests spilled from the cottage and through the yard. Natan could hardly see a thing from the back, but he was familiar with what happened. He shuddered at the thought of one day bedding his own wife with nothing but a curtain between them and their parents. It was enough for any sane person to remain a bachelor.

Cheers indicated the deed was done. Nasali caught Natan's eye and she winked at him.

Partying continued into the evening. As darkness fell over Ido, villagers threw logs onto the fire and took up a lively dance with clapping and singing. Someone found a drum kit, and the lute player from before joined in.

Natan clapped with the beat but sat off to the side. The fire held his attention with some primordial fascination. It was easy to slip off into a melancholic dream state, seeing images in the flames. He failed to notice Nasali until her hand rubbed his thigh. She leaned in, her breath playing hot across his neck.

"You're a quiet one," she said. "I like that."

"I don't feel well," Natan said. Nasali scowled. "Nothing personal," he added. "I think I'll go for a walk... alone. Need some fresh air and a clear head." Natan headed into the night away from the partying, wandering aimlessly along village paths, through orchards and fields. He came to a boundary marker and sat resting his hands and chin on his crutch. A cool wind rippled through his hair and he sensed the distinct first bite of autumn in the air. His thoughts turned to home. Out there, somewhere, Pao'an slept under the same sky. He stared upwards, wondering what his parents were doing. *Did they know Dasha was dead? Has Dan returned? Do they miss me? Wait, do they know I'm alive?* That sent a chill down his spine. *They'll think I'm dead.* He glanced down at the valley. From his position on the hill he had a good view of the wedding party. The bonfire burnt hot and angry, lighting the village square. Dark figures moved about it, but these were not farmers celebrating, these were armed men. Natan recognized some shapes, Pa'tavi included, backing into the shelter of a courtyard. He frowned. *That's not right.*

A scream drifted up to his ears. Natan swore to himself and tested his weight on his leg.

Dawn broke over the plains. A chill wind came from the south blowing drizzle in its wake. Po looked for a sign of their destination. Any number of villages could be folded into the landscape, but none were visible. The road wound on out of sight between hill and dale. At times were ruins of some old homestead, or what remained of a chimney, then only bricks one atop another.

"Where are we going?" he asked.

"You'll see," the man said. "Now keep quiet."

Po bowed his head against the wind. Ashara walked out in front with Dovo and Anjan behind. Po took up the rear, only feet between him and the dogs behind. He glanced over his shoulder. The blacksmith grunted and a dog snapped. Po quickened his pace.

The road rounded a knoll and descended steeply. The plains fell away and a great crack rent the land, broadening into a valley of rusty autumn trees. Po could not help himself.

"We're going down there?" he asked. No one replied. A wooden bridge crossed a stream and beyond that were two pillars, one on either side of the road, worn smooth with the ravages of time, though some shallow scars indicated where once characters had been chiseled into the surface. The road forked after this, one rising back onto the plain, and the other cutting deep into the forest with trees forming a roof above them.

"To the left," the blacksmith barked, indicating the forest path. After a few minutes Ashara stopped and Dovo bumped into her.

"We're being watched," she said.

"Yes," the blacksmith said, his voice less certain than before. "Keep going." Po hesitated. Leaves rustled and boughs creaked and groaned. Twigs snapped and all seven of them turned to the source. A figure shrouded in robes of black and gray observed them. His face was in shadow and his feet were bare against the forest floor. He raised a hand and extended a finger towards Po and his companions.

"Is this them?"

The blacksmith swallowed hard and tried a few times to get his words out.

"T—Th—These are them," he said. "As you requested."

"Good," said the man. "You can go." The blacksmith and his two followers touched their foreheads in a sign to ward off evil, thanked the figure, and fled the way they had come. Po looked to his companions. The four had unconsciously backed into a tight knot. Ashara's hand strayed to her sling.

"Don't," Po hissed. She flicked him a frosty glare. "Violence won't help us," he clarified. "Let's see what he wants."

"He's just one man," Ashara whispered. "I can take him."

"Po's right," Dovo said. "Stick together. No sudden moves." Anjan gave a squeak and Po felt fingers close around his elbow.

"Po," Anjan hissed. "There are more behind us." Po saw them too; not just behind but on all sides. Figures shrouded in dark cloth, tatty and rugged, approached barefoot and silent against the background noise of creaking trees and rustling leaves. The first figure drew back his hood to reveal a pockmarked, shaved head and dark sunken features.

"He's Ba're," Ashara yelped.

"Hold on," Dovo said. "Not every bald man is Ba're."

"Silence," the man said. "You are surrounded. Do not touch any weapons and no harm will come to you."

"Hear that?" Dovo said to Ashara. "Hands off." She snorted yet held her tongue. Po brushed a hand against hers and she squeezed it in reassurance.

"What is it you want?" Po called.

"You will come with us," the man said. "I will lead the way. Stick to the path and you will be safe."

"And where do you take us?"

"That, you will soon know," said the man. Po nodded. They were out of options. He hoped the others saw it the same way, and that he was not missing anything.

"Dovo?" Po asked.

"We do as he says," the monk said. "But stay alert."

Surrounded by shrouded figures, the four companions followed the leader. The path meandered this way and that, occasionally blocked by a fallen log, or grown over by vegetation. As they ventured deeper into the forest, a foul odor began to cling in the air.

"*Pew*," Ashara said. "It smells like Pao'an."

"More like an offal pit," Dovo said, twitching his nose. "Rot and decay."

"Pao'an," Ashara said again. Their hosts remained silent. Anjan pointed out a skeleton sitting upright against a tree. Shreds of sinew remained and wet rags clung to the bone. Soon they saw another. Both were in meditation positions, their legs crossed under them and their hands in their laps. Po began to grow suspicious. Something was nagging at him but he could not put his finger on it. In the back of his mind puzzle pieces were coming together.

They broke out into a forest clearing. Around the outside were two dozen raised platforms about ten feet off the ground and just big enough for a person to comfortably sit on. On each of the platforms was a figure facing inwards, their heads bowed and their fingers working reflection beads. In the center of the clearing was an ancient gnarled tree with rusty gold leaves. On a platform beneath this tree sat a man in solemn contemplation.

"I got it," Po exclaimed to his companions. "They're Tika Ba're. I've read about them. I'm sure of it. This forest is their monastery. And *that* is an Oblivion Circle."

"I knew they were Ba're," Ashara said, directing her words to Dovo.

"They're not Ba're," Dovo insisted.

"To be fair," Po said, feeling a rush of confidence returning. "They sort of are." Then to Ashara he said; "The Ba're you know are *Sudo* Ba're of the Great Path. The *Tika* Ba're are of the Narrow Path."

"So they're Ba're," Ashara said, confirming her initial assessment.

"A similar name does not a religion make," Dovo quipped. "We're as different as bread is to wine. Look at them."

"I think I slept through that class," Anjan said. "What's an Oblivion Circle?"

"It's their renunciation of life," Po said. "They climb onto those platforms and never come down.

"Never?" Ashara gasped.

"Never," Po said. Their guide turned upon them.

"Quiet!" he commanded. "We're here. Speak when you are spoken to and do as you're told." He walked them over to the man beneath the ancient tree. Their escorts withdrew to take up positions behind them.

"Kneel," their guide ordered, and they knelt. Po and Ashara exchanged glances. Po mouthed a word of support to her. She frowned and mouthed something he didn't understand.

"You kneel," their host said, raising his voice. "Before the Venerable Votna, Patriarch of the Vuku Tika Ba're." Venerable Votna raised his head at the mention of his name. The man was sickly looking, but not too old. His clothes were patched from bits of dark cloth; no two pieces being the same, and his feet were bare and crossed under him. Po shuddered to think how long Votna had remained on his platform. There were stories of them surviving for years in sun and rain, served by diligent supporters day and night.

"Speak, who are you?" Votna ordered. "And where do you go?" Dovo dipped his head and spoke for them all.

"I am Brother Dovo, this is Novice Po and Novice Anjan, and that is Ashara of the Kh'areen. We are on our way to Jan'a."

"And you are of the Sudo Ba're?"

"That is correct," Dovo said. "We come from Jan Moga in the Diocese of Pao'an."

"Yet you travel in the company of a Kh'areen witch."

"Witch?" Ashara said. "I'm not a witch." Venerable Votna made a point of ignoring her. He instead motioned to Dovo to explain himself. Dovo shook his head.

"She is not a witch," Dovo said. "Peculiar in her manner and customs, but not a witch. She was of assistance to our monastery and now she honors us on our journey."

"Does she believe in Tanri?" Votna probed. "Does she believe this *spirit* listens to her prayers, and does she invoke his name when she needs help? Does she not then try to manipulate the world using false, heretical spiritual powers?"

"I don't know," Dovo said. "You would have to ask her." Votna sneered and Ashara folded her arms. Po leaned over to Dovo.

"The Tika Ba're won't talk to women," he whispered in his ear. Dovo nodded and scratched his chin.

"I cannot answer you," Dovo continued. "For I don't know. But I find it irrelevant. We are lawful travellers on the Emperor's road. It's wrong to detain us and you must set us free at once."

"It *is* relevant," Votna said. "You are accused of being false monks, taking advantage of ignorant villagers and abusing their hospitality. This is our domain, and we will protect the spiritual wellbeing of the prefecture." Dovo bowed his head and murmured to Po for assistance.

"I'm but a cook. Po you are quicker with your tongue." Po locked his eyes with Votna.

"With respect," Po began. "The villages don't belong to you. I saw no Ba're structures, nor hands of Dasanika... but I did see shrines to the travel god Basatu and boundary markers dedicated to Nulagia. They are simple Vu'du folk who gave food to us, and in turn we helped with their basic, temporal needs. This is an ancient custom and well you know..."

"Enough," Votna growled. "You did so under false pretenses. We were told you travelled with a witch, that you deceived the villagers as to your status as monks. And this you did in our domain, making it our problem."

"We are monks," Po said. "And if you call my companion a witch again this audience is over. Now let me speak. You don't care about the villagers. They're scared of you. They don't understand what happens in this forest. Do they even understand you are Tika Ba're? No. You take their offerings and the moment competing monks step on your turf, you harass us and spread vile rumors to discredit us."

"Save me your insolence," Votna said. "You call yourself Ba're, yet you make bold pronouncements for a novice. A novice should be seen and not heard. What do they teach you in Pao'an? The Sudo Ba're is the great path to nowhere, with answers to nothing. You have become weak hiding in your cities, with fresh clothes in your fine monasteries. When was the last time you fasted, or sat the Oblivion Watch? When was the last time you meditated on a rotting corpse or sat in the rain reciting the sacred *Kyomo Kyara Khama Kho*?"

"We take refuge in the Five Tenets," Po said. "You miss his point if you swap his teachings for a veneer of similitude. There is nothing magical about the old language or manner of speaking."

"It's tradition," Votna said. "But come, let us see what is in those bags... for what possessions does a monk have need of, or is it contraband?"

"No," Po said. "Have you now become robbers?" There was a tug on Po's shoulder strap and he turned to see shrouded figures pulling at their bags. "Let go," Po shouted and pulled his bag from the nearest figure's grip. The figure let go and Po went sprawling on the ground.

"Stop!" Anjan called. "See, look in mine." He opened it and pulled items out one by one. "Food, a razor, a sewing kit, bandages, a bottle of *botke* oil for wounds..." Seeing nothing of interest, some figures turned back to Po.

"What's in there?" Votna asked. "What does a monk prize that he uses violence to protect it?"

"Just show them and we can go," Ashara said. Po looked Ashara in the eyes, pleading silently for her to understand.

"No," Po said, shaking his head. "I can't."

"Come on," she pleaded. "I just want to get out of here."

"Stand your ground, Po," Dovo called, himself in a contest for his own belongings. "They have no right!" A hand grabbed Po's bag and yanked him forward. It became a tugging match between the pair. Po watched others come to assist his opponent and knew it was only a matter of time. *Think*, he told himself near panic. *Think*.

A knife flashed and his opponent released the bag, sending Po sprawling a second time. The man gushed a torrid string of unholy abuse and waved his hand around for all to see the blood. Po scrambled up, his back against Votna's platform. Angry Tika Ba're disciples picked up sticks and advanced on the companions. Dovo walloped one with his bag. Anjan grappled clumsily with another. Ashara howled in wild release, her knife in one hand, a loaded sling in the other. Po hesitated. He was taught non-violence, but his friends were in danger.

"Kill the witch!" Votna shrieked above him. "She defiled the Circle. Kill her. Kill her!" Po grabbed the platform's supports and pulled himself up, hand over hand. His hands gripped the platform and he rolled himself over the edge. A foot connected with his stomach as Votna cried and raged.

"This is a sacred space," he yelled, kicking Po with each word. "You defile it. You will all pass the gates of Oblivion today." Po gritted his teeth and suffered the kicks. He slowly and painfully rose to his feet. Votna pushed him and Po pushed back.

"You disgrace the Ba're name," Po said.

"Lofty words for a novice," Votna responded, shoving Po a second time.

"Tell your followers to let us go. I mean it." Votna scratched Po's face and Po grappled with him. Both men grunted and groaned. They came perilously close to the edge and back again. Votna tried to trip Po with a flick of his foot, but Po sidestepped and stamped on Votna's exposed toes. The patriarch muttered under his breath and spat in Po's face. The pair tore apart and Po threw a feeble punch. Votna tottered and flapped his arms for balance. One foot stepped into thin air and the patriarch tumbled over the edge of the platform.

Po feared to look. He massaged his wrist. A half dozen Tika Ba're lay at Ashara's feet. Dovo and Anjan stood back to back defending themselves as best they could. From where he stood Po had a good view of the Oblivion Circle. Most the figures on the platforms stood watching them, unable to climb down due to their vows.

"I'm coming," he called to his friends and swung himself one leg at a time off the platform. On the way down he spotted Venerable Votna crawling away from the fight, his leg twisted at an unnatural angle.

"Ashara, let's go," he shouted. "This way." He shoved an attacker away from Anjan and returned Dovo's bag to him. Ashara extricated herself and hurried to join them. They ran to the forest path they had walked in on, Ashara slinging stones at anyone who came too close.

Once in the forest, Ashara took the lead. They ran as best they could. Po's sandal got stuck in the mud and had to be pulled out, tearing the strap. All three monks tripped on roots and overgrown foliage across the path. By the time they reached the fork in the road, all four were puffed and gasping for breath.

"Can we have a rest?" Anjan asked.

"No," Dovo said. "We can't stay here. We take the road left away from here. We can rest later when this place is far, far away."

From the fork, the road carried on back up to the plain, and from there, after a few miles, back into cultivated country. The companions hurried by the first three villages, mere clusters of hovels around a village well, and then came to a stop at the fourth. The village was larger than the others, some twelve cottages protected by a ditch and hedgerow. Children played with a kitten and the adults paid the four companions no heed.

"Looks safe to me," Dovo said.

"I'll see if they have food to buy," Ashara said. Po was about to accompany her, but Dovo put a hand on his shoulder.

"Anjan, take the kettle and go with her. See if you can fetch water from the well."

"I can do that," Po said.

"You need to think what you'll tell them," Dovo said in a hushed tone. "Sooner or later they'll want to know what's so important in that bag of yours."

Po said nothing, but sat cross-legged on the ground, got out his sewing kit and began to fix his sandal strap. Dovo got a fire going. Before long Ashara and Anjan returned.

"They're nice enough," Anjan reported.

"Warm bread and bacon," Ashara said, passing it to Dovo. "I spent some of my coins. That cheered them up."

"Well, this is the latest breakfast I'll ever serve," Dovo said. "You all did well back there. Ashara, you saved our skins."

"I — I don't know if you'd have had the problem without me," Ashara said. "Everyone thinks I'm a witch."

"Nonsense," Po blurted. "It's not your fault. They just didn't want other Ba're monks in their territory."

"You could've just shown them your bag," Anjan said.

"It wouldn't have ended there," Po said. "I —"

"Don't tell us you still wanted to keep it dry," Ashara said, rolling her eyes. "What've you got in there? You're awfully protective of it."

"You're keeping something from us, aren't you?" Anjan added.

Po gazed into the fire and was quiet for a moment. All eyes were on him.

"There's a bit more to going to Jan'a than I told you," he began nervously, and from there he told Ashara and Anjan about Judge e Unuga, how they met, and about the manuscript the judge's widow brought him. "It's in my bag."

🌲

Hands guided Savani to a chair and secured her wrists to the armrests. She looked about the room in confusion, a lack of sleep clouding her judgement.

"Did you sleep well?"

The speaker stood opposite Savani. She squinted up at him. He was large and fleshy, with a full head of silver hair and dressed entirely in black.

"Sleep?" she said through cracked lips. "No, I… yesterday, you…"

"Yesterday?" the man said, indicating himself. "I didn't see you yesterday. You must be confused."

"I —" She bit back her words. Her throat was parched and it hurt to speak.

"Would you like some water?" the man offered. Savani nodded and soon a tray was brought in and put on the table in front of her.

"You must forgive me," said the man. "I forgot to introduce myself. I'm Inquisitor Lukan. You can have this water when you've answered one, simple question." Savani looked up at him and nodded.

"Good," Lukan said. "This manuscript we're after — you know, the one your husband wrote containing spurious and highly inflammatory comments about our new Chief Minister — the last time we spoke, you admitted to taking it the day we raided your house. Do you remember taking it?" *I must have told them.*

"Well?"

"Yes," Savani said.

"Good," Inquisitor Lukan said. "See, now you get your water." He poured a cup and set the porcelain to her lips. Savani gulped it down.

"Can I have another?"

"How about we clear some other things up?" He sat on the edge of the table and picked at a stray thread on his coat. He began to talk in an offhand manner as if it was only a small thing for Savani to consider.

"When you were arrested in Tavana, you didn't have the manuscript. I guess that means you left it somewhere or with someone. It isn't something you'd easily lose. So where is it?"

"I can't tell you," Savani said.

"That's disappointing," he said. "You can't tell us who you gave it to?"

"No," Savani said.

"So you did give it to someone?" Savani recognized the trap too late. She shut her eyes and drew a deep breath. The lack of sleep was getting to her.

"No," she said clumsily, trying to cover her mistake.

"I suspect you were right the first time," Lukan continued. "So you did give it to someone. Now, where would that someone be? I guess we'll have to haul in your friends for questioning. Madam Kasa-Duna is of particular interest, perhaps —"

"It wasn't her. It wasn't one of my friends."

"Oh?" Inquisitor Lukan looked surprised. Savani bit her lip. *Focus,* she told herself. *These are silly mistakes.* She was offered another cup of water and she drank it.

"I understand your desire to protect your friends," Lukan said. "I really do. But without a reasonable alternative, we're left with no choice."

"I can't."

Lukan clapped his hands. The door opened and a virtueman popped his head inside.

"Fetch Madam Kasa-Duna. Rough her up a bit. We need her ready to talk when she gets here."

"Stop," Savani said. "I took it to the Jan Moga." She hated herself.

"Ah," Lukan said. "Forget Madam Kasa-Duna for now." He leaned in to Savani's face.

"You wouldn't lie to me, would you?"

"No."

"You know what happens when people lie?" Savani shivered. This appeared to excite the inquisitor.

"You don't want to know," he said. "Now, who did you give it to at the monastery?"

"Po," Savani said. She began to sob. "Let me go, I want to sleep. Just let me sleep."

"Po?" Lukan said. "We need to verify your story, then you can sleep for as long as you like."

CHAPTER 17

"Across the width and breadth of the empire, few men and women are more feared than the inquisitors. These are the most senior officials in the Ministry of Virtue and the mere mention of them strikes fear in the populous."

The Travels of Odam Yusufkas the Solari

Natan's heart pounded. He skidded in the dark and got back up. The screams had stopped, but he still heard loud voices from the wedding party. *Come on, come on,* he repeated to himself. *Don't be late. Don't let it happen again.* He threw open the door to his host's cottage and scrambled about in the dark to collect his gambeson, shield and axe.

Back at the wedding party the large bonfire still burnt. Natan approached with caution, sticking to the shadows and taking up a position behind a feed trough. He lay down his crutch and mentally prepared himself for the fight to come.

Armed men stood outside the courtyard where the village had celebrated the wedding earlier that day. Inside, other armed figures sat at the tables gorging themselves on the remains of dinner. From the chatter coming from that direction, it sounded like the guests had been herded into the family home.

A gate creaked and Natan spun to his left. A man led a goat towards the party. He did not see Natan but came within feet of him on the other side of the trough. Natan scanned him for colors or emblems but nothing stood out. *Probably bandits*, he concluded, but he resolved to find out more before he acted.

By a circuitous route he approached the rear wall of the courtyard and felt his way along the bricks to the corner of the cottage. The brickwork was old and in some places the mortar chipped. Natan put an eye to the holes until he got a view of the inside. There was light from a fire, but it was dim and the people within were shadows. Still, he now knew where the villagers were.

Carefully he stalked back to the front, taking every chance he got to try and identify figures. He figured there were about eleven, though he could not discount more in the corners of the courtyard or in the privy.

Natan returned to his position behind the feeding trough and watched for signs of anyone else. The two men at the courtyard gate began to relax their guard. Clearly they wanted to go join their comrades. They cast glances within and soon someone brought them a plate each. Minutes later a bandit lurched out of the yard. He burped and put his hand on a sentry's shoulder to steady himself.

"You're missing out," he said. "Good feast in there. I'll sleep well tonight. Never know, eh? Could bed a farmer's wife."

"You can hardly walk," the sentry said. "You won't, you know, perform. You leave them to me and Gaji here." The drunk one giggled, scratched his belly under his open shirt and fumbled with the ties of his trousers.

"*Eww*, not here," the sentry said, jumping away and spilling some of his dinner. "Go piss elsewhere." The man grumbled and lurched towards the feeding trough. Natan shrank back into the shadows, praying he was not seen. The man pissed, taking perverse pleasure in spraying it all over the food scraps for the pigs. He shook himself off and fiddled with his trousers again.

Natan sprang at him. With one swing of the axe the man's guts spilled from his stomach. Natan bounded over the body and charged the two sentries at the gate, careful to keep most of his weight on his good leg. They responded slowly, apparently assuming their friend had fallen over drunk. The first one went down with a strike to the face and a spray of teeth, blood and bone. The second almost retrieved his spear, but Natan drove him into the wall with his shield, stepped back and dropped the man with a blow to the neck.

Not daring to stop, Natan entered the courtyard. His eyes darted about, taking note of everyone's position. Faces looked back up at him in shock and confusion. Drinks spilled and plates clattered as bandits lunged for their weapons.

Natan was in his element. *This* was the fighting he was used to with his brothers; not the shield wall with spears, but a dirty brawl. Another man had his back to him. Natan struck the man between the shoulder blades and kicked him across the table. A bandit jumped onto the table and stabbed at Natan with a spear. Natan blocked him with his shield and sent his axe head through the man's leg. The bone shattered and the bandit toppled backwards with a crunch of his neck on the trestle bench.

Six more to go, Natan thought, mentally ticking them each off in his head. One came at him with a rusty blade and square shield. His blade broke on Natan's shield and Natan drove him back amidst the chairs. The bandit tumbled over them and landed with his feet in the air. Natan swung at his backside, opening up the flesh and exposing bone in a shower of red mist.

The remaining five bunched together and stood ready to take Natan on as a group. They raised a motley array of weapons and held their shields. Natan studied them and stalked around the yard. He was sure they were drunk, but he would take no chances. Natan ran at them and withdrew, then banged his axe on his shield and watched their responses. One was definitely soberer than the others. His eyes followed Natan and he kept a hatchet ready.

Suddenly the door to the cottage banged open and Natan spun about. The bravest men and women of the village poured out with knives, pitchforks and shearing tools. One screamed. Natan felt a blow to his shield and reeled back. A hatchet head protruded through the wood beneath the rim, missing his head by inches.

"Who the bloody hell are you?" the sober bandit roared, his hands now empty.

Natan advanced on him, mindful of the other four.

"I am Natan, son of Sato, Lord of Battle. I am the protector, the defender, and avenger. Prepare yourself." The man picked up a chair and Natan split it in two. A second bandit slashed at him with a sword, but Natan blocked and caught the man's hand with the rim of his shield. A chair crashed over Natan. He staggered back but caught his attacker unaware, expecting to find Natan's guard down. Natan's axe cut upwards, spilling the thug's intestines. Still, gravity carried the attack and Natan felt the blow of the club hit his shoulder. He cried in pain and jumped backwards, tripped and fell to one knee. His leg spasmed.

"Not now," he growled. "Sato protect me."

He plowed into the four remaining men, hoping his aggression and speed caught them off guard. Their reflexes were slow and the first fell to a blow to the head, the second had his hand crushed and the third tripped in the chaos and was finished by the villagers.

It was over.

Days passed in the village and Natan basked in his newfound status. People brought gifts and visitors came from as far as the surrounding valleys to see the hero who fought like a god. Natan felt like telling them the bandits were drunk, but the story got more dramatic with every retelling, then one night Jen'gu came in and hung his coat on the hook beside the door.

"I suspect," he announced to the room. "It's time for our guest to leave." There was a chorus of protest, but Natan rose above them and asked what brought on the sudden announcement. "Scouts were seen at Vaki. A farmer there said the Third Army was not far behind."

"How far's Vaki from here?" Natan asked.

"Over the hill," Jen'gu said. "Two miles at most. But if they're around they'll hear about you. My guess is they'll be going along the highway from Kunan to Mo'dan. Not far from there to Pao'an. It's the way the traders take the millet." The other guests nodded in agreement.

"If I had my way," Pa'tavi said. "We'd find a way to keep you here."

"No," said Natan. "Jen'gu's right. It's not safe. I'm needed with my unit."

"Duty's duty," a farmer said. "But when the war's over, think of us. You may want to return."

"I'll certainly consider it," Natan said. "You've treated me well. I like it here."

"Do you know where you're going?" Jen'gu asked, putting Natan on the spot.

"I — I guess I follow the road," Natan said. Jen'gu shook his head.

"I suggest you go south," Jen'gu explained, motioning with his hands for emphasis. "Go over the hills. There are some villages in the way, so best avoid them. But you'll see a pillar of rock about three valleys over. The road swings by there. Once with the road, keep your distance. Don't get too close. Mamot's men will be everywhere."

"And don't use bridges or river crossings," the neighbour said. "They'll be watched. Cross downstream. Take your time finding a good spot. Even the son of Sato is vulnerable when waist deep in a river."

"I'll remember that," Natan said. People began talking over one another; all wanting to impart their own wisdom. Natan looked from speaker to speaker but could not keep up.

"Enough," Pa'tavi said. "Natan's a big boy. We need to get him packed."

Half the village turned out to see Natan off. They took turns patting him on the back and wishing him well. Some tried to sneak sweet treats, pies and fresh fruit into his pockets and bag while others pressed on him the need to return when the war was over. Natan reached into his belt pouch and pulled his money out, concealing it in his clenched fist. Leaning in to hug Pa'tavi goodbye, he put all he had into her apron pocket. Pa'tavi tensed, as if she understood what he had done, but she was too proud to say anything.

Farewells said, Natan slung his shield over his back, wrapped his axe's blood knot around his wrist and stepped out into the fading light.

It was evening, just past the eighth bell. A chill wind blew, and a cat yowled in the darkness. Inquisitor Lukan stepped down from a wagon and regarded the black form of Jan Moga. Behind him, feet scuttled over the cobblestones. Someone lit a torch. Soon the street outside the monastery was full of virtuemen divided into three companies. Lukan adjusted his coat and approached the gate. He ran a hand over the ancient wood and paused before ringing the bell. There was no response.

"Break it down," he ordered.

"Stop!" a voice called from within. "I'll let you in. Just stop." Lukan shrugged, took a step back and the gates opened. A monk stood staring wide-eyed at the visitors. Inquisitor Lukan took the man by the ear and marched him into the courtyard. Virtuemen flooded in behind him, breaking into groups to search the monastery. Lukan was left with three assistants and the monk.

"Who's in charge here?" he demanded of the monk.

"That — that would be Master Dugen," the monk stammered. "Our abbot is sickly."

"I'll have him brought to me," Lukan said, releasing the monk's ear. He shoved the monk over to one of the virtuemen. "I'll be in the hall." The virtueman took the monk and hurried off.

Inquisitor Lukan looked about the courtyard and wandered over to the Great Hall. Shouts broke the night air and furniture crashed from open windows. A handful of virtuemen, their masks over their noses, carried armfuls of books and manuscripts outside and prepared a pile of them for burning.

Despite the chaos, the Great Hall was empty. There was not much in it to bother the virtuemen, and any monk with an ounce of sense would hide elsewhere. Inquisitor Lukan strolled about the drafty hall and arranged two chairs beneath the Hand of Dasanika. Under a small ceremonial altar, he found wax candles, and from a lamp by the door he lit them and set them up next to the chairs, melting a bit of wax under each one to hold it secure. He sat and waited.

An old monk with liver spots and glasses shuffled into the hall with a virtueman in tow. Inquisitor Lukan rose to greet him and offered his hand, but the monk refused it.

"Master Dugen, I presume?" Lukan looked down at his hand and withdrew it. "Please, be seated," he said. "This won't take long." The elderly monk brushed past the inquisitor and took the seat Lukan intended for himself. Lukan bit his tongue.

"Very well," he said, taking his seat opposite Dugen and dragging it forward. "Do you know why we're here?"

"I heard your men. They're looking for a former novice by the name of Po."

"That's correct," Lukan said. "We're looking for him. Where is he?"

"I couldn't possibly tell you," Dugen said. "As you know, we're no longer a school. Our students are all gone." Lukan reached into his coat and pulled out a folded sheet of paper. He unfolded it and balanced it on his lap.

"It says here he was one of your best students. The best even. I don't believe you let him wander off without even a referral letter." Dugen shrugged.

"There are many things in life that are hard to understand." Nothing about the monk's body language suggested he was lying.

"But I do," Lukan said. "I do understand. Po came into possession of something important. You sent him away — either to protect him, or to protect the object." The hall was silent, but the sounds of breaking windows and shouting continued to drift in from outside. Lukan snapped his fingers and a virtueman approach.

"Bring your equipment," he said. "We'll have to do this the hard way."

"That won't be necessary," Dugen said. "I've said those two would be the death of me." Lukan rubbed his hands together.

"Good, you've seen sense."

"All men break eventually," the monk said with the wave of a hand. "And your ministry is particularly skilled at getting answers." Lukan smiled. *Yes*, he said to himself. *We can come to an arrangement.*

"Very well, where is this Novice Po then?" Dugen sat up straight, widened his legs and set his hands into position of reflection. Lukan waited with bated breath.

"Have you heard of the Oblivion Circle?" Dugen asked suddenly, his eyes closed.

"It is a religious ritual isn't it?"

"Yes," Dugen said. "Part of the Ba're is coming to terms with our own mortality — our impermanence. The Tika Ba're use it as the center of their devotion, being the ultimate expression of their spiritual journey. But among the Sudo Ba're it is but a symbol, or a ritual used on the deathbed. It is a conscious decision: Here I am, I am mortal, I now die. There is a peace in that."

"And how does this information help me find Po?" Lukan asked.

"Po is far away," Dugen said. "You'll never find him." Lukan turned to a virtueman over his shoulder.

"He's playing us. I don't have time for this. Bring the equipment." The virtueman stepped forward with a leather case, knelt and opened it on the ground.

"I told you it won't be necessary," Dugen said, his voice now barely a whisper. "All living men break eventually. But oblivion does not surrender its secrets."

Suddenly Inquisitor Lukan understood. He jumped, knocking over his chair. Dugen looked peaceful, his eyes closed, his thin purple lips still. Lukan slapped the monk across the face. The skin reddened, but the body did not move.

"Do something," Lukan yelled. "Wake him up. What have we got there? Purge his stomach. Charcoal, give it here." The inquisitor braced his fingers around Dugen's mouth and forced his jaw open. The virtueman opened a paper sachet and tipped the contents down Dugen's throat, followed by the contents of a flask. It backed up and dribbled down the monk's neck.

"He's dead," Lukan said. "Heaven damn him. He's dead." He shoved the body off the chair. "How in all creation can they do that. You two — take the corpse and throw him on the pile with the books." Then to the third. "Find that abbot they talked about. Someone knows something."

Half an hour later, Lukan trudged up the stairs of the abbot's tower.

"He's very sick," a monk explained. "He sleeps most the day. He doesn't know what he's talking about."

"I'll decide his use," Lukan said. At the top of the stairs Lukan opened a door and walked directly into Venerable Biet's bedroom. The shutters were closed and the air stale, carrying with it the whiff of urine and body odor. Lukan ordered the windows opened and a lamp placed beside the bed. The waxen face of Biet was immediately visible. Lukan drew a silk handkerchief from his sleeve, held it to his nose, and leaned over the abbot.

"Well, he's alive," he reported. "Wake him up."

"No, no," the monk insisted. "He needs his sleep. He's of no use to you." Lukan pushed the monk aside and folded back the corner of the blanket, revealing the abbot's nobbly left foot. The virtueman with the satchel sat on the edge of the bed and set to work. He cut away a fingernail-size square of skin on the abbot's toe, then took a vial and cloth from the satchel's side pocket. He dabbed the cloth and applied the surface to the open wound. Biet's body stiffened, his chest heaved and his eyes popped open. The abbot let out a graveley moan. The virtueman packed away his implements, took out a flask and applied it to the abbot's lips.

"What are you doing?" the monk shrieked. "He's an old man."

"It's just *kaja*," Lukan snapped. "It'll keep him lucid. Now, out. Out! We'll call you if we need you."

The monk retreated from the room. When Lukan was sure the monk was gone he sat down on the bed beside Venerable Biet and held the elderly man's hand.

"Venerable Abbot," he whispered.

"Who is it?" Biet's reedy voice asked.

"A friend of the monastery," Lukan said. "Relax. You had a bad dream."

"Where's Brother Bidovi? I'd like some water."

"Brother Bidovi? Oh, he'll be right back," Lukan said. "Don't you worry. But you have a special guest on the way." Biet looked up, his face expectant.

"Who?" he said.

"Novice Po," Lukan said. "Your best student." Biet smiled and relaxed back down into the pillow.

"He was," the abbot said softly. "Is he back from Jan'a already?"

"Jan'a?" Lukan said. "He must be. I saw him myself."

"Was he well?" Biet asked. "Was he successful?"

"He didn't say," Lukan said. "Is this about..." Lukan lowered his head as if to speak of a secret. "... the book? The book he took to Jan'a?" Biet nodded ever so slightly.

"So it's done," the abbot said. "I must tell Dugen." Inquisitor Lukan patted the abbot's hand and arranged the bedsheets around Biet's shoulders. He picked up a spare pillow.

"Sleep well Venerable Abbot." He pushed it down onto Biet's face and held it there until movement stopped.

As darkness fell, mist lay wispy about the woodland. Dovo and Anjan got a fire going, and Ashara led Po in search of mushrooms to add to their supper. They had not gone far when she crouched, picked one, and held it for Po to examine.

"This is what we're looking for," she said. Po inspected it with a look of consternation on his face.

"Almost too dark to see," he said.

"So we've got to be quick. You hold the handkerchief and I'll pick them." Ashara set about passing what she found to Po. He trailed along behind her like a lost puppy. After a while they came upon a hedge. At the base of the hedge a rabbit had left fresh prints. If there was more light she could catch one and roast it for dinner.

"You okay?" Po asked.

"Of course I'm okay," she said. Ashara ran her fingers under a clump of grass and lifted it, hoping to see a rabbit hole. Nothing. She moved on to picking mushrooms again. They came to an irrigation ditch and a small

232

bridge cutting to a gate in the hedge. A milestone lay next to the road. Ashara straightened, massaged her lower back, and leaned against the marker.

"Why didn't you tell me earlier?" she asked suddenly. "Didn't you trust me?" The question had eaten away at her, but Po appeared confused at first, then his features dropped and he folded his arms. He stuttered before getting his words out.

"A— About what? The manuscript?"

"Yes," Ashara said. "The manuscript."

"I thought you said it wasn't important. *It's just a book,* you said."

"You know what I mean. I don't think the book's important. Who's going to believe it? But it isn't about that. You hid this from me. It shows you don't trust me. I thought we were friends. I told you why I had to leave Pao'an."

"I didn't hide it," Po said. "I just didn't find the right moment. Once the first few days passed, everything was just going so well. I didn't want to ruin it, and the longer we went, the more awkward it would be to tell you."

"What if the book was found? What would happen to me? I don't care about the risk. But did you think about it? Did you consider me? Or Anjan? We're your friends. If you told us, we'd give our lives for you. But you didn't tell us, did you?" Po cast his eyes to the ground. Ashara continued to study him.

"No," he said at last.

"I'm not even angry," Ashara continued. "More hurt. You're the most intelligent person I know. I've learnt more about the world in a month with you, than in a lifetime before. But your knowledge is limited to books. You don't understand real people. When was the last time you had a friend outside the monastery?"

"Never," Po said. "Until you."

"And when did you last see your parents?"

"I don't know. Five or six years ago. They write every New Year." Ashara pushed off from the milestone and took the mushrooms from Po. She began to walk back in the direction of the camp.

"And you think that's healthy?" she asked.

Po remained silent and hurried along behind her.

The four companions had chosen a campsite off the road between the spreading roots of a time-worn oak. On Ashara's return, Dovo and Anjan were crouched over the fire, toasting bread and waiting for the kettle to boil.

"Mushrooms," Ashara said, dropping the handkerchief into Dovo's lap. "Good sized ones too."

"Just you wait," Dovo said. "This is going to put all our other dinners to shame."

Po came and joined the huddle. Ashara noticed him silently crouch down and break twigs in irritation. The others did not notice. Dovo began to prepare the dinner, and Anjan got the cups ready for the ritual *kaja*.

"Anything happen while we were gone?" Ashara asked.

"Imperial riders," Dovo said. "Galloping towards Lugan."

"We're getting close to the Kh'areen border," Ashara said. "There are outposts strung out for miles from hilltop to hilltop. I guess we'll start seeing more riders and soldiers now. Best we keep our heads down."

"I'd think most have gone north to join the war," Dovo said. "You'll have no trouble getting through unnoticed when the time comes."

"How long do you think that'll be?" Ashara asked.

"Oh, another week. According to the mile marker at Kadan we've done over four hundred miles. Another eighty to Danma —"

A growl interrupted them. They looked up to see a dog stalking towards them from the direction of the road. Its lips curled back showing rows of teeth and its ears were flattened. Muscles rippled down the side of its body.

"Nobody move," Ashara said. "A Solari bear dog." She removed her sling from her belt and prepared a stone. Just then there was movement from her left. Another dog entered the firelight. They were both the same breed; black and white with broad shoulders and powerful limbs.

"Avoid eye contact," Ashara whispered. "Don't challenge them. They're bred for hunting bears. Humans are easy prey." A third dog moved in the shadows. One dog was easy to scare off. Two was difficult. Three was a pack. Ashara slid the knife Dovo had used to cut the mushrooms into the cook's hand, hiding the movement behind the monk's robe. Po tensed and inched his fingers closer to a stick of firewood. Anjan sat, paralysed, looking at Ashara.

"Help," he whispered. "I'm scared of dogs."

"Its okay," Ashara said. "No one panic." Slowly Ashara became aware of another noise; horse hooves, tinkling bells and the creaking of a cart. Lamplight glimmered through the woods and shadows danced off tree trunks. A voice cut through the night.

"*Oi!* Gasa, Gaki, Gana, come!" The dogs lost their edge and while they kept eyes on the four companions, they slunk back into the darkness. A cart stopped on the road, a stone throw from the campfire. It was an enclosed box on wheels painted in garish colors and pulled by a single draft horse. A lamp hung from a pole above the driver's seat, revealing a figure in a green coat and red Vu-cap, his face in shadow. He stood and waved.

"Sorry about that!" he called. His countenance was revealed in the campfire light; a dark face with a frizzy beard and heavy eyebrows. His cheeks were speckled red with tiny broken blood vessels, and a scar ran down from one eye to disappear beneath his beard.

"No harm done," Dovo said. The man climbed from the cart and the dogs emerged to nuzzle their owner. He fed them each a treat from his coat pocket.

"You're out late," Dovo noted.

"Late start. Was hoping to reach Lugan by nightfall."

"Not far to go now. Just up the road."

"Bit late for business," the man said in a disappointed tone. "Any of you need shoes repaired?" He indicated Vu characters on the side of his cart.

"Not us I'm afraid," Dovo said. Dovo pulled back his traveling hood and Anjan did the same. Visible beneath were their monk's robes, a clear sign they carried no money.

"Ah, noble monks," the man said. "I should have noticed something holy about you." Ashara bit back a snort. Only moments ago the three monks were pissing themselves in fear of three domestic dogs.

"And the lady?" the man asked.

"Me?" Ashara said. "My boots will last." The features on the man's face dropped. He seemed genuinely disappointed.

"More's the pity," he said. "Been a bad year for business." Dovo took the pan off the fire and showed it to the shoemaker. The mushrooms sizzled and spat with a mouthwatering aroma.

"Care to join us? There's more than enough to go around." Ashara started. She sensed Anjan and Po do the same.

"What are you doing?" Ashara whispered. "I thought we're avoiding attention." Dovo leaned back and murmured from the corner of his mouth.

"It's called hospitality." The shoemaker appeared not to notice the misgiving.

"I couldn't say no," he said with a hand on his belly. "There is a pleasure in making acquaintances on the road and sharing a meal at the end of a long day." The four companions stood, and Dovo stepped forward with a hand extended. The other three clustered behind him.

"I'm Brother Dovo," he said. "And this is Novice Po, Novice Anjan, and the lady is Ashara of the Kh'areen."

"Nice to meet you," said the shoemaker. "My name's Gutal Noda, itinerant shoemaker."

"Gutal Noda?" Ashara said, her curiosity overriding her apprehension. "Your family name is Vu but your first name is Kh'areen."

"Well observed. My mother was Kh'areen, my father Vu." He rolled up his sleeve and showed Ashara his wrist tattoo. "Prefix is for Baki, no? Lived most my life in Gai'an though, so can only muddle my way through the Kh'areen tongue. In Gai'an they called me Guta."

"I like Gutal," Ashara said. "What was your mother's family?"

"Garagar," Gutal said. "Of Zot Galat."

"My uncle married a Garagar," Ashara said. "I'm a Daladh'an of Baki." The man's eyes brightened and the pair hurriedly exchanged the names of relatives and places, though he was at least twice Ashara's age and his memory of all the familial connections was faded. Dovo eventually interrupted and suggested they eat before the meal went cold. Anjan

236

laid out the toasted bread and Dovo heaped the mushrooms on top. Po cleaned out a fresh cup so Gutal could share in their *kaja*.

"Excellent stuff," Gutal said.

"You have to make do on the road," Dovo said.

"That you do," Gutal said.

"So where are you going?" Ashara asked.

"I'm off to Baki. The way business is going in the central provinces, I decided to take the road to Kh'areen. Everything's so depressed with the war."

"You're going via Danma?" Ashara asked, hopeful he was going the same way as them.

"Danma?" Gutal said, as if the idea had just occurred to him. "No, no. That'll add about a hundred miles to the journey. I'm going through the Badlands. I've done it before — it's tough but there are fewer patrols and it saves time."

"The Badlands?" Anjan said. "But there's hardly any water and the place is infested with snakes, scorpions and spiders. *Argh.* I'd rather walk a hundred miles."

"The reputation is overblown," Gutal said with a dismissive gesture. "Where are you lot off to anyway?" Ashara and Dovo explained in turns that Ashara was off to Baki, and the monks were going to Jan'a. Gutal whistled.

"Jan'a," he said. "Heavens, you lot aren't afraid of travel. That's a long way."

"Another two hundred and fifty miles," Dovo said. "According to the last place I asked at anyway."

"You'll need new sandals before the journey is over."

"And new legs," Anjan said. "Do you sell those?"

"How much are you willing to pay?" Gutal asked with a laugh before turning back to Ashara. How are you getting to Baki? Don't tell me you're taking the long route."

"I am," Ashara said. "I'd rather not brave the Badlands alone. I've spent most my life on the road and that is one place I won't do by myself."

"We could go together," Gutal suggested. "I'd welcome the company and it isn't so bad on a cart."

"Together?" Ashara said. *That's a bit presumptuous.* She looked to the fire and considered her options, conscious of the eyes on her. Gutal seemed like a trustworthy individual, but she had only just met him. On the other hand, there were plenty of unknown risks to the trek from Danma to Baki alone. Both carried risks — *but a hundred miles off the journey*, she thought. *One hundred miles. I'll be in Baki before winter.*

"It sounds like a good idea," Dovo said, interrupting her thoughts. "I'd be a lot less worried if you were going with someone."

"You'd be home faster," Anjan said. Ashara looked to Po, but he avoided eye contact. That decided it.

"It's a deal," Ashara said. They shook on it. His hand was rough and calloused, reminding Ashara of her father.

"So we'll travel together to Lugan tomorrow," Gutal said. "And then part ways after that?"

"You know the road," Dovo said.

"Fine by me," Ashara said, pointedly glancing at Po for his reaction. *He can't expect me to stay around,* she told herself. *Maybe this is a good thing. It will be easier to part with him like this.*

"We'll miss you," Po said at last. "I thought we'd have longer."

"People always do," Ashara said.

CHAPTER 18

"Posan is a township on the road to Danma. Set in an arid plain, the township is strictly rectangular in shape and surrounded by an impregnable wall. It was originally a military camp, then settled by veterans in the pacification campaigns of the 7th century."

A History of the Vermilion Empire

Natan crawled up to the berm and peeked over the top. The road was clear, but it had not been for long. It was churned to mud and littered with rubbish. A smell wafted of human waste, reminding Natan of Pao'an. He approached cautiously. Flies buzzed. A body lay propped against a tree, a bottle in his hands. From the looks of him he was not long dead. The man had soiled himself and his face was crusted, waxen and yellow. Tiny blood vessels had burst beneath his skin, leaving it purplish and blotchy at places.

Natan recoiled in disgust. He had seen men die, but most were from visible wounds. This man was dead from something invisible, his companions stripping him of valuables and leaving him a bottle to drink away his final hours and speed up his death. Further up the road Natan found another. This one groaned, though his eyes were caked over. Natan decided to leave him. In a distant part of his mind he considered giving the man a soldier's death, but the horror of their fever dissuaded him.

Abandoning the road, Natan trekked cross-country past orchards and woods, and through fields of millet and rapeseed. Over three days he was almost discovered five times by hunting or scouting parties but always managed to lay low and wait for them to pass. Many of the men looked weak and more occupied by sniffles than with duty. One man urinated near where Natan stood. He grumbled to his comrade.

"Like pissing millet," he said. "You got any of that *vate're* left?"

"Piss off," said the other man. "You don't have the fever. You probably stuck your prick in the wrong woman."

"I tell you, I'm burning up."

"Here," the speaker said, reaching out for the other's forehead. The first man swatted the hand away.

"Not while we're pissing. Keep that hand away from me. Don't touch me."

"You should have said that to the woman."

"Real smart one you are. You'll be sorry when I'm dead." The second speaker buttoned his trousers. The first continued to strain, the concentration clear on his face.

"Look," said the other, waiting for his companion to finish. "If you're so concerned, do what Jato said and try a shot of vinegar each morning."

"Captain said it was bollocks."

"What does he know? Besides I say it is bollocks you have the fever."

"Bugger off," the first speaker said, finally giving up and buttoning himself. "I'd burp vinegar all day." They turned and returned down the hill. Natan dared not move. He waited in stillness for the best part of an hour. When no more patrols were forthcoming, he set off south, putting distance between himself and the highway.

More days passed and Natan saw more signs of the sickness plaguing the Third Army. Each camp they left behind had a pyre for the dead, and behind each day's march, a trail of sick and dying unable to continue.

One night he watched Kat'an burn. He did not know what crime the walled town had committed, but Mamot unlimbered his fire wagons and spent the night using the town for target practice.

The next day he witnessed the surrender of Mo'dan on the Blue River. The town opened its gates and Natan watched the sacking from a wooded hill a half mile away. *There's nothing stopping them,* Natan thought in a moment of depression.

Natan could not risk crossing the river so close to Mo'dan, so he turned from the town and began looking for a safe place to cross. He passed a number of villages, but no other bridges. Eventually, he plucked up the courage to approach one of the settlements, and there he found a villager mending a fishing net next to his reed coracle. The villager seemed unsurprised, and after a short period of bargaining Natan surrendered a handful of items from his bag and climbed into the round craft. The man came in after him and untied the mooring line, winding the cord about his hand and elbow.

"Where you off to?"

"Pao'an," Natan said, too exhausted to hide the fact.

"Be careful," the villager said, not elaborating further.

"I know." They shoved off and slipped into the current. Natan watched the brackish water that swirled about the craft, remembering it was the same water that flowed past his home.

"Careful you don't fall in."

Natan realized how far he had almost leaned out. He looked sheepishly about and turned his attention to getting the dirt out from under his fingernails. Shortly, the bottom of the coracle bumped against the muddy bottom of the opposite bank. The fisherman grabbed a branch and slowed the boat to a stop. Natan hesitantly got to his feet, steadied himself, and stepped over the side into the knee-deep water.

"Heaven's speed," the fisherman said with a wave of his hand. "Give me a push will you?" Water ran between Natan's legs, soaking his trousers, but Natan braced himself and gave the coracle a shove. It resisted at first, then was caught up in the current and drifted out into the flow.

Natan waded over to the bank and scrambled up into the thick brush. He had no time to dry his clothes. He wanted to get ahead of the Third Army, and that meant hurrying back the way he had come, just on the other side of the river. He dashed along, brushing aside branches and scrambling over logs. After a while he began to weary. His limbs ached and his trousers chafed. He found himself in woodland above the Mo'dan crossing. He slowed to a walk and regained his breath.

A bird called a warning. Natan fell to a crouch, his axe ready. The strain of constant vigilance was getting to him. He reprimanded himself for taking too many risks. His eyes darted left and right. Nothing moved. Natan took a deep breath and stalked forward. The woodland was tame with precious little cover. He felt vulnerable in the open.

The bird called again. Natan cocked his head. He thought he heard insects clicking, their pattern somehow artificial. He paused and this time remained deathly still, his senses strained to the maximum. The wind blew through the trees, picking up fallen leaves and blowing them about the forest floor. *Nothing.* Natan let out a long slow breath. He placed one foot forward, then another. His eyes were busy. His ears were attuned to the slightest noise.

The forest floor launched at him. An arrow drew back on a bow. Two eyes looked out from a formless, mud-smeared face. Grass and leaves clung to the figure's hair, making it one with the woodland. More movement. He was surrounded.

"Put your weapons down and place your hands on your head."

Window shutters rattled and wind whistled through the rafters. Dovo, Anjan and Po crouched around a fire on the barn floor, wrapped warmly in their clothes. Light flickered over the walls, casting dark shadows into the corners where unseen animals stomped and grunted. Po sighed.

"Cheer up," Dovo said, poking the fire with a stick. "We'll be in Jan'a in a week."

"He's still got his mind on Ashara," Anjan said with a friendly jab in Po's direction. Po brushed his friend's hand away.

"No," he said. "Just things I wanted to say." The kettle began to whistle and Dovo poured three drinks.

"This is why," the monk said. "Venerable Biet taught against attachment."

242

"I'll be fine," Po insisted. "It's not attachment. Just a lot to process." Dovo smiled but did not reply. Po knew he sounded silly. Of course he had been attached to Ashara.

"Well," Dovo said at last, passing around the cups. "Drink up before it gets cold."

Suddenly the latch on the barn door clicked and it banged open against the wall. The sudden gust of wind sent clouds of dust, grit and dried grass eddying across the floor. The fire flickered and responded violently, pitching this way and that. The three monks stumbled to their feet, shielding their faces with their arms. A man stood in the doorway, grabbing for the door he had lost control of, his clothes flapping about him.

"Sorry," he shouted. It was the farmer who owned the barn. "Just two more visitors," the farmer added, retreating back out into the dark. "Won't be long."

He returned with two horses which he led down the back. Two figures appeared, rubbing their hands against the cold.

"Virtuemen?" Anjan said, almost inaudible against the wind. Po's stomach froze. The men wore black coats with hoods and red masks up to their eyes. Instinctively Po stepped in front of his bag. Dovo put a hand on his arm.

"Hello," one called, pulling back his hood and lowering his mask. "Cold night eh?"

"Very," Dovo called back. "Would you like to join us. We've just brewed *kaja* beans." The second virtueman closed the barn door and stuffed his gloves into his coat. Dovo indicated the cups they had prepared, then tipped his cup into the straw behind him.

"I'm, *er*, afraid the dust has got into it," he said. "We'll make some more."

"Can't say no to that," a virtueman said. The two newcomers squatted down by the fire, warming themselves. Anjan and Po returned to their positions. Dovo took the kettle.

"I'll be back," he said. "We'll need more water." Po watched Dovo go, then looked about the barn wondering what to say. He stuck out a hand.

"Po," he said. "Ba're novice."

"Tovo," the virtueman said, shaking Po's hand.

"Basadare," the second said. Anjan introduced himself and the absent Dovo.

"Do you drink?" Tovo asked, drawing a flask from his coat.

"No," Po said, holding up a hand. "It's against our vows."

"A shame," Tovo said, taking a swig and passing it to Basadare. Dovo returned with water and conversation turned to dinner. The kettle boiled and the last part of a loaf was toasted over the fire.

"So what brings you here this night?" Dovo asked at last over their meal. Tovo looked into the flames, his face flushed from the drink.

"Don't know," he said. "Some big assignment. Pigeons arrived at Jilan and now we're being recalled."

"Where's Jilan?" Anjan asked.

"About fifteen miles north. Prefecture office." Anjan's face turned ashen. Tovo slapped a hand on Anjan's knee.

"You look like I said your mother died," he barked with laughter. "You sure you're not someone we're looking for? Maybe I should bring you in just in case."

"No," Anjan said. "Just my geography is not so good."

"I'm joking," Tovo said. "I'm exhausted. Time for sleep."

The next morning cold rain came in showers, the drops driven almost horizontally by the wind. Po stood out on the road feeling the soothing bite of water splash across his uncovered face. Anjan and Dovo joined him, their hoods up and bent against the wind.

"You'll catch a cold," Dovo warned.

"So, what's the plan?" Po asked, ignoring the advice.

"Posan Township," Dovo said. "The farmer said it's a good five hours. Can't avoid this one."

Po spied the dark, ant-like figures of the two virtuemen winding their way up a distant slope on the way to Jilan.

"Let's make it in four," Po said. "I don't like whatever business they have in Jilan."

"Time will tell," Dovo said. "But not sure the weather will hold. We'll have to weather the storm in Posan."

Dovo was right. The land around Posan was arid, with carefully irrigated fields and dry rolling hills. Within sight of the walled township, gray clouds rolled over and showers turned to lashing rain. The town gate was left unguarded. Po glimpsed the guards huddled in the gatehouse over a game of *sa'na* and the three companions entered Posan unchallenged.

The town spread out before them in a grid pattern, its streets all regimented in tidy rows. It was a convenient layout to find the town square and soon they were settled in a small shrine to Basatu. Dovo tried to get the fire going, but the driving rain kept extinguishing it. Po shivered and looked about the square. A door opened and a man came out to greet them. He invited them into his house.

"It would be my honor," he said. "Come. Is that everything? Yes? Good. Pass me your hoods. I'll dry them by the fire. Good. I'll show you the guest room."

The house was large and airy, a mansion it seemed for some bureaucrat with tiled floors and carved wood panels. Po followed the owner up the stairs to a second floor guest bedroom. Anjan approached one of the feather beds.

"I dare not touch it," he said. "But this is the best thing I've seen… ever."

"The servants are preparing baths," the man said. "I'll fetch some spare clothes for afterwards. These robes of yours need cleaning."

"We're happy to wash our own," Dovo said.

"Rubbish," said the owner. "My house, my rules." Po agreed for Dovo, and the three were called downstairs. Five tubs lined a wall in the basement, three of which were full with steaming hot water. Having stripped off, and the clothes removed, they climbed in.

"I think I've died," Anjan said. "Paradise is real."

"Don't get used to it," Dovo warned, scrubbing his skin.

Po laughed and ducked his head under the water, rubbing off weeks of grime and grit. A thought occurred to him. He sat up and gripped the sides of the tub. *My bag's upstairs*, he thought in alarm.

"What's wrong?" Dovo asked.

"Nothing," Po said, for he did not know who was listening. He rubbed himself down, stood and climbed out of the tub. Water pooled about his feet on the floor. He took a towel and dried himself off, conscious all the time of not looking too anxious.

"It's too hot," he said. "I'll see you in the room."

The owner of the house had left spare clothes by the door. Po sorted through them and picked out what he thought would fit. They felt soft, but were decorated in gaudy primary colors, not the sort of clothes the monks were used to.

As he approached the guest bedroom, he heard someone inside. He snuck to the doorway and peeked around the corner. Two servants were making the beds, and the owner stood over their bags. He knelt down and opened one of them. Po gasped.

"What are you doing?" he said, walking hurriedly into the room. The man looked offended. He stood and threw up his hands.

"Just checking for dirty clothes," he said. "I don't mean to offend you, noble monk."

"I overreacted," Po said, casting his eyes to his feet. "It has been a long time on the road."

The owner grunted and left the servants to their work. Po watched them and wondered if he should say something to Dovo and Anjan, but if he did, he did not know where in the house was safe to talk.

Dinner was spiced lentils, barbecued lamb and buttery cabbage. As Po ate, he listened to Dovo and their host engage in conversation. It turned out the host's late wife had been Ba're and monks sat by her on her deathbed.

"So, I have an abiding respect for your order," the man explained. "One good turn deserves another."

"Any advice for the road ahead?" Dovo asked.

"Be careful," the host said, pausing between mouthfuls. "Odd things happen out there now. Bandits are becoming bold. There are rumors the Kh'areen are restless. We've lost some outlying villages over recent weeks."

"To bandits, or Kh'areen?" Dovo asked. Their host chuckled.

"Is there a difference?" he asked. Po bit back a comment and focussed on his food. It was only when the host pushed back his chair and stood that Po returned his attention to the room.

"I've some business to attend to," their host said. "Your clothes will be ready in the morning. Sleep well."

He dabbed the corners of his mouth with a white cloth and departed.

"We should get an early night," Dovo said, wiping his fingers on a napkin.

"I'd like an early start," Po agreed. Anjan looked to his two companions, shrugged and shoveled more food onto his plate.

"I'm not letting this go to waste."

Upstairs, the three monks reflected on the day, then went to bed. Po had trouble sleeping. Something didn't seem right. *What were the virtuemen in a hurry about? Why was the host so hospitable? What had he seen in the bags?* He could find no answers, but the suspicions nagged at him. He got up and sat by the window, peeking out through the shutters at the city beyond. Lights flickered in the government building opposite. Figures moved past the windows. Down in the square someone carried a torch. The firelight sent shadows over the walls. Po caught the flash of steel, and he thought he heard the soft padding of hooves. He squinted and focused on the town square. *Yes.* He spotted horses — *perhaps a dozen*, he thought. *No.* There were more than that. They trotted in via the main street until their number was beyond count. *An army. Cavalry. Well, it is the border.*

Downstairs a door banged. Po listened. Someone talked in the hall. The voices stopped. *Footsteps.* They faded. Po breathed a sigh and brought his legs up to hug his knees. He rested his head against the wall and did not know if he fell asleep or not, but started at a sudden tapping at their door. *A rat? No a person.*

Po got up and lifted the latch.

"*Shhh.*" A woman's face appeared, an index finger across her lips. *One of the servants.* Po gave her a quizzical look, keeping his foot behind the door in case of trouble.

"What?" he mouthed. She indicated he should come closer. Po leaned in.

"You need to go," she whispered. "I've left the garden gate open. They're coming for you."

"For us?" Po asked, forgetting to whisper. The servant screwed up her face.

"Keep your voice down. I don't know what you've done, but they're looking for three monks."

"The army's looking for three monks?"

She rolled her eyes and pulled him close by the collar.

"I don't know, alright?" she hissed. "Just go. You didn't see me, and I don't know you. But keep me in your prayers, okay?" Po nodded. He waited until the servant's shadow disappeared down the corridor, then went to wake Dovo and Anjan.

"You're sure that's what she said?" Anjan asked.

"You're right, those are cavalry," Dovo said, peeking out the window.

"Keep those shutters closed," Po warned. "It doesn't make sense. But she was serious. They're looking for three monks. It must be us." Dovo backed away from the window and slipped on his borrowed clothes.

"Seems a bit rude to disappear in the middle of the night with his clothes."

"We can't risk it," Po said. "Carry your sandals and don't make a noise."

Dovo went first out into the corridor, followed by Anjan, then Po. They felt their way along to the top of the stairs, then followed the railing down to the entrance hall. A cough came from the dining room. Candlelight cast the silhouette of a person sitting at the dining table. Po froze and Anjan tugged silently at his sleeve to get him to move. Dovo pointed at a side door, which looked like it led to a servant's passage, for it was plain and seemed to merge with the wall. The older monk tried the door handle and slid the door open. Anjan pushed Po to the front, and Po entered the corridor, his heart pounding. Dovo shut the door behind them.

A bell rung. Shoes echoed off the tiled floor. *The front door*, Po realized.

"Where do we go?" Po whispered. Anjan pushed him.

"Just keep going."

Feet pounded on the stairs above, and the sound echoed through the building. It was not just a servant, but a host of people hurrying upstairs. Po broke into a run, his hand trailing along the corridor wall so he kept his balance and direction. A dark shadow warned him of a wall ahead. Anjan bumped into him and Dovo tripped, crying out in the darkness.

"A window," Po said, grabbing Anjan. "Get that open." Dovo crawled along the floor and Po helped him up, pushing the older monk towards the window.

"It won't budge," Anjan said. "It's stuck."

"Here," Po suggested. "Give me your shoulders."

Po put his arms around his two friends, lifted his legs and kicked the window as hard as he could. It banged and rattled but did not open. Dovo and Anjan understood. They braced themselves against the wall behind. Po tried again and again. Something snapped and Anjan elbowed the shutters open.

Outside, the monks stuck to the flowerbeds. The paths were gravelled and made a crunching noise. Po felt sorry for the gardener. At the end of the garden they found the gate, and as the servant said, it was unlocked. Turning back, Po glanced at the house. Lights flickered in the windows, and shouting echoed off the garden walls. Whoever was in there now knew the monks had escaped. It was only a matter of time before they came out looking.

"Run," Po said, shuffling his companions out into the alley.

Holding their sandals, they ran barefoot through town. They splashed through puddles and slipped on cobbles. Dogs started to bark, alerting the whole town to their presence. At a corner they saw the south gate by the light of braziers and a signal fire. Guards stood by warming themselves. An officer in a crested helmet was giving them instructions. Po grabbed his friends' hands and ran for the gate, not having time to think up a better plan. He lifted the bar, grunting, and dropped it. Anjan and Dovo shoved the gates open, and they ran out into the night. Shouts followed them, but they dared not stop. They left the road, running across fields, leaping ditches and skidding down banks. Po's feet went numb from the bruising and cuts.

"Don't stop," Dovo called. "They'll have dogs out soon."

"Hold up," Anjan cried. "I need to catch my breath."

"Just keep going," Po shouted. "We can't wait." They rounded the top of a rise and came into a shallow depression. Shadows were thick across the ground and the companions had to slow lest they break bones in the dark.

"I smell smoke," Anjan said suddenly.

"Can't smell a thing," Dovo said. Po stopped and sniffed. A hand clamped over his mouth and a body pulled him to the ground. Dovo and Anjan's screams were cut short. Po thrashed about, but the more he moved the harder the grip.

Sand blew in gusts up the valley, scouring the pancake rocks and stinging Ashara's eyes. Despite the discomfort, she could smell home. She wasn't sure if she imagined it, or if the steppe beyond the Badlands really had a flavor she could taste. The three dogs, Gasa, Gaki, and Gana ran alongside the cart. From her perch on top, Ashara watched them startle a rabbit and give chase between the rocks and sand drifts.

"If you ever come this way yourself," Gutal Noda called over his shoulder. "The art is never leaving the road, not even for an instant. You'll get lost"

"It doesn't seem so bad," Ashara called back.

"Winter brings some drizzle, the air is damp. In summer you'd already be dead."

"How do the border patrols survive?"

"With difficulty." Ashara fitted a stone in her sling, spun it and released. The stone sent up a puff of sand by a dead tree.

"Damn it," she said.

"Good shot," Gutal said. "You'll be useful in a fight."

"I missed," Ashara said. "If that was a bandit, he'd still be alive." Gutal shrugged and poked out his bottom lip.

"It's a moving cart. It takes some skill."

The cart continued down the road, though it was more a broken trail and Gutal had to avoid the drifts of sand. Ashara reached beneath her seat and took out her water skin. She washed the grit from her mouth and rubbed her tongue over her teeth. *I'm almost home*, she reminded herself.

"Something up ahead," Gutal said, though his posture remained unchanged. Ashara fitted another stone to her sling and checked her knife. "Load the crossbow." The crossbow lay in a box behind them. Ashara removed it, fitted a bolt and cranked it up. She then placed it on the bar by Gutal's hand.

"What do you think it is?" she asked.

"Dunno. See the carrion birds. They're looking down into the next valley."

Gutal whistled for the dogs and the three canines returned to the cart. Gaki had a rabbit between his teeth. They seemed to sense the danger and moved in close formation.

"If I left the track I could flank them," Ashara suggested.

"What did I just say? We stick to the road. You want to get killed?"

"No," Ashara said testily. "But if it's danger we should be careful."

"Yes. Stay on the cart, keep your weapons ready, and stick to the road."

They rounded one of the large pancake rocks and looked down into the next valley. Ashara's breath caught in her throat. The valley floor was scattered with the carnage of battle; bloodied corpses, broken weapons and horse carcasses, mixed with drifts of sand two days deep. A dozen men led their horses over the field, picking over the bodies and placing anything of value in their saddlebags. From time to time they shooed away a vulture, or stood to re-secure their robes against the constant buffeting of the wind.

The cart rattled down into the valley and one of the men looked up. He drew a sword and hurried towards them with a hand up.

"Halt! Halt! Stay right there."

Gutal stopped the cart and whistled. Immediately, Gasa, Gaki, and Gana pricked their ears and scooted to the front, their lips curled back in snarls. The man stopped short and braced himself. His companions joined him, one notching an arrow to a bow, another mounting his horse and hefting a spear.

"You're in the wrong place," the first man called, his scarf flapping about his neck.

"Bollocks," Gutal said, placing a hand on his crossbow. He nodded towards the battlefield. "What happened here?"

The man regarded Gutal with steely eyes.

"Found 'em this way. Been a battle."

"Between who?"

"Soldiers and Kh'areen." Ashara stood and Gutal tugged her down again. She wanted to get a closer look at the bodies.

"Why would Kh'areen be here?" Gutal called.

"War, isn't it?" said the man, edging closer. "The Oracle rallies at Zol Ba'az. They won't accept Jano — 'tis rebellion."

"And how do you come to be here?" The man glanced over his shoulder as if suspecting all the talking was a delay for an ambush. One of his followers nodded and began trudging up to a prominent stone ridgeline.

"That's our business," he replied. "Now we have us 'ere a problem."

"What's that?" Gutal said, stretching out his legs as if in leisure.

"You're armed. We can see that, and those dogs have nasty teeth. Let's settle this business-like and you can pass." Ashara stood again. The men tensed.

"I hate bandits," she said. "Move or die."

"Sit down," hissed Gutal. "It's a simple transaction."

"Listen to your old man," barked the bandit leader.

"My old man was killed by a bandit like you," Ashara called back. "I have no time for you."

The bandit snorted and turned to his companions, then back to Gutal.

"Get your whore —"

Ashara's sling snapped in the air and the archer spun where he stood, crumpling to the ground. She immediately had another stone ready and took down the rider. The others yelled and ran forward. Gutal whistled and his three dogs tore into their midst, barking and biting at flesh. Ashara leapt down from the cart and ran to join them, snapping out stones and screaming her ancestor's warcry.

"*Tanri gosh ba!*"

This was not a fight for self-preservation, it was a matter of vengeance and justice for her father and brothers. Her knife cut into flesh and her sling cracked skulls. The battle was over as fast as it began. Ashara fell to her knees crying in rage as the dogs wrestled with the bandit leader.

"Off," Ashara cried, crawling towards them. Gutal whistled and the dogs withdrew, leaving the body with strips of flesh hanging loose. Ashara looked down into eyes bulging with terror. She gripped the salt and pepper hair at the back of his scalp and slapped his cheek.

"Witch," he hissed. "Demon-warrior."

"How many Kh'areen were here?" she demanded. He spat at her. Ashara took her knife, buried it in his shoulder and twisted it.

"Two hundred," he said. "On horse." Ashara stopped twisting.

"A raiding party?" He nodded. "Where did they go after this?" The bandit leader gagged and his eyes rolled back in spasms of pain. Ashara laid him back and slapped his cheek to keep him awake.

"I... I... didn't see them, but the tracks went east. Please..." he tried lifting a hand. "Mercy..." Ashara wiped her blade off on the bandit's clothes and ignored his pleas for a quick death.

"They're definitely Kh'areen," Gutal said. She had not noticed him join her. He was inspecting the bodies.

"Imperial troops — you can tell from the armor. A border patrol most likely. These are Kh'areen though. That there's one of their — our — horses. These horses are Imperial." Ashara followed Gutal's gestures and trod among the corpses. She spotted something in the sand and dug about with her fingers. It was an iron bullet from a sling stamped with a craftsman's mark from Baki.

"It's true," she said, straightening. "It's war."

Gutal Noda and Ashara spent an hour rounding up the bandit's horses, coaxing them with oats and carrots. Once they were together, and their valuables sorted, Gutal tied them up to string along behind the cart. Ashara picked through the pockets and belt pouches of the dead, retrieving coins, rings, and the odd broach. As she did so, she considered the consequences of the war. Her thoughts turned to Po, Anjan and Dovo. They were alone, unarmed and within raiding distance of the border. *Do they know what they're doing? Do they know the danger? How far have they gone? Are they safe?* The questions nagged at her.

"We're ready," Gutal called. "Let's get going before the vultures attract more company."

"I can't," Ashara said. "My friends are in danger."

"The monks?" Gutal asked. "What can you do to help them?"

"The Kh'areen are my people," Ashara said. "I can keep them safe."

"You'll get yourself hurt. It's a huge border area. Chances of them being in trouble are tiny. The chances of you finding them are smaller still."

"I can't risk it," Ashara said. "Besides… I left things unsaid." Ashara ran a hand over the rear horse. Gutal's shoulders sagged. "Can I take this one?" Gutal said nothing but untied the rope and handed her the reins. Ashara thanked him and handed over the pickings from the battlefield.

"Be safe," she said.

"Don't leave the road," Gutal said. "Tanri's speed, Ashara Daladh'an."

Crowds packed the streets and filled every balcony and window space, jostling for a good view. Parents carried children on their shoulders and youths took to the rooftops. The noise was overwhelming. People whooped and cheered; fireworks crackled, and every bell in the city tolled. Muni Mei-Uduga waved to the crowd and basked in their adoration, showered in confetti, petals and millet. Captain Vatoni led her on a royal white horse, followed by Adan rocking along in a palanquin, and General Nulu bringing up the rear with her honor guard.

She was a long way from the Dili Valley. Li'an was her hometown, and now, she hoped, the base for regaining the Imperial government. Every supporter, every chance to engage with the people, every soldier to her cause mattered. They all mattered. On her horse, Muni was dressed to convey power, not in the dresses of state as First Lady, but in quilted white shirt and polished steel breastplate. On her head, unwilling to usurp the dress of an empress, but unsuited to the helmet of a general, Muni wore a steel ring.

Muni Mei-Uduga rode up to the governor's mansion, and Captain Vatoni offered her his hand to dismount. She slid gracefully from the horse and curtseyed to the governor. He in turn bowed and kissed her gloved hand.

"A pleasure," he said. "To see you here again."

"The pleasure is mine, Governor Gato." He took her hand and walked her up the steps to a balcony looking out over Covenant Square. The crowd roared at seeing her. The noise was deafening. Muni felt her body tingle at the excitement, and her stomach tickle with nerves. The governor held his hands up, and as if ordered by a god, the square fell to a deathly quiet.

"Li'an," the governor roared. "Our greatest daughter has returned — the widow of the deified martyr Tomi Mei-Uduga! It is the will of Heaven, by the blessings of the Great Serpent, that she should survive to return to us. This is a sign, as sure as the shooting stars that heralded Tomi's death and deification. The war is not lost. We will resist. The usurper will be defeated. And let the world know — Li'an holds the battle standard."

The crowd erupted again and any hope of Muni speaking was drowned out in the cacophony of trumpets, drums and firecrackers. Governor Gato picked up her hand and held it high for the people to see. Muni swallowed her words and basked in their adoration. She closed her eyes and breathed deep.

"That's about enough," Gato said, lowering her hand. The pair bowed to the crowd and left the balcony.

"That was a nice addition, the shooting stars I mean," Muni said.

"Thanks," Gato said with a grin. "The people like a good story."

CHAPTER 19

*"In times of trouble, the Kh'areen sort themselves into warbands.
These form around a strongman figure which they call a gosh or
lord. Beneath the gosh are companions who each command dozen
or so warriors."*

Master Suvu's Life of a Scholar

"Let go of me," Natan cried. "Get off me."

A gloved hand clamped over Natan's mouth. He tossed and turned, trying to dislodge the attacker from his back. Someone grabbed his hands. Another booted him in the shins. Natan hit the ground. He rallied his strength and pushed upwards, briefly freeing himself from their grip. They fell upon him again; gloved hands and booted feet struck him. His attackers piled on, crushing him with their weight. Natan lost the use of his limbs and air burst from his lungs. *You've lost*, his brain said. *Survive…* Natan relaxed and embraced his fate.

Hands hauled him to his feet. His vision went dark, a sack on his head, and they secured his arms with rope that cut into his skin.

"Don't resist," a voice said in his ear. Natan struggled to keep down panic. A hand guided him forward and he took slow, careful steps. This appeared to annoy his captors, who gripped his arms and dragged him forward at a brisk walk. He stumbled three times before they reached a stream and carried him across.

By the time they stopped, Natan had no idea where he was. He had lost all sense of direction, made worse by the way his captors now turned him around on the spot and positioned him up against a tree. Someone bound him to the tree with rope, and another removed the sack from over his head. Natan gasped, gulping down fresh air. They were in a clearing. A small fire heated a camp kettle and twelve horses were tied up in the shade of an gnarled oak.

"Out with it, what's your name?" Natan squinted at the man in front of him. The man's face was smeared with mud and he had twigs in his beard. Only his teeth and the whites of his eyes stood out as human.

"Natan Luka-Tudo."

"With General Mamot?" his captor asked.

"No." The man grunted and stepped back. Natan worried that this was the wrong answer. He watched the other men for a reaction, but they stood impassively, regarding him.

"Deserter then?" Natan shook his head.

"You come from Mamot's camp?"

"I've seen it," Natan said. The man sighed and turned his back to Natan.

"Sergeant," another suggested. "He might be a bandit."

"Nah," the sergeant said. "He's a fighter." The sergeant turned back to Natan.

"So what're you bloody doing here?" Natan explained, mindful he was unfamiliar with the allegiance of his captors. They listened, stone faced. Only the sergeant seemed agitated, cutting Natan off.

"The 37th Auxiliary, 14th Banner?" the sergeant clarified. "Seventh Army?" Natan nodded and the sergeant turned to his men, jerking a thumb in Natan's direction.

"Any you boys know their commander?" They shrugged and muttered, shaking their heads in ignorance. The sergeant dismissed them and peppered Natan with questions. Natan answered as best he could, as honestly as he could.

"He's no use to us," an observer growled. "Cut his throat and we'll get another."

"Our orders are clear," said another. "He's no use." A lanky man with missing teeth flashed Natan an evil grin. He drew a knife and advanced on Natan.

"Here, let's get this over with."

"Hold it," the sergeant barked, placing a hand on the man's chest. "We're rangers, not murderers. If his story checks out, he's on our side."

"Not our problem," the lanky man said. "We're after Mamot and the Third, not stragglers from the Seventh. Besides, I don't trust him."

"I —" Natan began to protest. The sergeant silenced him with a glare.

"Here's what's going to happen," the sergeant said, looking about his squad for agreement. "We'll leave him here, go back, nab a *real* enemy soldier, and then skedaddle. Pao'an and hot meals by morning. How about that?" To Natan's relief, the man returned the knife to his belt.

"Alright," he said. "But if he risks the mission, I slice his throat."

"Deal," said the sergeant. "Get ready. We're going out again." The men shuffled off and prepared for another foray. They helped each other reapply leaves and grasses to their camouflage. The lanky man pulled out a small pot and heated the remains of a stew for the squad to scoff down. The sergeant retreated and came back with a water skin. Pulling the stop out with his teeth, he offered it to Natan. Natan took a mouthful of the brackish water.

"So, we have a friendly," the sergeant said.

"Can you untie me?" Natan asked hopefully.

"No. Don't trust you that much. We won't be long. You'll be in Pao'an by first light, then we'll see if you're telling the truth."

"I am."

"Save your breath." The sergeant returned to his men and they filed from camp, merging into the shadows.

"Hello?" Natan called after a while. No response. He was alone. The leaves rustled and the horses shuffled about. Natan tried to shut his fear out. He turned his mind to Pao'an. *Did he really say we'd be in Pao'an by morning? Hot kaja, a cooked breakfast, fresh bread, cold millet beer…* he could taste it.

Movement caught Natan's attention. A large rat scuttled into the clearing and rummaged through the bags before finding a ration cake. It sat eating it, then spotted Natan and scampered off, cake between its jaws.

The horses acted irritated, snorting and stamping their hooves. Suddenly the forest exploded with crashing of bushes and stamping of feet. Horns blasted and screams cut the air. The rangers — now only eleven in number — rushed into the clearing with soldiers in hot pursuit.

"To the horses!" the sergeant cried.

"I'll hold them off," roared the lanky man, his sword drawn and a knife in his other hand. The first of the pursuers sprinted into the clearing. Steel clashed on steel. A ranger fell to an axe blow; another to a spear in the neck.

"Help!" Natan squealed, still unable to move. No one looked his way. The sergeant cut the ropes tying the horses to the oak, and called for his men to mount.

"Don't leave me here," Natan screamed. For an instant the sergeant made eye contact. He paused, reins in hand, and dashed to Natan's side.

"You want to die a soldier?" the sergeant asked. Natan had no time to reply; the sergeant cut at his bonds and Natan yanked himself free. Natan grabbed a sword and shield from the camp and joined the rangers. They were pushed back. Enemies moved in from all sides. One ranger, the sergeant, remained, his back to Natan, the pair fighting for their lives. With every breath Natan reminded himself of the massacre these men carried out in the Dili Valley. *Nimi...*

Cold steel cut his flesh, and blood splattered his skin. Other soldiers arrived, now more coordinated. They formed a shield wall and a captain ordered the front ranks of attackers back. They broke and ran, leaving Natan facing the shield wall, bristling with spears. At his back the sergeant swore.

"I believe you now," the sergeant called above the shouting. "Oblivion awaits."

"For Jano," Natan cried back. "And the Vu'tai."

"For the Seventh! All under Heaven!"

The shields closed in. Natan did not wait, but charged into them, his brute strength breaking the wall. Again and again his blade found its mark. A spear grazed his neck. Another lodged itself in his shield. From the corner of his eye, Natan glimpsed the sergeant fall. He cried out a final battle cry and expected the end to come. But it did not.

"Enough!" roared a voice beyond the carnage. The attackers jumped back, their weapons wavering with nervous energy. Natan flicked his eyes around, his sword ready, not daring to believe the fight was over. A large man with bushy beard, an extended belly and yellow silk over chainmail pushed his way forward.

"You want to live?" demanded General Mamot. "You fight like an aurochs, with the strength of ten men. I need men like you."

"I'd rather die," Natan spat. The general clapped his massive hands as if applauding a mummer.

"Bravo," he said. "You've got guts and a temper. Now think like a man, not an angry boy." Natan shifted his weight, unsure what to do. It was true, he would rather not die. But Mamot would never break him.

"I'll surrender," Natan said. "But I'll never fight for you."

"A warrior and a pragmatist?" Mamot laughed. "That's not common."

"I'm a survivor," Natan said. "And while I yet live, I can still kill you."

"A mouse roars to a lion. You hear that?" The soldiers laughed on demand. "I like him. Take him. I want him alive."

Natan buried his sword in the earth and dropped his shield, too exhausted to feel shame, only relief that he yet lived.

Po squirmed, unable to move. He was wrapped up in a blanket and bound tight, like a caterpillar in a cocoon. A piece of cloth kept him from crying out. It began to rain. Water dripped down his face, and a puddle formed around him. Their captors had dumped them, bound and gagged, in a depression, they knew not where. Anjan shuffled restlessly. From the snores, it sounded like Dovo was asleep. *I wish I had that skill.*

Po withdraw within himself, willing himself to be calm, to face his fate with the composition of a monk. *Kime ki're kima ka. Kime ki're kima ka.*

He woke, cold and shivering. A man stood over him, and Po knew instantly it was not a virtueman or a soldier. The man had a broad face with chiseled features. While his skin was a dark tan, his cheeks were burnt red from a life under the blazing sun. His captor grinned down at him, showing a mouth full of black and broken teeth.

"Who are you?" Po asked. The man didn't reply. Instead he picked Po up by the ropes that secured the blanket around him. Blood rushed to Po's head and his world spun. He caught a brief glimpse of Anjan and Dovo being picked up as well. Three captors; three monks. They were carried into a camp of trampled earth. Horses and men milled about in the cold morning drizzle. *Kh'areen.* They dumped them unceremoniously on the ground.

"*Oi,*" Dovo cried out next to him. Their captors exchanged guttural laughter. Po wriggled around to look at them, but one of the men landed a boot on Po's back and pinned him down. A crowd gathered, but Po could see no more than their boots sloshing about in the mud. All of a sudden he was drenched in ice cold water. Po drew in a sharp breath and squealed. His captors laughed again and emptied buckets onto Anjan and Dovo. One of them leaned over and made a sign with thumb, nose, and index finger to say he thought the monks stunk.

"Let us go," Po demanded, finding his voice. As if on order, the monks found themselves hauled to their feet and their bonds removed. They reached out and helped each other stand, for their legs had gone numb, as they struggled to maintain their balance.

The attention of the gathered crowd switched from the monks to a large warrior. He stood, arms folded, watching his captives. Muscles bristled along his exposed arms and bright silks glistened beneath a shirt of scale armor. Po held the man's gaze, then broke it, for the malice within was evident. He looked down to the warrior's boots and skin breeches.

"Gosh Azraik," one of the warriors said. Po looked up, but did not understand. The man pointed to the large warrior.

"Gosh Azraik," he said again. A hand landed on the back of Po's neck and forced him to bow. On either side Dovo and Anjan did the same. They straightened again and looked up. The man frowned and spoke. He turned to an attendant and beckoned him as if calling a dog, barking an order as he did so. The attendant left and returned with the monks' bags, casting them on the ground at the leader's feet. The leader crouched before them and checked the contents, leaving a pile of belongings next to him. He came across the canvas bag with the papers inside and discarded it in a puddle.

"No," Po yelped. He surged forward but hands pulled him back. The leader glanced up and retrieved the canvas, taking a sudden interest. He passed it to an attendant and returned to the bags. When they were empty, he stood and rubbed his thumb and fingers together.

"Money?" Dovo asked, miming a coin. The leader nodded. Dovo, Anjan and Po turned out their pockets in a display of poverty. Not satisfied, the Kh'areen pushed in and rubbed their hands all over the companions, tearing off strips of fabric and cutting holes in the lining. They found nothing, and quickly lost interest. Po and his two friends were herded away.

A corner of the camp was set aside for prisoners. Po surveyed the motley group of half-starved captives. There were eight of them. From their clothes, Po guessed five were formerly officials in some capacity and three were army officers. The officers were still in their tunics, but those had been ripped and muddied. One had his arm in a sling and a bandage wrapped around his head. It seemed the Kh'areen did not bother to tie them or restrain them in any way. There was nowhere to go, no way to escape. The warriors made a show of parading the new captives, then pushed them in with the rest.

"Hello," Po said once the Kh'areen had left. No one replied. They stared at him with sunken eyes. The officer with his arm in a sling coughed up phlegm and swatted a fly from his face. There was something mad about him that startled Po a little. *Is this what captivity does to people?* The prisoner eyed Po as if hearing his thoughts.

"Welcome to the party."

Dovo put his hand on Po's shoulder and steered him from the prisoners as far as they dared go. The companions sat, crossed their legs, and fished about for their reflection beads, at once looking up at each other.

"I think we left them in Posan," Po said.

"Well —" Horns blew, cutting Dovo off and stirring the camp to life. Warriors mounted their horses and two old warriors fetched the prisoners.

"Where are we going?" Po asked as they were herded to a rallying point.

"Do you think they tell us?" asked a sallow-faced prisoner. The man wore a white shirt, tied at the neck, of the sort worn under a bureaucrat's robes. Without the adornments of office it looked more like a nightshirt, and a soiled one at that.

"No, but..."

"Just do as they say."

Po frowned and looked about. For every Kh'areen warrior, there were four or five horses. The spares, along with the prisoners, were kept in the middle of the formation, under the charge of the eldest warriors of the warband.

"Looks like it's north," Dovo said as they set off.

"Posan?" Po asked.

"I guess so. Can't be far."

"They're in for a surprise," Anjan said with a smile. "The Kh'areen I mean —"

"*Shush*," Po said, poking his friend. "We don't know how much they understand."

The prisoners trudged on in silence. Before long the warriors up front reigned in and shouted in excitement. Peeking between the bodies of those in front, Po saw the square form of Posan dominating the wide open valley. Smoke rose from the chimneys and figures ran along the battlements sounding the alarm. Bells tolled a warning, and guards at the gates hurried to stand aside.

"Why aren't they closing the gates?" the officer with a broken arm asked.

"Wait," Po replied, earning a jab from Anjan. The guards at the gates threw their hands up in salute and ranks of cavalry trotted out, forming on the plain before the walls. The Kh'areen hooted and jeered, standing in their saddles and waving their weapons in challenge. The two armies inched forward, forming a nomansland about two hundred yards apart. From the Imperial ranks trotted the commander, flanked by two bannermen, driving a bearded resident of Posan before them. From the glimpses Po caught, the man looked nervous and unarmed, his hands up beseeching the gods with every second step. The commander stopped and called out in a booming voice.

"My name is Commander Vitan of the Imperial Seventh Army." The bearded man translated, calling out the words in Kh'areen. "You're in open rebellion. Put down your arms and go home." He said more, but Po could not hear through the jeering of the riders around him. "Whatsmore, I have money for you ... three monks ... yes, three monks ... if you see them, or have seen them, give them to us and you get this bag worth fifteen gold *gotti*." At mention of the three monks, Anjan gripped Po's arm, and Po bit his tongue to stop himself from crying out. They turned to the Kh'areen leader for his response.

The Kh'areen leader raised his hands for calm and pranced his horse out in front of the army. Calling in Kh'areen, he addressed the Imperial commander, while the bearded man translated. Po strained to listen, but the translator's words were soft and caught in the wind.

"I am Lord Azraik of Clan ... warband of the Great Horde ... beyond count ... the land is thirsty for blood ... once ... my ancestors watered horses at Kh'ot Galad, *er*, Posan. Their bones feed the earth ... our wyvern hunted the skies. Who are you, millet eater? ... to order us? ... the people of the steppe."

"He's..." Anjan started.

"Shhhh," Dovo hissed. Po took an involuntary step forward, hoping to hear the translator better.

"We have no monks," the translator called. "And why would we barter for three, when the whole land is in dispute?" Po stood dumbfounded.

"Eh?" Anjan said. "Why would he say that?" They turned to Dovo, who looked equally confused. Dovo fumbled for words, then his eyes brightened.

"Well look at us. We borrowed these clothes, and when was the last time we shaved?" The truth dawned on Po. *We don't look like monks.*

"So," said the officer with a broken arm. "You're the three monks?" Anjan flashed him a wink.

"I think so," said Po. Dovo touched Po's shoulder.

"You shouldn't have said that." Already the captive officer was getting a warrior's attention. He waved three fingers at the captor and pointed wildly at the three companions. The warrior looked puzzled, then angry, then intrigued.

"*Oi*, what are you doing?" Po demanded.

"Freedom," their fellow captive said. "We're going home."

"You can't do that," Anjan said, rushing at the officer.

"*Kadash!*" a Kh'areen warrior yelled and, jumping from his horse, struck Anjan a blow across the back of the head. Anjan yelped and fell to his knees, clutching his scalp. Warriors grabbed the trio and dragged them, accompanied by the wounded soldier, to Lord Azraik, who in turn whistled for a cohort to follow him. The two sides met, a small party with each, in nomansland.

"Are these the three monks?" Lord Azraik asked via the interpreter. Commander Vitan looked from Po to the Kh'areen lord.

"Is this a joke?".

"You think I jest?" the interpreter asked.

"Look at them," the commander said, his hands out in annoyance. "They're not monks." He turned on the interpreter "Are you translating this right?" Before the interpreter could respond, the officer with the broken arm dashed forward.

"Please!" he cried. "They're in disguise. I heard it from their own mouths!" The commander frowned and looked about the gathering, then down at the man.

"You were once a soldier?"

"I am a captain in the 12th Frontier Force."

"But you allowed yourself to be captured?" the commander turned up his nose at the man and returned his attention to Lord Azraik. "I'm sorry," the commander continued. "But these three are not the ones we're looking for."

"It's battle then," Lord Azraik said via the interpreter, and with that the Kh'areen delegation turned to leave.

"Wait!" came a voice. "Wait!" Po turned to see figures hastening towards the commander. He froze with terror, realizing two were virtuemen. Commander Vitan leaned over to speak to the translator, and the translator shouted in Kh'areen after Lord Azraik. The Kh'areen delegation turned back.

"Lord Azraik wishes to know what's changed," the interpreter said once the two sides stood face to face again.

"We'd like another look at your prisoners," Commander Vitan said. Kh'areen warriors pushed Po, Anjan and Dovo forward. A virtueman stepped towards them, removing his hood as he did to reveal a head of white hair. He smiled gently to the trio.

"I'm Inquisitor Lukan," he said. "Do the Kh'areen keep you well?"

"They do," Dovo said. Po and Anjan nodded.

"Good," Lukan said. "Show me your wrists." The monks rolled up their sleeves, and Lukan reached out to check them. Po shivered at the touch. Lukan's hands were soft and grandfatherly. The inquisitor's fingers paused with Po.

"Hello, Po. We meet at last," he said, then turned to Anjan and Dovo; "And you must be Anjan; a defector, I believe. Weren't you serving in a medical capacity with the Seventh Army? And Dovo, a monk in the kitchens of Jan Moga. You're unlikely candidates to defy the Vermilion Empire. I must say I'm very surprised." Po avoided the inquisitor's eyes.

"And where is the manuscript?" Lukan asked.

"I can't tell you," Po said. Inquisitor Lukan shook his head and *tut tutted*.

"*Oh* Po, we want the manuscript, not you. You tell us where the manuscript is, and we buy your freedom." Po wiped his nose and turned to point at the Kh'areen.

"They have it," he said. Lukan patted Po's hand and spoke with Commander Vitan. The commander nodded, and called over the interpreter, who in turn ran to speak with Lord Azraik.

"He says no deal," the interpreter said.

"Fifteen gold *gotti*," Commander Vitan said.

"He says for that, you get the three monks. If you want their belongings also, you must add another fifteen." Vitan's face reddened.

"Twenty, all included." The interpreter passed this on and shook his head.

"Lord Azraik has changed his mind. These monks are valuable. He wishes to keep them."

"He can't do that!" Inquisitor Lukan spluttered.

Azraik shouted in Kh'areen and his warband leapt to action. A warrior yanked Po onto his horse and three others snatched Dovo, Anjan, and the officer. In the chaos, the translator was grabbed from behind and hefted kicking and screaming onto a horse with another rider. From the far end of the plain, the remaining warriors of the warband thundered towards them.

Po screamed. The horse under him broke into a trot, and then a gallop. Unfamiliar voices shouted, and the air buzzed. His world spun. The horse wheeled this way and that, following the Kh'areen formation. The warrior behind him guided his mount with his legs, and used his free hands to load and fire his sling. Po hung on for his life.

Screams cut the air and a rider fell from his saddle. A horse reared and threw its warrior, an arrow sticking from the animal's heaving breast. Po had no more breath to scream. He felt sick. His muscles tightened and he tried to make himself as small as possible. He imagined at any moment a dart piercing his lungs.

A shout went up, repeated by all the warriors, and Po's rider switched his sling for an axe. Po twisted his head; Imperial cavalry bore down on them, their horses faster and better at the gallop. Just before the two armies met, the Kh'areen horses veered hard right, keeping formation and giving their riders first swing with their axes. Po clenched shut his eyes, drowning out his thoughts with the *Kime ki're kima ka.*

The battle roared, throwing up a storm of blood-curdling screams, clashing steel, and thundering hooves. The noise became physical, vibrating deep into Po's skull, overriding his attempts at deflection and controlling the very center of his being. A cold shiver ran through his veins, and his body felt weightless, as if about to float into the blue beyond. *So this is what death feels like.*

A horn blasted, jerking Po back to reality. The Kh'areen warband broke from combat. The Imperial cavalry tried to give chase, but their mounts were exhausted and frothing at the mouth. They fell behind and were soon lost to Po's sight. Yet the Kh'areen continued to gallop, kicking up dirt and grass under hoof, joining with the baggage horses, and continued for the best part of an hour. Po was impressed with the stamina of the Kh'areen.

Eventually, Lord Azraik called a stop and the warband sought refuge in a wooded valley. Po slipped from his horse and collapsed to the ground, his energy and adrenaline spent. He gagged and tried to vomit, but there was nothing to throw up. He rolled over, felt the dirt against his back and gazed up at the gray sky.

"Po," came Anjan's voice. His friend ran over, his cheeks white and his hands shaking, but his face carrying his familiar grin.

"I lost a sandal," Anjan said.

"I lost both of mine" Po said, glancing down at his grubby feet and wiggling his toes. Anjan slid down beside him and together they gazed at the sky.

"I can't believe it," Anjan said. "Did you see the cavalry charge, and the control they have over their horses?"

"Incredible," Po said. "Have you seen Dovo?"

"No," he said. The pair got up to investigate. The Kh'areen warriors were too busy to mind the prisoners. Already fires were flickering and food bubbled in pots. Horses grazed on the rich grass of the valley, while birds flitted anxiously about in the trees.

"Over there," Anjan said, pointing. Lord Azraik stood in a knot of warriors, a head taller than everyone else. As the prisoners approached, the Kh'areen looked up and parted. Beyond them were bodies in various states of dress.

"Dovo," Po cried, recognising his friend. Dovo stared at the canopy above, his eyes lifeless and glassy. His mouth hung open in a dying scream.

"Dovo," Anjan said, joining Po in falling at their friend's side. They checked his body and closed his eyes. Po snapped the arrow shaft buried in his friend's chest, and lifted Dovo's hands to his breast, securing shut his mouth for a more peaceful demeanor.

"Lord Azraik is sorry for your loss." Po glanced up at the interpreter with tears in his eyes. Lord Azraik stood grim-faced beside him.

"I..." he fumbled for words. "He's..." He caught sight of the officer with the broken arm, peering out from between two warriors.

"You!" Po yelled. He rushed at the man and it took three warriors to pull him off. Po did not care. His world was already broken, his mission failed, and one of his best friends dead. Sobbing, he collapsed at Lord Azraik's feet.

"I don't know your custom," the Kh'areen lord said through the translator. "But your friend died in battle. We'll rest here this day, so you can get on with the funeral rites. But tomorrow we ride, and we will look to the Great Horde at Zol Ba'az. The Oracle and Gosh Ovrak will know what to do with you."

Campfires flickered and sparks drifted into the black night. Soldiers laughed and quarreled, some played dice, other's *sa'na*. Sentries stood watch, wispy clouds of white steam puffing from their mouths. Occasionally an officer strolled between the fires.

Natan shivered, the cold prickling his skin with goosebumps. He looked down at his bare skin and ran a hand over the scars. They'd healed well — he just wished he was allowed a shirt. When asked, General Mamot's steward shook his head.

"Not now. Maybe when we trust you." It required constraint not to floor the cocky little man, but Natan new that would only get him in trouble. It was not worth it. He was going to escape, and *then* they would regret the way they treated him.

"*Oi,* Aurochs." Natan looked up. A cook approached with a silver platter, piled with steaming meat and vegetables. "Here," said the cook. "They're waiting."

"Smells good," Natan said, taking the platter. The cook gave him a menacing look.

"Well it ain't for you, is it?" *Don't start a fight,* Natan reminded himself. *Their time will come.* He turned to Mamot's tent, brightly lit in a circle of braziers. Two guards watched him approach and with a rustle of canvas the steward appeared, his face a picture of agitation.

"At last," he said, holding back the flap. "Quickly. Come on in." Natan mumbled an apology and stepped through onto the coarse woolen carpet, stained and frayed from weeks on the road. At once the heat and pungent aroma of incense and body odor hit him. Eight men, all government officials, sat around a table dominating the tent floor, nursing their cups while General Mamot regaled them from the head of the table.

"...and our fire wagons..." General Mamot paused and looked Natan's way. "Aurochs!" The guests turned, apparent relief on their faces at the interruption to the story. Mamot swept aside a jumble of cups and bottles.

"Here, put it here," he said. "Gentlemen, you'll remember Aurochs — we talked about him. Caught him after he killed twenty-seven of my men. He's a beast. Go on — show them."

Natan set the platter down, raised his arms and turned around, just like he had done a dozen other times before the legions of officials Mamot hosted. The guests marvelled at the scars crisscrossing his body, and his muscles rippling beneath the skin. A soft hand, unfamiliar with a hard day's work, ran itself over Natan's abdomen. Natan tensed. His eyes fell on a knife on the table. His fingers twitched. *Don't,* he told himself. *You'll die. Escape is a far better revenge...*

"A worthy prize," a guest said. "Twenty-seven men though? Really?"

"And twice as many wounded," Mamot said. "One day I'll break him."

"He looks tame enough," said another.

"A pet saber tooth can be tame," Mamot said. "But you don't turn your back on it." They chuckled.

"Still," said the first guest. "One less to worry about. The whole Seventh Army is dug in around Pao'an. You've got a challenge ahead of you." He paused, perhaps thinking he had gone too far, then continued. "How are you planning to take the city?" Eyes turned to Mamot. The general drummed his fingers on the table and turned his lips in a scowl. Natan stepped back, hoping no one would notice his departure, but Mamot raised a hand to stop him.

"Do you question the Third Army?"

"Me?" said the speaker, shrinking back into his chair. "I — I, well, I merely ask what your plan is, for — for I know you will have one, and perhaps could impress us with your military, *er*, wisdom."

General Mamot stood, and in silence crossed to a side table where he picked up a pile of porcelain plates. He returned to his guests and started laying the plates in front of them. Every eye in the room watched him. Mamot took his seat again.

"The art," he said slowly, measuring his words. "Of war is never fighting a battle you do not have to fight. It is as much here —" he pointed at his head. "— as it is there —" he pointed at Natan. "A good general never gives away his secrets."

"Of course," said the official. "I understand."

"I'm not sure you do," Mamot said. "Take this platter of vegetables. It smells wonderful doesn't it?" Heads nodded in approval.

"Could I," Mamot continued. "Move all those vegetables with a single fork?" He dangled his fork around before them, and heads shook. Mamot smiled in approval.

"Oh?" he said. "It's a matter of outthinking your opponent, and finding a weak spot." He stuck his fork into a potato at the bottom of the pile, and dropped it onto his plate. The vegetables above rolled across the table. Mamot looked to each of his guests with fire in his eyes, thumping a fist and squashing a stray parsnip. The violence startled his listeners.

"My Third Army," Mamot said. "Is not a fork. We are the fist of the gods. And I intend to apply no more pressure than a flick of the wrist." In a single motion Mamot stuck his fork once again into the potato, and put it in his mouth.

"You have a secret master stroke?" the official asked. Mamot smiled, his cheeks flapping about as he chewed on the potato. He tapped his nose with a finger.

"I have a plan," he said. The general's attention turned back to Natan. Natan stiffened at attention. "You're still here?" he asked through a mouthful, holding up an empty bottle. "Go get us more drink."

Later that night, after the guests had left, Natan went to clean up the dining tent. It was a mess, food trodden into the carpet, bottles rolling about and puddles of millet beer dripping from the table. From the smell, someone had relieved themself in the corner. The other prisoners grumbled, but Natan set to work with grim determination, deep in thought. *So, General Mamot isn't going to attack Pao'an*, he thought. *What's he going to do? We can't be more than a day or two from the city, an easy horse ride. Something must be happening. What am I missing?* The answers eluded him.

"Hey, Aurochs," the soldier supervising them called. "Here, take this bucket of scraps to the pigs."

Outside, the temperature continued to drop. Natan picked his way between the campfires, now dying low with sleeping figures wrapped up around them. He caught brief snippets of hushed conversation, and by the latrine pits he heard the moans of soldiers still suffering from typhoon fever. They reeked of dysentery and vomit, enough to turn Natan's stomach, but the pigs nearby did not seem to mind. Sniffling and grunting, they fed off the camp scraps. Natan tipped the bucket into the pen, adding to the already sizeable pile.

On the way back to the dining tent, Natan passed the cooking pits and supply tent. Five horses shuffled nearby, puffs of steam rising from their nostrils. Natan paused. *Are the guests still here?* He was unfamiliar with horses, but knew they were not the typical stocky warhorses of the Third Army. They were sleek and lean, each with a quilted blanket over their backs. Natan approached, careful not to startle them. Voices wafted from a nearby tent. One in particular was familiar. *General Mamot?* Natan questioned, drawing near yet sticking to the darkest shadows. He peeked into the tent where he saw five people huddled around a single candle. Drawing back into cover, Natan listened.

"— not the original plan," a thick Solari voice said.

"Adding Jano will increase the risk," said a second Solari voice. "Are you sure?"

"Yes," Mamot whispered. "If you can promise me success." There was a long pause.

"No," the first voice said. "One we can do. Not two."

"When the Emperor disappears," said the second. "Everyone 'll be on alert. We'd never reach Jano."

"I pay you," Mamot hissed. "And you're telling me it can't be done?"

"One, we can do," a third voice said. "But I agree with my comrades. It is risky enough grabbing the Emperor, and we have the cooperation of his staff. Grabbing the Emperor *and* reaching Jano, that is harder."

"Fine," Mamot said, louder this time. "But I'd pay more of course. How's one hundred gold *gotti* sound?"

"For…?" a Solari voice trailed off.

"Kill Jano." The men whispered among themselves.

"We can set up a diversion," the first man said. "Jano will be attacked, ambushed, at the same time we grab the Emperor. But we cannot guarantee a kill."

"Deal," Mamot said. "So in three days. My cavalry will advance under the cover of night. You know the signal. When you're out of the city, flash the code and they'll pick you up."

"Agreed — and the matter of payment?"

"I told you before," Mamot snapped. "Payment on completion."

"But," said the Solari, pausing. "You have our request ready?" Mamot grunted.

"Ten thousand," said the general. "Copper *jet*, half freshly minted. Five hundred silver *li* produced under the current Emperor. Two hundred gold *gotti*, unclipped — and a bank draft from the Honorable and Worshipful Bank of the Merchants of Gai'an to the sum of a further two hundred gold *gotti*. Yes, I remember. And yes, it's ready." Someone blew out the candle and Natan heard movement. He slipped around the side of the tent and froze perfectly still. He did not know which side they would exit from.

"— you better be grateful," Mamot said, clear and crisp in the night. "I sacked a dozen cities to raise the funds."

"Your Emperor will appreciate your dedication."

"Our Emperor," Mamot corrected.

"Indeed." The Solari mounted their horses and rode off into the night. Mamot watched them go, his features hidden in the darkness. Natan lowered himself further into the shadows. As he did so, his knee rubbed against the canvas of the tent. General Mamot jolted at the sound and turned on his heel, glancing into the shadows. Natan held his breath and closed his eyes, willing himself to be invisible. Somewhere in the camp a dog barked. Mamot muttered to himself, and foot falls faded into the distance. *He didn't see me*, Natan though with relief.

"Three days," he whispered to himself. "Three days." Natan knew what he had to do. He had to escape — and he had to do it soon.

CHAPTER 20

"Before the First Emperor, the Vu lands were ruled by petty kingdoms. The most powerful was the Kingdom of the Plain centered on the ancient capital of Vada-Manke, now a ruin. Their kings were buried in the Valley of Kings."

A History of the Vermilion Empire

Ashara looked down at her reflection in the water. She hardly recognized herself. Her fingers probed a scar along her cheek and a bruise on her temple. *How did that get there?* She rubbed at it, but it was definitely a bruise. The surface of the stream broke as she dipped her hands in and washed her face. The cold water numbed her skin and prickled her cheeks.

Her horse snorted, drawing Ashara's attention back to her surroundings. Thick brush rose up the sides of the valley, leading to the snow-capped mountains of the border regions. She squinted, seeking out anything that may have caught the horse's attention. Wind rippled the leaves and swayed the bushes, making it hard to tell if anyone approached.

Standing up, Ashara wiped her hands on her clothes and pricked her ears, listening for even the slightest sign of human contact. She heard nothing other than the rustling of the foliage.

"Come on," Ashara said to the horse, mounting it. "Time to go." She followed the stream, keeping a careful watch on the ridgeline. Fortunately she had come across few people over recent days. Most of the villages, if not deserted, were locked up tight behind ditches and palisades. In such cases she always felt wary eyes watching her. *Poor people*, she thought. *They didn't ask for this.*

A goat track diverged from the stream and led up to a shallow ridge above the valley. Ashara encouraged the horse up the hill and gazed at the rolling expanse of grassland laid out before her. She could see for miles and miles. The horizon eventually blurred in a wall of gray cloud. Some five miles off was a walled town, while smoke indicated a dozen odd villages.

The main road, Ashara thought. *It'll pass through the town. That's where Po would have passed.* Ashara set the horse off at a canter, caring no longer about being watched. Before long she was riding over barren fields, past the uprooted foundations of store sheds and farm buildings. Ahead, the town walls loomed, shutting out the world, with figures patrolling the battlements. Ashara looked to the gate, but it was closed. Helmeted heads looked down at her and pointed. She turned her back on them and skirted the town, avoiding the cesspits, and came to the south gate. It too was closed. This time the watchers challenged her.

"What's your business? The town's closed."

"What town's this?" Ashara called back. The sentry waved to someone and squinted down at her, taking a closer look.

"Posan," he yelled in reply. The men on the wall exchanged words. Ashara thought she heard the word "*Kh'areen.*" They turned anxiously about and disappeared behind the crenelations. There was no way she was getting into the town. She trotted her horse to the road, then noticed what she had at first missed. The dirt before the gate was torn up with water pooling in the troughs. Further along, the ground showed signs of a stampede, a violent struggle that got worse the further she rode. Having been around horses all her life, Ashara read the scars on the earth as if they were written words. She dismounted and felt the dirt between her fingers. *Two or three days*, she thought. *Still fresh.* Probing about she discovered the familiar shape of a sling stone. *Kh'areen.* Ashara stood in a panic.

"Po!" she yelled.

Her voice echoed off the hills. She cast about for other clues. Half trampled into the ground she found a broken arrow shaft. *The Imperial Army fought a battle here.* She chose a particular set of prints and followed them. *Here,* she said to herself. *Here they fought. Here the horse collapsed. Okay, the Kh'areen would go — there. They broke contact.*

Ashara jogged back to her horse and jumped into the saddle. She followed the tracks south, finding signs of a camp. *Definitely Kh'areen,* she noted, identifying the position of pickets and the way the horses had been corralled. She dismounted and checked the dirt for any sign she could draw on. Someone had discarded sheep bones and a broken flask. Someone else had chipped a piece of pottery. She sighed. There was no sign of the monks, and without access to the town she had reached a dead end. *Did they get this far?* She straightened and rubbed her back in irritation. A piece of red cloth caught her eye. Ashara approached and bent to pick it up. Her heart stopped and she choked back a sob. Her fingers dug through the mud and pulled out Dovo's sewing kit. *They came this way. They were with the Kh'areen.*

Without checking the rest of the camp, Ashara bounded to her horse and galloped south following the trail, pausing only to collect three dirty but familiar sandals.

Ashara looked down at Dovo's body, and whispered a brief prayer to Tanri. *No more than a day, or so,* she thought, noting the condition of the body. Poor Dovo… He had been buried it seemed, but then exhumed and left stripped naked next to the water-logged hole.

"I wish I could give you a proper burial," she said aloud. "And had time to get to know you better. May Tanri keep you, my friend, and give your soul rest." She saw no sign of Po or Anjan, and assumed they were still with the Kh'areen. From all the signs, the Imperial Army had not caught up with them, and the Kh'areen were making good progress. Ashara took a second look at the abandoned camp, and resumed her ride south.

Fire flickered through the trees, sending a soft glow into the night sky. Ashara tethered her horse and wriggled forward on her elbows. From her position she could see down into the camp and count the fires. *Definitely Vu,* she thought. *Kh'areen don't camp like that.* It concerned her however that she could not see the individuals in the camp. They could've caught Po and Anjan, and she would not know. Ashara bit her lip and considered her options. The easiest way was to pass them, rejoin the trail, and continue her pursuit of the Kh'areen. But then if it turned out her friends were in the camp, she'd never catch them if they returned north.

"Tanri, give me strength," she whispered. Deep down she knew there wasn't a choice. Before she went on she had to discover if her friends were down there.

Ashara stood in the shadow of an old pine and stripped herself down, removing everything that made noise. She wrapped it all up in her coat and left it by the horse. Then she crouched down and scooped up dirt from between the roots of the tree and smeared it over her cheeks and knife blade. Butterflies fluttered in her stomach, and she felt the sudden need to relieve herself.

"*Tanri gosh ba,*" she repeated to herself. Satisfied she had done everything she could to prepare, Ashara crept into the vale, sticking to the trees and undergrowth for cover. Drawing near, she heard voices from the camp. Soldiers talked around their fires, and somewhere a man exchanged harsh words with a comrade. Unseen, however, were the sentries that Ashara knew would he lying in total darkness, their ears and eyes peeled for anyone approaching the camp.

Ashara slipped down onto her belly and crawled forward on her elbows, pausing every few feet to listen. Suddenly she spotted movement, a dark patch against the night.

"You okay, Davi?" a voice asked.

"Alright, Captain," replied another.

"Tana will be along shortly with hot *kaja* and a bite to eat."

"Thanks." Footfalls passed Ashara's position as the captain continued his patrol. She had a good lock on the sentry's position, only a dozen feet from her. An insect crawled over her hand, but Ashara lay dead still. It tickled and she bit her tongue. *Not now… please not now.*

Almost indiscernible, Ashara heard the rustle and crunch of feet on grass.

"Davi, you there?"

"Yeah."

"Get this down you." After a pause, the feet moved on. The sentry sipped at a drink and chewed on his food. Ashara inched forward. She could almost see his shape crouched in a slight depression. *Just a bit further, you can do it.* Her breathing slowed. Her muscles tensed. Ashara focused all her energy on the moment, drawing on her experience hunting with her brothers. The sentry's smell told her she was almost on top of him.

"Tana, that you?" Ashara froze. "Tana?"

Steel brushed against leather. Ashara moved. Davi was too slow to respond. Ashara's hand clamped over his mouth, her weight driving him into the ground while her knife sliced deep across his throat. As the life drained from him, Davi hit her limply with his cavalry saber, each blow getting weaker until it fell from his fingers.

Ashara shivered and lay still, sprawled over the body. She listened for movement. Nothing. After a few minutes she slipped to the ground and crawled towards the fires; coming close enough to hear individual voices. It was the usual mix of oaths, obscenities, and camp banter, but nothing much of use to her. Further along were two men standing, their backs to the fires, deep in conversation. Ashara edged closer and lowered herself down next to a short screen of grass.

"We need to be out there," one man was saying.

"I've explained already," said the second. "Our horses don't have the endurance. Short spells, yes. But the Kh'areen can manage ten miles at a gallop."

"Then they've escaped us already."

"No, Inquisitor. We'll catch them. They're overconfident. Most likely they'll see a village ripe for plunder, or turn aside thinking we've given up the chase."

"You're the one that's overconfident, I think, Commander Vitan. We should've taken up the chase as soon as they broke from battle."

"What?" Commander Vitan said. "And have them turn on us as soon as our horses were tired? No, this is the way we do it. You're welcome, Inquisitor, to take your virtuemen, and carry on the pursuit by yourselves if you wish."

"Our orders come from Jano himself," said the Inquisitor. "You know that's not an option. We either return with those monks, or we don't return at all — and that applies to both of us."

A cry carried across the camp and others broke out in yells and shouts as alarm spread. Commander Vitan whirled on the spot, sweeping out his saber in one fluid motion.

"Positions!" he roared. "Defensive positions!" *They've found Davi,* Ashara realized in a panic. *That was quick.* She fought every impulse to get up and run. The primal urge to scream was almost overwhelming. Shapes moved around her, not concealing their movement. A cavalry boot stepped near her head. The owner stood over her, spear pointed into the night.

"Torches," Vitan roared. "We need light." The man standing over Ashara appeared to have second thoughts and ran back to the fires. Ashara used the opportunity to scuttle in the opposite direction. Flickering light jumped across the grass, and shadows crawled up a nearby rock face. A burning brand landed on the ground nearby.

"Over there!" someone shouted. Ashara did not wait to see if they'd actually seen her. She ran. A horse neighed, and an arrow whistled past her ear. Her heart pounded and her lungs burnt with the exertion. Another arrow shot past. At any moment she expected to feel the bone-breaking impact of cold steel. She reached the rock face and scrambled up the grassy bank beside it. A shaft buried itself in the ground beside her hand.

"It's a trap, fools," Vitan roared. "Hold your positions! Hold, I said!" She was in pitch darkness again. Gingerly, Ashara removed her sling and loaded a stone. The soldiers were easy targets, silhouetted against the firelight. She snapped a stone out towards a mounted soldier. He fell from the saddle as his comrades watched dumbly on. Ashara ran, chose a new position, and loosed another stone, then another, changing her angle of attack with each shot. As she hoped, the Vu cavalry men started snuffing out their torches and taking cover.

Her pouch exhausted, Ashara backtracked a way, looking for her horse. It took some time stumbling around in the dark. She began to fear the cavalry would realize they were not in immediate risk and come out after her, but this did not happen. Eventually the sound of the horse, agitated at the sound of distant soldiers, drew Ashara to it. She calmed it with a gentle touch.

"I'm back," she whispered in its ear. "We can go now."

Thunder rumbled on the horizon, waking Ashara from her sleep. She sat up, taking a while to remember where she was. The brown-gold grass of the plains stretched on, rolling like the waves of the sea to the distant mountain ranges of the border. Ink black clouds blotted out the sky to the southwest, while about her everything was gray and menacing.

Ashara stretched and yawned. Her stomach rumbled, but yesterday she had eaten the last of her supplies. Warily, she rekindled the fire from the night before, and went in search of water from a nearby stream. While there she restocked her pouch with pebbles for her sling.

"Tanri, make today the day," she prayed. She started off optimistic, then her spirits dampened with the arrival of cold showers, chilling her to the bone. The showers passed, and towards midday were the tell-tale signs of horses a distance ahead.

"Not long now," she said to her horse, barely containing her excitement. The horse snorted and shook its head in irritation. Its breathing was hard, and the nostrils flared. "I know," Ashara said. "I know. Just a bit further." She worried the horse might not make it. Vu horses just did not have the endurance of those bred by the Kh'areen. After a mile, Ashara reluctantly dismounted and led the horse on foot. This was easier on the horse, but harder on Ashara. *Just a little further*, she kept reminding herself.

The sun passed unseen overhead, and towards midafternoon the clouds parted, casting golden shafts across the plain. Ashara drank the last of her water, and promised herself she'd hunt the next rabbit she saw, mindful that every distraction took her further from catching the Kh'areen.

Ashara struggled up a gentle hill with a broad, sloping top. She bent over and held her knees, willing herself on. Straightening, she pulled at the rope, but her horse had sat down.

"Come on," she said, but it refused to move. "Fine." She sat down in the grass beside it, and imagined what it would be like to chew on the wild flowers. Her father had never suggested it, so she supposed it was a bad idea. "You know," she said to the horse. "If it rains, we're awfully exposed." *Am I going crazy?* She almost expected a reply.

Wind rippled through the grass, whistling over the hill. Ashara thought she heard words. *I'm so hungry,* she lamented. *I'm starting to hear things.* She lay back and closed her eyes, but the sound didn't disappear. Suddenly, she sprang to her feet. They were Kh'areen voices. Ashara ran across the top of the hill and looked down into the Kh'areen camp.

Horns blew. She was spotted. Returning to the horse, Ashara persuaded it to its feet.

"One last walk," she promised. She met three Kh'areen warriors halfway down the hill.

"Halt!" one yelled in Kh'areen, then followed up in Vu. "Stop there." Ashara stood her ground.

"Good afternoon," she said in her native tongue. "I've been looking for you." The warriors looked to each other, confused.

"Who're you?"

"I'm Ashara Daladh'an, daughter of Kh'am Daladh'an, friend of Takich Kh'undit, late priest of Tanri in Pao'an." It was a line she'd dreamt often of saying.

"And you look for the warband of Gosh Azraik?" asked the warrior.

"I believe he has my friends." The warriors listened to her explanation, and walked her down into camp. Passing through the picket, she drew the attention of the band, and soon a crowd formed around her. Lord Azraik pushed through them and came to stand before her. Behind him came Po and Anjan.

"Ashara!" Po yelled.

"Hi, Po."

Azraik gave Ashara a quizzical look, and listened while his warriors recounted what she said. When they finished the warband leader scratched his chin.

"I think," he said at last. "We need to talk."

Natan woke to trumpets heralding a new dawn, and another day of marching. He groaned, hating the slow monotony of such an army on the move, cramming the roads and spilling over into fields, with thousands of baggage carriers, wagons, soldiers, and cavalry all jostling for space.

"*Oi*, Aurochs," a supervisor yelled. "Quit your whining."

"The name's Natan," he said.

"I'll bloody call you what I like. Now off to the cooking pits. Go!" There was no point arguing. Natan trudged after the other prisoners, the mud underfoot already ankle deep with the passage of men and animals. The air that morning was particularly foul, with the wind carrying the stench of the latrines over the command section. *Escape,* Natan told himself, recalling the night before. *There has to be a way.*

General Mamot met his senior commanders first thing in the morning. Natan served breakfast while listening to the officers talk about the day ahead.

"Hey Aurochs!" General Mamot bellowed across the tent at one point. "You'll see Pao'an tonight. How's that make you feel?"

"Homesick," Natan said. The commanders chuckled over their breakfasts and avoided eye contact. General Mamot gazed around, his eyes bloodshot and his cheeks yellowing. *The bastard's still drunk.*

"Homesick?" Mamot barked. "I heard he cries in his sleep. Is this the best Jano can send against us?" *I do not,* Natan fumed. He scanned the officers, tittering like children, and then narrowed his eyes at Mamot. *They only laugh because you feed and pay them. They don't respect you.*

"I heard," Mamot continued. "Jano's wife left him for a shoemaker. If he can't command a woman, how's he command an army?"

Though the ground was damp, it turned to dust under the thousands of feet. Flies buzzed about the column, drawn to the animals and the odor of the porters. Natan labored under a heavy load, assigned to baggage duty after his encounter with General Mamot that morning. The overseer roared and raged, strolling up and down the line with a leather strip, driving the prisoners onward. Natan grunted and sweated, his bad leg prickling with pins and needles, his skin chafed raw. Still, there was little rest and no chance of escape. The beedy eyes of the overseer watched his every move, and mounted men patrolled the route with bows and arrows ready.

The sun was already touching the western ridgeline when the line of porters arrived at the evening camp. Natan stumbled to a stop and blinked the sweat from his eyes. He dared not believe it was the end of the day's march. In front, a flustered camp warden raised a hand and came towards them.

"Who're you lot with?"

"Headquarters," the overseer said.

"Okay, proceed over... hold on, stop!" A company of infantry tried to overtake the porters, joining the columns of men and animals converging on the camp.

"Stop!" the warden repeated. "Who're you lot with?" The captain gave his unit number. The warden looked about and scratched his head.

"Seventeenth? You're on picket — see the valley? We're holding the ridgeline. Everything inside is friendlies. Go up the track there. You'll find your commander at the top. Hurry, he arrived a while ago." The captain grunted and led his men off up the track. Natan squinted and looked to where the captain was going. The valley had steep hills on both sides, thick with yellowing scrub, that almost hemmed in the entire valley floor. Some ancient breastwork partially blocked off each end. There was an air of artificiality about it; an almost perfect symmetry.

"Right, porter's who're..."

"Headquarters," the overseer barked a second time.

"Yes," said the warden. "Proceed through the gap. You'll see the general's standard — center of the valley, by a well." The overseer nodded his thanks and yelled at the column to continue. Natan groaned. He wished they had never stopped. His legs almost refused to move, and his load felt heavier than at any time during the day.

I'm never going to escape this valley, he said to himself, gazing up at the natural defenses. Pao'an was close, but he had never felt so far away.

"Here you go," barked the overseer. "Baggage down. Pile over there. No, don't sit down. Who said we're resting? Firewood, go on, I want a stack of it. I'll tell you went to stop."

They collectively groaned.

"Where we get that?" said one, picking a boil on his foot. The overseer rolled his eyes and pointed to the valley wall.

"There's plenty there." They shuffled off, complaining to each other in low voices. Natan led the pack. Though tired, he was eager to see how easy the hills were to climb. The prospect of escape lent his limbs energy, and his mind a new sense of clarity. Together they began tugging at the dead branches littering the hillside beneath the scrub. Natan worked his way up, his feet raw from the days walk, and now bleeding from the many cuts. The going was tough. The others stopped and moved methodically, clearing out patch by patch, but Natan left them behind.

"Aurochs," one called. "Where you going?" Natan raced for an excuse, looking about the ridge above. He saw it.

"See the lone pine?" he called back. "There'll be some nice thick branches under that."

"One's as good as another," the porter said, shaking his head. "Your skin."

Natan continued to pick his way upwards. Thick columns of rock broke from the scrub, some of it dressed as if the ruins of an ancient building worn with age.

Maybe, maybe I can find a spot to hide. Disappear during the night, then escape before dawn when they're least on guard. He thought about it, but decided it would never work. He would be missed, and they would comb every nook and cranny of the valley to find him. And double the guard. *No, I'd be caught. And killed. And made an example of.*

Natan headed back down to the porters, picking up bits of firewood on the way. He stopped. *A hole.* It was by the base of one of the smaller ruins, one he had missed; too big for a rabbit hole, too small for anything larger than a wolf. Natan pulled back the grass and twigs and peered in, half expecting a growl and gnashing teeth, but nothing came at him. In the remaining light was the faintest hint of rock, indicating the depth of the hole. Natan snapped a piece of firewood in two and chucked both ends in. Nothing. Satisfied he was not going to be attacked, Natan dug his fingers into the earth around the hole, looking for signs of what lived within. He hit smooth, hard stone and brushed the dirt away, uncovering a square stone rim.

"Someone made this," he said, puzzled at the find.

"Aurochs, where are you?" Natan stood and waved. He would have to find an excuse to come back.

"Coming," he called. Back down with the workers, Natan dumped his firewood.

"There's snakes up there," he said casually. The others looked at him. Some jerked back from the scrub.

"There's what?"

"Snakes. I saw a nest of them."

"Did they have yellow stripes?" Natan, being from the city, did not know what that meant, but he went along with it.

"Yeah, you know..." He did a vague motion to indicate a generic stripe. "Do you think I should go back and fire the nest?" Seemingly glad Natan volunteered, the others nodded enthusiastically.

"That'd be best." Natan acted reluctant and rubbed a hand over his face. Beseeching eyes watched him, waiting for his move.

"Alright," he said. "Wouldn't want someone bitten taking a piss." He crossed over to the nearest campfire where a squad of crossbowmen prepared their evening meal. "...just up there," Natan explained, becoming confident in his story.

"You know what you're doing?" the sergeant asked suspiciously.

"Done it before," Natan lied.

"You'll need a good torch. Not one of these," he said. The sergeant jerked his head at one of the men, who returned with a pine resin torch. Natan accepted it, glad he had not been questioned further. His knowledge of killing snakes was even less than his knowledge of the snakes themselves. Heart racing, he crossed to the baggage crew.

"Good luck."

"Thanks," Natan said. "You'll come get me if I'm bitten?" The men looked aghast, muttering and shaking their heads.

"Bugger off. This is on you."

"No point in others dying," said another. "If it was me I'd let the soldiers do it. This ain't my war." Natan snorted in apparent frustration but actually swallowed a laugh. He turned from them, the heat of the torch scorching his face. Gingerly he climbed the hill, heedless of the branches and twigs that scratched his skin. *This is it*, he told himself. *No going back.*

At the hole Natan wasted no time. Legs first he slid in and brought the torch after him. It was larger inside than he had presumed — a tunnel going back into the hill further than the torchlight travelled. Clearly humans made it; the stonework cast irregular shadows off the vaulted ceiling. Natan glanced back at the entrance, then cast about with the torch. There had to be a way to close it. *No one makes a doorway without a door.*

Sure enough, his eyes fell on a stone plug. Leaving the torch, Natan picked it up and pushed it into the square gap. It fell out. He inspected it. Someone had once used mortar to secure it. He did not have access to that. Instead he pulled branches in to partially cover the opening, and took sand from the floor to wedge the plug as best he could. It stayed. *For now.*

Without natural light, the passage appeared far less encouraging. Natan thought he heard something. *Probably rats.* Retrieving the torch, Natan ventured into the dark. The passage led upwards, ever so slightly.

He came to a chamber lined with alcoves. Whatever had once been in them was long gone. The passage continued on the other side. Up it went until Natan arrived at a second chamber. This far exceeded the other in size, and the domed ceiling disappeared into the gloom above.

Jade, Natan thought, approaching a large panel on the wall. Some ancient worker had engraved words into the surface, barely legible with age. Though Vu had changed somewhat, Natan still recognized the words.

> *We are Makan-Dapa, King of the Plain.*
> *We conquered nations, destroyed cities.*
> *Ja'pa is turned to ruin, its crops withered.*
> *Tavana is humbled, its prince pacified.*
> *No other king is greater than us.*

By the panel, Natan noticed stones missing from the wall. He bent over and looked inside. There was a chamber beyond, a large marble box in the center — a sarcophagus. The hole was almost big enough for him to fit in, but for all his curiosity Natan knew he could not linger. If the torch went out he'd die alone, lost forever in some pre-imperial king's tomb.

The passage continued through the other side of the chamber, this time gently sloping downwards. Natan began to hope for the first time the passage actually took him under the hill and might have another entrance on the other side. He passed side rooms and more alcoves, pillaged long ago by grave robbers. Then he came up against it; a brick wall sealed off the passage ahead. The only option was a smaller tunnel that skewed right off the main passage. Natan paused. So far, he had not turned any corner or dared do anything that might get him lost. But he had no choice. He entered the smaller tunnel, stooping with the low ceiling. Necessarily, the torch came close to him, singeing his hair.

The tunnel dropped down into a chamber, and beyond that was the familiar square plug he had discovered at the other end. He ran his fingers over it, secured a grip and pulled. It did not budge. It was lodged firmly in place. On closer inspection, Natan noticed mortar still in the cracks. *The grave robbers must have come the other way. I'll just have to break it.*

Natan cast about for a stone, but the chamber and tunnel were clear of debris, as clean as the day the ancient king was sealed away. He hurried back towards the main chamber, dashing in and out of side rooms, looking for something — anything he could use. The torch flickered and hissed. Natan glanced at it; he would not have long. Soon he'd be in total darkness.

Panic set in. *Breath deep,* he told himself. *Control yourself. Focus.* He took a deep breath and measured his steps, trying not to run. At the main chamber Natan found the gap in the wall where grave robbers had broken in. Stone chips lay scattered around the base of the wall, none big enough to be useful. Natan knelt down and stuck an arm through the gap, feeling about for something bigger. His fingers brushed a chunk of stone the size of his hand. Grabbing it, Natan returned to the tunnel and the exit plug. He hammered away, sending chips flying.

"Come on," he hissed, putting all his strength into the strikes.

With a puff the torch died, leaving an amber glow. Natan blinked, the final image of the chamber wall burnt into his vision as a heavy darkness enveloped him like a wet rag. His lips quivered and his stomach cramped. He felt light headed. *The end is near...*

"No," he screamed, rallying himself for a final effort.

Grit showered his face and caught in his eyes. Suddenly, the plug shifted. Two more strikes and it landed with a muffled thud at Natan's feet. The expected rush of fresh air did not come. Instead the chamber filled with a damp, earthy smell. Natan groaned, realizing the implication, and tested the packed earth with his palm. There was nothing else he could do. He could not go back, so he started digging.

He tore at the earth, scouring his skin and snagging fingernails on roots. For once Natan was glad the torch was out; he could use two hands, and he did not see the damage he did to himself. He was up to his elbows when he felt sweet, cold, fresh air breeze over his fingers. It did not take long to widen the hole after that. Natan boosted himself and squeezed through the gap, rolling into grass on the other side. He lay there, looking up at the night sky, sucking in air and wiping tears from his eyes.

After composing himself, Natan sat up; the hill at his back. Before him the great plains stretched out, cast in deep shadow under a starless night. Only the distant glow of Pao'an gave Natan a sense of direction, as a beacon welcoming him home. He gripped his knees and stood, then walked, stumbling along like a drunk returning from a night out. Every fiber of his being wanted him to stop. Every breath became painful, but Natan refused to give in. As dawn broke he leaned against a boundary marker and caught his breath. He looked back to where he had come from, then towards Pao'an. Three horses galloped towards him, green pennants streaming from their lances. Natan straightened and walked towards them.

"Halt!" one cried when within hailing distance.

Natan stopped and raised his hands. He was home.

Firelight glistened in the eyes of the warriors. Lord Azraik walked among them, his thumbs stuck in his collar, and his chest puffed out. His words were unintelligible to Po, but the passion of the lord's speech was evident. His warriors hung on his every word. Azraik stopped and focused on each in turn, the silence pregnant with anticipation. He said two words more and returned to his camp seat, a head and shoulders above those seated on the ground.

Ashara rose and picked her way between the tangled limbs. Po had hardly heard her speak her native tongue before, and when Ashara opened her lips he saw a different side to her. Gone was her accent and stilted choice of words, replaced with confidence and cadence.

"I hear our names," Anjan whispered.

"It's about us," Po replied. "But I can't hear... yes, I can. Your name."

"And your's," Anjan added. Po raised an eyebrow and glanced at his friend.

"Bokos," Anjan said. "Haven't you picked that up yet?"

"No," Po said. "But that's not my name."

"It's what they call you," Anjan said with a grin.

"Better not be anything bad."

"I think it means pig." Po jabbed an elbow at Anjan, and Anjan drew back. A warrior grunted and cuffed Po over the back of his head. Po ducked and shrunk down into his shoulders.

"Sorry," he whispered, exchanging sideways glances with Anjan.

Ashara came to stand by them, and with a final statement yielded to one of Azraik's companions, but remained standing. Po touched her foot.

"What did you say?" he hissed.

"*Shush*, let me listen," Ashara said.

"Fine," Po said, eyes downcast.

Azraik's companion drew back his shoulders and puffed up his body as he walked back and forth before the warband. He emphasised his points with a single clap of the hand, or a finger jabbed into the air. Po wished he could see Ashara's reaction, but her face was dark and turned away from him.

"They're discussing what to do with you," a voice said, startling Po. Hand on beating heart, Po spun about on his backside. It was the translator, crouching at his shoulder.

"What *are* they going to do?" Po asked once recovered.

The translator shrugged.

"It's up to Azraik. But he'll listen to opinions first."

"What's the mood? What're they saying?" The translator frowned and indicated the companion.

"He thinks your friend's story is too convenient. He wants you taken as prisoner to Baki, to be traded at the end of the war for Kh'areen prisoners."

"And Azraik?"

"I already said. He's non-committed, cautiously testing the band."

"You believe us though, right?" The translator raised his palms and leaned in closer.

"I've not seen the document they talk of."

"Didn't Azraik show you?"

"He's Kh'areen. They don't write sensitive information." He tapped his temple. "They keep it here. Your problem is convincing these warriors that your mission is as important as your friend says it is." Po folded his arms, feeling his ribs beneath his skin. He'd lost a lot of weight. He did not know if he could survive a trek across the open steppe in winter — not without a change of clothes and a good diet.

"Here we go," the translator whispered. Azraik stood and took some time to tuck his thumbs back into his collar and clear his throat.

"What's he saying?" Po asked nervously.

"The time is late, and he's heard enough. He'll discuss it more with his closest companions." Warriors began to stand and dust off their breeches, filling the air with chatter.

"I guess we wait," the translator said.

Po and Anjan sat by the fire, struggling between them to turn four squares of canvas into passable shoes.

"No, it's like this," Anjan said, exaggerating the movement of the needle.

"That's what I did," Po said. Anjan took Po's shoe off him and completed the loop himself.

"How'd you do that?"

"Like I showed you."

"You two eaten?" Ashara asked, emerging from the darkness. Po nodded towards the bones by the fire. Ashara sat beside them with a roasted leg bone between her teeth.

"I'm starving," she said from the corner of her mouth. Po watched her eat. *She really is beautiful.*

"You didn't have to come back for us, you know." Ashara regarded him but continued chewing.

"It was my choice," she said.

"You were almost home," Po continued. "You'd be in Baki now if it weren't for us. I mean, we're happy to see you. But, well, you know." Po berated himself for not choosing his words better. Lowering the bone, Ashara furrowed her eyebrows.

"And you were going to save yourself?"

"No."

"So, I came back." Anjan jabbed an elbow into Po's side and leaned across to Ashara.

"I think," he said as Po winced. "He means we're grateful you came back. Whatever happens, you've given us a second chance."

"Thanks, Anjan," Ashara said.

"That's what I meant," Po said. "Thank you." Ashara's features softened, though Po sensed an inner tension remained as if she fought to relax. Her fingers fidgeted with the bone, and she turned it over in her hands.

"I shouldn't have left things as I did. I was angry. I..."

Anjan coughed nervously.

"I'll clean up, shall I?" he said, awkwardly getting to his feet. They watched him go.

"I'm sorry," Ashara said. "You never meant to hurt me."

"No, I'm sorry," Po said. "I should've been open with you. It seems like so long ago, but I was told telling anyone would put them in danger. I didn't want that. If you were caught, I didn't want them torturing you for information."

"They'd do it anyway," Ashara said. "I... no. I don't think we should do this again. It happened. We all make mistakes. Only Tanri knows how much time we have left together, let's not part again in anger." A lump caught in Po's throat.

"I'm glad you're here, Ashara."

"I can't say the same to you," she said with a smile.

"Will they release us?"

Ashara leaned over. Her hand touched Po's knee reassuringly.

"I don't know," she said. "But I've done the best I can." Po placed his hand on hers.

"I'll miss you," he said. Ashara looked away and sighed.

"Me too." Po did not want the moment to end. The spell was broken. A hand squeezed his shoulder, the fingers firm and commanding.

"Bokos," Azraik said, forcing his way between the pair and sitting with his feet out towards the fire. "*Kh'olun da?*" Po glared at him, barely containing his irritation at the interruption. Azraik appeared not to notice.

"He wants to know if you've eaten," Ashara translated.

"Tell him I have," Po said. "Thank you." The translator joined them, taking Anjan's spot, looking distinctly less relaxed than the Kh'areen lord. Anjan returned and sat opposite.

"He's made a decision," the translator said, prompted by the lord. A knot tightened in Po's stomach and his fists balled up. Lord Azraik clapped him on the back and laughed, saying something to the translator.

"He says don't be so nervous. Sick prisoners aren't worth as much."

"What?" Anjan demanded. "They're not letting us go?"

"Quiet," Ashara hissed. "Listen." Azraik clamped a hand onto Po's knee, squeezing it, and leaned over, talking sternly with his eyes locked on Po's. Po met his gaze and held it. Azraik stopped and let the translator speak.

"Lord Azraik says, his people fight with iron. They charge their enemies on horseback and trample them into the dirt. This is the way of war." Azraik continued, so close Po could smell the spice on his breath. "He says, he grew up with an axe in one hand and a sling in the other. He is a warrior. But a man who will not fight is a suckling goat ready for the fire pit. In the wild the terror bird and the wolf prey on weaker animals, so in life the strong dominate the weak."

Po did not blink, not even once. He stayed focused on Azraik, drawing on his Ba're training for concentration. He did not know what game the Kh'areen lord was playing, but he knew if he looked away he lost.

"You, Po, are his prisoner. While he fights with iron, you rely on words. Words did not save you from him, and yet you claim the words written on sheets of paper will win the war. When have words ever won a war?" Po waited for Azraik to continue, but the lord fell silent, watching him. When it became obvious Azraik didn't plan to continue, Po spoke.

"Tell him this: war is what happens when people run out of words. But even then, words have power. I've seen you encouraging your warriors. I saw you speaking today. You know your words matter. Your enemy is Jano Maretaki. My enemy is Jano Maretaki. These *sheets of paper*, as you call them, speak the truth, compiled by one of the most trusted men in Pao'an, and will weaken Jano's moral authority."

"His what?" the translator said. Po searched for a better word.

"His command," he said. "These words will weaken his command." Azraik listened to the reply and opened his mouth to speak, but Po cut him off. "Gosh Azraik, let me weaken your enemy. Then you use iron and horses to scatter him across the grassy plain as dust beneath your feet." Po hoped his words sounded as compelling in translation as they sounded in his head. Azraik remained silent a long time, his eyes not moving, his lips as firm as cured leather. Then he broke into a wide grin.

"*Da bana kel abeega,*" he said. "*gidh'di abee gosh dabi u din.*" The translator cleared his throat.

"You think you can bargain with him, but Lord Azraik is lord of war, keeper of the gates of war." Po broke eye contact and turned to the translator. Though a cold night, the man sweated and tugged at his collar.

"What does he mean?" Po demanded. Azraik spoke.

"You go free, not because you bargain, but because Lord Azraik, bountiful in his mercy, wills it. Because he thinks it is good."

"We can go?" Anjan squeaked.

"Really?" Po asked. Ashara fired off questions in Kh'areen and soon everyone talked at once. Azraik silenced them.

"You leave this night. Your monastery is not far from here — in the mountains to the southwest. In daylight you will see them. Take this document and make the secrets known. May the monks there print ten thousand copies so all the world can read it."

"I think there's more people than —"

"Po!" Ashara barked.

"Sorry." Lord Azraik stood, and the others followed.

"Lord Azraik says, your name should not be Bokos, but Bo'chin." Po glanced at the smiling faces and sensed he was the butt of a joke.

"What's that mean?"

"Bokos is pig," Ashara said. "Bo'chin is monkey. He thinks you talk like one." Po looked down at his bony, wraith-like body.

"And pig? Why did they name me that? I don't look like one." Azraik understood without need of translation. He cupped two hands to his mouth and squealed like a pig stuck with a branding iron. Everyone except Po laughed at the imitation.

"I don't sound like that!" Po protested. "I don't! Do I?"

It was just before dawn. The land was still dark, with nothing but the slightest gray glow on the horizon. A small party gathered beyond the Kh'areen pickets. Po stamped his feet and rubbed his hands.

"It's not far, a day or two at most," Ashara said. "How are the shoes?"

"They'll do," said Po. "Thanks for the hood." Po couldn't see Ashara's face, but he heard a puff of air suggesting a smile.

"You don't have tinder and flint do you?" Anjan asked.

"No," said Ashara. "No fire. It's not safe."

"I agree," said the merchant of Posan. "You don't need the attention."

"Not even for a hot cup of *kaja*?"

"There's none anyway," Po said. Grass crunched and they turned towards the dark shape looming from the night. Lord Azraik was flanked by two of his companions. He spoke in a low voice, and Po felt a roughspun bag pushed into his hands.

"He says the document's in the bag."

"And our referral letters?" Po asked.

"He says all papers are in the bag."

"Bring fire," Po said. "I'd like to check."

"No. Eyes could be watching the camp. We don't know how far the imperial scouts are from us. You'll have to go as far and as fast as you can before the light reveals you're gone."

"If," Anjan postulated cautiously. "They have eyes on the camp. Won't they notice us missing in the morning and give pursuit?"

"Possibly," the translator said without waiting for an answer from the lord.

"Speed," Ashara said. "Don't slow down. Just go as far as you can and don't stop."

"How about..." Anjan began, but Lord Azraik cut him off. Ashara translated.

"If the enemy is close, we'll delay them." Po paused. He did not know how to say goodbye. He sensed the tension around him.

"Well, we better start," said Anjan. "Dawn can't be far off."

"Stay safe," Ashara said. "May Tanri watch over you."

"We'll meet again," Po said, struggling to keep his voice from cracking.

"Don't say that," Ashara said. Po wished the others would leave him alone with Ashara one last time, but he knew the time had come. He forced himself to turn his back.

"Po, Anjan," Ashara said. "We part as friends. I'll never forget you."

"Neither will we," Anjan said.

Words caught in Po's mouth and he blinked back tears, refusing to reveal the depth of his emotion.

"Bye," he said.

Lord Azraik said something and turned back to the camp, the translator in tow. Ashara lingered a moment, then went after them. Po sniffed. Anjan put his arm out and together they set off on the final leg of their journey.

In the light of morning, the distant Graytalons rose bleak and rugged, shrouded in a haze of pearly mist. It reminded Po of the painting back at Jan Moga. He could even picture where the monastery lay, tucked within the folds of the mountains. Towards late morning they left the grassy plain and entered the wooded foothills. Occasionally they saw a distant village or terraced fields, but it felt safer amidst the trees with plenty of cover. The atmosphere loosened and they began to talk freely.

"Hard to imagine," Po said. "Early Ba're monks choosing these mountains. They're so far from anywhere and not very welcoming.

"If you want peace and quiet, where would be better?" Anjan suggested.

"Do you think they'll recognize us as monks?"

"A few days rest, fresh robes and a haircut and you'll look the part."

Po ran fingers through his beard, the first one he had ever grown.

"It's prickly. I don't know how men keep it."

"I like it," Anjan said. "But I'll be glad when life's back to normal."

"Will it be?" Po asked. "Normal I mean."

"Sure it will. Back to monastic routine. I never thought I'd miss it."

Po sniffed the air and glanced the pine-clad slopes. Something was not right.

"What is it?" Anjan whispered.

Po held up a hand and, sensing the direction of the breeze, and pointed to a nearby rise. They crept forward, keeping their bodies low to the ground, their canvas shoes silent on the pine needles. *Smoke. Fire. Danger.* Anjan touched Po's shoulder and motioned for him to stay. Po crouched and watched Anjan approach the edge of the rise, sheltering his approach by the trunk of a tree. Anjan jerked his head down, held it, then came back.

"There's a road," he whispered, making signs with his hands. "Runs by a small lake. They have a roadblock. Three horses. Must be three soldiers. Little fire."

"Do you think they know we're headed this way?"

"Well they must suspect it," Anjan said with a shrug. "They're not taking any chances."

"Bother. We'll have to go round."

Anjan nodded and led the way. For the rest of the afternoon they proceeded in silence, not daring to make a sound. There were villages, another roadblock, and what Po thought were bear tracks, and with every passing hour the hills rose higher and higher until they gazed out over the bleak country below, dim and cheerless with rain.

"They're out there somewhere," Po whispered.

As night fell, Anjan convinced Po they had to rest. They picked a tree and hollowed out a space between the roots, their backs to the wind. Without fire it was the best they could do.

"Tomorrow in Jan'a," Anjan said, holding up a piece of dried beef.

"Tomorrow in Jan'a," Po repeated.

"Do you think it'll make a difference?"

"What?" Po asked, chewing stale bread.

"This book. Out here, it doesn't seem so important."

"The world must know of Jano's crimes."

"Will it make a difference?"

"I think so," Po said. "Maybe not for everyone. But it sows doubt. People will whisper behind his back, and those who knew Judge Bodai will say he was a great man."

"Can I see it?"

Po unwrapped the roughspun bag and pulled out the contents. There was Master Dugen's copy of the *Sudo Ba're Datai*. Po ran a hand over the ancient leather cover, peeling at the edges, and returned it to the bag. There were three letters, written in immaculate handwriting and stamped with the seal of Jan Moga.

"I guess Dovo won't be needing his."

"Keep it safe," Anjan said. "In his memory."

Po nodded and returned the letters to the bag. Last there was the manuscript, water stained and torn in places. Lord Azraik had not looked after it.

"Is that it?"

"Yeah." Anjan flipped through the pages, stopping from time to time to read a page or two, muttering to himself.

"The army won't be happy."

"Why?" Po asked.

"If Jano's borrowed so much money, what happens when he can't pay them?" Po shrugged, accepting the manuscript back.

"They're already committed. I don't think they'd just turn on him." Anjan rubbed his bare arms against the chill. Po returned the manuscript to the bag and offered Anjan an arm. They snuggled together, Ashara's hood being big enough for the both of them.

"It's snowing," Po said after a while. There was no reply. Anjan was fast asleep. Po checked that the hood covered them both, and closed his eyes.

A horse snorted and pawed the ground. Po started awake and sat up. Beside him Anjan stirred.

"Hello Po," said Inquisitor Lukan. "You thought you'd escape us, didn't you?" Virtuemen strode into view, their black coats flapping in the wind. Po squinted, trying to comprehend what was going on.

"What time is it?" he asked, confused. Lukan dismounted and drew back his hood.

"That's a weird question. Come on, get up. It's over."

CHAPTER 21

"Upon arriving at Jilan I saw Vu cavalry on parade. They rode in companies of one hundred, ten abreast and ten deep. Each carried a spear, saber and bow."

The Travels of Odam Yusufkas the Solari

"To arms!"

Ashara jumped up, her prayers forgotten. Around her the camp burst into activity. Warriors stumbled into their britches and fumbled with the ties of their laminar armor. A priest in his robes called out exaltations, and one of the companions lifted his warhorn and blew a staccato tune. Ashara pushed her way between the warriors, looking for Lord Azraik. She found him by his fire.

"Where should I go?" she asked. "I want to fight." The warleader glanced at her, roared a command to a companion, and then looked back.

"Go with the supplies," he ordered. "Quickly."

"I can fight," Ashara persisted. "Give me armor and a horse." The Kh'areen lord shook his head and pointed to a companion.

"Orslan, take her to the supplies." The companion raised an eyebrow at Ashara and grabbed her by the arm. He was as large as Azraik, with plaited hair and an angry red scar running from one ear down to his chin.

"This way, miss."

"What's happening?" Ashara asked, hurrying to keep up with him. "I can fight."

"The Imperials stole a ride on us," Orslan growled. "Closer than we thought." Ashara felt sick. Po and Anjan had only left the camp in the early hours of the morning. She desperately hoped the cavalry under Commander Vitan would miss their trail. Just as she was about to ask another question, Orslan pushed her towards a youth with his arm in a sling.

"Son, take her."

"Yes, father," the youth said, taking Ashara by the forearm. Ashara resisted, but the youth tightened his grip.

"This way," he said, almost politely.

"I want to fight," Ashara said. "Let me go."

"You haven't trained with the men. You're safer with me."

"That's not the point. My friends are out there." The youth ignored her. They came to the corralled horses, protected by the elder men and those too young or injured to fight. The men raced to have the horses tied, the supplies loaded, and the prisoners secured to the saddles. From among them the priest appeared, beseeching those who would listen to call upon Tanri for protection.

"Tell them I can fight," Ashra said, gripping the hem of the priest's robes. "Isn't it written..."

He snatched back his clothes and hurried off, casting a wild glance in her direction. Ashara turned back to the youth.

"What's your name?" she asked. They stopped in the midst of the chaos.

"Bavgai," he said. "That was my father, Orslan."

"Tell me Bavgai, can you help me?"

"How?" he asked, clearly suspicious.

"Just a little thing," Ashara said. The youth looked about frantically at the activity.

"We've got to go," he said. "See, the warriors take their horses. Soon we ride out."

"I'll ride with them," Ashara said. "I've been in battles before. I can fight. Trust me."

"No," the youth said, avoiding eye contact. "My father..."

"Let her go," an old warrior shouted. "One less mouth to feed."

"Tanri favors the brave," called another. "Let's see what she's made of." Ashara regarded the two old warriors atop their mounts.

"Flesh and guts," she said. "I assure you."

"You're only young once," said the first. "She's got a fire in her." Bavgai considered the two men, then turned to Ashara.

"Damn it," he said. "Okay, you've got to be quick." He released her forearm and hurried to his horse. From the back of the saddle he removed his laminar and leather armor.

"It's a bit big for you," he said. "Pull this over your head. Here. Tie these. Okay, the helmet's too big."

"Here," called one of the old men, removing his own. "Try this. Fetch." Ashara caught the offered helmet and felt the sticky leather. It stank of body odor, but when she pulled it on it fit snuggly.

"Now look after yourself," Bavgai said. "Don't let father see you."

"I won't," Ashara promised, adjusting the belt for her knife and sling.

"You'll need an axe. Take mine."

"I'll use my sling," Ashara said. Bavgai sighed and turned pleadingly to the older warriors.

"Take the axe," the first one said. "You'll need it." Ashara grunted and accepted the offered axe. It was heavier than the weapons she was used to. She gave it a few practice swings and Bavgai adjusted her grip.

"No time for more," he said. "Take my spare horse. Go gently with her. She was a birthday gift — name's Ayanga."

"Ayanga," Ashara repeated as Bavgai helped her up into the saddle. "Thanks." She paused a moment to thank the two old men and trotted off after the last of the warriors.

"Don't let my father see you," Bavgai called after her.

Ashara reined in amidst the last ranks of the Kh'areen warband. The warrior on her left gave her a confused look then nodded his head. She turned to the right and started in her saddle. Of all the two hundred something warriors, she had chosen Orslan's section. The companion considered her, scowled, then huffed his ascension.

"Too late now," he grumbled. "Stick with me and look after my son's horse." Ashara swallowed hard.

"Ayanga's safe with me," she said. Ahead, Lord Azraik raised his axe and the warband hushed. The front ranks bristled with spears, the rear ones prepped their slings. They faced a nearby ridgeline. Two warriors lay prone at the top. All of a sudden they ran back to their horses.

"Advance at a walk!" Azraik shouted. The ranks of Kh'areen horse stepped forward, the riders careful to keep their lines. Ashara glanced to the left and right, conscious of her inexperience at riding in formation. When she looked up again, the front row of warriors were breasting the hill.

"Advance at the trot!" Azraik shouted. The pace increased and Ayanga responded beneath her. Ashara reached the top and felt the ground flatten out, then she was on the other side, the valley before her with Vu cavalry in their loose lines, their riders circling.

"Advance to engage!" Azraik roared, and the horses quickened again. Horns echoed and the Vu cavalry twisted in their saddles and raised their bows. The air filled with black, whistling shafts.

"Hold steady!" Orslan commanded. The ground shrunk between the two armies. Arrows thudded into man and beast. Warriors pitched from their saddles, and a horse cartwheeled forward, tail over head, dumping its rider. Ashara heard the crunch as her own horse trampled one of the fallen men. She felt sick. She felt the sudden urge to pee and wished she'd skipped breakfast. She did not have long to think about it.

A cry arose and Ashara whirled her sling. A hailstorm of stones arched towards the Imperial horses. Once, twice, three times they fired. Ashara imagined the damage they caused.

For Po, she told herself. *For Anjan.*

"Spears!" Azraik ordered. "Axes! Charge!"

Ashara tucked her sling into her belt and brandished Bavgai's axe. The horses thundered, their hooves kicking up clods of turf. The Imperial cavalry wheeled and formed ranks, facing the coming onslaught. Ashara opened her lungs and yelled along with the warriors. The Imperials answered, their warcries drowned out amidst the din of the charge.

"Tanri gosh ba!"

Crunch.

Horses whinnied. Bones cracked. Blood sprayed from wounds. Ashara struck at an oncoming rider. She was rewarded with a bone-jarring *thunk*. A saber flashed and Ashara dodged, nearly falling from the saddle. Others stampeded past her. The shouts and cries were deafening. Suddenly Ashara realized they had broken free and galloped over open ground, the Imperials behind them.

"Follow my lead!" Azraik yelled. "Wheel about! Ready slings!"

Ashara fumbled with her bag of stones and scattered the contents, swearing under her breath. She caught one of the sling stones and loaded her sling. Just then, the warrior to her left yelped. She turned in horror. He sat forward in his saddle, an arrow embedded in his breastplate, blood dripping from his open lips.

"Ashara, you okay?" Orslan called. Ashara turned to the companion, a look of shock on her face. She nodded. There was no time for further discussion.

"Form ranks!" Azraik yelled. "Keep your lines!" Orslan and the other companions took up the cry and Ashara closed ranks with the riders on either side. She could see two dozen horses without riders, and others where warriors sat slumped in the saddle. The horses were so well trained they kept going.

"*Tanri gosh ba!*" the warriors yelled.

"*For Po! For Anjan!*" Ashara shouted. Orslan glanced her direction and took up the cry, rising high in his stirrups.

"*For Po! For Anjan!*"

The sides collided. This time the fighting splintered, the ranks broke apart and the horses slowed. Ashara drove into the thick of it, fighting hand-to-hand. Beneath her Ayanga tensed up, the muscles rippling between Ashara's legs, her ears pinned back. She knashed her teeth and barreled into the Vu horses, kicking and biting. Blood splattered across Ashara's face and dripped down her fingers. Orslan yelled and ploughed into the fray beside her.

"*For the Oracle and the Chobi! For the Chobi Ghada!*"

Ashara pushed Ayanga ever deeper. Her hand tired. The gore-splattered axe became heavy. Her vision tunneled. Ashara shook her head, fighting back the fatigue. If Po and Anjan were to escape, she knew they had to bloody Vitan's cavalry. It was all that mattered.

The figure of Commander Vitan rose up out of the battle, crashing his armored horse into the warriors. Orslan swung his axe at him, but Vitan deflected it off a small round shield. The companion didn't have time to recover. As Ashara lurched to his aid, Vitan's blade slashed across Orslan's face, showering his horse with fresh warm blood. Orslan opened his mouth, his teeth red, and bellowed to the sky. Ashara pushed between him and Commander Vitan. Vitan slashed at her, but Ashara kicked free of the stirrup and dodged his attack. He corrected and went for her breast. The sword struck her laminar armor, driving the wind from her. His blade came round and went for her unprotected throat above the larynx. Ashara swept out her knife and caught the blade just above the guard. Vitan looked at her in surprise, then his face exploded in a mess of blood and bone, Ashara's axe lodged in his skull.

"Orslan!" Ashara yelled, returning to his side. The companion clawed at his face, his fingers slick with blood. Ashara grabbed his reins and spurred the two horses out from the fight. They rode over bodies, some still moving, others dead and trampled. As they withdrew, horns blew and cries in Vu went up.

"The Commander's dead!"

"Break!"

"No! Hold! Regroup!" But no matter what the officers screamed, the Imperial cavalry broke north, galloping across the grassland, stragglers cantering after them, some riderless. Ashara watched them, her chest heaving. Warriors lingered around them.

"Orslan," a warrior cried, dismounting and running to the companion's side. "Can you hear me? Are you okay? Speak to me."

"He'll live," Ashara gasped, panting for breath. "Just a —" she indicated a sword swipe with her hand. "The helmet took most of it —"

"What are you doing?" Azraik yelled, cantering into the huddle of riders. "After them! Take out the stragglers! Don't let them regroup."

Ashara put a hand to Ayanga's neck and brought it back, red and sticky with blood.

"Can you do it, Ayanga?"

The horse gnashed her teeth and stomped, still excited from the battle. Warriors peeled off and gave chase. Ashara dug in her heels and galloped after them, determined despite her fatigue to finish off her enemy. The Kh'areen warriors streamed after the remnants of the Imperial cavalry, picking off the slowest riders with sling stones. They rounded a hill and swept down into the subsequent depression. Ahead, a section of the fleeing cavalry split off from the rest. Their leader appearing to be a captain, a green horsehair crest shimmering in the wind.

"They're forming a rear guard!" a warrior yelled. "At 'em!" The defiant captain addressed his ranks and raised his sword. Ashara sensed victory. There was no way those dozen cavalrymen could hold off the Kh'areen.

"Tanri gosh ba!"

Arrows thudded into the pursuers. Men went down. Ashara gritted her teeth and lowered herself in the saddle, her axe ready. The gap closed. *Come on, come on, nearly...* A sudden weight hit her, throwing her back in the saddle; only the reins stopped her from toppling back off the horse. Her body went numb and her vision glassy. A warm sensation grew in her chest, then bloomed like fire, searing her insides. She looked down. A shaft protruded from her breastplate. Ayanga slowed to a trot. The axe fell from Ashara's hand. Icy waves chilled her fingers and toes. Breathing was difficult, though in some moment of clarity she realized she still had the use of both lungs.

"Help," she wheezed.

Her vision swam. The horizon rolled like an ocean swell. Ashara eased herself forward and rested her forehead against Ayanga's mane and wrapped her arms around her neck. For a moment she felt the world stabilize, but it slipped away. Her father called her. Her brothers shouted her name. *Welcome home.* The pain faded. Though her eyes were closed, light filled the corners of her vision. Peace.

CHAPTER 22

"Punishment within the Imperial Army can be swift and brutal. On the road to Ma're I spotted a series of bodies hanging from trees. They were, I was told, soldiers who had disobeyed orders."

The Travels of Odam Yusufkas the Solari

Sentries called a challenge and the riders answered. Hinges groaned as the gates swung open, and the sentries dived out of the way as the horses galloped through.

"Bastards!" one yelled. "Slow down." Natan gripped the rider in front of him and buried his face in the back of the man's jacket. He looked up as they reined up on a parade ground in front of a ruddy pavilion.

"Here," one of the men said, offering Natan a hand. "You have never ridden a horse before?"

Natan shook his head and swallowed down acidic bile. He stubbornly swung his leg over the saddle, lost his balance and fell into the man's arms. His feet landed in a puddle, splashing them both.

"Sorry," he mumbled.

"Eat shit," the rider growled. "These are fresh britches."

"Alright you two," barked the patrol leader. "No time for hurt feelings. You can have a cry on your own time. To the duty officer. Go." Natan steadied himself on his feet and followed the patrol into the pavilion. Clerks perched at their slanted desks, scratching away at orders. A tea boy hastened past with bandy legs, carrying a large iron pot.

"Who's in charge here?" the patrol leader asked. The clerk waved his pen at an officer leaning over a central table, his back to them. Perhaps sensing the visitors, the officer turned, the folds of his uniform falling loosely about his manicured frame. After a brief exchange, the patrol leader gave his report, gesturing with his hands and careful with his words. In response the duty officer grunted and held up a hand.

"Who'd he say he was?" he asked, wrinkling his nose.

"Seventh Army," the patrol leader said. "We —"

"Looks like a bloody carcass. You dig him from the grave?"

"No, sir. He claims to have escaped the Third Army."

The duty officer raised a plucked eyebrow.

"I doubt that. He can't have come far."

"They're not far," Natan mumbled. "Sir."

"Did I tell you to bloody speak?" the duty officer snapped. Natan shook his head, his eyes falling to the officer's boots.

"If I may," the patrol leader said, directing the officer to the central table. "He said they're in a valley — this map, hold on. Yes — here. We picked him up here. He came from there around — here."

"The Valley of Kings?"

"Yes. I'm certain of it." The officer pinched the bridge of his nose.

"Well, he's lying."

"Say again? — Sir?"

"These counters are the Third Army," the duty officer said, indicating a series of wood markers painted yellow.

"Maybe the counters are wrong," the patrol leader suggested. The officer snorted.

"No, they're bloody well not. Now charge this man with desertion and take him to the lockup."

Natan's legs wobbled and he felt light-headed. He grabbed at his scalp to hold it still, and his primordial groan caught the attention of everyone in the room.

"No," he screamed, balling up his fist. "I'm not a deserter. They're close. They plan to grab the Emperor. They'll do it soon. You have to —" The officer's hand cracked across Natan's cheek with a teeth-shattering ferocity. Tangy blood burst onto his taste buds. Natan sunk to the floor, hoicked back phlegm and spat out a molar. His tongue probed the empty space it left.

"See?" the officer yelled. "The story changes. Daken, where are you? There — come. Get this man's number and run it to Commander Va'sa. I want a court martial by tomorrow. See it done."

A hand seized Natan's wrist and yanked it from his head. Natan pulled back, but the man called Daken twisted it around, sending bolts of pain up to Natan's shoulder.

"Le' go of me," Natan shouted, spitting blood and mucus at Daken.

"Alright," barked the patrol leader. "We'll take care of him. Let him go. You've got the number? We'll take him to the jail pit." Daken paused, his grip still tight around Natan's wrist.

"Deserter, alright," he sneered. "Need to teach him some respect."

"We'll do that," the patrol leader said sternly. "Come on boys, pick him up."

The other two picked Natan up. Natan squirmed and refused to go quietly.

"I told you! I'm no deserter! Ask Captain Mako — 14th Banner! He'll tell you. Shit, where are you taking me? Hey, look at me —" One of the patrolmen clamped a hand over Natan's mouth, muffling the screams.

"He's half dead," the jailor said. "Where do you find these sorts?"

"Court martial tomorrow," said the leader. "They're writing up the orders."

"Shame," said the jailor, shaking his head with pity. "Looks like he was a fit young man. It's a cruel world. Here get these clothes on." Natan accepted the outfit with trembling fingers and sniffed it, catching a faint whiff of rosewater and sulphur. It reminded him of home. Without a word he slipped the clothes on and wiped his eyes with the back of a hand.

"Be a man," the leader said. "Don't cry." Natan glared through a salty haze.

"When I'm dead," he said with an icy tone. "Then you'll know. You'll know I was right — I'm no deserter. I escaped. I risked everything. But it will be too late."

"Easy now," the patrol leader said, holding up his hands. "I don't make the decisions. I follow orders. As you should've."

"What'll you do when Mamot seizes the Emperor?"

"How? The Emperor is safe in his palace surrounded by guardsmen."

"They betrayed him once." The patrolmen snorted, and the leader rolled his brown eyes.

"His brains've gone to shit," he said to his two companions. "Come on. If we're lucky breakfast's still hot." The three plodded back to the command pavilion. Natan watched them go.

"Here," the jailor said. "Get this food in you." Natan eyed the half loaf and bowl of stew. He had seen worse, but the prospect of death curdled his stomach.

"Why bother."

The jailor's baton struck the table, jumping the bowl.

"I says you eat, you eat. Got that?"

Natan shivered through the day, a roughspun blanket clutched about him. The wind howled and the canvas whipped one way then the other, straining at the ropes secured to the jail's palisade wall. For a time it rained an icy drizzle, near horizontal in the gale. Unable to sleep, Natan sat up and hugged his knees, pulling the blanket over his head, and wrapping it under his chin. He wondered what his parents were doing. If he survived he promised himself he would visit them.

Somewhere in camp a trumpet sounded the changing of the watch. For one wonderful moment Natan felt the need to report to duty, then he remembered the wicker cell, the chains, and the locks. He had nowhere to report. No one cared.

The prisoners stirred, rising ape-like and pressing their noses between the bars, their fingers clawing at the air beyond. Natan stood, wondering what everyone had heard. A gate slammed. The jailor sauntered into view between the wicker cells, whistling to himself a tavern tune. Hooked digits reached for his sleeves, but the jailor knocked them back with his baton and shouted at the offenders.

"Back! I'll have you squealing like a baby. Kuvu you old bastard! I'll break your other arm. You try me. Mato you gap-toothed rat, how'd you like another hole in that smile?"

He stopped before Natan's cell door and fiddled with the lock and chain.

"I see you're alive," he said with a smirk. "I thought the gods would take pity on you."

"They're far too cruel," Natan said, backing towards the rear wall. The jailor yanked on the chain and swung the door back against the wicker weave. His baton pointed to the walkway.

"Where we going?" Natan asked, fingers touching the wall behind him.

"Where do you think?"

"The court martial is tomorrow," Natan said.

"Not any more." Natan sank to his haunches and hung his head.

"Any last requests?" the jailor asked. Natan studied the jailor's eyes.

"Is it true you shit yourself when you're hung?" The jailor looked taken aback. He fumbled for a response.

"It happens from time to time," he said.

"Then when it's time, can you take these clothes off me?"

"You want to be naked?" Natan shrugged.

"I don't want these clothes ruined for the next fool to wear them." The jailor gave Natan an odd look and stooped to pull him to his feet.

"If it'll make my job easier, I'll do it."

Natan sat on a low bench, his arms resting on raw knees. He glanced about, nervously eyeing each person in the tent. The jailor stood by the entrance, sharing a flask with a clerk, and two soldiers leaned on their spears. Clerks came and went, fussing over a desk at the back of the tent, ready for the officer in charge. Natan looked down at his hands, swollen, bloody and broken-nailed, quivering with a life of their own. He self-consciously clasped his palms together. *Don't show fear*, he told himself.

The back flap rustled and an officer entered, stooping his tall frame. He carried a stack of papers under one arm and, paying attention to no one else in the tent, dropped them on the desk and took his seat.

"Natan Luka-Tudo?" he asked, pinching the corners of a sheet of yellow paper. "I'm Commander Va'sa." He scanned the paper before continuing. "You're charged with desertion, how do you plead?"

"How do you think?" Natan said. Commander Va'sa looked down his bulbous nose and absently dipped a pen in ink.

"Don't make this hard on yourself," the commander said. "You were in the 14th Banner, you're now sitting in front of me without your uniform. Your excuses are incoherent. How do you plead?"

"Fine," Natan said.

"How do you plead?" Va'sa repeated.

"I said it didn't I?" Commander Va'sa sighed and rubbed a bloodshot eye with a balled fist. Natan waited, eyes ahead.

"Guilty," Va'sa said at last, recording the word for the record. "You plead guilty."

"Thanks," Natan said, at peace with his fate.

"Well, Natan Luka-Tudo, you've been found guilty of desertion. You'll be taken from this tent to the place of your sentence, and there hung by the neck until dead. May Heaven give you rest." Va'sa blew on the paper, folded it and passed it to a clerk. "Quick justice is effective justice," Va'sa added. "The backbone of the Seventh Army is discipline. Let this be a lesson for all." Voices mumbled agreement and Natan felt a finger on his shoulder.

"Come on lad," said the jailor. Natan stood, rubbing his hands to stop them from shaking. The jailor led him out into the twilight and back to the jail, next to which was the gallows. The wooden frame stood dark and dreadful.

"Does it have to happen tonight?" Natan asked.

"You heard the Commander," the jailor said. "Quick and effective."

"Are they ever wrong?" The jailor snorted and ran a grubby hand under his nose.

"At this age? I'm wise enough to keep my head down."

Boots squelched in the mud. Natan and the jailor turned to a squad of troops marching up. A captain called a halt.

"Sergeant! Dress the lines! Face the gallows!" The captain shook hands with the jailor and looked Natan up and down.

"Ready?"

"Would you be?" Natan asked.

"Very funny. Over there."

"Hold on," Natan said, catching the jailor's eye.

"Strip off then," said the jailor, reaching for the clothes. The captain watched in amusement and soldiers whispered among themselves. Natan handed the garments to the jailor. The cold air chilled his skin, but numbed his fear.

"Sergeant, prepare the gallows." Amidst the motion, Natan caught the jailor's arm.

"Will someone tell my parents?" The jailor jerked away, but then shrugged and straightened out his sleeve.

"Not a high priority," he said. "Now go stand over there."

They bound Natan's wrists and helped him onto a stool beneath the noose. Natan felt the rope graze his face and tighten about the flesh of his neck. Behind him, the sergeant shouted at his men to hold the rope. Natan closed his eyes, not knowing when to expect the stool to disappear from beneath him. He bit his lip so hard he tasted blood.

"Soldier," the captain said, adopting a pompous, official tone. "You're to be hung and your body put on display. In this you'll perform your final duty as a warning to all who consider desertion. Now sergeant, on my order."

Fresh urine trickled down Natan's legs and he wondered if it was the last thing he would feel. He waited.

"Why the bloody hell is he naked?" The outburst shocked Natan into opening his eyes. Captain Mako strode onto the execution grounds, one hand on the pommel of his sword, the other with folded paper between two fingers.

"Excuse me?" the captain in charge demanded, his face darkening like a beetroot. "Who're you?"

"The execution's over. Back to your tents."

"I think not," the captain said. "You'll answer to Commander Va'sa for this."

Mako thrust the paper under the captain's nose.

"And you'll answer to Jano," he sneered. "Care to read it or do I shove it up your arse?"

The captain snatched the paper from Mako and read the contents. He did not move. His eyes narrowed. Natan watched the jailor take charge.

"Execution over," shouted the jailor. "Sergeant release this man."

"But," stammered the captain. "My orders."

"You have your orders," Mako said, tapping a badge on his harness. "I have seniority. Now bugger off." Hands helped Natan down from the stool and removed the noose from his neck. Even gone, the rope continued to prickle his neck. Natan rubbed at it trying to forget the sensation.

"What happened?" Natan asked, fighting back the bile in his throat. Mako ignored him, instead pointing at Natan's sallow chest.

"Soldier," he barked. "Where the fuck are your clothes?"

"Here," the jailor said awkwardly.

"Bloody hopeless. Are executions always such a shitty mess?"

"Not my department," muttered the jailor. "Always thought he was innocent."

"Well," said Mako. "I'd love a chin wag, but we've got an important meeting."

The two soldiers entered a grand pavilion lit by crackling braziers and hazy with smoke. Dark shadows milled about the perimeter, fussing over a horseshoe of trestle tables, the occupants of high backed chairs cast in harsh relief.

"Were those guardsmen?" Natan asked, glancing over his shoulder as Mako led him towards the tables.

"Who?" Mako asked, distracted. "Oh yes probably. Now you speak only when spoken to, alright?"

"What's this..." Natan stopped, frozen to the spot.

"Is that him?" a voice asked, cutting through the heavy air of the pavilion. Bushy eyebrows rose over black eyes and skin pulled taut across high cheekbones. It was a face Natan instantly recognized, though one he had seen in person only once before.

"Reporting, Your Grace," Mako said.

"So this is him," Jano said. "Natan Luka-Tudo, no? I believe you have something you want to say to us." Natan felt his mouth go dry. The smoke tickled his lungs.

"Did they cut out your tongue?" Jano asked.

"No, Your Grace," Natan managed.

"Well, go on then."

"What do you want me to say? I..."

"Start from the beginning."

So Natan began. He tried his best to stick to the hard facts. When he got to conditions inside Mamot's camp, those seated started to ask questions, sometimes two or three at a time competing for Natan's attention, until Jano raised a hand.

"Stop. Natan, proceed." Natan continued his story until his capture that morning. At this, Jano cleared his throat.

"That's enough. Captain Mako, can you wait outside?" Mako turned on his heels and Natan hesitated. "You too soldier." Embarrassed, Natan hurried in Mako's wake. Once outside he took a deep breath and slowly let it out.

"What just happened?"

"Buggered if I know," Mako said. "The leader of the patrol that picked you up found me. I knew you weren't the type to desert so I started knocking heads together. Besides, you owe me."

"About that..."

"*Bah*, I trust you'll pay. You *will* pay, right?"

"It might be installments," Natan said. "It's been a difficult few weeks."

"You'll do better than the scouts. Turns out they got the enemy positions wrong. Commander Dovanti gave them a right bollocking.

One of their captains is getting kicked back to the ranks. Eight years until retirement and back to one *jet* a day. Poor bugger." A clerk called them back in.

"You first," Mako said. "Now we learn our fates."

"Our fates? I'm the one in trouble."

"And I jumped in the shit with you."

Returning to the trestle tables, Natan found half those seated had gone. Jano sat brooding over a long-stemmed pipe, the bowl nested gently between three fingers.

"It's been decided," Jano said. "We trust your report."

"Thanks —"

"So you're going back in tonight," Jano said, cutting Natan off.

"Tonight?" Mako echoed. "We are?"

"Speed's of the essence. You're to report to 5th Banner's HQ. Departure within the hour."

CHAPTER 23

"Wyvern are an ancient creature now limited to the mountains and wildlands on the borders of civilization. At full size, they grow to around 300 pounds, but some are significantly smaller. Many Vu believe them sacred."

Master Suvu's Life of a Scholar

Lukan's eyes blazed with a quiet ferocity. His hand reached out for the bag and Po pulled it away, clutching it to his chest.

"Hand it over," Lukan said. "This doesn't need to be unpleasant."

Anjan's eyes snapped open and he sat bolt upright. For a moment they stared at each other, comprehension slowly spreading over Anjan's face.

"Po! Don't give it to him." Lukan motioned to the surrounding hillside.

"Resistance is quite useless. You're surrounded."

It was true. Po watched the black cloaks edge along the ridge and through the rocks. He counted eleven. One bent over and picked something from a cleft.

"Inquisitor!" the man called from above. "Look what we have here." Lukan broke eye contact with Po for just an instant.

"Put that down. If it's not the bag, I'm not interested." The virtueman ran down the hill in leaps and bounds, his hands cupped about his discovery, until he skidded to a stop amidst the pine needles at Lukan's side. Po could not see what it was in the man's hands, but the look on Lukan's face was one of revulsion.

"They're worth a lot," the man stammered. "At least a *gotti* in Pao'an. There could be more."

Inquisitor Lukan brushed the man aside and drew a length of rope from his belt.

"Very well, we'll secure them, then go looking — on your feet and hold out your hands."

Po inched his knees up to his chin, and Anjan laid a hand on Po's shoulder.

"We're not getting up," Anjan said. "You're not taking us."

"I'm afraid," said Lukan. "You don't have any choice." There was a moment of uncertainty, then Po shrugged off his friend's protective hand and rose, pushing his back up the tree behind him.

"Good," Lukan said. "Now —"

A shriek rent the frosty air, rising into a deathly scream that echoed off the slopes and shook the trees, loosing the accumulated snow on their boughs. Lukan's horse reared and bolted, kicking up clods of dirt and needles as it galloped downhill. The inquisitor spun about and grabbed for the reins, but he was too slow and fell with an *oomph* to the ground. Po saw his chance and, grabbing Anjan's hand, they ran directly over the inquisitor's prostrate body and for the rocky ridgeline. They got halfway when a blur of motion and flapping of wings stopped Po in his tracks.

It darted right for them, then swerved and changed tack. The virtueman with the little bundle in his hands screamed and threw the baby chick into the air as the adult wyvern leapt at him. Po did not wait to see what happened, he grabbed Anjan again and ran. Behind him the shrieks of the wyvern and the screams of the man intermixed in a hellish cacophony.

They reached a rock face and Po began to climb. Anjan hesitated.

"I can't," he said. "I can't climb."

"Yes you can," Po said, his voice catching. "Quick. Follow my actions."

Anjan took hold of a stone beneath Po's feet, and Po looked back to the clearing where they had spent the night. The virtuemen stood in a circle, batons out, fending the angry wyvern away from their fallen leader. Inquisitor Lukan nursed his elbow and pointed at the fleeing monks.

"They'll be after us soon," Po said. "Don't look back. Climb."

Po's hands grasped at roots and he pulled himself up onto a ledge. He offered Anjan a hand and hauled him up too. They rested a moment, panting for breath. Beneath them the wyvern had disappeared and the virtuemen ran for the rock face.

"This isn't going to slow them down much," Po said. "We have to keep going."

He tested the tree clinging to the ledge and put a foot on the lowest bough. It held and using the branches Po easily completed the climb to the top of the rock face. The ground levelled off after that, and they were both once again running across needles and scattered rock.

"We slept by that all night," Anjan managed.

"Lucky I guess we didn't light a fire," Po said. "Or it was saving us for breakfast." After a few more yards Anjan stopped and held his knees.

"How — how can we be sure we're going the right direction?"

"It's like the painting," Po said, rubbing his back. "This is the foot of the first Graytalons. We've already seen the second peak. We just have to head in that direction. You'll see soon enough."

"I think I'm going to walk," Anjan said.

They continued on, taking every chance they could to put distance between them and their pursuers. Occasionally they heard the shriek of the wyvern, but any sight of it was lost amidst the trees. It did not make it any less scary, and Po found himself chanting slowly under his breath, rallying his focus on the mountain ahead.

A mile further they came across a deep ravine. White frothy water stormed beneath over jagged rocks. They stood at the edge and looked down at the raging torrent.

"See," Anjan said. "You can't just walk in a straight line. We should have given this more thought."

"When did we have the time?" Po said. "We can't exactly follow the roads. And neither of us have a map. Now which way should we go?"

"Up?" Anjan said. "It's worked so far. Until now." The companions set off following the ravine higher into the mountains. Before long, Po noticed the roar of the water become louder and louder. They rounded a hillock and let out a collective groan.

"A waterfall!" Po exclaimed.

"Well that's a dead end," Anjan said. "Try the other way?" Po wondered how much time they had before the virtuemen caught up. He dithered.

"The pool — there's still water before it cuts into the rock and forms the ravine. Perhaps there is some shallows there that can be crossed."

"You keep lookout," Anjan said, rolling up his trouser legs. "I'll be back."

Anjan darted for the catchment at the bottom of the falls and followed the river back towards the ravine. His toe touched the glistening surface, then his ankle went in. He tested each step until he was up to his shins. Po held his breath, wanting to call his friend back. Anjan stopped and glanced back at Po's position, grimaced, and took one more step. He wavered and slipped, disappearing in an instant under the bubbling surface.

"Anjan," Po yelped, running for the bank. There was no sign of his friend. A piece of wood sped past, betraying the strength of the river beneath the surface.

"Anjan!" Po called, louder this time as he desperately searched the bank. "Can you hear me?" No reply. Something breached the surface a few yards downstream. The water foamed about it like a rapid. Po raced towards the tint of human flesh and could just make out Anjan, his elbow wrapped around the root of a tree, bubbles streaming from his lips.

"Hold on," Po cried. "I've got you."

Po threw himself on his belly and thrust his arms into the ice-cold water. He felt Anjan's body, tense and slippery at his fingertips. His hands found purchase and he pulled. Anjan's head broke the surface, spluttering and gasping for air. In an instant he was back under and then out again.

"Stop fighting," Po yelled. "Let me pull you. I can't hold you much longer." Anjan gargled and spluttered, choking out intelligible words. Po's fingers began to slip, just as he felt the body make contact with the bank. His fingers scratched at Anjan's skin. His friend's head went under again.

"Hold on," Po cried, though he knew Anjan was deaf to his plea. Soft flesh slipped from his hands and the current took Anjan in a kaleidoscope of skin, clothes and refracted light. There was nothing Po could do but bite back a scream of agony. He lay there in the sudden stillness; the strength gone from his body, the will to continue vanished. Ever so slowly Po edged from the bank and sat there, his back against a tree.

Numb with grief, Po imagined himself back at Jan Moga before everything fell apart. He remembered the candle-lit halls, the classes, and Anjan laughing at some practical joke. His friend always had something to smile about. All that was gone. *All things are impermanent. This is the way of the Ba're.*

"There he is," someone shouted. "There, under that tree." Shadows fell over him. Po gazed up at the faces; Lukan and two virtuemen returned the stare.

"Where's your friend?" Lukan asked. Then he glanced at the river. "Oh. What a pity. The undertow in those things can be very deceptive. I guess monks aren't taught such things."

"It's the bag alright," the man to Lukan's right said. "See."

"He won't escape us again," Lukan said. The Inquisitor knelt and slipped a noose around Po's hand.

"There might be some climbing involved," Lukan said. "So I'm only tying one hand. You behave, okay?" Po nodded. They helped him to his feet and prodded him in the direction they had come.

"I must congratulate you," Lukan said. "This is the most expensive investigation the Ministry has ever engaged in. It's nice to think it hasn't been wasted."

"All this for a book?" Po asked. "Is your leader so thin-skinned?"

"Perception is everything," Lukan said. "As a monk you'd know this. Isn't the heart of your religion the battle between perception and reality?"

"We don't kill," Po said. "We don't murder. We help and cure. We teach and care."

"Your Abbot didn't care much when he told us where you'd gone."

"He wouldn't do that," Po snapped, but from Lukan's expression he knew it was true.

"I killed him," Lukan said. "So don't worry, no one else heard his betrayal." Po had no reply. His heart had hardened like stone, and a cold chill numbed every inch of his body. His feet plodded on, but he was only aware of the motion, not the steps themselves. Slowly even the motion became irrelevant, hidden behind a veil of tears.

Inquisitor Lukan yanked on the rope, forcing Po to stop. They stood at the brink of a cliff jutting out over a wind-rippled lake. The roar of a waterfall wasn't far off. Unbidden the image of Anjan swept over the edge sprung to mind. Po's stomach turned and his legs wobbled.

"Infuriating isn't it?" Lukan said. "Just when you think you're getting somewhere. Never mind... we'll follow this till we reach the main road."

"No," Po said. "I'd rather join my friend. Why not throw me and the book into the lake and end this." Lukan looked visibly shocked. He held a hand to his chest.

"Why Po," he said. "That isn't how we do things. There needs to be a full debrief. Reports have to be filed. Maybe there were other conspirators. We don't know what you know." Po took a step to the edge. The rope tightened at his wrist. *Lukan will never let me jump.* As if to test the inquisitor, he took a step into thin air and felt his body pulled back from the brink.

"No," Lukan said "I..." A familiar shriek echoed off the mountain slopes. A black shadow passed overhead.

"Damn that creature," Lukan sneered. "You two, distract it and meet us at the crossroads by Na've."

"Yes, Inquisitor!" the virtuemen said and drew their batons. The wyvern dropped between them, arching back its head and baring its teeth. The talons tapped the ground in a death rhythm. Its eyes darted from one person to the next.

"Here, Inquisitor," one of the virtuemen said, tossing Po's bag.

The wyvern lunged at the object, but before it could get its teeth into the canvas, the virtuemen set upon it, beating it with their wooden batons. The creature shrieked and returned the attack, blurring scales and flesh. Lukan picked up the bag and gave it to Po.

"When I might have to fight," Lukan said. "I don't like my hands full. Carry that, will you? I know you won't try and drop it." Po clutched the bag to his chest, more on reflex than a conscious decision, and hurried after Lukan. They had gone only a few yards when motion blurred towards them and Anjan appeared, dripping wet and dressed only in his loincloth.

"Let my friend go," he shouted between blue lips. Lukan wheeled about and raised his baton to protect himself.

"Stand back," he cried. "My men will catch up soon. Better you hand yourself in now than fight." Anjan approached, his fists clenched, and Lukan backed away, the edge of the cliff behind him.

"Let Po go," Anjan growled.

"Anjan," Po said. "Don't be stupid — save yourself." Lukan drew Po to him and touched the baton to Po's temple.

"One more step and I'll break your friend's skull." Anjan took one more step.

"I mean it," Lukan cried. "Back away!"

"Po! Duck!" Po only had the briefest comprehension, but he slipped from Lukan's grip and hit the ground. Anjan barreled overhead, carrying Lukan with him. Po rolled, kicked and tangled with their feet until he felt the earth give way beneath him. He fell and landed with a bone-jarring crunch. The rope snapped tight, yanking his wrist with it. The flesh around his hand felt like it would tear. Po grabbed with his other hand and pulled, relieving some of the tension. Out of immediate danger he finally looked about, comprehension slowly dawning on him. He was on a ledge just beneath the cliff top. The rope disappeared over the side. They had fallen over the edge of the cliff. *Anjan never saw we were tied together,* he realized.

"Help!" It was Lukan's voice.

"Hold on," Po managed through gritted teeth. He braced his feet and hauled hand over hand, gathering up the lax rope as it came in. Curses came from over the edge.

"For Heaven's sake, pull!"

324

"I'm trying," Po said, not once questioning his decision to save his pursuer. "Can you grab hold of anything?"

"I'm slipping. Faster. Kive have mercy!" Blisters stung and every muscle protested, but Po kept up the effort, drawing on his Ba're training to accept the pain. *All things are impermanent and this too shall pass. Kime ki're kima ka.*

Fingers appeared over the edge, and then a hand.

"You're doing it," Po said. "Just a little further." Lukan groaned with effort. His fingers clawed at the rock. Po twisted his body, maintaining tension on the rope while leaning into the edge. Lukan's eyes met his, wide with terror, the pupils straining at the edge of the iris.

"Give me your hand," Po said. "You're almost up." Po reached out to the hand Lukan held wrapped around the rope.

"I'd have to let go," Lukan cried. "I can't."

"You have to," Po said. "Lift. I'll take your wrist." Their skin met and Po's fingers crawled over his bunched fist. He lifted Lukan's hand to the ledge.

"You'll have to let go of the rope," Po said. "Hold the rock. Then I can help you up." Reluctantly, Lukan surrendered his lifeline and hooked his fingers around the rock. Po tugged at the inquisitor's clothing, but he gained little purchase. Lukan groaned, his strength beyond complaint. His arms shuddered with exhaustion.

"Nearly there," Po said. "One more pull." Lukan's left hand slipped, then his right broke free of the rock. Po released the cloak before he was pulled after him. Lukan fell, bounced once off the cliff face, then crashed into the rocks jutting from the white-capped water at the base. Po had no energy left to scream. The inquisitors body was splayed in sickly fashion next to the body of his friend. *Anjan…*

There were no tears left to cry. Po took the bag, coiled the rope, and climbed back the last half-dozen feet to the cliff top. Movement startled him, and Po sought refuge behind a large pine. The two virtuemen worked their way along the clifftop, scanning the lake. They had clearly seen something, but Po could not tell what. As they drew near he began to hear parts of their conversation.

"Two of them alright," one said.

"Bloody balls of Kive," said the other. "How'd that happen?"

"Bag must be down there as well."

"Well I'm not getting it."

"Come on," said the first. "We've both taken a beating. If we go now we can be with the horses by lunchtime. There'll be safety in numbers and we can report them both lost — those secrets are as safe as they'll ever be down there."

"Bloody oath," said the second.

Po watched them leave. He waited until they were out of sight, then returned to the ravine. He soon found the spot where Anjan had climbed out. The rock, otherwise dry, was still wet, and Anjan's clothes lay on the bank. A tree had fallen into the river and, braced between two rocks, had formed a sieve picking up everything larger than a pinecone that came its way. It formed a passable bridge, and the ravine there was shallower than other places and the sides had partially collapsed. Jagged rocks and tangled branches hid the crossing from view and Po moaned at the sight, upset he had not seen it earlier when he and Anjan were scouting the banks. He stood in silence fighting his anger and regret. He tried to justify himself, but in truth he thought they had probably been distracted.

With the help of Lukan's rope, Po climbed down to the fallen tree, tied a broken branch to the end of the rope, and threw it across the river. It did not catch, but two more attempts saw it lodged firmly between a fallen boulder and the roots of the tree. Po tugged on it and the rope held firm. He tested his footing and took his first steps in crossing the river. The log beneath him groaned and Po picture himself falling into the frothing water. Hesitantly he lowered himself to all fours and, keeping a firm grip on the rope, crawled across.

On the other side, Po recoiled the rope, swung it over his shoulder and turned his sights towards Jan'a.

Evening was gathering when Po came to the gates of the monastery. A nearby village lay quiet and shuttered. Roadblocks lay abandoned, the soldiers called away. Po crossed a rickety wooden bridge and approached the double-doors set into the mountainside. A sign above the door read:

JAN'A. ESTABLISHED BY VERMILION CHARTER.

Nervously, Po rang the bell. After a pause, the bolts on the other side clicked. A monk appeared, flanked by two lay members armed with spears.

"I'm here to see the abbot," Po said, handing the monk his letter of recommendation.

CHAPTER 24

"The Ministry of War is by far the most impressive building in Northgate. Facing onto South Avenue it bristles with towers and arches. Despite its fierce facade, inside it is mostly bureaucrats passing papers from one office to another."

A Traveler's Guide to Pao'an

"G'me a hand," Mako grunted, struggling for breath. Natan clasped the captain's outstretched arm and tugged until Mako was red in the face.

"You shouldn't have had that pie before we left."

"Very funny. One more pull." Natan braced his feet, lowered his center mass and heaved. Bit by bit Mako inched forward, bringing dirt and pebbles showering down over the rim. All of a sudden he was loose, and Natan cushioned his fall.

"Bloody hell," Mako said. "Is the other end that tight?"

"Not nearly as bad." Mako picked up the lantern resting on the chamber floor and looked wide-eyed around the stone walls. He was about to speak when someone hissed from the other end of the entrance hole. Natan peeked upwards.

"Sorry," he whispered. "All clear. Pass the kits." Invisible hands in the pitch black above shoved through carefully wrapped packages of animal skin. Natan took each package and laid it on the chamber floor, away from where the soldiers would enter. Inside were protected weapons and armor for each man.

"That it?" he asked when no more came. There was no answer, then a foot was inches from his face. Natan jumped back and waited until the boot was clear before helping the soldier out.

"Alright?" Mako said. "Get your weapon and stand by the passage. Let us know if you hear anything." The soldier gazed about, mouth slack, then shook himself back to his senses.

"Yes, Sir," he said, and busied himself with one of the packages. More figures appeared, each one helped by Natan into the chamber. Soon there were too many for the little room and Mako told Natan to start leading the way.

"Me?" Natan asked.

"Yes, you. You weren't brought along for your dashing looks. You know the way, now be of use for once and show us." Natan took his kit, ducked his head and felt his way along the passage. Captain Mako followed, the light from his lamp casting dancing shadows along the stonework. Other soldiers followed in the rear. They proceeded a good two dozen feet before Natan stopped. He rubbed his eyes and squinted into the gloom.

"What?" Mako asked.

"I keep thinking I'm seeing things."

"We've got your back," Mako said. "Keep going." Natan hugged his kit closer to his chest and felt for the axe handle within. He continued down the passage until the first signs of the corridor appeared ahead. Again, he stopped.

"That's it," he whispered over his shoulder. "The main corridor."

Mako did not reply, but pressed his fingers against Natan's back. Natan didn't move. He blinked, then ground his eyes with the palm of his hand. Colors danced and sparkled in his vision.

"What's wrong?" Mako whispered.

"That drink the surgeon gave me. I feel weird."

"Keep going or I'll give you more to worry about." Natan's heart fluttered and his limbs tingled with nervous energy. He slapped at a phantom itch. He took one more step, then another, easing his way towards the dark gulf ahead.

"You know," Mako said. "Some soldiers in the rebellion took that every day."

"I'm okay," Natan insisted.

They passed under the low archway and entered the wide corridor with vaulted ceiling. Lantern light searched the furthest corners and Natan realized after a few moments that he was holding his breath, his chest tight with anticipation.

"All clear," Mako yelled back down the passage. "Everyone form up."

Stooped soldiers hurried from the passage and took up positions, finally able to stand straight in the murky bowels of the tomb. Two sergeants appeared, lanterns aglow, and set about their men.

"Dress the lines! Look sharp!"

"Headcount?" Mako queried.

"Forty-six," the senior sergeant said. "Plus you two."

"Good," Mako said, motioning for Natan to stay in his place. "Now listen up. It looks like they haven't discovered the tomb. Keep your wits about you. Move fast. Our strength is in surprise. I don't need to give you encouragement. You bastards are the toughest sons of whores ever handpicked from the Seventh Army. Dawn can't be far off. Let's give them cold steel and their own blood for breakfast."

The men cheered and Mako reddened.

"Shut your gobs and listen. Once we reach the other side, you're all silent. Whispers only in the cave. Keep those kits close to you. I'll gut the first man who risks giving our position away before we're ready. I don't give a rotten dog's kidney which one of you it is. Sergeants, move out."

No one cheered this time. Natan looked to the grim faces — every one of them scarred and misshapen. Natan was unsure if they were the best the Seventh Army had to offer, but he was sure they were the meanest, roughest brawlers available, men who officers did not want in the shield wall but who could hold their own with axe or meat cleaver in a tavern free-for-all. And he was going with them into the heart of the enemy camp.

"Nothing more I need to know?" Mako asked as the column set off.

"No," Natan said. "I've told you everything."

"Better," Mako grumbled. They entered the burial chamber and saw the inscribed wall, but the soldiers paid little attention. Natan nodded in the direction and Mako grunted in understanding.

"Focus on the task," the captain mumbled. Arriving at the far chamber on the other side of the hill, the column stopped. Natan pushed his way to the front and identified the exit plug. In hushed silence they watched him loosen it, and before it could drop to the floor a sergeant took the stone and laid it down carefully on the ground. Natan hesitated, feeling the chill air breath across his face. He listened. All he could hear was the rustling of animal skins as soldiers returned their weapons and prepared to squeeze through the gap before them. The valley was quiet.

"Problem?" Mako breathed, barely a whisper.

"Quiet," Natan said.

"They're not expecting us. Go on then. Give me your kit."

Natan parted with the protective bundle and hauled himself through the shaft. His fingers felt the stone rim, then his hands grasped at roots and prickly branches. Soon he was back on the hillside from which he had escaped the day before. The Third Army camp lay beneath him. A thin layer of mist cloaked the valley, mixing with the hazy wash of campfire smoke.

"Ready?" a voice whispered.

Natan took the package offered to him from the hole and laid it down. He unwrapped it and picked his way carefully through the contents. By the time he wore the mail shirt, coif, buckler and helmet, other figures had emerged into the cold night air. Natan shook out the animal skin wrap and wore it as a jacket. Lastly he took the axe and wrapped the blood knot around his wrist.

"Look at them all sleeping," Mako said at Natan's side. "You did bloody well. Go down there and cover us while we kit up."

The raiding party advanced through the slumbering camp in the direction of General Mamot's headquarter tents. In the absolute stillness, the sound of their chainmail chinking and their boots squelching in the mud felt deafening. Natan gripped the axe handle, expecting a challenge at any moment.

"Easy now," Mako ordered. "No one expects us." Natan let the handle slip to his side. He wondered if they were visible to the sentries on the surrounding hills. If so, they were nothing more than a dark smudge on the valley floor.

They neared the first of the tents. For the first time someone stirred. A shadow moved, black against the deep gray of the tents.

"Identify yourselves."

"Patrol reporting," Mako barked back.

"You don't report here. What's the password?"

"Special patrol. Reporting direct to General Mamot." The sentry backed away and raised his shield to cover his center mass.

"Password," he said again. "Sergeant, can you —"

"Bugger this," Mako said, drawing his sword. "Get him." The shadow squealed and ran between the tents. Natan sprinted after him, joined by others in the raiding party. They went down in a storm of thrashing limbs and splattered mud, their faces cloaked in the darkness. Fingers clawed at Natan's face and teeth clamped onto his forearm. Natan tried to use the axe, but he did not know where to strike. The shaft of a spear battered uselessly at his helmet and soiled fingers dug into his mouth.

"Don't move!" a voice yelled, then warm blood spattered Natan's face.

The fingers in his mouth went limp. Beneath him the sentry jerked and gargled as his life bled out. Natan spat the vile taste of vomit and another man's blood from his mouth and stumbled to his feet. Around him men screamed and campfires stirred to life. Mako bellowed to rally his men.

"First squad, seal the perimeter. Second squad, on me. Natan — where's Natan?"

"Here," Natan said, catching his breath.

"Don't fucking run off like that again. Where's the general's tent?"

"Should be this way," Natan said, directing his captain with his axe.

"Get a move on. Quick."

They'd gone only ten paces when torch-bearing guardsmen charged from one of the tents. Natan had no time to stop. He barrelled into them and shattered the first man's shield. The second dropped his spear and went for his short sword, but Mako caught him in the center of the face an inch from the man's nose guard.

"Keep going!" Mako roared as they finished off the remainder. "Don't slacken. Take no prisoners. Go!"

Natan recognized the general's command tent. A fire glowed within and a screen of spearman protected the entrance. Beyond, trumpets rent the night as the Third Army was called to arms. They were forty-eight men soon to be set upon by more than fifty-thousand; outnumbered more than a thousand to one.

"There," Natan said, but Mako was already on top of things.

"Surround that tent, don't let him get away."

The raiders were at a disadvantage. None of them carried spears, but while others dashed to cut off any chance of escape, a hardcore of brawlers set about the spearmen with everything they could snatch. Natan joined them, seizing at camp furniture and burning logs from the fires, and throwing them at the soldiers. Whenever they saw the opportunity, someone slid between the spears and struck with sword or axe. The lucky ones caught their axes on the rims of the enemy shields and yanked the defenders out of the shieldwall. One by one the spearmen fell to the gore-stained earth, yet the raiders paid a heavy price. Seven lay dead or dying before the path was cleared to the entrance.

"Inside!" Mako yelled. "No time to lose!"

Natan stumbled over the bodies of his fallen comrades and swept aside the tent flap. There was a blur of motion, and Natan fell to one knee with a skull-cracking blow to his helmet. Bright dots sparkled in the corners of his eyes and his vision lanced in and out of focus. He lifted a bloodied hand to his head and felt a dent the size of his fist.

"Aurochs!" a voice boomed.

The voice. Natan's stomach contracted in a violent seizure and hot acidic vomit blew from his lips. He wiped his chin with the back of his hand. *Get up*, he told himself. Clashing metal rang in his ears. Shapes breezed past him. Men fought across the floor of the tent. Natan crawled forward until he came across a body. It was Mamot's steward, his neck half severed. By his hand lay an iron war club. *The little bastard,* Natan swore as he realized where his head wound came from. *Up,* he told himself. *Up.*

Natan's body demanded rest, but the surgeon's potion sizzled through his veins. Mako's shouts of command focused Natan's attention. He retrieved his axe, dangling by the blood knot, and got to his feet. His head swam and he tottered for a moment before finding his balance.

Chaos reigned. Braziers spilled their burning contents across the ground and flames crept up the damp canvas walls. Through smoke bodies twisted and turned, their weapons crashing as they fought with animal ferocity. General Mamot dominated the space, a chair in one hand and a short sword in the other. A soldier lunged, but his blade caught between the chairlegs. Mamot snapped him forward and kicked the man into Captain Mako.

"You're too late," Mamot yelled. "Soon I'll have the Emperor and you'll be dead men."

"No bloody chance," Mako shouted back over the din, untangling himself from the fallen soldier at his feet. "Kive awaits your soul."

Captain Mako attacked, blocking the chair with his buckler and thrusting for Mamot's exposed chest. The general danced about the blade, surprisingly agile for his bulk, and cut down into the captain's right thigh. Natan heard the scream as he ran to his officer's aid. Mako went down, his leg buckled beneath him, and General Mamot stabbed at the base of Mako's neck. As his sword touched the skin, Natan crashed into the general, sending both of them sprawling amidst the embers of the burning tent.

Pain jolted Natan's leg, reviving memories of his battle wound. Mamot struggled, but Natan lay atop him. He jabbed his buckler into the base of Mamot's skull and pushed with all his might. The general gasped and wheezed, his face reddening. His plump fingers grasped for his short sword. Natan released his grip on Mamot's neck just long enough to make room for his axe to cleave through the back of the general's skull. Bone crunched and blood spattered, speckling Natan's face.

It's over, Natan thought with a wave of relief. His shoulders slumped, his mouth hanging loose as blood dribbled over his lips onto Mamot's nightshirt. He raised his axe and kissed the haft, leaving a bloody lip print.

"Aurochs-like Sato," Natan prayed. "Lord of the Battle. Accept my sacrifice."

"Lad," Mako groaned, pulling Natan back to the moment. "Help me."

Natan looked about the tent as bits of glowing canvas drifted down around him. They were alone. The ground lay slick with blood, and the air heavy with the acrid scent of death.

"We need to get out," Natan said. "Here."

"No, listen."

Natan ignored his captain. He wrapped his arms around Mako and dragged him from the tent to the carnage outside. A knot of two dozen soldiers gathered around.

"Is that the captain?" one asked. "Fuck."

"Where's your sergeant?"

"They're all dead. First squad's fallen back. We're surrounded."

Natan turned his face from his comrades and concentrated on staunching Mako's wound. *Think*, he told himself. *Don't panic. Think. Find something to say.* The blood continued to flow. It did not look life-threatening — at least not immediately — but, all things considered, they probably did not have long to live anyway. Mako made eye contact with him.

"Take charge," Mako said through gritted teeth. "Rally the men."

"We'll wrap you up," Natan said. "You can lean on me. They need you."

"No," Mako said, swatting away Natan's hands. "I'll look after myself."

"But —"

Mako's hand snatched at Natan's coif and suddenly Natan was nose to nose with his commander.

"Do what I say or I'll break that thick skull of yours. You hear me?"

Natan glared back, then tugged Mako's hand away and rose to his feet.

"What do you want us to do?" asked a soldier.

"What's your name?" Natan asked.

"Tivo. Tivo Luka-Ban."

"You're my second," Natan said. "Is this everyone?"

"All that's left."

Twenty-four men, Natan counted. *Not good odds.* Still, the odds had never been good. The difference was they were now his responsibility.

Aurochs-like Sato, Lord of the Battle... Natan removed his helmet and probed the dent that had come so close to claiming his life. The steel had fractured at the point of impact. *Shit.* He took a deep breath and surveyed the survivors.

"You've done well," he said, addressing them. "Mamot is dead, our mission is accomplished. Now we make our stand. Take what you can from the dead — retrieve their shields and their spears. Replace anything that is broken, and prepare the ground here around our captain. Keep it tight. We don't know what they'll bring against us."

"Let's do it," Tivo said, his face not reflecting the excitement in his voice. "Quick while they organize. This lull can't last."

The men did not wait for Tivo to finish. Already they were salvaging what they could from the dead. Natan joined them. He unbuckled his buckler, returned his axe to his belt, and armed himself with a spear and the familiar long shield of the infantry. Once the rest were similarly equipped, Tivo directed half the men to clear a circle, while Natan took the other half to pile up the dead around the perimeter and jam the gaps with handcarts, shields and wagon wheels.

"Wedge those together," Natan said. "Make it solid."

"Any spare shields?" Tivo asked.

"What do you need them for?"

"Extras. And spears."

Natan jabbed a finger at three of his men and they ran off, only to return moments later.

"They're coming!"

"How many?"

"The whole bloody army." They didn't need an order. Everyone piled inside the crude defenses.

"Shields together," Natan said. "Mind your sectors."

"Keep yourselves low," Tivo added.

"Give 'em a good bashing for me," Captain Mako barked.

Natan had almost forgotten the wounded officer, he had been so quiet.

"You alright there?" he asked, glancing down at the sitting form.

"Lovely," Mako said. "Absolutely charming view from down here. Two dozen arses in my face and nothing but mud to sit in."

The men tittered.

"We could get you a camp chair," Natan suggested. "But it might spoil your view."

"Don't mind —"

"I see them!"

Natan in the middle of the circle looked over the man's shoulder. A wall of shields marched from the murky half-light. Only the remaining tents broke their formation. Natan checked all approaches. They were surrounded.

"Stay strong," he hissed. "They don't know our strength or what condition we're in."

"They'll know soon enough," one remarked.

"They're pulling down the tents," warned another.

"Just clearing the field," Tivo said. "No problem there."

Natan knew he had made a good choice for his second-in-command, however arbitrary it had been.

"Steady," Natan said. "If anyone's got water, pass it around. It'll be a while before we get another chance."

A half dozen canteens made the rounds. As they drank, the first rays of the sun gilded the tips of the western ridgeline in a golden glow. In the stillness Natan took a moment to say goodbye to the world.

"Attention!" a voice boomed over their heads. "You're surrounded. Put down your weapons and approach our lines with your hands on your heads. You'll not be harmed."

"Piss off!"

"Or what?"

"Bastards!"

"You're outnumbered," the voice continued. "No one more needs die today."

Tivo cupped a hand to his mouth.

"Why?" he yelled. "You scared? Come get us."

The voice did not respond. Natan put a hand on Tivo's shoulder.

"You think you can carry my weight?" he whispered.

"I can try," Tivo said.

Natan explained what he wanted and Tivo knelt in the middle of the circle, his shield across his knee and his hands gripping either side. Natan stepped onto the shield.

"Look at me," he yelled. "You know me. I am Aurochs. Your general is dead. I killed him —"

A murmur washed over the ranks, rising to a roar with shouts of *'lies!'* and oaths of vengeance. Almost lost amidst the din, Natan heard trumpets and the dull roll of drums.

"Here they come," he yelled to his men, jumping back down into their midst. "At least they don't have crossbows."

"Not in this light," Tivo shouted back over the tumult. "But if we wait they'll have clear shots."

"Thirty paces," one man cried. "Twenty-five. Twenty."

The beat faltered. Some continued the advance. Others stopped and looked to their officers. Sergeants raged, shoving those under their command back into order. Eyes began to turn eastward. Natan noticed the confusion on their faces and exchanged glances with Tivo. Tivo shrugged.

"The hills!" a soldier cried.

Natan spun about. The eastern ridgeline, black against the rising sun, flickered with firelight. Wooden watchtowers went up like funeral pyres and torches dotted the summits.

"They've done it," Natan yelled. "Jano's taken the heights!"

It took a moment to dawn on the rest, but then the cheers of the survivors merged with the general commotion beyond the circle.

"Stay focused," Natan warned. "We're not safe yet."

The blood-drenched earth shook and Natan looked to his feet, wondering if he imagined it. *No.* The puddles formed by their footprints rippled. A new sound entered his awareness. *Dreadbeasts?* He could not be sure, but then the attention of the enemy began to shift to the north and the sound of battle became more distinct. Men craned their necks and officers stood paralyzed, their command structure broken.

"Goddess of Mercy, what's happening?" Tivo said.

"Watch your sectors," Natan barked, glaring at those who turned to the head of the valley.

Confused trumpets echoed off the valley walls. Natan was unfamiliar with the signals of the Third Army, but even he could tell the orders were chaotic and contradictory. The enemy soldiers arrayed around them turned to their officers and one by one the companies to the north about-faced and marched in the direction of the fighting. Those to the south wavered, with some standing their ground, and others withdrawing to regroup.

Two companies, around four hundred men, remained to watch Natan and the encircled raiders. Their two captains conversed openly, then prepared their lines for assault.

"What's happening?" Mako asked.

"Jano must have attacked the valley entrance," Natan said.

"Look's like they're coming," said Tivo. "Don't celebrate —."

"Dreadbeasts!" one of their number yelled. "Look!"

The massive animals rose above the heads of the Third Army and plowed into view, sundering the lines and throwing bodies into the air. Men broke and over the din came the thunder of horses as Seventh Army cavalry cut into the routed foe. The two companies set to guard the raiding party threw down their weapons and ran.

As cavalry neared their position, Natan realized the danger and climbed once again onto Tivo's shield and waved a green strip of tunic.

"Seventh Army!" he yelled. "Friendlies!"

Horses stampeded past and in their wake came a rider with an emerald green plume and cape about his shoulders. The horse stopped before the tight knot of survivors.

"Commander?" Natan said in stunned disbelief. "Sir."

"Are you it?" the commander snapped. "Are there others?"

"We're what's left," Natan said. "Twenty-four men and a wounded officer."

"Hold tight," the commander said. "I'll get help."

The officer wheeled his horse about and spurred it on back the way he had come. The sun rose and flies buzzed about their position. The sounds of battle faded as fighting carried itself to the end of the valley and into the fields beyond. After the best part of half an hour, the officer returned with an escort and three empty supply carts.

"How you lads doing?" the commander said. "Get in the carts. You're out of here."

Military training kicked in. No one questioned the officer. They abandoned the circle and carried Mako and their arms to the carts.

Natan slept against Tivo's shoulder. Tivo's head rested against his own. The carts rattled and jolted, requiring the occasional adjustment of their bodies. At one point Natan thought he heard voices at a checkpoint, but his eyes burned and his eyelids felt like lead. Eventually the tailgate banged open and Natan jolted awake. They were not moving. The cart swayed as a city watchman stood on the back step and scanned the survivors. For a brief moment their eyes made contact, then the watchman stepped down and bolted the tailgate shut again.

"Tivo," Natan said, shaking his companion. "We're in Pao'an."

Tivo stretched his arms and yawned.

"Not back in camp? Where are we?"

"I think it's Northgate."

Other soldiers stirred and Natan nudged Mako sleeping at his feet. The old captain grunted and rolled over.

"What are the black flags for?" Tivo asked.

Natan followed his gaze to the gatehouse.

"Northgate," he confirmed, then he noticed the flags also.

The carts continued down the broad street and crowds parted. They looked glum. *Don't they know the war is over?* Natan asked himself, concerned. Something was wrong. *Why aren't there celebrations?*

"No street vendors," a soldier noted.

"Goddess of Mercy," Tivo muttered.

Natan felt he was missing something. Realization appeared to strike the others in the cart, but he looked about beseeching them with his eyes for an answer.

"What?" he said at last.

As they rolled up to the Ministry of War, Tivo whispered what everyone else had realized.

"The Emperor's dead."

CHAPTER 25

"When all Kh'areen come together they form the Great Horde and at the head of the horde are the Chobi and the Gosh u-Gosh. One represents the spiritual, the other the temporal."

Master Suvu's Life of a Scholar

Demons swirled in a storm of souls. Fire lanced from the maelstrom and thunder shook the earth. Ashara screamed.

"Get her on the table," a voice boomed.

"She won't make it."

"You fix her or this house burns down around you."

Pots clattered and jars smashed. Fingers tugged at her. The demons came for her. They pulled her. She gasped. Hardwood made her bed. A lantern glared in her half-closed eyes.

"There's movement!"

"I can't see if it's hit a major organ."

"Bring the tools - hold her down."

The world spun. Ashara's flesh bristled with fire. Worms burrowed in her skin, pulling it this way then that. Their weight drove her down. She fell.

"Hold it there! Clamp it!"

"You sure you're doing it right?"

"Hold! Where's my apprentice? The jar! Get that into the wound."

Acrid black water flowed over her body, clogging her mouth and nose. It seeped into her eyes and filled her lungs. Her nerves fired off. Something ate at her, gnawing at the tissue down to the bone.

"Her mouth!" a voice screamed, bubbling through the liquid.

Two beady eyes glared down at her like pinpricks through the darkness. Claws latched onto her jaw and tentacles reached into her mouth, tugging at her tongue and pressing against the uvula. Ashara tried to resist but her body did not respond.

"Hold! Careful — hot brand coming through."

Ashara's skin fizzled and white-hot pain consumed her. The demon exploded into stars of glistening light, growing ever larger until they blanketed her vision. Then —

"Hail Tanri, Lord Above," droned a priest.

A candle flickered in the corner. Ashara's head lolled to the side.

"Milk," said the priest. "Hold her still."

Hands straightened her head on the pillow. Voices intoned the *Chobi Ghada*, and a spoon smeared a sickly sweet milk over her tongue. Ashara choked and spluttered.

"Water," she rasped. "Water."

Fingers stroked her forehead, burning her skin.

"Hush. The pain will cease."

"Can you do anything?" a voice asked.

"I told you, she's in the hands of Tanri now."

"No," Ashara screamed.

They had come for her, the demons again. This time they threw her about, laughing at her pain. They tore at her and prodded her. Their stench was overwhelming. Light flashed and thunder rumbled as they drew her into the maelstrom. Then a figure approached, shining white as if the Oracle herself.

"Po?" she mumbled.

The face became clear. The demons fled. Po directed her to a bed on a chariot of plush cushions and gaudy velvet. His face radiated as the sun and her skin crawled with the kisses of life. Her body lurched and Po vanished.

"Don't fight," a voice hissed.

"Bavgai?" Ashara rasped.

"You're on a cart. We're moving you."

"Where's my father?" she asked.

"Hush," he said. "You're confused. You need rest."

His fingers stroked her hand. She tried to pull away but found her hands wrapped around a solid object heavy on her chest.

"What is it?" she asked, fear spreading.

"Your sword," Bavgai said. "If you died, you'd die a warrior. Father ordered it."

"Sword? I don't have a sword."

"You killed Commander Vitan. His blade is rightfully yours."

"Battle?"

Bavgai gave her a quizzical look.

"What's the last thing you remember?"

"Po," she said. "He was here."

"You need sleep," Bavgai said.

With the passing of days Ashara became more aware of her surroundings. More memories returned, but her body remained frail. Bavgai traveled with her, sitting beside her in the cart. After a few days he tried sitting her up, partially at first and then higher with each successive day. New vistas became available to her; the sweeping grasslands of her homeland, flocks of sheep and goats, swollen winter rivers, and the soaring buzzard that shadowed the warband. Lord Azraik came to visit from time to time. As did Orslan, his face wrapped in bandages. One night Bavgai brought her hot soup with chunks of fatty meat.

"Little at a time," he warned. "Not too fast."

"What are they celebrating?" she asked, nodding towards the warriors.

"Tomorrow we rejoin the Great Horde. They celebrate a successful raid."

"A sweet reunion for some," Ashara said.

"Come on," Bavgai said. "You must have family somewhere. There'll be Daladh'an in the Great Horde. Uncles or distant cousins, maybe?"

"Maybe," Ashara said with a painful shrug. "What will they want with me though?"

"You're family, and you're a hero — the slayer of an Imperial commander."

"More like a young woman," Ashara said. "Without family, battered and useless, crawling back from a raid on the back of a cart."

"Wounds heal, and family is what you make it."

"You're just trying to make me happy," Ashara said. "I thank you, but I know how it'll go. First they smile. Later you become a burden."

Bavgai climbed down off the cart, empty soup bowl in hand.

"I'll show you," he said. "Tomorrow I'll bring you your family."

The next day they saw the Great Horde, its tents and pavilions sprawling beyond count. On seeing them, horses galloped with riders ululating across the plain to meet the returning warband.

"It's not Baki," Bavgai said to Ashara. "But look at it. The Kh'areen united under one banner."

"I've never seen so many," she said.

"Get used to it. Next time it won't be just a raiding party. We'll be going to stay."

Ashara could believe it, there were so many of them. As they drew close, crowds swarmed from the camp. Family opened their arms and merchants haggled over plunder. Lord Azraik pranced on his horse, rearing it here, and whirling it there, regaling the masses with tales of their deeds. Warriors interjected and children stood spellbound. Ashara became engrossed in the theater and forgot her pains for a blissful moment.

"Bavgai, I —" she said, turning.

Bavgai was gone. He must have slipped away. She called his name, but no one answered. A merchant caught her eye and strode over to the cart.

"How much for the sword?" he demanded.

"It's not for sale," she said.

"I'll give you two silver li," he said.

"I said it's not for sale. You don't even know the condition of the blade."

"Here, give us a look."

Ashara scowled.

"I'm an invalid," she sneered. "Not stupid. This is mine and it's not for sale."

"Very well," he said. "You change your mind, you ask for me."

Other merchants came and went, inquiring about her sword and general plunder, but she rebuffed them. Everything in the cart belonged to Bavgai and his family. Only the sword was her's, and it was not for sale. An hour passed and the crowd thinned. Orslan approached the cart, his head swathed in bandages.

"You seen my son?" he asked.

Ashara shook her head. Orslan grumbled.

"Damn kid's run off."

"I think he's looking for someone," Ashara said.

Just then, Bavgai's head appeared. He pushed his way towards the cart, a lanky warrior in tow.

"Where've you —" his father started, but Bavgai raised a hand.

"Ashara, look who I've found."

Ashara met the warrior's gaze.

"Bayar?"

"Ashara?"

Her bother scrambled onto the cart and they embraced, mixing their warm tears and stammering uncontrollably.

"I… I thought you were dead."

"So…. so did I. How… how's this possible?"

"I saw the bodies. I thought you were among them."

"I heard they saw you being beaten in the scrub."

They fell silent, pawing at each other as if checking the other was truly there.

"Uncle Nugai is here," Bayar said at last. "And cousin Sammi. I'm with them. They're waiting. Can you walk?"

"No," Ashara said.

"I'll carry you," he said.

Before Bavgai or Orslan could object, Bayar began clearing his sister of blankets. His hands found the sword. He picked it up and examined it.

"Nice," Bayar said, offering the blade to Bavgai. "Don't lose it."

"No," Bavgai said, raising his hands. "It's not mine. It's your sisters."

"My sister —?" Bayar said. "Ashara?"

"She killed an Imperial commander for it," Bavgai said. "In battle."

"To save my life," Orslan added. "Fierce warrior you have there. My family owes her a debt we can never repay."

Brother and sister exchanged looks. Ashara nodded and Bayar beamed with pride as he scooped her up in his arms.

"We have a lot to catch up on," he said.

"We do," said Ashara.

She wrapped her arms around her brother's neck and rested her cheek on his shoulder. Bayar stepped down from the cart and thanked Orslan and his son.

"When she's fully recovered," he said. "She'll visit you."

"No, we'll visit her," Orslan promised. "Lord Azraik as well. The respect is ours."

The thinning crowds parted for Bayar with Ashara in his arms. She clung to him, warmed by his pretense.

"Ashi," he whispered. "Welcome home."

CHAPTER 26

"The Covenant sealed in the vermilion blood is the Empire, and the Empire is the Covenant. None may be emperor unless the gods will it."

A History of the Vermilion Empire

Snow caught on the leadlight and ice frosted the glass. Natan pulled the blanket extra close and rolled over to watch the fire crackling in the grill.

"Cheer up," Mako said from the next bed over. "Maybe no exercise in the yard today, but I hear there's cake. Who doesn't like cake, eh?"

"When do you think they'll let me out?" Natan asked, sitting up.

"You in a hurry? I'd rather be here than doing field exercises out there."

"It's so boring," Natan said. "Three meals a day. Occasionally someone changes the sheets. Exercise when fine. People come and go. And in between just sleep. I don't even belong here."

"The surgeons disagree. You should've seen the work they needed to do on that head of yours."

"No," Natan said. "I mean I'm not an officer. People give me weird looks."

Mako propped himself up on an elbow.

"You bloody killed General Mamot. The least they could do was put you in here. If it were me I would be demanding a lot more."

"And the Emperor."

Mako glanced at the other beds, the whites of his eyes showing.

"You can't say that. Not in here. He killed himself."

"You know what I mean."

"I fucking do not. No. If you want out of this hospital you learn to shut that mouth of yours."

The door to the ward banged, startling the two men. The surgeon and his apprentice strolled up the rows of beds, checking here, muttering there. They came to Natan's bed and the surgeon pulled up a stool.

"How are you feeling?" the surgeon asked.

"When am I allowed out?"

"Five hundred beds," the surgeon said, shaking his head. "And five hundred patients. You're the only one that wants to be discharged."

"I'm sure," Natan said. "Someone else could make better use of this bed."

The surgeon had Natan swing his legs out of bed and roll up the legs of his woolen pyjamas. The apprentice watched over the surgeon's shoulder as his fingers probed Natan's joints.

"Open your mouth."

Natan obliged.

"Well," said the surgeon, standing and wiping his hands on his apron. Apart from the questions, you've been the perfect patient. Healed up well. Some god is looking after you."

"So?" Natan asked.

"There's an officer downstairs asking after you. I'm to report your condition. I think you're ready to be discharged."

Natan beamed with excitement. The first thing he was going to do was seek leave to visit his family. Not that he should seem too eager to see them, of course, but a visit was socially expected.

A draft wafted the curtains and a gust rattled the window frames. Natan busied himself with a razor, trying to make himself look presentable. He squinted into the mirror and ran a finger over the white scar stretching a thumb's length along his shaved head. They had said he was lucky to survive.

"Hurry up with the mirror," another patient said. "It's for shaving, not for gawking."

"Oh lay off," Mako growled. "He's expecting discharge papers. Can't go out looking like a beggar."

"That ugly mug? No chance a razor will fix things. Go on bugger off."

Natan ignored the insult but Mako swung out of bed and grabbed his crutches.

"I said lay off. Do I need to bloody beat it into you?"

The offending officer bristled and squared his shoulders.

"You're lucky you're a cripple," the patient sneered. "Or I'd break that jaw of yours."

"Cripple?" Mako spat. "I could break that turnip you call a nose with my little finger. Come on. Show me what you've got."

"Please," Natan said, stepping between them. "I'm finished."

"More like he's finished," Mako said.

The double doors at the end of the ward slammed open against the walls.

"Everybody on your feet."

The three men froze mid-argument and slowly turned their heads. A captain in full battle-kit stood in the doorway with his hand on the pommel of his sword. As patients piled out of their beds the captain marched down the aisle.

"Next to your beds," he barked at Natan and Mako. "At attention."

More soldiers entered the ward and trotted after their captain, their hobnail boots muffled by silk handkerchiefs. They spread themselves out and faced each other at equal distances from one end of the ward to the other. The surgeon was next. He hurried over the tiles and stood at the foot of Natan's bed.

"What's happening?" Natan whispered, starting to feel uneasy.

The surgeon did not look his way, his lips pressed shut. More movement at the door. Two heralds took positions on either side and banged the floor with their serpent staffs.

"Our god-like 63rd Emperor Gotti VIII, ruler of all under Heaven, keeper of the Covenant, most blessed of mankind. May he live ten thousand years."

Across the ward men bent the knee. Natan focused on the polished tiles, and from the corner of his eye he watched Jano sweep into the room cloaked in white and black ermine. The velvet boots drew near and stopped beside the surgeon at the foot of his bed.

"Arise, Natan Luka-Tudo," said the Emperor.

Natan trembled as he rose to his feet. Jano had been his general, but now as Emperor he was the living embodiment of the divine.

"You have served us well," Jano said. "Your courage on the field of battle and your loyalty in the face of death are examples for all who march under the Imperial banner. It is therefore with great pleasure that we grant you the rank of Captain with all the perquisites and benefits therein."

The Emperor took a scroll from a cushion held by a servant and passed it to Natan.

"Furthermore, in acknowledgement of our thanks for services rendered, and to allow for your physical comfort and recuperation, we grant you this one-time bonus from the Imperial Treasury. Spend it wisely."

The Emperor passed Natan a bank draft written up in his name and a heavy purse that *chinked* with coin. Natan fell to one knee once again.

"My Emperor, I am unworthy."

Jano held out a hand and presented his boney fingers adorned in jewelled rings.

"What we call worth, do not call unworthy. You may kiss the divine hand."

Natan's hands shook and he felt a lump form in his throat as his lips brushed the surface of the Emperor's skin.

"Arise, Captain Natan Luka-Tudo."

The Emperor Gotti VIII turned and swept from the ward, conferring on the way with an aid as to his next engagement. Two sergeants remained behind, laying out Natan's new uniform on the bed, along with captain's sword and harness. Before they left, the senior of the pair addressed the stunned captain.

"The hospital will sign you out tomorrow. You're to settle your affairs and report to the Ministry of War at the fourth bell of the afternoon. Trouble's brewing in the south so by spring you can expect a long deployment."

"Thank you," Natan managed to say, not quite believing what he was hearing.

Alone once again he turned in stunned silence to Mako. Mako held out a hand.

"What?" Natan asked.

"You've got a debt to settle. Nothing personal. Just business."

Natan opened the purse to the glint of gold, silver and bronze. *Is this really all for me?* He took out the appropriate coins and dropped them into Mako's outstretched hand.

"What?" Mako said. "No interest? I know you're good for it."

"Sorry," Natan said with a grin. "Interest was never part of the terms. Nothing personal. Just business."

Mako laughed.

"Maybe there's something in that thick scalp of your's after all."

The next morning, the seventh bell tolled, softened by the fog. Natan straightened before the mirror and adjusted his emerald uniform.

"Not bad," Mako said. "You scrub up well."

"I haven't seen them in months," Natan said.

"Get used to it. Once you're deployed it could be years."

The surgeon's shoes squeaked on the tile floor. Natan turned.

"Your things, sir?" asked the surgeon.

"Dispose of them," Natan said. "Burn them. Return them to the army. I came with nothing. I leave with this. It'll be a fresh start."

"If I could just get your signature here. Thank you."

"Remember, Ministry of War, fourth bell," Mako said. "Pays to be early. First impressions matter."

"Captain," the surgeon said, waiting. "My apprentice will walk you downstairs."

Outside, the chill bit Natan's skin and his breath turned to white frost. He leaned against the wind and clutched his cape as he set off in the direction of Eastbank. The going was hard, but Natan felt light-hearted at his sense of freedom, despite the weather. It was only when he entered his street that a stone settled in his stomach. He imagined his parents' reaction to his return. Would they treat him like a child, or respect the man he had become? Would they forgive him for enlisting, and if they

did, was he willing to forgive them for everything he had suffered under their care? He did not know.

In deep contemplation he approached the gates to the trading house. They were locked. He looked up at the sign, snow bunched about the letters. No lights were in the windows and no smoke issued from the chimney. Natan rattled the gate and turned for the alley, hoping for more luck with the kitchen door. He approached with an increasing dread. His gloved hands knocked on the peeled paint. Nothing. Cobwebs formed around the frame — no one had opened the door in a long time.

Natan returned to the alley and traipsed back to the street. He stood there for a while, deep in thought. *What had happened?* He wondered. *Where are my parents?* Next door a latch clicked and a plump woman backed out of a doorway, a sack of millet in her fleshy arms. She started at Natan's appearance on an otherwise empty street.

"Can I help you?" she asked.

"This house," Natan said. "Where are the owners?"

"Them? Gone before I moved in. Three sons died in the war. Mother taken with fever. Father locked up for his debts in the Decimation. Beyond that you'd have to ask someone who's been here a little longer."

"Are you sure it was that family?"

"Was what I was told. We adopted one of their cats."

"You mentioned the Decimation, what was that?"

"Punishment," the woman said. "For supporting the Reformers."

"But I'm an officer in the Seventh," Natan said. "My brother fought for Jano as well."

The woman shrugged and turned to leave.

"So you're one of the sons then? There's no logic in life. It just happens. May Heaven give you answers."

Natan thanked the woman and turned back to the house, pinching the bridge of his nose between gloved fingers. He was glad the frost camouflaged his tears. His limbs felt numb, and a creeping cold tightened his chest. Despite Natan's acquaintance with death, he had never really considered it taking his mother. Not while he was away. Not without him there beside her. *Mom...*

The clerk did not look up when Natan entered Eastbank Barracks. Snow whirled through the entrance until the door slammed behind him, ruffling the posters on the walls.

"Can you tell me," Natan said, standing before the counter. "Where you pay the Decimation?"

"Here," said the clerk, eyes on his work. "Every second day between second and fifth bell in the afternoon."

"That's not going to work for me," Natan said stiffly.

"Too bad. Come back tomorrow."

"My father's detained. Can you tell me where he's held?"

"Look," said the clerk, putting down his pen. "I —"

He froze. Natan sensed the sharp intake of breath. The clerk jumped from his chair.

"I'm sorry, Captain. I didn't see you."

"You saw me," Natan said. "You ignored me."

"An unfortunate mistake," said the clerk, bobbing his head in apology. "Let me get the Captain of the Watch."

The clerk returned moments later with a disheveled officer in the black and red of the city watch. Natan explained how he'd only just returned to Pao'an and found his father gone, caught up in the Decimation. The captain rubbed his stubble and scratched his head.

"Well you see," the captain said. "It's not actually our jurisdiction. You'll need to come back tomorrow between second and fifth bell. They'll then be a bailiff here from the Ministry of Works. He'll sort you out. And that's assuming your father's still in Pao'an. Some have been dispatched to labor camps already."

Natan ground his knuckles on the counter, his face coming dangerously close to the captain's. The captain flinched but ultimately stood his ground.

"I'm reporting for duty this afternoon. I want this sorted today."

"Then go to the Ministry of Works. They'll sort you out."

The door to the hall opened and the clerk grabbed for his papers before the wind swept them away. Natan turned to the woman who entered, a baby in her arms. He bowed courteously to her and glared back at the captain.

"I'm hoping they do."

The Ministry of Works was a large stone edifice off South Avenue in the Inner City. Natan stormed up the steps and shoved his way through the double doors into the public foyer. Clerks looked up, disturbed from their work, then returned to their scribblings. A woman approached.

"You look like you need help," she said. "Please, take a seat."

Natan caught his breath and waved her away.

"No, I'm not taking a seat. I've just learnt by father was held in the Decimation. I want him freed immediately before I go back on campaign."

"Certainly, sir. If you just take a seat someone will be along in a moment."

"I don't —" Natan was cut off.

"Excuse me," said a bureaucrat, spectacles balanced on a crooked nose. "Just this way."

The woman smiled in obvious relief and returned to her desk. Natan followed the bureaucrat into a room of raised desks, flickering lamps and a glowing fireplace. He was offered a seat.

"What was your father's name?"

Natan obliged, and the official disappeared before returning with a file.

"The original debt was twenty-nine golden *gotti*, seven silver *li*, and ten copper *jet*. I see all that remains now is seventeen *gotti*, one *li* and three coppers. How would you like to pay?"

"There must be a mistake," Natan said. "My brother and I fought with the Seventh. Only one brother fought for the Reformists, and he died."

"Look," said the official, knitting his hands. "I'll be honest. You probably have a case. But you'd need to go before a judge, and then there's bribes and waiting lists and filing fees — you're best just to pay it. If you clear this debt now, I can have your father free within the hour."

"It's obviously a lot of money," Natan said. "And my father isn't a rich man — anymore. Perhaps the Ministry would accept a settlement for a lesser amount paid in full."

That got the official's attention. The man's eyes glistened and his finger absently drew a circle over the desk.

"I'm sure there'd be a processing fee," Natan added.

"How much do you think your father could realistically afford?" asked the official.

"Five *gotti*," Natan said. "Paid now. Hard coin."

"And for consideration — *er*, filing?"

"One *gotti*. Again, hard coin."

"I'm sure something can be arranged. I won't be a moment."

The official returned with a form and proceeded to fill in the blanks. Natan read upside down. *Date of death?* Then he realized. The official was declaring his father dead and the debt wiped. All six *gotti* would end up in someone's pocket. He should have made a lower offer.

"Sign here please," the official said. "Just as next of kin. And the money?"

Natan drew out his purse and counted the required coins. The official frowned but held his tongue.

"Six *gotti*," Natan said, sliding them across the desk.

"I'll have you wait in the foyer," said the man.

People came and went. Natan sat on a public bench, crossing and uncrossing his legs. Passersby nodded respectfully towards him, which confused Natan until he remembered his change of uniform. He wondered what his father would say.

After a while Natan went out onto the street and bought a pouch of *dama* leaf and a carved pipe. He slid them into his officer's tunic and returned to the ministry's foyer. Two men, bailiffs by their uniform, stood with their backs to him. Between them hung a weak, old man.

"Avi," Natan said.

The head turned. The unruly black hair that Natan remembered so well hung thin and gray.

"Natan?" Avi said, his voice hollow. "Is it you? By Heaven. A captain? They said you were dead."

Natan threw his arms around his father and pulled him into an embrace. This time he could not hide the tears. Both of them cried. Avi smelt of piss and body odor, but Natan ignored the effects on his new uniform. His father was the last surviving family he had left.

"Excuse me," said a voice off to the side. "Sorry to interrupt. Here's the key to your house, and a certificate saying your debt is cleared."

"Give it to him," Natan said. "It's his house."

Avi took the offered key and pressed it to his lips.

"I never thought I'd see you again," he said as they walked down the steps to the street.

"Let's hire a cart," Natan said. "I don't have long. I'll leave you money to get everything started and hire help. But I'm reporting to the Ministry of War at the fourth bell. Things are turning sour with the Kh'areen and I'm told to expect a long deployment."

South Avenue was busy and they had no trouble waving down a passing buggy. Natan helped his father into the back.

"Eastbank," he said. "I'll pay you extra if you wait outside for me."

"Right-oh, sir," said the driver.

CHAPTER 27

"Many a mystery surrounds Jan'a. This not helped by the abbots, who have delighted in keeping many things secret. They appear to know all that goes on in the outside world and their influence is not diminished by distance."

A History of the Vermilion Empire

High in the mountains, deep within a cavern carved into the living rock, candles flickered as monks chanted their mantra. From time to time brass bells chimed, marking the passing of hundreds and of thousands. Po sensed a disturbance in the air. Someone in the vast network of passages and halls had opened a door. He flinched and his heartbeat quickened before he remembered he was secure in the mountain stronghold. The bells chimed. Po raised his eyes over the shaved heads of the monks, to the bronze hand of Dasanika glistening in the candlelight. Memories of Pao'an and all the friends he had left flooded back. Jan'a was home now. *Kime ki're kima ka.*

Monks shuffled silently from the hall. Po fell in among the novices and joined the line weaving its way to breakfast. The passage took them through cut rock and natural cave, past classrooms and workshops, and out onto the windswept mountain where steps led up to High Jan'a, the monastery itself built against the elements. Here and there lay terraced fields, and paths diverged to lookouts and solitary retreats.

Po climbed the final steps to High Jan'a and entered the foyer. A monk, the warden of Po's dorm, stood by the passage to the kitchens counting off his wards.

"Novice Po," he said as Po drifted by. "Abbot Vaina would like a word when you're finished. He'll be at Beggar's Perch."

Po nodded and rejoined the flow of novices. For those he now dined with, being called to see the abbot was a big deal, but Po remembered his days spent with Biet. Vaina would never replace him.

Po set off alone to Beggar's Perch. The path led him higher up the mountain, past the remains of fallen watchtowers, grottoes and crumbling tombs. The Perch itself stood on a pinnacle of rock divorced from the Graytalons, accessed by a swing bridge. As Po took his first steps on the aged timbers, he saw the form of Abbot Vaina sitting in reflection, his back to the novice. Crossing the bridge, Po sat facing the abbot with his legs crossed.

"You called for me, Venerable Abbot," Po said.

Vaina's eyes flickered open, but the focus was blank.

"Spring is late this year," he said.

"It is," said Po. "I mean I've heard it is. I'm unfamiliar with the mountains."

Vaina rearranged his robes and picked at a piece of lint.

"I've finished reading the manuscript," he said at last. "We're making copies and a brother is designing a broadsheet. They'll be distributed far from here, just to hide the connection."

"And if Jano finds out?"

"We're on sovereign ground," said the abbot. "No opposing army has ever entered our monastery. Some institutions are too strong even for the Emperors to break."

"The Emperor?" Po asked. "Don't you mean Jano?"

"Emperors," Vaina said. "We have two now."

"Two?"

"Jano has crowned himself Gotti VIII in Pao'an, and we have Emperor Adan I in Ja'pa."

"Adan?" Po said. "But he's only four years old."

"Is he?"

"I knew his grandfather."

"Then you know more than I." A familiar shriek echoed off the peaks. Po flinched.

"It's just a wyvern. Do them no harm, they do you no harm. They prefer mountain goat and valley hares to humans."

"Memories…" Po muttered, fighting to keep his eyes from scanning the skies.

Vaina folded his hands and Po sensed the real reason he had been summoned was about to be revealed.

"And how are you settling in?"

"Alright."

"The truth, Novice Po." Po cocked his head, wondering how much Vaina understood his thoughts.

"How'd you expect?" he said.

"You've glimpsed the abyss," Vaina said. "And you can't unsee it."

"Yes."

"Can I suggest," Vaina said as if breaching a delicate subject. "We give you a break from studies. Six months, a year, however long it takes. The teachers say you're distracted and can't keep up. It'd be good for you."

"No," Po said.

"No?"

"No," Po repeated, gathering his strength for the discussion ahead.

"Can you explain? I'm making the suggestion now, but if this continues you'll have no choice."

"I want to rejoin the laity," Po said. "You're right. My lessons suffer and I can't concentrate at reflection."

"Well," said Vaina. "I'm disappointed. I really am. Venerable Biet said you were a mature, responsible student. You can't rush such a decision. What will your parents think?"

"They haven't seen me in years," Po said. "This is my decision to make."

"Once done, you will not be able to return," Vaina said. "You'll be alone and have to fend for yourself. Out there beyond the sanctity of this monastery, the world is not an easy place."

"I've seen it. Don't you think I know?" The abbot lifted the hem of his robe and stood. Po scrambled to follow Vaina's example.

"While you are here you're under my authority," he snapped. "And while under my authority, you'll treat me with a modicum of respect. I don't know if it was under my late friend, or if it was your time on the road, but you've been spoiled."

"Sorry," Po said.

"Two weeks in the grottoes," Vaina added. "That will perhaps give you some clarity."

Scattered across the mountains, the grottoes opened to the elements; wind-scoured and smooth with age, they represented the austerity of Ba're life. Po selected one and lay his mat beneath the visage of an ancient sage, so old and ghastly he wondered if it pre-dated the coming of the Ba're to the mountain vastness. *Two weeks*, Po thought. He grinned. In some ways Abbot Vaina had already tacitly accepted Po could leave. All he had to do was stay committed. *Fourteen days*. It was not easy, but neither did it break Po's resolve. Each morning an elderly monk climbed the high paths with a bowl of soup, and each morning it was cold and gluggy by the time it got to the grotto. Po would eat, set the bowl aside and sit in quiet reflection listening to the wind. The nights were the hardest time, when the wind howled and the bitter cold seeped through to his bones. The cries of wyverns occasionally kept him awake and sometimes he woke to the sound of grunting and sniffing about the mouth of the grotto, as if some creature of the night was on the prowl.

On the fourteenth day he heard the abbot's approach before he spotted the black robes. Vaina approached the entrance, a familiar canvas bag in his hands.

"Novice Po," he said. "Are you well?"

"Well enough," Po said, eyeing the contents of Vaina's hands.

"I have your things," said the abbot. "Do you return to your dorm, or do we walk to the gate?"

"I feel like a walk," Po said. "Stretch the limbs."

Vaina handed over the bag, disappointment etched on his face.

"Not a lot there, I'm afraid. Your copy of the *Sudo Ba're Datai*, a sewing kit, some other things you'll need for the road. We found clothes for you. I suggest you change before we go down the mountain."

The gate opened a crack and Po stepped out into the sunlight. His nostrils took in the first breaths of spring. Wildflowers blossomed along the stream bank and bees hummed their melody. Beyond, peasants worked their garden plots and smoke hung over the chimneys of the hovels. Po glanced back.

"Are you coming any further?" he asked the abbot.

Venerable Vaina shook his head.

"This is where I stop," he said.

Po dipped his head in recognition.

"This is it then," he said. "Thank you."

"No second thoughts?" asked the abbot.

"None," said Po.

"Well then, may the peace of Dasanika, and the blessings of the Ba're be upon you."

The gate closed and Po headed down the lane and over the bridge into the village. On the other side he came to a fork in the road. He paused, considering his options.

"Where are you going?" a peasant asked.

"I don't know," Po said. "I'm just pleased to have the choice."

FEEDBACK

If you enjoyed this book, please consider posting a review on Amazon, Goodreads or a relevant book blog. Your feedback helps other readers discover this book. You can also connect with the author via their website www.vermilionempire.com where you can find more information about the series, sign up for updates and engage on social media.